"YOU SUMMONED. I AM HERE."

Long-needled branches swayed, then parted. Alorie saw a wisp of shadow both light and dark. The unicorn broke his cover and stood before her. When he spoke, the air trembled with his voice that was not a voice. "Are you the Dancer?"

"Once," Alorie said. She cleared her throat. "Have you come to bless the marriage?"

"I carry no blessing, Dancer, but a curse. You are a daughter of the prophecy and you fail us all with your lack of courage. Find it again or the Corruptor and the Despot will plow us under in salted earth."

"No, I've lost everything but Rowan. I've done all I could. The prophecy is nothing."

"The prophecy is hope. Without hope, nothing can live. I have been sent to remind you, Alorie Sergius. . . ."

DAUGHTER
OF DESTINY

R.A.V. Salsitz

A SIGNET BOOK

NEW AMERICAN LIBRARY

SIGNET TRADEMARK REG. U.S. PAT. OFF. AND FOREIGN COUNTRIES
REGISTERED TRADEMARK—MARCA REGISTRADA
HECHO EN CHICAGO, U.S.A.

SIGNET, SIGNET CLASSIC, MENTOR, ONYX, PLUME, MERIDIAN
and NAL BOOKS are published by NAL PENGUIN INC.,
1633 Broadway, New York, New York 10019

First Printing, November, 1988

1 2 3 4 5 6 7 8 9

PRINTED IN THE UNITED STATES OF AMERICA

Prologue

In the soundless deeps of a world that had forgotten its name, had been wounded and crawled back into itself until all that remained was a land the elves call Bethalia, a lamp glowed.

Held in the hand of a cowled and caped sorcerer, it cast a low and wavering light upon a leathern sarcophagus, a monstrous cocoon, in the bottom of the cavern. The sorcerer set the lamp down unconcernedly as the wick sputtered. He was used to the dark.

He rolled his sleeves to his elbow and began to chant. The stone about him seemed to swallow both the sound and light into its innermost recesses. Slowly, agonizingly, the chitin of the cocoon peeled back. Webs and dust layered off as it crackled and opened.

The sorcerer sucked in his breath as the being inside was revealed, his arms folded over his chest, his chin dropped down, and his skin withered and dark like that of a dried fruit. The sorcerer felt an empathetic stabbing that iced through him for a second and was gone. He pulled a small knife from his sash, put the point to the ball of his thumb, and pricked it gently. A single crimson drop welled up.

He drew near the casing and the man it held, hesitating, his hand outstretched. Then, with a swift, contemptuous movement, he smeared the blood across the being's lips. He stepped back, his sleeves falling back down his arms, hiding all but his fingertips, and waited.

The response was a long time coming. It came dregged from the stone itself, for that was the binding upon the being. When the voice came, it sounded low and gravelly, the movement of one rock plate upon another when the world quivers. "How long?"

If the sorcerer was surprised, he did not show it within his cowl. "Long enough," he answered. The toe of his riding boot nudged the oil lamp. "Long enough to see that your hopes and plans have gone awry."

The being moved. Emaciated arms fanned out, grasping at the light and the air. The frail chest inhaled and expanded, holding the air greedily, unwilling to let go of its life. "What?"

The sorcerer smiled, a cruel gash across his pale face, uncaring if his captive saw his expression or not.

"A wedding is planned . . . soon to be celebrated. The last of the House of Sergius goes to her fate, the one she has molded herself, and you cannot stop it! I will leave you with that despair." He made a pass with his hands, abruptly, and the layer of the chitin snapped shut, closing off the being. Taking up his lantern, the sorcerer laughed and climbed out of the cavern.

In the darkness the cocoon quivered and shook and fell, its binding of stone and dark magic replaced. But a hairline crack appeared at the edge. Dark fingers wriggled through desperately as the occupant fought to free himself and his voice echoed into the darkness: "No! It cannot be!"

One

The bride woke from her Bridal Nap in terror. She lay on her simple cot, eyes wide open in the shuttered, dusky room, waiting for the noise and smells of the tavern below to chase away her nightmares. She could not remember her dreams. They had slipped away from her like dark river water through her fingers. All she knew was they had been enough to awaken her early on this, the eve of her marriage.

She rolled onto her side, her dark hair spilling over the rough cot's edge, and listened to the merriment wafting up from the tavern. Barrel lived up to its name: a crossroads village, rich in farmlands and with a reputation for making brew that made a peasant's life as good as a king's. Fumes of beer snaked up through the planked floors and shutters. She did not envy the barmaids working tonight. The marriage custom of "one for me and one for the land that keeps us free" made for a lot of spillage, although no serious celebrant downstairs was going to pour a whole mug onto the flooring, no matter how well they wished Alorie and Rowan.

A piper began a tune, and she could hear voices, off-key but making up for lack of pitch in volume. A drummer joined the song. Still half-asleep, Alorie lay listening to the drum's rolling beat, like that of horses' hooves. Her breath suddenly caught in her throat as her dream came back upon her.

It was the dead of winter, the land—broken timber and rocks and rills—sheeted in snow. But not white snow. It was dirty, befouled. The wind shrilled off the tors and passed through her body. Then she heard the yelps and howls of a hunt.

The unicorn thundered past her, its head flung up in

7

desperation, blood spurting from its nostrils as it ran. Its heat seared her. Before she could flinch or turn away, the beast fell, gasping as it rolled in a drift. She could see clearly then how pure the beast was against the besmirched snow. Alorie closed her eyes and tried to shut out the sobbing breaths of the dying creature. The yelps and barks of the hunters drowned them out for her.

She knew she dreamed but stood in fear, unable to run away, as the reken and hunting dog pack swarmed the unicorn. They nipped and tore until the ivory hide glistened with blood, and then a harsh shout made them back away. The reken stood on their rears and took the dogs by their collars, forcibly hauling them from the kill. The unicorn thrashed and rolled an eye—and she swore it saw her standing there. It tucked its legs under itself. Alorie felt hope for an instant, knew the beast was gathering itself for a break.

The pack master strode up the hill. She caught her breath, sinking back, praying *he* could not see her, or the malevolent presence that followed him. That miasma at his back hovered about the ground, shielded from sight by its umbra, which parted now and then as a tentacle licked out, searching for quarry. It was a malison and it followed the Corruptor as if it were one of the hunting dogs.

The sorcerer, wrapped heavily against the winter, approached the unicorn. They eyed one another. The beast jerked his hand up, menacing with his spiraled horn. Then the sorcerer reached out and snapped the horn off.

The unicorn screamed in agony. Icicles trembled on broken branches. Snow on the crags vibrated with its bugling. The Corruptor held the horn in its gloves, steam rising from the white and gold heat. He laughed between his teeth.

The reken pack leader echoed his satisfaction and said, "You have conquered it, Master."

The sorcerer looked up. "Perhaps," he answered. "There are unicorns, and there are Unicorns, however." He tossed the horn to the reken, who batted it away and let it fall to the icy ground.

The malison quivered. Its movement brought the Corruptor's attention to it. He waved at the unicorn that lay quivering at his feet. "Be my guest," he invited.

Alorie jerked away, dream or not, and began to run as the malison lowered itself to the quavering beast. She tripped and fell. Then the dream changed, as dreams do.

*   *   *

She stood in a meadow.

A darkness on the grassland, a darkness more foul than night galloped toward her, ebon spear lowered to skewer her, wine-dark nostrils rank with the scent of carrion: a black unicorn, its Mystery corrupted into Death. And she was its target.

She turned and ran. Bordering shrubs and branches whipped at her eyes, stung her hands as she flung herself through the brush. Sinobel lay ahead, graceful ringed city of her forefathers. If only she could gain its walls!

The unicorn's breath scorched at her heels. Her skirts tangled about her ankles. She felt the rip of her hem as it must have lanced her, piercing only fabric. Alorie gasped for breath as she raced across the clearing and trade road that separated her from safety. The unicorn's hooves pounded in her hearing, drumming, drumming. . . .

And then she was in her grandfather's halls, scarcely remembering gaining the walls or passing through the circles of the city. There were merrymakers in the great room. They baffled her passage and when she cried with protest, they only laughed and clasped her shoulders.

"Stay awhile, milady. You'll miss the entertainment!"

Alorie shook off the faceless courtiers and gained the curved staircase to the rear of the room. It led to her wing and that of her father and grandfather. She took the stairs two at a time and paused, winded, at the top when the front doors splintered, bursting inward, and the black beast thundered through. Sergius, High Counselor, rose to his ancient height and pounded his iron-footed staff on the stone tiles. Its belling cut through even the pounding of the beast's hooves, and Alorie felt its resonance in her chest. This was her grandfather at his best—and his worst.

"Halt! Who invited your passage here? Begone!"

Alorie saw then that a rider had joined the unicorn, a wide-shouldered blond with narrow, arrogant eyes, wearing blue and silver. She leaned over the railing to scream, "Father! Run! It's Aquitane!"

Her father, sharing the throne dias with Sergius, began to turn as though he heard her over the din of the crowd and the shrilling neigh of the engaged unicorn.

He turned slowly and inexorably, too late to see the death charge of the ebon creature that skewered him and tossed his body aside like that of a straw doll, then plunged toward the old man and cleaved him in two. Even as he toppled and fell, her grandfather called out to her from beyond his death: "Run, girl! Last of the house of Sergius—run!"

Her knuckled grip froze her to the bannister even as Aquitane pivoted his mount and they came at the stairs. Where was Rowan? Rowan would save her—*had* saved her—but there was no sight of him. The enemy galloped after her, drumming, drumming, drumming. . . .

Alorie bolted upright on the cot, gasping for breath. The song below her erupted in laughter, then the piper began another tune with the drummer taking a more sedate tempo. She held her hands in front of her, still half-clenched in a dream-entranced grip. Her heart gave a shudder within her breast. The Nap was over for this Bride!

She staggered to her feet, took a deep breath, and steadied herself. Homespun clothes lay over a chair at the foot of her cot. At midnight's eve, Mary Rose would come to get her, dress her in her disguise, and send her into Barrel's night to find her lover, also in disguise, symbolizing the search for true love. They would go from tavern to tavern, open house to open house, wined and feted, guided and misguided at every step until sometime just before dawn, they were destined to find each other. If they found each other before then, to preserve the luck of this commoners' ritual, they would bypass until the skies lightened and the celebrants tired. Then, under the canopy representing the aproned lap of the Mother, she and Rowan would say their vows.

But she was not a commoner. She was the last of the House of Sergius and, it seemed, she would be the last to be allowed to forget that. The clothing slipped from her fingers as she looked across the shuttered room and saw, in the darkness of early eve, a muffled light.

It peered from under the lid of her chest, a trunk nearly empty, for she'd had no one to pay her bridal price. But what it held was worth more than the lands her grandfather had once ruled in place of the long ago defeated High King. Alorie sucked in her breath. She went to the trunk and threw it open. The light blazed out, blinding her, then was gone, but not before she saw its source.

She lit a taper. Her fingers were numb with an inner chill, and she had trouble setting the candle back into its base. Its mellowed illumination spilled over the corner of the room and into the trunk as she reached into its depths.

Wrapped in one of Mary Rose's embroidered cloths, a

sigil ring glowed. Its radiance went out as she touched it gingerly and then took its warmth into the palm of her hand. Had it been a reminder that she was not a peasant and could not forget all that she had gone through to get here, this eve of spring and marriage? She curled her fingers around it, thinking of the lost Brock, Rover mage shorn of his power but not his wits, his skin as dark as the newly loamed soil and eyes of greenwood and smoke. Holding his ring like this, Alorie could not accept reports of his death. She never had. She never would. It was her legacy to him.

Beneath a quilt, another handicraft from the clever dwarf-ish fingers of her maid, lay a long and thin wooden casket. Alorie put the ring aside in a corner of the trunk as she knelt to touch the casket. As she began to open the lid, her hands failed her and turned to stroking the oiled wood of the sword's casement instead.

"Three years ago," she whispered. "I put you down three years ago. A lifetime! Now I have nothing but planting and harvest to worry me. No kingdom but that of the seasons. I will not take you up again!"

A cutting howl sounded from the edge of Barrel's fields, echoing through the woods that cupped the north end of town. It sliced through the merriment below and Alorie froze in hearing it, an echo of her dreams. A reken! What would a furry-coated servant of her enemy be doing here?

She listened tensely for an answer to the howl. No signal came. The din from below enveloped her again as a shout for a toast reached her. Alorie shook her head. She'd heard an owl perhaps, nothing more. The nightmare had unnerved her. As for the sword, she had to hold it tomorrow, her Lord Rathincourt and her husband-to-be Rowan had both agreed the heroic weapon should be displayed for the cere-mony. Then she would lay it aside once more, an heirloom to be given to her children.

Her heart would not loose its chill. She needed Rowan, she thought, and closing the lid to the trunk abruptly, stood. By custom she had not seen him for three months. She needed to talk to him, to see the auburn glint of his hair warmed by candlelight, to feel the warmth of his arms around her.

Custom be hanged! This lost lover was going in search of her mate early. Alorie smiled fleetingly as she thought of Mary Rose's vexation when she would come upstairs to dress her and find the bride already gone!

*   *   *

"Hurry! Hurry with that butter, child! I want this carted into town and laid to storage before the even star comes up." A short, plump, and curvacious dwarf woman looked fondly off the seat of the wagon as the human girl, all coltish legs and elbows, tugged at the flats of molded butter she carried.

But the girl didn't mind her urging. She was flushed, even in the still biting cold of an early spring night, and the ends of her hair stuck out from her braids. With an "oof" and an "uff," she dropped the flats into the back of the wagon. "Only one more, Mary Rose," she said and disappeared into the barn. As she staggered back out and dropped the last flat, she grinned. "That's the best sweet butter churned for days around," she announced. "Ma and Dad said only the best for the Lady Alorie's wedding." She pushed her straying bangs from her face. "Can I drive in with you? *Please*?"

The dwarf woman held her foot on the brake, hesitating. "Got permission?"

"Oh, yes! And I'll do all the unloading. I want to see how Barrel is all decorated and . . ." The girl hesitated. "I heared from—from others . . . that on a quiet night, when the moon is hid, you can see the unicorns across the fields. White as dew on the grasses, they've come to celebrate the wedding."

Mary Rose kept her smile to herself, thinking that the wagon was not likely to fulfill the requirement of quiet. "Did you, now?"

"Yes!"

"All right, then." The dwarf held out her callused and yet strangely gentle hand. "Come up with me."

Carpets of littlefoot crunched underneath the wagon wheels once it left the open dirt yard of the farmer's homestead. Eileen leaned down to sniff the fragrant scent. Littlefoot grew green and blossomed bright yellow only in the spring, barely a handspan high, yet thick and luxurious. She liked to lay in it and watch the clouds overhead, but farming life gave little time for such luxuries.

She twisted back on the wagon seat. "I want to see the wedding canopy and everything," she announced.

Mary Rose shook her head. "The wedding's not till afternoon. The canopy won't be put up till then. No sense letting the wind batter it down."

"Oh." Eileen's face fell in disappointment.

Mary Rose clucked to the horse, which still wore his shaggy winter coat. "Nay, child, there'll be plenty more to see. There's the golden water clock sent by King Bryant from the Delvings! That's a wonder indeed."

"Is it true the figurines go round and round and it strikes at sunrise and sunset?"

"Truer than that." Mary Rose puffed out her apple-colored cheeks. "My kinsmen in the Delvings spared no workmanship nor gold making it."

"Ma says it's better now to make clocks than armor or swords," Eileen said, with the frankness of a child. She stretched and looked up at the dark sky overhead. "I think Rowan is handsomer than anything, even if he is a Rover and can't own land."

That was quite an admission from a farmer's daughter, to whom land was almost everything in life. With none of the reserve an older woman might show to the dwarf who was Lady Alorie's personal maid, Eileen gossiped. "Everyone's coming," she said. "Even though there's not so many taverns or as big an inn this side of Roaring Bridge for days, Ma said the place would be fuller than a tick. She was happy to give sweet butter for the feast and even made Dad carve a new molding board. She wanted his name to stand out, she said, when the Seven True Races sat down to butter their bread!"

Mary Rose laughed and clucked at the cart horse to pick up the pace.

Eileen's fat braids bounced on her shoulders. She looked at the dwarf. "Is it true," she asked shyly, "about the unicorns?"

The dwarf shrugged. "I've never seen one, but my husband Pinch has. He's armsman to Rowan, you may know, and a couple of the Rovers coming in off the trails say they've seen 'em, but far off through the trees, like a smoky mist. If they come closer at all, it'll be because of my lady."

"What is the princess really like?"

"Well, for starters, she's not a princess. She's a lady, her father and grandfather being the high counselors of Sinobel before the massacre."

"I heared Dad telling about that, how they was killed by the reken and the malison and renegade soldiers. Have you ever seen a malison?"

Mary Rose shuddered, despite her sturdy body. "No . . only their leavings. Never ask to see a malison, child."

"The princess—the lady—then, tell me about her."

"Well, she's young and willowy. She has dark hair, like a raven's wing, and eyes of gray-blue. Gray when she's stormy, but her gown will be of sky blue, and that'll bring the blue out. She's plain-featured, and pale. Her skin doesn't brown in the summer, but she'll have a dusting of freckles, like you, before harvest moon."

"And she wears the sword all the time!"

"The sword made of a unicorn's horn? No, child. That's been kept away since she faced the army of the Corruptor and scattered them to the winds. No . . . there's a kind of fire in the sword and it's magic, so it's to be used sparingly. She wears a longknife, though, and she's good with it."

"But is she—is she royal?"

Mary Rose looked at the hard-worn farm girl a moment before choosing her words. "There's a spine to her," the dwarf said finally, "a determination. And people trust her. She looks not only to herself, but to all of us. But when she's with Rowan, she'll be beautiful, like any young bride in love."

Eileen let out a sigh. "It's all so, so wonderful," she said and leaned sleepily against Mary Rose's shoulder.

"What'll it be, gentlemen?" the innkeeper boomed, the tavern behind him loud and cheerful in its celebration, but his attention not diverted to the fact that the pair in front of him, though travel-worn and mud-stained, were of gentle bearing. "Drop your hoods, find a seat, and I'll draw you two of the best. The Weary Rover's fair bursting, but we've always room for one or two more."

The tall, burly man did as he was bid. His icy blue eyes were too small for the flesh of his square face. He was fair, his hair a pale blond that flowed to the collar of his cape. The second gentleman was much shorter, of a height with the innkeeper, and he shrugged into his black wool cowl. "The nights are still chilled," he said with a voice as flat and cold as the night he spoke of. "We don't wish to be disturbed."

His words sent a quickening down the innkeeper's back.

"I have mulled wine still hot," he blustered then. "There's a quiet table to the far corner, where the candle's gone out. I'll have my girl relight it for you—"

"No," said the caped man. "I like it that way."

"Right." The innkeeper wrung his rheumatic hands. "Will you gentlemen be needing lodging?"

The tall, big-shouldered man in blue smiled and said, "We've already made arrangements."

The innkeeper was relieved. "Good, then. Well, I've other guests to attend to. My girl will bring the wine right over." He made a bow and waddled off hurriedly.

With a tight, amused smile the big man watched him go. He took the caped man's elbow and steered him to the corner. Far across the massive wooden floor of the inn, celebrants joked and cheered near a roaring fire. The faded black and silver outfits of many of the crowd, their green and russet cloaks thrown to one side, helter-skelter over benches and the backs of chairs, showed the men to be Rovers, rangers of the roads.

"Rovers," the fair man said as he lowered himself into the shadowed booth.

"It's to be expected. Rowan is favored by many of them, Aquitane."

"I don't like it," the man said. He placed his large hands on the table and waited until the serving maid had shoved a large mug into them and scurried off before he said anything further. "What if I'm recognized? They want my head."

"By one of them? Not likely. Only the girl has seen you before and she won't be here. She's busy with the women getting ready for the ceremony." The man in dark wool reached over and patted his wrist. "Do you think I'd put you at risk?"

Aquitane settled for a long draft of the wine instead of an answer.

His master did likewise.

Aquitane put his mug down. "If you wished," he said lowly, "you could lay a seeming over me—"

"And sap my strength foolishly? No. Besides, I have my reasons for wanting you to be known later."

The big man's fist tightened about the mug until his knuckles whitened. "We've been nearly three years rebuilding—"

"Nothing will befall our plans. The road is paved, the pathway nearly clear for my master to return. And that—" the man's voice lowered to a near-hiss— "is my concern."

But the human lord was not one to back down easily. If he had, he would have been of little worth to the other. "And the Lady Alorie is mine," he said.

"When I get the sword, you get her. We have the reken surrounding Barrel. All you have to do is stand forth and make your claim on the bride when the time comes, and I guarantee chaos. We'll each gather up the prize we covet."

"What if the sword . . . harms you. Your experiments have not been as successful as we hoped."

The man in dark wool, whose face he could barely glimpse in the depths of the cowl, gave a bitter smile. "I am the Corruptor, am I not? It will turn for me, as all living things I bend my will to must do. As for the girl, she's yours when I'm done with her."

The Rovers broke apart after a lusty song. Their voices carried through the crowd of revelers as they lifted their foaming mugs. "To the Lady Alorie!"

Aquitane and his master lifted their drinks and echoed them darkly.

"Quite a rumpus they're kicking up tonight, eh, Trumpet?" the white-haired man inquired as he looked about the tavern.

The innkeeper swelled his chest. He wasn't called Trumpet lightly, but the swelling came from the pride of having a great warlord like Rathincourt staying at his establishment (as well as the bride herself). The lord and his detachment had ridden a hard road and gone to bed, sleeping through most of the afternoon, but now Rathincourt looked refreshed and in search of revelry. "Yes, milord," he said. "But I allow it was noisier last night. We even had a knife fight."

The bushy eyebrows arched, sending a deeply etched wrinkle into the forehead and puckering a scar that caught Trumpet's attention. A sword scar, thought the innkeeper, no doubt deflected by his lordship's helm. Trumpet nodded about the matter at hand. "The groom, Rowan himself, broke it up. A fair gentleman, that one is."

"Yes," the warlord agreed and clamped his hand down on the innkeeper's shoulder. "They don't come any better than Rowan. What's about tonight?"

"Don't know, milord. There's been some talking of getting up a unicorn hunt while the lovers search for one another—"

Rathincourt broke into hale laughter. "If her ladyship hears about that, she'll be the one knocking heads! Well, give me a trencher of that savory I keep smelling and a cool head of beer, if you've any left."

Trumpet grinned. "I won't be running out for this wedding," he promised. He turned on his heel, remembering the two foreboding gentlemen in the corner. "Your lordship—"

Rathincourt, as alert to changes in temperament as well as in the winds of war, stopped in his tracks. "What is it, man?"

"Well, Barrel being full of all types for the wedding, even elves, it's said, well, I'm not one to be worried about appearances. But with the gold water clock from King Bryant and the other gifts . . . thieves as well as guests are bound to be about."

"True enough. Have you a suspicion I might look into for you? Discreetly, of course."

Trumpet heaved a sigh of relief. "Two gentlemen in the far corner. Quiet types . . . they toasted her ladyship, but, well, things aren't as they seem."

The white-haired man swung about. The corner table stood empty. "It appears we're too late."

Trumpet looked and then scratched his head. "Well, thank you, your lordship for the consideration. The first mug of beer is on me."

"Thank *you*, Trumpet." Rathincourt straightened his dark red tunic. "Do you remember their faces?"

But the busy innkeeper had seen too many faces that night and shook his head. The warlord sighed and headed toward the Rovers. He needed to find Rowan as soon as possible. Without putting a damper on things, he wanted to talk about protection ringing the village. Enemies as well as allies could be expected at an occasion like this.

Trumpet's wasn't the only tavern in town bulging to the seams with the Seven True Races come to attend the wedding. Storytellers told all the old stories, of All-Mother who made the Seven True Races and held them in her lap in the sky until the evil one frightened her and she stood up to flee; the races fell from her lap to the lands that held them now, where All-Mother gathers them up still, one at a time, to take back to her. Tales like that meant dusty throats and Barrel carried out its name several times over.

The only ones not drinking were the Mutts, the doglike humans, for drinking didn't go well with their gentle constitution, and a few of the revelers looked askance at the Lady Alorie's personal guard led by a Mutt named Jasper, for he was a soldier and even more foreign to their way of thinking than strong drink.

In her rooms above the Broken Barrel inn, a seamstress sat with her daughters around her, each of them with a section of a wedding gown over her knees, taking tiny stitches. The room was ablaze with light and still she frowned and picked at a stitch, taking it out and painstakingly putting it back in again. If all went well, she'd have the gown finished soon. Then she could sleep early and wake in time to enjoy much of the celebration. Rayna straightened and flexed her back. She smiled as a youth entered the room with a fresh lamp to replace a flickering one. It didn't take sorcery to see that he planned on going out.

"Where are you going, Barth?"

He shrugged diffidently. "Just out. Any of the taverns are full tonight. Maybe down below. Pinch is down there telling tales again."

The seamstress' worn hands lay idle in her lap. She had met the dwarf several times. She knew her son couldn't ask for more honest company, but Barth's interest in the dwarf and the Rover Rowan worried her. The whole wedding seemed to have turned her life upside down, though she could never have asked for a nicer employer than the Lady Alorie. Her ladyship was exacting but patient—and who would have thought she had led an army and scattered the host of evil from out of Cornuth and the Barrowlands? But still, there was something disturbing about the presence of Alorie and her lover Rowan. Prosperity was back again. The green shoots of first planting had come a-cropper, and there was talk about the farmlands that there would even be a second harvest this year. And there was other talk. She hesitated to say anything to her son, and her daughters silently watched her face as though they knew they had to learn this—to learn what to say to sons and husbands whose feet itched to travel the roads elsewhere in search of glory and themselves.

But Rayna failed them as she smiled wearily. "Don't believe everything you hear," she said finally.

"Aw, Mom! They're just stories about Gavin Bullheart and the Unicorn sword and stuff like that."

"I know. And I overheard you talking yesterday about Cornuth, and maybe going up there to kill a monster or two yourself. Leave that be! There'll be heroes enough to clear out the old king's city. You've cobbling to learn."

His fleeting smile as he ducked out the doorway told the seamstress he'd not listened to her. With a sigh the woman and her daughters returned to sewing.

The dwarf Pinch would have been a handsome man, if he'd been born a man. As it was, he was a hale and handsome dwarf, with curly yellow hair as bright as the newly forged water clock of gold from the Delvings. His silvery, opaque eyes were a little disconcerting until one knew the dwarf, for it seemed at times he could look right through a man. Now he held reign in the common room, his boots resting upon a squat three-legged stool as he quaffed a dark amber ale. He wiped his mouth carefully on a handkerchief and one of his audience yelled out, "Tell us about the unicorn again."

He cocked a silvery eye on the lad, saying, "Ye look like a maiden, boy. Go out and seek 'un yerself!" But as the drinkers burst into laughter, he dropped his feet to the sawdust-covered floor. "I'll show you, bucko, what few have ever seen." His listeners quieted as he shrugged off his mail surcoat and pulled up his bright blue shirt. Even in the lantern light of the tavern, the wound under his rib cage looked purple and ugly, but he smoothed out the scar tissue unfeelingly. It was clear to all who looked that it had been a death wound. "I was gored, do ye see? But when the lady Alorie brought back the unicorn horn, she healed me. These are good times now, bucko, but don't you be forgetting the past." He dropped his shirt and lifted his mug again, then made a wry face. "Why, this be empty!"

"I'll take care of that, master dwarf!" the lad said and jumped up to refill his drink.

But even as he joked and talked, worry rankled at Pinch. He eyed the front door a number of times, wondering where Mary Rose could be. She was working for this wedding twice as hard as he was—all woman's work, but he worried still. She'd gone out to get freshly churned sweet butter for the feast, but she'd promised to join him. And though he'd made light of his old wound, sometimes it pained him still and brought a dark worry on him. The eve before a wedding was no time to be feeling it.

Mary Rose was just as concerned that she was late. The wagon bumped Eileen awake. The pathway to the town was dim and uncertain here in the woods, and Mary Rose thought she heard brush rustling and shrubbery crackle as though something trailed her. The horse uneasily flicked his ears to and fro.

Finally she pulled the reins back and put her foot on the brake. She handed the reins to Eileen. "I'm going to take a look," she said. "If anything happens to me, you get to town, you understand?"

Eileen blinked sleepy eyes. "Maybe it's the unicorns!"

"No, lass," the dwarf said. "It's not unicorns." She swung out of the wagon with the skill of one used to making it in a world not sized for her. Born to the underworld, she needed no lamp to see well in the darkness. With the wagon halted, the night had an unseemly quiet. She stepped off the pathway. A branch crackled. She thought she heard a pant, then quiet. Mary Rose hesitated. She wore a hunting knife at her belt the way Alorie wore a longknife at her side, and she put a hand to its hilt now.

She narrowed her eyes at the sign in the damp night earth. Then she stumbled over the body of a kill—sucked dry of blood, gutted and stiff in the night. Its odor overwhelmed her and she staggered away.

Mary Rose held up her skirts and ran back to the wagon. She would have to tell Pinch as soon as she reached Barrel, if, indeed, her husband didn't already know. Reken were in the area. Old allies of evil, rust-coated and sharp-fanged, reken could be found scattered throughout the lands, but they hadn't ranged here . . . yet. She didn't like what she'd seen.

She took the reins and snapped the end of them against the horse's rump. "Get on, now!"

When they rattled into town, she found two strong backs willing to unload the wagon for Eileen. She left the farm girl in charge of their fuzzy noggins, for the two lads had been drinking a little, but the girl was full of common sense. Eileen would see the butter safely laid down before she went exploring. Mary Rose had urgent matters to attend to.

She hurried through the doors of the Broken Barrel. Pinch caught her up and swung her around, her fair ash-brown hair floating as he spun her, but the look of joy on his face had melted into a frown before he set her down.

The expression wasn't lost on the two men cooling their heels in a relatively quiet corner of the tavern.

Aquitane turned to his master. "This is the third tavern we've been in, and no nearer learning what we need to know. I tell you, if the sword's anywhere, it's with her. And that means we have to act at the wedding or not at all. I don't like it."

"I agree with you." The Corruptor stood up after dropping a coin on the table to pay for their supper, though it was near enough to midnight eve to almost qualify for breakfast. "You should decide what it is you intend to say when the time comes. If the time comes."

Aquitane straightened, pulling his cloak about him. His blue eyes considered his master's figure. "What do you mean, *if*?"

"I have the same reservations you do, my lord. Do you think I'd bring you here and expend you now, just now, with our troops poised in the north? I have better things to do than to waste my time or your life. My power is close. I have but to grab it."

Aquitane fought the instinct to take a step backward. "For the Iron Liege."

"Yes. Of course," the sorcerer said. "But the wedding's our concern now, and if all goes as I planned it, another . . . diversion will occur. You won't be at risk at all." He pulled his hood down, shading his face even further. "This sound of merrymaking grates at me. I don't intend to waste the rest of the night. I have work to do."

In a last, lowly tavern, whose reputation for inferior beer and toothless serving maids meant for a smaller crowd, a Rover sat alone and pondered a board of *rool*, overlooking the carved pieces. He kept an ear out for the shout that would start his part in the celebration, but for now he sat alone and melancholy, missing the graceful young woman who would soon be a bonded part of his life.

A shadow fell on the board.

"Play a round?"

Rowan looked up. "It'll have to be a quick one."

"I'm the impatient sort," the hooded and cloaked stranger said. He brushed the longknife in its scabbard off his hip as he sat down on the opposite bench. "You set."

Rowan did so swiftly. "Light or dark?"

"Tonight? Dark, I think." The stranger's voice was hoarse, as if he'd been recently ill or perhaps had been injured once in the throat.

"Can I get you a mug?" Rowan asked as he turned the board to put the dark wood pieces before the other player.

"Nay."

"Not celebrating?"

"Another man getting chained to a woman? I think not, and I'm surprised you would be."

Rowan grinned. "You know little of Rover women and even less of Lady Alorie, I'd say."

"Perhaps." Dark wool muffled the smaller man's face. "Draw for first move."

Rowan inclined his head. "I'll pass the move to you, stranger."

The gloved hand reached out decisively and moved a piece.

Rowan eyed the board and matched his move, thinking of long ago when Brock had first taught him the game of *rool* and all its subtleties. It had been a game to remind the players of the role of the High King and a quest to recapture his throne. Over the hundreds of years since the downfall of Cornuth, *rool* had gone in and out of popularity. Few played it now.

He'd asked for a quick game, and the stranger gave him one, his moves cold and deceptive, leading him on until they stood at the edge of final confrontation, with the kingpiece in deadly peril for each.

Rowan said then, "I have you."

The stranger shook his head. "Not yet, friend." He moved his queenpiece out, sacrificed it to the opposition, and salvaged his king.

The move shook Rowan to his core. No one—no one—sacrificed the queenpiece. It simply wasn't done. There was no inheritance of the dynasty of the king without a queen. He came to his feet, stunned by the ill omen. "No one takes a queen for a fall," he said. "Who are you?" He tore back the hood.

Her dark hair came tumbling down and Alorie grinned at him, saying, "And you know even less of your lady than you think!"

Two

What amused her infuriated him. "What do you think you're doing?" he said lowly, and now it was his voice that was hoarse, with rage. "We're star-crossed enough without adding ill omens."

Alorie pulled her hood back and began to tuck up her dark curls within it, though now he could see her face and her gray eyes darkening to dominate her ashen countenance. "I wanted to see you," she answered. "Three months has been far too long for me. I thought perhaps you felt the same—" She turned away, he caught her gloved hand.

"Alorie."

She paused. He kept the rough-hewn tavern table between them. "*Rool* is more than a game, and this is more than a marriage."

"Oh, aye," she said. "That I know." She twisted her wrist free and reinstated the light king. "I did what I had to do."

"There is no kingdom without a queen." Suddenly he regretted keeping her there because he feared what she was saying. "Do you understand me? Without his queen the High King is nothing!"

She shook her head. "Not the way I learned to play it from Grandfather. All that counts, all that is important, is that the king is restored. No piece is beyond sacrifice." She leveled her gaze at him. "And that's the way I play the game."

He did not respond.

"Dammit, Rowan." Her boot heel clicked on the hearth's edge at her back. "You're letting the prophecy unman you! Stop it. Our part's done. We've scattered *his* troops to the four winds and set him back years in his plans. It's to our children and our children's children to deal with it. Not us! I've—we've—lost enough."

He still could not force an answer through his clenched teeth. Alorie had not heard what she had read on the wall of Cornuth when they had made their ill-fated quest there to find a weapon to defeat the Corruptor. She spoke in tongues, and none of them had heard all of the prophecy, but each his part: Kithrand of the elves, Gavin Bullheart, Pinch, and himself. Rowan would never repeat his portion. He had buried it in his heart and hoped that it would never come to pass. If he were fortunate enough, he might school it into his son, and pray that it never came to pass for him either.

Gavin Bullheart had not had such fears. He had taken the sword of Frenlaw, the broken half sword, and watched it reforged, unafraid to fight the war with it. It had killed him.

He made a gesture then, a Rover gesture, as eloquent as a shrug, meaning he would leave it to the wind along the road. Fated. Tension left the lines of Alorie's body. A smile curved her lips.

"I can think of other games to play this night."

He remembered then how much he'd missed her. He returned the smile.

"Reken? Are ye sure, lass?"

Mary Rose tossed her head. "I read the kill. You cannot miss the signs."

Pinch frowned. He scouted the tavern and saw no one sober enough to take with him. He took his wife by the elbow as he went to the cloakroom and recovered his sword belt and traveling cloak.

"You can't go alone!"

"Neither can I raise the entire village," he said. "I'll find Rowan."

"He's got to be readied for the Search."

Pinch stopped outside the tavern's swinging gate. A chill in the night air raised a blush on his dwarf wife's face. Her eyes were bright. "Ye take care of the Lady Alorie. We'll be along presently. I'll take care of the bucko, never fear." He strode away purposefully, trying not to feel her too-bright gaze between his shoulders, for he knew it was not for Rowan or Alorie she feared. Aye, that was what a man or dwarf did to himself when he loved or married. He shrugged into his cloak and headed for the maverick tavern on Barrel's outskirts where he'd last seen Rowan.

He found Jasper leaning against a wall. The Mutt turned

to him, his paw trailing indolently over his sword hilt. Pinch beckoned him to fall in.

"Trouble?"

The dwarf nodded briskly. "Sign of reken."

"Spying?"

"Probably."

Jasper's black-skinned lips pulled back off his teeth. "I'll do for 'em."

"We'll be going out along the north road. Ready a couple of horses."

The Mutt nodded and agilely dodged from Pinch's side and headed for the livery. Across the scraggly end of what could be described as Barrel's rough end of town, he saw the rugged outlines of the Stove Inn. He had not approved of Rowan's decision to pass his time there, but the Rover lad got wayward now and then and he could do little about it. Any trouble he met in Barrel, Rowan could easily handle.

As, indeed, it appeared he was doing a little handling now. Pinch pulled up abruptly in the shadows and watched as Rowan and a companion sauntered in the narrow alleyway between the Stove Inn and the rest of the district. The companion was too short and lithe to be another swordsman, though she dressed like it. The dwarf frowned as they leaned together. A curse on the bucko, though Pinch knew well the jitters of the marriage harness settling around a man. He approached them and thrust the slighter body aside, saying in his deep, rumbling voice, "I'll be sayin' nothing of this to the lady, Rowan, but ye better be comin' along with me."

The woman laughed softly. "Ah, Pinch! Still protecting my virtue, are you? Well, you've caught us."

He ground his boot heel in as he pivoted. "Alorie! Ah, this is a bad business."

Her gray blue eyes sparkled in the tavern's spillover illumination. "What?"

"Reken," he growled. "I'll be taking the bucko here with me out to take a look."

Rowan, the bucko in question, had straightened severely but said nothing, his mouth in an amused twist. Now, however, his eyebrow arched, but his comment was cut off by Alorie's exclamation.

"I thought I heard one! Where—the north end?"

"So Mary Rose pointed me. She found a kill."

"They'll be spying," Rowan said. "We've expected this."

"Aye," rumbled Pinch. "But that doesn't mean we have to let them get away with it."

Jasper rode up, the reins of Pinch's pony and a nondescript gelding in his paw. The Mutt pulled his slat-sided mare to a halt and saluted Alorie. She nodded.

"Jasper."

"With your permission, lady."

She nodded. "Of course." She kissed Rowan swiftly and watched them mount and ride, thinking that her nightmare had been an omen that her years of respite were ending. She should have known that the harsh simplicity of a peasant's lot was not meant for them. She clenched her hand about the hilt of her longknife, and prayed that it was not so.

A Month Earlier

"I do not approve." Drussander kept the sun to his back, dappling shadows across the burled pillars of the council hall, and Kithrand frowned, unable to read either his opponent's face or his antennae. Around the low table where one either knelt or lay, elves stirred but said nothing in defense of Kithrand's request.

The elfin lord was angered, but he dared not show it in council. He had not gone to the table so he paced the platform's edge. A wind had arisen and leaves stirred all over the city, new leaves bannering to the season. He looked across a sight no eyes other than elfin eyes had ever seen: forbidden Charlbet; its beauty swelled his heart. He feared to think it might ever change. "It is only right," he said when he was sure his voice could keep an even timbre. "The homeless children have no greater ruler left than the Lady Alorie. If I wish to go as their friend and quest companion, you could not stop me—"

A whispery voice muttered, "Then go, Kit, and leave us be!"

Which muttering Kithrand ignored as he said, "All I ask is leave for my attendance to be official." Try as he would, he could not keep his antennae still. They feathered the air above his brow with his passion.

Gillus said, from his gold- and silver-threaded splendor at the head of the table, "Your friendship is hasty and unwise. We feel as you do, but we know from experience that we must examine our feelings and the portents closely before we act."

Kithrand stood, enrobed in maroon and rose, his fair hair rippling down to his shoulders, his booted feet planted firmly. "They live hasty lives, wise ones. If I wait for examination and decision from the lot of you, they will have grown old and died first!"

That whispery muttering: "Kit, Kit, Kit."

Gillus, however, took affront. He stood. Years had made him potbellied, though the rest of him was still elf-slender. His jet hair was silvering heavily. His dark blue eyes were as wide and aslant as they should be, but clouds rode the vision of his right and he was losing his sight in it. "You take a different measure of my words than intended. You ask for more than passage to this wedding of children. You ask to be an ambassador, our envoy. We have not done such a thing since the death of the High King—which I scarce remember and you were not yet conceived. It is not that we do not wish to extend our hands in friendship; it is that the homeless children have a history of which they are not even aware, and we suffered grievously in that history." As librarian of Charlbet, he rolled out the word history in all its pomposity.

The mutterer sat up at the foot of the table. She sniffed imperiously. Her robes of deepest green flowed unwrinkled to her sandaled feet, and the air filled with the perfume of the movement of the scented cloth. She was easily the oldest elf in the room. Her pale blond hair had gone to snow white. Her antenna quivered indignantly and severe lines creased her heart-shaped face. "Faugh," she said. The tree-uplifted platform quivered as though the branches felt her agitation. "We, as well as the High King, suffered putting down the evil that now shifts restlessly in his barrows. The Corruptor looks for the key that will unlock that one, and his searches will not be barren forever. Our time grows short. Go, Kithrand, be off with you and fill my ears no more. Go where you will and say what you have to say! Warn them. Remind them that the past few years have been but a pause. Our scouts say the malisons have returned to Cornuth from the north. If the souleaters have crept out, can the Corruptor be far behind? As for the rest of you—" she swept the hall with her haughty gaze—"we had best be catching up with what is left of our kingdom. *A ship landed twelve days ago—*"

Kithrand did not hear the rest of her speech. He grabbed a vine, wrapped it about one slender but well-sinewed wrist, and swung down off the platform, skimming through tree branches that sensed his passage and made way for him. He had his permission and did not wait to see if the Lady Orthea would be debated.

And on that same day, deep inside lifeless caverns that carried only the soundings of life as vibrations from above, a footfall echoed. It was followed by a dragging, staggering scrape, then a panting breath as if from torn bellows. Then another footfall. A pause. A sob from a dessicated throat . . . or perhaps it was a curse. Then a scrape from a limb that refused to awaken. Step. Halt. Drag. A gasping pause, until the cavern was filled with the sound of the being's agonizing progress.

Sound and life echoed in depths meant to imprison.

The even star reached its zenith as Mary Rose and Alorie met at the foot of the tavern's backstairs.

They each pulled back with a gasp and then Alorie let out a breathy laugh. "You're late!"

"And you're absent! Milady, they'll be ringing the bell for you any moment now."

"Then we'd better hurry."

Mary Rose followed her lady up the stairs with a little more difficulty—curse these human stairs meant for strides of long-legged weeds!—and arrived out of breath. She closed the door behind her even as Alorie shucked her breeches, went to the basin, and began to lave with rose-scented water. It had chilled since Mary Rose had brought it up, found the room empty, and begun to search for her charge. Alorie gasped and the dwarf maid barked an unsympathetic laugh.

Pinking as she washed, Alorie cast an eye as Mary Rose picked up the blouse and skirt. The mask dangled over her arm. It was not a mask that would fool anyone, but it was the first Alorie had seen of it, and its decoration was a clue as to the public face she wore. It had been stylized as a beautiful lady and they had left in the frown line between her brows that characterized, she supposed, both her stubbornness and her nearsightedness. But she'd seen beautiful girls wearing the masks of nags and hags and, on one occasion, seen a shy and homely girl painted as a radiant beauty. Mary Rose spied her glance and with a disapproving cluck threw her blouse over the mask.

"You know you're not to look."

"I know, I know." Alorie stood. The tapers lit when the bathing water had been brought were burning low. "Are they back yet?"

Her maid froze on sturdy legs.

Alorie tossed her thick, dark hair back over her shoulder as she reached for an underblouse. "I saw them ride out, armed."

Mary Rose took a breath. "Aye, they're back," she said, echoing her husband's soft burr. "Dowsed with blood and fairly scared my growth out of me, such as it is. But it was all of the enemy."

"Good." Alorie shivered and grabbed away the long skirt. "Reken?"

"A patrol of three, they said, and taken care of. Pinch said to tell you—he said to tell you he found other signs in the wood. 'Horn rubs against a tree.' He said you would know what he meant." Mary Rose stepped behind her and cinched the skirt's waistline. She said, "Up with your arms now," and slid the blouse over. Then, taking care not to display the mask again, she reached for a bone comb. "How about a love knot in your hair? I think I can tie the mask above it."

Alorie obligingly sat so that Mary Rose could reach to comb. She tried not to think of reken howls in the woods, and of the signs of unicorns.

Three

"One for me and one for the land that keeps us free," Alorie toasted dutifully and splashed the mug's contents upon the landlord's hearth. A rousing cheer followed her declaration in the Broken Barrel, but the contents of the mugs raised to her were promptly poured down throats after a desultory splashing to the floor. She smiled behind her mask, though the wearing of it hid her expression. "And now my good people, I search for my lost love, my husband-to-be. Have you seen him this night?"

Across the room she could see Jasper watching her, his doggish face unsuited for a drinking mug, but sipping ale from a clay bowl, always on guard yet enjoying himself this eve as well as anyone else in the town. She was immediately baffled with answers and riddles and laughed in spite of herself, though it was near dawn and she'd had enough of the game. Deanmuth, one of Lord Rathincourt's men, she thought, swung her upon his massive shoulders and carried her out of the Barrel. The linked mail of his surcoat bit into her hips through her skirt, but she ducked her head to avoid the eaves and the front doorway, obliging in the fun. Rowan could count the circular bruises in the afternoon when they were finally allowed to retire to their bower.

She thought she saw a masked man ducking behind Jasper as the crowd followed them out into the fresh air, but it could have been anyone—there were several masked girls parading about Barrel to mislead Rowan, and she knew of at least three Rovers wearing masks to deceive her. But there was much, much more to Rowan than his face. She knew his way of going, his alert tilt of head, the swing of his shoulders balancing his lean body. And besides, in the shadow of that shadow she thought she'd caught the gleam of butter-yellow curled hair and silvery eyes as a dwarf followed after.

30

Alorie threw her head back as Rathincourt's man straightened, and she inhaled deeply of the last of the night air. Yes, the edges of the sky lightened—earlier every day as it was wont to do in this month. As the soldier pivoted slowly, she saw the taverns and shops and homes emptying all over Barrel, in all directions, coming to the square and the masked men gathering. Her heart did a funny jump as she realized the Search was coming to a close. The soldier whirled faster and the crowd became a dizzy blur.

The drink went to her head as well. Just before she closed her eyes, she thought she saw the bulk of another man standing aloof at the edge of the celebrants, his traveling cloak muddied and frayed, hiding the clothes beneath. The vision burned itself into her eyes. She gasped and opened them wide, but Deanmuth whirled even faster and individual forms became giddy swirls in the graying dawn. Alorie took a deep breath and told herself what she felt could not be true.

There was no way Aquitane would dare to be in Barrel that morning.

Just when she thought her bearer would lose his equilibrium, the massive soldier halted. The ring of masked men pressed closer as the adjunct lifted her down. Giddiness clung to her and she pushed her mask off, gulping down the still chilled air to bring her senses back.

"Choose, choose, choose!"

Alorie saw Mary Rose pushing her way to the fore, taking no guff from bigger townspeople, and she looked to her a moment, but her husband Pinch was nowhere to be seen. She turned a half step, and spotted the seamstress Rayna, who had been working on her bridal gown. Her rangy son Barth all but dwarfed the woman.

The ring of masked men milled about and Alorie cried, "Unfair!" Her protests were drowned out by the roar of laughter from the onlookers. She laughed then, too.

She could rule out the arthritic masked man with grayed wisps of hair edging out from his mask. So, too, the beanpole of a farm boy who walked as if he still fought to keep a plow in the ground to lay a furrow. Trumpet, stocky innkeeper of renown, had donned a mask, too, unless her eyes deceived her. So that left a handful of Rovers to pick from and they protected their own as only a Rover could—landless, homeless, rangers of hill and stream, the long ago exiled guard of the High King. Her marriage to one was a sign of their redemption.

"Choose, lass, or have ye changed your mind?"

Pinch's jeering rumble brought on more cries of "Choose, choose!" but Alorie had already picked out the masked form that drew her gaze, and, following the tug of her emotions, made her way to him, put her hands upon his shoulders, and pulled him inside the ring with her. She reached up to pull the black cloth mask off his face, even as Rowan's pleased chuckle warmed her. The Bride had found her Husband.

Alorie paused at the top of the stairs. Mary Rose pushed and fussed about her. "It's just about dawn," she said. "Have I time for myself?"

The maid paused. "The breakfast table's waiting, and the canopy's to be put up yet. You might have a pause or two coming to you." She brushed a straying tendril of hair from Alorie's brow and rubbed the frown mark with a callused forefinger. "You'll have a terrible line there if you don't stop that."

The girl wrinkled her nose. "My face was meant to wrinkle. Grandfather had the deepest creases in all of Bethalia. He said it was indicative of profound thought processes."

"Not age or distemper."

"Never!" She leaned into her room and saw the dress Rayna had arrayed upon the cot. It took her breath away and she crossed to touch it, her fingers trembling. Lying next to it was a shift and hose of the finest thread. She had not thought to see such things again after the fall of Sinobel. Her roughened hands snagged upon them and she pulled the yarn back into shape quickly with a curse that Mary Rose coughed at, saying, "Milady!"

The dress beckoned her, but not nearly as much as the forest at the north end of Barrel. She had unfinished business there, she feared, and before the mists of dawn curled away, she wanted to be there. She paused long enough to take her cloak, belt, and longknife that she had worn earlier.

Jasper straightened at the foot of the stairs, but she lay a hand on his silken arm. "Not this time."

His brows came together. "The reken—"

"I can deal with them if you left any behind. I have something to do this morning and no time to argue. Walk with me to the edge of the forest, if you wish."

The Mutt made an awkward bow. "I do." Nor could she

shake her guard as they hurried through the last of the night as it lightened to give way to the day.

The forest was deeper and darker, heavy, overhanging branches still a roof over the grasses and shrub, and the dew there was like a blanket over the coltsfoot. Dawn lingered here beyond its time as Alorie made her way into it. That the reken could hide here she did not doubt, and she listened to her passage, made stealthy by years of practice, though any Rover child could do far better. No signal passed to mark her entrance. If something waited for her now, she bet her life it was not reken.

Horn rubbings upon bark, serrated slashes cutting into rough wood. Alorie paused as she followed Pinch's trail, for he had marked the way for her with a bent twig here and a braided clump of grass there, as if knowing her heart. And so he should, for it had been a black unicorn that had given him his mortal wound, and a white one that had cured him. She touched the slashes and stood on tiptoe to look closely, hoping the beast might have left a hint behind—a thread of forelock perhaps—and if it had, would it be of blazing ivory or darkest ebony?

Her nightmare pressed close around her, and Alorie forced a shuddering breath into her lungs as if to dispell it.

Whether the beast was light or dark, it had called her and she had come to meet it.

The branded tree stood at the edge of a lea, and she stepped into it, foolstaff dappling her boots with its dew. It gave off a sweet scent as her steps bruised it, and as she looked across the grasses, she could see another's steps imprinted, a deeper, more verdant green. Hoofprints.

Her mouth dried. She loosened her longknife in its sheath, though it had been a long time since she'd had to pull it.

The meadow was small. A horse could cover it in five running strides. That gave her some advantage.

A twig snapped. Its report echoed loudly in the copse beyond the meadow. Alorie stood, bathed in the rosy glow of morning that streamed down through the forest ring. Sunrise had come even to the densely wooded strand. She put up both hands, hesitated, then lowered her hood.

She called out softly. "You summoned. I am here."

Long-needled branches swayed, then parted. She saw a wisp of shadow both light and dark. Her pulse quickened at the sight. The beast broke his cover and stood, but it was difficult to tell if he was light dappled with black or dark dazzled with the first rays of sun. She wavered.

The stallion pawed. His feathers caught the dewdrops and scattered them, gemlike into the air. He spoke, and the air trembled with his voice that was not a voice but filled the silence. "Are you the Dancer?"

"Once," Alorie said. Her voice thinned as if it would fail her. Yes, once she had dared to share his thunder and majesty in dance, though not this beast, for he still carried his lance upon his brow. The one then had surrendered his horn to her, though it diminished him and he had faded away, as insubstantial as the mist once she had taken it. Alorie cleared her throat. "Have you come to bless the marriage?"

He thrust his way bodily into the meadow and stood, head up, neck taut, his mane and tail cresting thickly over his form. He reminded Alorie of her nightmare and the Corruptor's hollow voice saying, "There are unicorns, and there are Unicorns."

"I carry no blessing, Dancer," the stallion said, "but a curse. You are a daughter of the prophecy and you fail us all with your lack of courage. Find it again or the Corruptor and the Despot will plow us under in salted earth."

"No." Alorie pressed one hand to her throat, the denial pained her so. "I've lost everything but Rowan. I've done all I could. The prophecy is nothing."

"The prophecy is hope. Without hope, nothing can live in Bethalia. I have been sent to remind you, Alorie Sergius. Go now and look for joy among your wedding presents!"

With this, the unicorn trumpeted and charged. Alorie, Dancer, meant to stand her ground and, if need be, grasp that serrated horn and tumble herself out of the stallion's way as she had done once, but her resolution shattered and she turned and ran.

Four

By the time he had ordered an appropriate gift and clothes fit for rejoicing a marriage, Kithrand had less than seven days in which to make the journey from Charlbet east and south to Barrel. He whistled up his two best horses from the valley below Charlbet: a husky, deep-shouldered gelding whose temper had been sweetened the hard way, and a strapping mare who almost matched the gelding in size. He planned to ride one and lead the other loaded with spare supplies so that he could switch off easily and make better time. He stroked their gleaming necks after they raced to him. Kithrand knew that time was of the essence, but he would use neither bit nor spur. They would do their best for him because that was how elfin horses were bred—for speed and loyalty.

And so he traveled, across swollen rivers and muddy fields, through forests heavy with spring rains. They were mired once, but he was able to leap to across the bog and rope them out. The horses slept soundly at night, nodding over his form, protecting their master even in his sleep, though elves sleep lightly. They labored over mountain passes not quite thawed for the season, hock deep in slush. They raced over newly greened meadows, jumped thickets for the joy of it, and scattered flocks of birds to hear the *whirr* of their wings frantically seeking the air.

He knew he was close to Barrel when the roads began to show heavy usage, even this early in the trading seasons, wheel ruts fresh in the soft earth. A host of travelers had gone before him to attend the wedding. He checked his rope clock, counting the knots. If he was right, he had a day left. If he was wrong . . . Kithrand shrugged.

As they entered the deep forest north of Barrel, he turned deliberately off the trading road. He preferred the needled

35

footing of the forest floor to the muddy and channeled road. Besides, he did not wish to be part and parcel of the humanity bustling south. It was an elf's nature to be secretive and solitary.

The woods cut off the light early and dusk fell quicker, though his eyes saw well enough. A quietude fell with the early evening and it was then his mare took a wrong step, bobbled, and threw up her muzzle with a sharp whinny.

Kithrand kicked off the saddle pad and landed lightly beside her. He rubbed her withers. "What is it, Misty?"

She hung her head and shifted her weight off her right foreleg. Strider came to an impatient halt. He shoved his nose into Kithrand's back. "All right, all right," the elf lord said to him. "Taste the littlefoot." He dropped the gelding's reins and then moved to the mare's right front hoof to see what the matter was.

She lifted her hoof obligingly. He ran his hands about her pastern; it was warmish, but that was to be expected with the heavy traveling they'd had. What was not to be expected was the pointed rock lodged in her frog . . . lodged deep enough that blood freshened as he slipped his wrist sheath knife and prodded it out.

Kithrand made a noise to himself. He'd have to put a poultice on the hoof—bruises were bad enough, but a cut could fester. She'd walk well enough if he wrapped a bag about it, but it looked as though he'd not make the evening festivities. Walking at Misty's pace would take them until dawn.

Brush crackled. Kithrand called over his shoulder, "Don't be a pig, Strider, leave some grass for the forest beasties," as he crushed some littlefoot blossoms and packed them in to ease the pain.

But Strider had not left the mare's side. He had frozen there, white ears pricked forward, dark eyes alert to the shadowed woods about them. Kithrand looked up even as the rank scent hit him as a pack of reken moved out of the bramble.

"Ah," he said to no one in particular. "It looks as if I'll be even later than I thought." He moved his cape away from the scabbard of his low-slung sword.

The reken milled and snarled, their tusks clashing as they moved forward.

Kithrand smiled. It was a good thing he already had his throwing knife in hand.

*   *   *

Alorie spread the deep blue gown about her with shaking hands. Mary Rose caught one of them up and patted it.

"I couldn't love you more if I was your own dear mother," the maid said.

Alorie looked down. She tightened her fingers about Mary Rose's. "Thank you," she answered, and found her throat very tight. She had not thought about this day without her father, Nathen, and her insufferable tyrant of a grandfather until then. Then it swelled up inside her until it threatened to overwhelm her. Once she had wanted to take up the Unicorn sword and annihilate Aquitane, as if it could erase all that the renegade lord had done to her and her family. She had chosen Rowan's love over vengeance. After what the unicorn in the woods had said to her, she feared to touch the sword again. She would never master it.

And she trembled to be its servant.

As if reading her thoughts, Mary Rose threw open the lid of the trunk and lifted out the casket.

"No," Alorie said. "Leave it. A sword has no place at a wedding."

The dwarf maid pulled herself up, affront written all over her apple-cheeked face. "This one does, milady! And I thought we settled this once."

Alorie turned back to the polished shield that served as a mirror and addressed her tumbled hair again. "You settled it. I didn't. And I won't have it."

Mary Rose planted herself in the doorway, casket abreast. "You'll not be leaving without taking it."

Alorie put in a last comb and turned, eying Pinch's wife. "Then I'll take the window."

"You'll not!"

"Think so?"

Mary Rose's lips pursed. To Alorie's gaze she never resembled her kinsman, King Bryant of the Delvings, more than this moment in her pride and her stubborness. The maid said deliberately, "If I have to tie you to the cot and go get milord Rathincourt and Rowan, you'll be wearing the sword."

White-maned Rathincourt would brook no nonsense from her. One of the last lords left of the old guard, he'd been most insistent. Alorie faltered. She did not want the warlord looking on her as a willful girl.

Shuddering, she turned away from Mary Rose in defeat.

"All right," she murmured and waited for it to be brought out.

"Ye'll not be getting nervous, now, would ye?" Pinch cast a silvery look at his armsman as Rowan adjusted his short cape of black and silver, especially made by the Rover women of the haven Stonedeep to be worn at his wedding. Rovers customarily wore green and russet over the colors of their exiled post.

Pinch crossed his legs and sat back atop an empty keg, as he tamped his pipe down. Blue-black smoke curled up presently as he watched Rowan continue to fuss with the cape. "Good weed, this."

"You'd smoke littlefoot if you had to," Rowan muttered. The water basin made for a poor mirror. The skirmish with the reken had sobered him up more than a little, so he had no excuse for the pounding in his temples and fumble in his fingers. Would that Brock was here! Like a father the dark-skinned man had been to him. The Rover mage would undoubtedly have a word or two to say to him. And, equally undoubtedly, Rowan would find exception with some of it and be left to ferret out that which would prove valuable.

"You're frowning, bucko. What be ye thinkin' of?"

"The dead," Rowan said. "I know, I know, an ill omen."

" 'Tis only natural. The two of you have a lot of history together . . . a war, even. Wars mean death."

He took a deep breath and gave his fingers one last chance to button his cape. They accommodated him.

Pinch blew a smoke ring and jabbed the pipe through it for emphasis. "But this be a wedding, and weddings mean life! Oh, I know you and the lass have been with one another . . . but not so often as to start a family. Now's the time to start, Rowan. We're not getting any younger."

"Speak for yourself, Pinchweed."

"Well, I might. If ye stop dragging me about the country-side, 'twould help. Mary Rose is making noises about getting a cottage of our own."

"Why not go back to the Delvings?" Rowan asked as he turned and buckled on his sword belt and adjusted its sling.

Pinch had paled slightly. "Not the Delvings." He shook his head vigorously. "I cannot live underground."

"You're about the only dwarf I know who can't."

"Then ye know little about the dwarfdom I come from!"

Rowan nodded. "True again. Even the sorcerous city of

Veil is more open than your birthplace or Charlbet." He
checked his draw. "And speaking of which, where do you
think Kithrand is? I thought he'd be here."

Pinch shrugged as he jumped down from the keg. "Elves
are tricksy," he answered. "He'll be here if it fits his whim,
which is more than I can say for the rest of his ilk." He
stood on a crate to fold back the edges of Rowan's short
cape, then got off after eying the Rover critically. "Ye look
as ready as you'll ever be."

"Thanks," retorted Rowan. "I think."

The canopy had been strung in the main square. The
townsfolk let out a peal as Rowan and Pinch arrived. The
ranger looked across, under the canopy, and saw Medra
standing quietly, waiting for them. The rawboned Rover
woman had been chosen by both Rowan and Alorie as the
healer to represent the All-Mother for them. She was dressed
severely, for Rover women were upon the road as Rover
men, stealing time in the havens they could find in the
wilderness or outlying parts of sympathetic realms. She had
brought the canopy of Stonedeep with her. This part of the
ceremony was perhaps the only portion to be the same
whether Alorie was marrying royalty or commoner.

An aisle formed before them. Rowan squinted in the bright
noonday sun, but even as he squinted, wisps of cloud scuttled
across the sky and the day was dappled light and dark. He
hesitated to step forward, but Pinch grumbled at his side.

" 'Tis time, bucko."

He hooked a thumb in his sword belt and tried to look
nonchalant as he approached stern-faced Medra. The canopy shadowed him completely as he stepped under it, though
it rippled slightly in the breeze. He had just gained his place
in front of her when he heard the murmurs greeting Alorie
as she stepped out of the tavern.

He turned his head and remembered with a shock the first
morning of his meeting with her, and how even then those
stormy gray-blue eyes had captured him—him, the freest of
the Rovers. Had Brock foreseen that when he'd sent Rowan
to Sinobel to bring her from the beleaguered city? Perhaps.
Rowan would not discount the story if told that way. But
then she'd been a girl on the threshold of womanhood. Now
as she stepped forth in a sky-blue gown, her dark hair a
cloud about her oval face, her eyes seeking him, he felt a
stirring. By all the gods, she was beautiful in that dress!

Alorie stepped out hesitantly, the Unicorn sword a heavy
drag upon her waist. She wore it ornamentally, its spiraled
length along her right hip, incorrect for a draw but she had
no intention of using it. Its weight dragged at her as though
she carried an anvil, and she looked forward to handing it
back to Mary Rose, who would give it in its casket to Medra
to use as an altar over which their wrists would be bound.
She heard the murmurs the moment she was sighted. Were
they for her—or the mystical weapon at her side? Was she
beautiful or only a curiosity? She looked desperately for
Rowan, found his face, and held to it as though it were a
beacon as she moved toward him.

The pipers began to play and someone had even found a
harp. The drummer kept pace with her solemn steps or
perhaps she kept pace with him. She felt a tensing of power
along her thigh. The sword quickened. It thrilled against
her, alive as it had never been those last days of war when,
victorious, both it and she had been totally drained. She had
done all she could, elated by their triumph and saddened by
the knowledge she could never provide all the sword needed
to be the weapon it had truly been prophesized to be.

And now they wanted her to take it up again.

Alorie hesitated in her march. The music took her up
swiftly, made the stumble seem a curtsey before walking
beneath the canopy. She gathered up the shreds of her
resolve and started forward again. Faces along the aisle
were a blur. She thought she saw the seamstress and her
daughters who'd made this beauty of a dress. And Rathincourt,
her warlord, in full dress, his helm underneath his right
elbow, his left held out to her, to stand by her in place of
her deceased father. His snow-white hair showed no sign of
thinning, and his immense eyebrows pulled together over
his deep blue eyes as if he saw her hesitation. Several of his
massive adjuncts winged the area, including Deanmuth.

The air under the canopy was chill upon her face as she
stepped under it. She welcomed its touch, for it brought her
focus back upon Rowan. He smiled and her worries fled.
All that had ever been truly good in her life waited before
her. Alorie smiled back and went to him as Mary Rose took
the sword off her belt, lay it in the casket, and gave it to
Medra for the ceremonies.

"We gather to witness and strengthen a bonding that is
nearly as ancient as our lives here upon this earth since our
fall from the All-Mother. The earth is fixed below, the

All-Mother above. The only mutable part of this ceremony is the flesh that partakes in it. Who names this man?"

Pinch rumbled, "I do. This is Rowan."

Medra's face creased, an expression that flashed by as quickly as it had appeared.

"And who names this woman?"

Rathincourt said crisply, "I do, your honoress. This is the Lady Alorie of the House of Sergius."

Again, that fleeting glimpse of humor across the healer's face. Then she looked solemnly out across the square and the multitude gathered there. "This is a grave bonding to enter into. The All-Mother asks of you before you make this commitment that you both have fulfilled whatever obligations you may have made before. Rowan?"

He nodded. "I am free to this bonding."

"Alorie?"

Her voice failed her. She tried to speak, could not, and merely nodded her head.

Medra held the Unicorn sword in its open casket. Before she presented it, she said, "If there is anyone present who knows differently, now is the time to speak."

One of Rathincourt's men stirred, the burly man hidden by shadow, drawing Alorie's startled gaze. Rowan looked up also, but before the man could say anything, if speak he would, the sky clouded. A faraway rumbling spoke of rain soon to fall. Alorie blinked and shuddered, once, inside her bridal dress.

A wind swept across the square, scattering townspeople here and there, a dark funnel of a wind that expired as it reached the canopy, streaming both Medra's and Alorie's hair loose of their ribbons. The dust devil cloud opaqued, solidified, into a mask as big as a man.

Its mouth stretched open. "Stop! I forbid it!"

Alorie's eyes widened. She clung to Rowan's arm. He tried to shake her off so that he could draw his sword as the good people of Barrel cried out, "Sorcery!"

Pinch growled, "Foul mongerer," and drew his axe to cleave it, but Alorie trembled as it spoke again.

"This must not be! She is the last of the House of Sergius!"

Pinch raised his axe.

"Don't!" Alorie cried out.

Five

"Don't destroy it!" she said and broke away from Rowan to stop Pinch as the dwarf axe quavered in midair.

"I'll not let them profane your wedding day!" the armsman swore.

"This is sorcery most foul." Rathincourt added to Medra, "Your Honoress, ignore this blasphemy!"

The mask turned as if sighted through the gaping holes that served the mask as eyes. Alorie met the horror squarely.

"What is it you want of me?"

"Milady . . ." the voice paused, thinned, gasping. "You have promises to keep—"

"That does it," Pinch thundered and raised the axe again.

"No!" She grabbed it by the haft, even though the weight of it nearly tore her arm from her socket.

"Are you daft, lass?" Pinch protested.

Alorie shook her head wearily. She turned to Rowan. "Listen," she said. "Can't you hear him? I don't know where he is or how he's sending, but Rowan—that's Brock!"

Rowan thrust himself between Alorie and the mask with a roar. "No! I won't give her up!"

The mask's maw closed, then opened again. "Marry then, if you must . . . but find me first. Listen to what I have to say . . . then, blessings upon you—"

Before either of them could react, Medra let out a high, piercing scream. She toppled to the ground as a thief plucked up the Unicorn sword from the casket in her limp arms and held it triumphant in the air as he leaned from his horse. The destrier reared and kicked out, clearing the area and bringing the canopy down off its poling. The destrier stamped its way out triumphantly as Alorie whirled to meet the arrogant stare of ice-cold blue eyes.

42

"Before that, milady Sergius," Lord Aquitane said, "I have a prior claim that should be discussed."

Even as Alorie cried out, Rowan threw himself forward.

The Unicorn sword twisted in Aquitane's hand. Crimson already shone along its spiraled length, blood that matched that stain pooling under Medra's body. Rowan aimed a cut at the lord's stirruped leg.

Aquitane laughed harshly as he parried it, saying, "Unfair, that one, bastard. Perhaps you'd like to meet me on even ground?"

"Never," Rowan ground out as he freed his blade and jumped back.

The warlord Rathincourt fairly snarled as he came out from under the canopy, but his lunge at the mounted man was blunted by Mary Rose, who threw herself headlong at Aquitane. The Unicorn sword flashed and Alorie turned her face away as blood spurted, and the diminutive maid fell beneath the destrier's hooves in the dirt. Behind her Pinch gave a cry of anguish and there was the sound of an axe whirling through the air.

Aquitane ducked and spat out coarse words as he threw up a mailed fist. The weapon skimmed him and the crowd shattered with a scream as it went wildly into their midst. Young Eileen was not fast enough and it felled her as she gave a high, piercing scream abruptly cut off.

"Enough!" shouted Aquitane. He heeled his stallion, which careened directly at Alorie.

She froze. Her ears roared as time halted in its passing. The renegade lord held out a massive arm for her. She could not move. She would not be impaled as had been Medra and Mary Rose, but worse, captured . . . and she could not move!

And then a blur that was Rowan was between them, and the massive arm twitched, and the hand filled with the Unicorn sword swung down.

"Rowan!" she screamed as his body fell and the dark stallion gathered to leap over her as she knelt by Rowan's form. The air crackled about her. The sword drew her gaze, its ivory and gold-shot length stained with death. Without thought she plunged after it to rip it from Aquitane's hand.

The dark horse pivoted under his rider and Aquitane shouted. His voice pounded at her temples, buffeting her to her knees beside Rowan's body. She felt a dark pressure as Aquitane shouted again. Thunder clapped and then he was gone, pounding out of the town square of Barrel, death and misery in his wake.

"Stop him!" she cried even as Jasper plunged past on his mare, the Mutt's elbows pumping as he hurried her on. She shrilled and reared high as they reached the spot where Aquitane had disappeared, throwing the Mutt to the ground as she toppled, as though repelled. The two thrashed in the dirt but a second as townspeople came to their aid. The mare staggered to her feet and stood, muzzle hanging.

Rathincourt stood over Medra's remains. "That bastard took no mortal road out of here," he said darkly. He ordered his men to strip away the wedding canopy.

Gentle hands pushed Alorie's hands away from Rowan. "He'll live, milady—if we can stop the bleeding."

Alorie looked at her trembling fingers, stained crimson with his life stream. Beyond them she saw Pinch kneel grief-stricken at Mary Rose's crushed form. He pulled her apron over her face, then stumbled onto the stricken farm girl's body. Her parents cradled her, the murdering axe at their scuffed and booted feet.

"How can I ever—" he forced out and stumbled to a halt.

"It wasn't your throw, armsman," the man said flatly. "I seen the magic turn it. It was only bad luck Eileen was in its way."

The woman looked up, tears streaking her careworn face. "Bad luck," she echoed. "You have grief of your own."

And even though they denied his wrongdoing, they huddled close together as if to shield him from further hurting their child's body. Pinch cleared his throat several times and turned away. He left his axe in the dirt.

The detail Rathincourt had ordered came to a halt in the now nearly-empty square. The white-haired lord swung up on his horse. "With your permission, milady."

Alorie looked between Rowan and the warlord, momentarily confused. "I—I don't know—" She looked away as Rowan gave a short gasp—the only healer left in Barrel peeled away his mail coat. The Unicorn sword had bit into it as a hot knife through butter. But its stroke had been blunted, and she saw a deep score along his ribs and into the flesh of his waist—a gaping, ugly wound, but not mortal except for the bleeding. "He was wearing mail," she murmured.

"Aye, lass," Pinch said. "We all did, even under the finery. But we didn't want to fuss you ladies, so I didn't . . .

I didn't tell Mary Rose—" His voice choked away as he knelt beside her again.

Rathincourt's war mount pawed the dirt and did a dancing step away from her. "Milady," he repeated firmly.

But as Alorie looked up, she was interrupted by the clatter of hooves as a rider hurried into Barrel and pulled up, rearing, at the scene of mayhem. The faery gelding let out a snort as he came to ground and his rider leapt off. The circlet about his pale blond hair had stopped a slicing knife wound across his brow, and his jacket had not fared much better, its sleeves all tatters, as the elf lord went to his knee before Alorie.

Before she could say anything, he sprang up, and his antennae wove a pattern about his pale face. "This place stinks of sorcery," he said. "I apologize, milady, for being late. Too late."

Rathincourt said, "It looks as though you've been in a scrape yourself, Lord Kithrand."

"The woods are rank with reken. Did they do this?"

"No," the warlord answered him as the soldiers in his detail began to grumble at his back. "Lord Aquitane was here."

Kithrand leaned over, took Alorie's blood-marked hand in his, and drew her to her feet as he joined her by Rowan's side. He watched a few seconds as the healer moved swiftly, her hands cleansing the wounds and then taking a few stitches to stem the flow of blood. "He'll make it," the elf lord said. "One less tragedy we have to face."

Rathincourt interrupted harshly, "Milady, if I'm to regain the sword—"

"Yes," she answered softly. "Follow Aquitane if you can." Her gaze went to Jasper, who had remounted. "Go with them."

Rathincourt's soldiers shifted uneasily as the Mutt kneed his horse into rank with theirs.

"Suffer him," she requested, "for me."

They looked at their lady, their faces hard and pale beneath their helms and said nothing further, although no man would look back at the Mutt. Kithrand said then, "They'll not find a trail."

But Rathincourt ignored him, wheeled his horse, and led the way out of Barrel northward, and this time no invisible force daunted their passage. Kithrand waited until the clat-

ter of horse hooves had faded, then went to Pinch's side as
the dwarf remained bent over his wife's body.

The squat being said without looking up, "Ye missed the
action, Kithrand."

A wry smile flickered over the elf lord's face. "I found a
spot of it myself. Is this Mary Rose?"

"Aye. What's left of her." *And my heart*, the dwarf might
well have said, but didn't.

Stunned by his loss as well as her own, Alorie stepped to
her maid's form. She peeled back the apron already soaked
with blood, and looked at Aquitane's handiwork. The apple
cheeks were already ashen with death. She'd taken the
sword in the throat, nearly decapitated. Alorie swallowed
convulsively, then reached down and smoothed the dwarf
maid's hair. Two of Jasper's Mutts came up with a litter to
take her body and Medra's. Eileen's had already been loaded
onto the farmer's wagon, and it rolled slowly past them. The
man and woman did not pause as Alorie called out, "I'm
sorry. Oh, gods, I'm sorry!"

As Mary Rose's body went onto the litter, her arm swung
free. Pinch took it up and held her callused hand tightly a
moment before tucking it under her apron.

"I don't want her underground," Pinch said brokenly.

"She has to be buried," Alorie told him. "And the quicker,
the better. We've reken to clear out of our woods."

The dwarf shook his head, yellow curls bouncing. "Not
underground!"

Kithrand put a slender hand on the armsman's thick shoulder. "Come with me, Pinch, and I'll give her elven fire."

Pinch hesitated but a moment, then nodded brusquely.
"That'll do."

Alorie stood, torn, as the healer's litter with Rowan lifted.
His unconscious face was pale, his dark auburn hair a slash
of color across his forehead.

The elf lord sensed her dilemma. He looked at her, saying,
"This is private, milady, if you don't mind."

"I—I'll be with Rowan, then," she stammered and followed after. As she gathered the long skirts of her sky-blue
wedding gown, she saw it had been dyed to purple with the
splash of blood. The Rovers gathered, waiting at the steps
of the Broken Barrel, where the healer signaled for Rowan
to be taken upstairs. She took a breath.

"What are you waiting for?" she demanded. "There are
reken out there. Dispose of them."

As she sailed past, they straightened with indolent grace, echoing, "Yes, ma'am!" and left in a swirl of green and russet cloaks over lean, shadowy forms as she went upstairs after her stricken lover.

The healer dried her hands and said, "The stitching's done. It's not a bad piece of work. The ribs shouldn't pull when he draws a bow or his sword. Time and rest will tell."

Alorie left her post by the door and joined her. "Thank you."

"No thanks needed, Lady. Just ask for Karlin if you should need me later. I'll tarry a bit and be taking a draft downstairs before going home if he wakes feverish. If not, I'll be checking on him tomorrow." The silver-haired, brown-eyed wisp of a woman paused. "Too bad you don't have the sword," she said. "You could have healed them all."

Without a word Alorie closed the door after her, then went to the windows and shuttered them. She sat by her emptied trunk and kept watch on Rowan's still form. No one could hold the sword but her unless sheathed. How could have Aquitane? Then she remembered his mailed hands. The gauntlets must have been ensorcelled. She thought of her dreams. Had the Corruptor been finding ways to combat the talisman's magic?

How long she sat bowed in the corner in silence and thought after the healer left, she could not tell. But a clatter rose in the square and she heard Rathincourt bellow, "Milady Alorie!"

His voice disrupted Rowan. He moved as she brushed past the cot to go to the window.

Throwing open the shutters, she leaned out. The dusty horsemen milled around below her.

Rathincourt had taken off his helm. He looked up now, his snow-white hair sweat-plastered to his brow. "There's no sign of him!" the warlord said. "It's as though the earth swallowed him up."

"He's taken a different road," Kithrand interrupted as he stepped out from the tavern with a mug in his hand. He gave Alorie an ironic bow. "I told you the air reeked of sorcery."

"Do you know where he's gone?"

"Mayhap. I can show you the way."

She found a sudden clarity to her thoughts. "Then do so, my lord of Charlbet. I'll be down in a moment. I've a horse in the livery—dappled. Someone tack him up and bring him around."

Jasper looked up, his soft ears swinging with the snap of his head. "I'll ride with you, milady."

"Then get a fresh horse."

Pinch came out of the tavern, wiping off the foam of a mugful from his upper lip, his bowed legs a little more bowed than usual, but his silvery eyes still clear. "I'll be going with ye, too."

Kithrand said, "That'll be enough. If I may suggest that Rathincourt stay behind? I bring warnings as well as greetings from the hidden city."

"Rathincourt?"

The warlord swung down wearily. "As you wish. Aquitane may be a decoy, as it is."

Alorie pulled back from the window and began to unlace the bodice of her dress. "Where is it you're taking us, Kithrand?"

The elf gave an ironic smile. "I'll be pointing the way, but alas, I cannot go with you, milady. Elves cannot go the way of mortal flesh."

Six

As Alorie pulled away from the window, her fingers chilly as she finished stripping off her befouled wedding gown, Rowan stirred. She saw his eyelids flicker as she began to pull on the breeches and shirt of her disguise for *rool*, but didn't know if he were fully conscious yet or not.

She had her answer when he said, weakly, "Where are you going?"

"After the sword and *him*."

"No."

She pulled on a leather surcoat and laced it quickly, the ties stiffened from age. It too had come from the bridal trunk, laid there years ago when she'd finished her warring. "I have to."

He caught the hem of her cloak as she shrugged it on, and pulled her close. "Then it's not love that burns in you anymore," he said, his voice a hollow husk of what it had been. "It's revenge."

"Rowan! He murdered my father and grandfather and tried to do the same to you! I can't let him go!"

Rowan shook his head. His fingers lost their grip on the cloak and his arm fell back to his side. "It's not Aquitane. It's the Corruption that burns in him. And in the Barrowlands, that other. Awakening. And it's not revenge that's taking you. It's the Prophecy."

"Never!" she hissed. Then her voice caught, and she leaned close over him. "If you could ride—"

"You'd not be going alone," he finished.

She put her hand upon his brow, testing for fever, and, finding none, stroked his temple gently. "I'm not alone, exactly. There's Pinch and Jasper."

"Mary Rose?"

"Dead," she said shortly, then found her longknife and belted it on. At the doorway his voice caught her.

"Is there another healer?"

"Yes. She did the job on you."

"Fetch her, then. Have her marry us. Don't leave me without marrying me."

Alorie closed her eyes briefly, then said, "I can't, Rowan. Not now." *Not like this.* "There isn't time." She crossed the room swiftly and gave him a lingering kiss good-bye, her heart aching at the fear she'd heard in his voice. "I'll be back." She shut the door between them quickly, praying that she'd not hear his soft voice through the wooden planks, begging after her. That would wound her worse than almost anything that had happened that tragic day.

Kithrand gave her a leg up and as she settled into the saddle, Pinch trotted up behind her. His pony was nearly horse-sized yet small-barreled enough for his shorter legs. He'd gotten his pack and sported a new axe. The old, treacherous weapon lay still in the dust, and he did not look in its direction as he joined the riders. Jasper and his two guardsmen, dark, curly-headed Bounder and Mick, his flaming chestnut hair carefully combed and kept back with a leather thong, saluted Alorie. Kithrand patted the toe of her boot.

She looked down at the elf lord. His expression was carefully noncommital, but she thought she saw the glint of fear behind it. He'd given way to cowardice, she knew, more than once, but it had to be difficult to a being who viewed mortality and immortality entirely differently. Even his dreams while sleeping were disparate. Though he had and would live centuries longer than she, could she deny him a fear of death? Yet he had saved her life before and if she had to stake it on him, she would again, though not without reckoning for that breaking point.

Rathincourt had changed his clothes and came out. He frowned down at the elf lord, his massive white eyebrows moving on his brow like thunderheads boiling on a horizon. "You said you knew the way. What is it?"

Kithrand did not look to the tall warlord, but kept his gem-blue eyes on Alorie's face. "I am not versed in power," he said evenly, "as you know. Nor am I as talented as those ones of your kind and my kind who study in the sanctuary at Veil. Still, this is a road that was opened so that Aquitane may ride upon it, and whoever closed it off did so improperly. I can open that track and once you are upon it, you will be seized as one of the first party, though you trail far behind."

"What track? Where?"

A feeler danced upon Kithrand's brow. "I'm not sure where," he answered. "I think perhaps it leads to the Paths of Sorrow."

Even Rathincourt paled at that. Jasper shrank back in his saddle enough to make his paint gelding toss his head restlessly. Only Pinch remained unmoved and Alorie thought perhaps that was because the dwarf would relish walking the land of the dead if he could meet his wife there. She brushed her forehead with the back of her hand, felt a drop or two of nervousness smear. She had dead of her own to go walking with there. No wonder the elf lord could not go with them.

"Are you sure?"

"No."

She nodded.

"Milady . . ."

She met his eyes. "Kithrand."

"I am not sure if this track was closed improperly or if . . . one was trying to ensure you'd follow. If you find yourself on the Paths of Sorrow, I think it safe to say you will not be returning unless you win the sword. It too has powers—"

"We ride the hellroad," Pinch rumbled. "Milady does not belong in hell, yet. I'll see she makes it back."

The elf hesitated yet another moment as if he might disagree, then changed his mind. He squeezed tightly the toe of Alorie's boot. The gesture was so like that of Rowan, tears blurred her eyes suddenly. She dashed them out with trembling fingers. "Find me this treacherous road," she ordered, and wheeled her horse about. The stallion hitched about nervously and lashed out, keeping Bounder's gelding away. She curled her fingers about the reins tightly.

Kithrand strode to the alleyway where Jasper and his mare had taken an abrupt fall. He made a pass and in the dusky air before him, a violet sign glowed. It blew apart in the late afternoon wind. He made a second pass and this signature of cobalt blue vanished almost before he finished the last stroke. The elf lord shuddered. Alorie sensed a shifting in the air about her. Her ears popped faintly.

Her horse tensed, muscles rippling across his back and withers just as an archway of sparks and darkness tore across the air in front of Kithrand. He jumped, patting down the smolders on his already battered jacket. Then he bowed. "The track, such as it is."

Alorie put her heel to the stallion's flank, then stopped him from moving forward.

"Tell Rowan—" she began, but the elf lord said angrily, "I'll tell him nothing! You come back and tell him yourself what you wish him to know."

She smiled thinly and it faded almost as quickly as the elven magic had. "All right," she said, and released the stallion so that he could move forward onto the road that beckoned him eagerly.

Kithrand watched them ride by, his heart tight in his chest, if indeed an elf had a heart. As the last passed by, he made another pass and the archway snapped shut on their heels. He staggered back, his shoulders to one of the hovels these men called buildings as the release of power sent his pulse fluttering. He shook his head and wondered to himself just what he had done. There was no doubt in his mind that there would be an accounting for this.

He looked back to the inn where Rowan rested. It was just as well he retire for the moment and taste whatever of wine and wench was available. The Rover would have questions as soon as he was able to ask them, and Kithrand able to think of an answer.

As the elf lord left the empty street, a lithe, compact man, as heavily caped and cowled against the afternoon as he had been against midnight, stood out from the shadows. The cruel line of his mouth stretched happily as he surveyed the work Lord Aquitane had done that day. Too bad the dead had been so mangled. They would have had uses. He made a sign that crawled upon the air, a sickly, poisonous green, and the archway opened. He stepped into it even as he summoned Ungraven he had not had to pass by. The road to hell would be extremely well traveled that dusk.

Seven

They rode in a vortex of wind and rain and lightning. The sparks that had fired the elf lord's clothing now stretched into flashes that seared the whirling tunnel cocooning them. The air stank of the levin bolts, and Alorie's hair rose with a crackling sound and danced upon her shoulders with a will of its own. Rain pelted them in immense droplets that stung as they fell and evaporated as quickly, for their clothes stayed dry. The wind roared about them with a voice of terror and destruction.

Jasper cried out to Alorie, "We ride a cyclone!"

She did not have enough utterance left to respond. The reins cut into the palms of her hands and she cursed leaving behind her gloves in her haste, but there was no turning back.

The horses ran, but they showed the whites of their eyes as they did, and lather flecked their necks and flanks copiously. Their hooves appeared to skim over nothingness, setting off lightning even as they struck, but without the reassuring thunder of hoofbeats upon solid ground. Alorie looked down, once, grew dizzy, and fought to tear her gaze away before she fell from the saddle. She bit her lip to quell the nausea roiling in her stomach and the pounding in her temple. As her tooth pierced her bruised flesh, the horrible feeling left, and she sucked the flat, iron flavor of the droplets of blood welling up.

No one asked, nor had she the wonder, why this road of magic was not used more often to travel upon. When, if, they made it to their destination, they would be lucky to be sane and well enough to fight Aquitane to reclaim their sword. Nor, Alorie sensed, was the power to make such a track easy to find. All Kithrand had done was crack open the doorway to it, and she'd seen him reel back, his eyes rolled up in his head though still on his feet, as though the effort had nearly killed him. She would not be taking the road now if need did not spur her.

It pricked at her as her teeth had into her lips. Need to take back the sword and calm all that had gone wrong, as if having the sword in her hands again would bring back Mary Rose and Medra, the slight farming girl, and the marriage . . . her life to be patched together as if it were a quilt. But even as she hunched down in her saddle and felt her horse's legs driving under her, she knew that the prophecy found her wherever she hid. It would not be denied. All she could hope for now that somewhere in the portent there would be a place for her love for Rowan. A month or two. Perhaps even years, snatched here and there. She was greedy and selfish, she supposed. What extra time would Eileen's mother have stolen if she'd known of her child's imminent death?

Time ceased. Alorie thought it had been snatched away in the wind. She rode until her thighs and knees went numb and her hands crabbed about the reins. The horses all slowed into a ground-eating pace from the headlong gallop they'd been in. Pinch kneed his pony close to her dappled stallion. He was shadowed in the gray light of the vortex. The wind had matted his curly golden hair into a mass that looked like a comb could never get through. His silvery eyes were bloodshot and hard.

He passed a water bag to her. She sucked the water quickly, found it warm and somewhat brackish.

"How long?"

He shook his head as he took back the water. "Maybe half a day's riding, maybe more. This be sorcery, milady, and it has its own hours."

"We'll lose that whoreson."

Her words brought a grim sparkle to his expression. "Not," he said, "if I have to make my own magic!"

Kithrand stirred as Rowan moved, then pitched about as though to sit up. "How far ahead is she?"

The elf lord put his slim hand on the man's shoulder, but when his fingers tightened, they felt like steel. "You're not going anywhere."

Rowan lay back. His free hand scrubbed at his eyes. "How long have they been gone?"

"Three days, so far. But time is not said to matter on the road they travel."

The man under his hand grew tense. "What do you mean?"

"If you promise to lie still, I'll tell you."

"I promise to cut your liver out and roast it over a fire for my breakfast if you don't start talking."

Kithrand grinned and released Rowan's shoulder. "Perhaps," the elf lord said, "you've recovered enough to sit up."

Rowan did so without help, but when he swung his legs over the cot for his feet to touch the floor, a cold sweat broke out on his forehead and his arms trembled as he braced himself in place. "Who did she go with? And what are you talking about?"

Kithrand lowly began to tell him.

The vortex slowed about them. Pinch unwrapped a hand from his saddle horn to point.

"A blight on the horizon in front," he rasped. "Aquitane?"

She frowned to see. "Perhaps. How much farther can the horses go?"

He stroked the bobbing neck of his laboring pony. "They're not blown yet, milady, but soon. This is not natural for 'em."

Or any of them, she thought. Her horse moved under her in a traveling canter that ate away the distance, if the cocoon about them had distance to consume. She had no desire to break their mounts' wind, but until they drew near enough to see if they closed on Aquitane, she feared to pull up. There would be no tracking by sign on this hellish road unless it was by sight. They passed over and through the vortex as though nonexistent. And, perhaps, they were.

The wind and cloud about them began to open up and thin. Looking ahead, she could indeed see a man on horseback, his cloak streaming out behind him. The sword in his hand attracted the lightning, for the levin bolts streamed out and around from its point. She could hear the crackle and smell the discharge. He pulled his charger about and brought it plunging to a halt. The vortex took hold of his cloak and spread it about his body like immense black wings.

The crease deepened in her forehead. She found enough strength to knee her mount onward, prodding her to move faster. Pinch kept pace with her. She eyed the figure until she could see Aquitane's face well enough to know if he was indeed the silver-blond lord of what had once been the reach of Quickentree. The reach had been abandoned by

Aquitane when he'd massacred her city of Sinobel, and the wars later had razed the kingdom.

"It's Aquitane. Do you think he sees us?"

"Do ye see him?" Pinch grumbled. " 'Course he sees us. A pox on weddings, milady," he added. "I left my bow at the inn!"

As they slowed on the vortex pathway, it began to buckle under the horse hooves. Jasper called out, "Take care! There's an edge to this track!"

She looked to the Mutt. His brown and white pelt was disheveled, but his dark eye met hers in determination. At his back, Bounder and Mick wheeled their horses to guard their flank. They pulled their swords.

She had never known Mutts to be anything but gentle servants, as doglike in loyalty and trust as the canines they were rumored to have descended from. Only Brock's memories of the stories of the Twelve Races claimed that Mutts had been bred to be soldiers, to do the warring that men did, thus saving the lives. It caught in her throat now, a festering lump, that Jasper was fulfilling the fate of his race—though it would kill him.

Yet she knew the Mutt well and that he would have it no other way. He drew his lips back from his teeth now.

"Let us show his lordship that we can fight and die as well as any of the Twelve Races," the Mutt snarled, as though he was privy to her thoughts.

"Not yet," she answered softly. "Aquitane is my meat." She reined her horse around.

Aquitane's black destrier was so whited with foam and lather that he looked as dappled as Alorie's mount, though a negative of it. Yet he pulled at the bit and trumpeted out a challenge as they approached the lord. Behind the warhorse and lord, a miasma boiled that she found it difficult to look into. The end of the road? And if so, where did it lead?

The wind died down to fitful gusts. She could hear Aquitane clearly as he called out, "Once again, lady, I am impressed by you. You are brave to follow me alone." He crossed his wrists over his horse's shoulders, the Unicorn sword arrogantly held in his right hand.

"Not alone."

He smiled broadly. "You might as well be—half a man and dogs that walk on hind legs and paw at swords as if they might be bones."

Pinch growled behind his yellow-gold beard.

That made Aquitane's smile even wider. "Or perhaps I have confused man and dog," he said.

The dwarf's hand twitched and he drew forth his new axe. He hefted it. "I have not yet blooded this beauty," he said. "Yours will do nicely."

The renegade lord shook his head. "I think you will find other targets." Even as he spoke, Mick let out a sharp cry like a yelp.

"Trailers!"

Aquitane stood in his leathers to look over the top of their heads. Then he nodded. "My master is prepared for you. He has sent his best, the Ungraven, to welcome you."

A shiver pricked the nape of her neck and slithered down her spine, bringing an ache to muscle and bone already tired beyond endurance, but she refused to turn her head to look back. "We are not leaving until I have what I want!" She dug her boot heels into her stallion's flanks and charged even as Aquitane began to answer in his indolent tenor, "And what is this?"

She screamed in anger, "Your death and my sword!" as Aquitane shifted his weight and his destrier moved quickly.

Not quickly enough for her stallion. They collided, two heavy, lathered bodies, even as Alorie reached up to snatch the sword from Aquitane's grip. His gloved fist smashed into her face and scored across her cheekbone, but she grabbed him and clung determinedly even though her vision swam and her horse went down, rolling at her feet.

The stallion got up without her. Alorie kicked violently and pulled Aquitane out of his saddle with her.

"Bitch!" Aquitane kicked her in the hip, and, as she went to her knee, pulled free; as quickly, his left forearm was about her throat as he yanked her back to her feet. He held the Unicorn sword in front of them like a shield between them and Pinch and the Mutts.

Alorie's breath came in angry spurts. "Run!" she cried huskily, and the brutal shaft across her throat tightened even further.

The lord laughed harshly and gestured with horn tip. "Jump," he said. "I think not. That way lies the Paths of Sorrow. Retreat, and the Ungraven will drink deeply."

"How about," Jasper said, and his voice was punctuated by the drawing of his sword, "we go through you."

"If you wish it. The doorway there leads to a realm you

may find interesting, even stimulating . . . just before the malisons reach you."

Alorie fought to breathe. She suggested, "Or you could surrender, traitor, and throw yourself on my mercy."

"Mercy? Milady, you have a lot of admirable qualities, but mercy is not one of them. No. Though I will say this: if it had been you wearing the hat of Counselor, I would not have turned traitor. The Corruptor would have had little to entice me with. I would simply have married you and had it all."

A drily amused voice behind them said, "Keep the girl, Aquitane, and give me the sword."

Alorie felt a quiver run through the burly form that held her solidly. The lord made a sound in his throat as if pleased. "Master. I've been waiting for you."

The Corruptor answered, "I've been busy. You've done well, but I believe the time has come to end this game."

Alorie moved her right hand slightly, trying not to let the movement telegraph along her whole arm. Pinch's gaze wavered slightly, then away from her abruptly as the dwarf swung down from his pony. He tossed his axe from his right hand to his left and filled his right with sword hilt, the axe held as easily as a longknife in his left. "Come and get me," he challenged. "I'm thinking you've used all the sorcery you can summon up just holding the road open. Shall we see?" He planted his booted feet firmly upon the track, sending up a distracting shower of sparks.

Distracting enough that Alorie pulled her longknife clear of its sheath. At her back she could feel Aquitane's muscular form keenly. Smell his strong scent and that of his destrier. Feel his excitement and the swell of his chest as it filled with air.

Aquitane shifted weight from his left to his right boot heel and began to pass the sword to a presence gliding into position behind.

Alorie took a deep breath, twisted about, and buried her longknife in the suddenly opened and vulnerable spot just under the right rib cage. Aquitane staggered back a step as she wrapped both hands about the longknife's hilt and ripped it to her right as she faced the lord. As his tunic and stomach ripped, she gutted him effectively, twisted the knife for good measure, and pulled it out with a sickening *slurp*.

Even as the Corruptor reached for and snatched the falling Unicorn sword out of Aquitane's grasp, the human buckled in two and tried to hug back his cascading intestines. "Master," he gasped.

The Corruptor stepped away from him quickly. As hot blood splattered her face and then spilled out upon her boots, Alorie said with satisfaction, "For my father and my grandfather. For Medra and Mary Rose and young Eileen. For everything you've ever touched with your filthy hands!"

Aquitane keeled to the hellroad with a grunting moan. His destrier bolted away and plunged through the doorway, disappearing with a squeal of equine terror.

Leaving Alorie face-to-face with the Corruptor.

He stood with the sword in hand, running his gauntleted fingers over the hilt. His dark heavy wool cape and cowl baffled him from her sight. Then he paused and put back his hood.

Once she'd mistaken him for Brock, but now she saw there was no mistaking. The mage's face was as white as hers, not rich brown, and it was pitted and scarred. His eyes were dark, flat, and cruel, his mouth a thin-lipped slash.

He watched her intently a second, then said, "The sword is mine. No matter what happens now, remember. It is mine."

He took his free gauntlet and ran it lightly down the length of the unicorn horn. The mailed glove began to steam, then smolder, and then she saw the links melt away, as if a forge heated the weapon, and the serrated edges bit deeply into the flesh within the glove. The sorcerer let out a cry and dropped the weapon. Alorie fell on it and snatched it away, heedless of danger.

Pinch vaulted his pony and charged at the Corruptor. The sorcerer danced back, tracing a sign into the dead air between them, and cried aloud a word that sent pain jabbing into Alorie's eardrums.

Her stallion jostled into her. She grabbed for the stirrup leathers and pulled herself half onto the beast, unable to mount fully. Beyond Jasper and the Mutt guards she could see riders, fell riders, and she cried out, "Follow me!"

As she swung on and fought to put her toes into stirrups, she reined the dappled stallion around and kicked him off the track into the plunging, swirling vortex. With a curse Pinch followed her. The howls of the Mutts came after them as they dropped into nothingness.

Eight

The stallion stretched as though he hurdled a fallen log, his forelegs tucked under and his back lengthening under the saddle. The clouds tore around them. Alorie blinked as she leaned forward, wrapping her hands into his mane, preparing for a tremendous jolt when they hit. Color bled out and then returned—the stallion was dark as the dapples overcame him, then snow white again, then sepia, then dappled again. The sword in her hand glittered gold and ivory and the air about them crackled, though they drew no more lightning the way Aquitane had.

Her lips tightened. She felt hollow inside, victoryless. The Corruptor had merely sacrificed the human lord to get what he wished: the sword. And though Alorie had regained it and avenged herself on Aquitane besides, there was no triumph to it. She had gutted him, plain and simple.

She thought and prepared herself as the storm whipped away from them and the rich brown and green of new earth hurtled toward them as they broke into the light of day.

They landed with an immense pounding and the stallion bobbled, then righted himself and kept his balance by bounding forward until he could slow. As she wheeled him round, she could hear the sounds of Pinch and then the three Mutts landing. One of the horses spilled. It cried out sharply and thrashed to regain its feet, but one foreleg dangled limply and it did not understand what had happened to it. Bounder drew his sword across its throat quickly as Mick pivoted his horse and rode back. He took an arm up and the two rode double. Alorie tried not to look at the fallen mount, its crimson blood staining the ground too brilliantly to be watched.

Pinch joined her.

"Where are we?" Her voice fell on air too quiet. She

balanced the sword across the saddle and took to weaving her hair into a long braid, though it snapped and sparked as she did so. She tore a strip off her cloak hem to bind it back.

The dwarf rubbed his face. His silver eyes crinkled as he did so, weather-worn lines creased at their outward corners. He shook his head, then added, " 'Tis not natural. No birds or insects. No sound but what you and I make." He moved in his saddle and the creak of leather was sharp in the air.

Alorie looked about. She threw her head back and glanced above, seeing nothing of the track that had carried them. A few wisps of clouds eddied across a sky so clear it made her head ache. Yet there was no warmth to the day. She pulled her cloak about her and shrugged into it.

Jasper flanked her. His sharp face pulled into a wolfish grin. "If his lordship is to be believed, this is hell."

"If it is," Pinch answered, "I've had a hand in populating a part of it."

Alorie found it difficult to breathe. She let out a sound like a strangled sob.

Pinch reached over and patted her wrist. "Don't fash yourself, lass. Did you really think it would all be easy?"

She remembered the feeling she had had when she'd first grasped the sword and walked out of the forests, knowing that the secret races had approved of her and given her their talisman. And then she remembered the long and winding road of war and death and sacrifice and love that had led her there. She shook her head. "No." Gathering her reins, she said, "Let's follow the river."

"Aye," the dwarf armsman agreed. "But be taking no rides from any ferrymen."

The landscape remained eerie, alike and yet unlike, alive and yet unalive. Forest dwindled to marsh grass and nettles and a wide, slow river with water so blue it was nigh black. The banks were sandy and crumbled easily, as if the river had eaten them away. She saw no gnats or frogs in the reeds that clumped here and there. She heard no birdsong or squawk of raven. No mice bolted away from their hooves as they rode through tall grass and drying spring flowers.

Her stomach cramped. It reminded her that she lived and hungered, too. Other than water, they had not been provisioned. As the river curved and they followed it, they came out of the forest. The grass fields faded away into sienna sands. Ahead stretched an immense mountain range as blood red as the stains on her riding clothes. Pinch let out a low whistle.

"Just when I was beginning to think hell might not be so bad after all."

She could feel the parched heat of the desert reflecting back at her face. There were shadows boiling under those red cliffs, but she could not see if they were mirage or umbra . . . or something else yet. The river stretched in that direction and widened into an immense, flat lake. She did not think its waters drinkable. None of the horses had inclined toward its banks in the hours they had been riding. Pinch passed her his water bag, as if knowing that just looking upon the horizon blistered her throat. She lifted it and squirted a few sparse drops down, then passed it back.

Jasper kneed his mount closer. The Mutt said, "If we don't starve to death first, that will be the end of us."

"There's nothing in the brush or air," Pinch answered.

"The river?" Alorie knew her guardsmen had experience fishing. Jasper made a negative motion.

"Dead water" was all he said.

It confirmed her earlier suspicion. She heeled her mount back into motion, following the rough lane that led from forest into desert. The Paths of Sorrow, indeed.

The tall grasses wavered. Her horse shied and came to a stop, trembling, nodding his head up and down. Pinch backed his horse to shield her, putting himself between whatever it was in the grasses that had frightened the horse and her.

Jasper dismounted. With his sword tip he parted the grass so heavy it bowed, revealing a dark blotch upon the ground.

"Welcome, my Lady Alorie."

Her eyes widened and she put her hand to her mouth to keep from screaming. The spread-eagled man on the ground had lifted his head to speak to her. He showed no sign of bloodshed or a death wound but seemed oddly transfixed to the ground; all that he could move was his head. His icy-blue gaze pierced her.

"I seem to be hell's latest arrival," Lord Aquitane said.

"If once wasn't good enough," Pinch offered, "I'll be glad to gut you again."

"Oh, it was quite sufficient," the human answered. "I'm dead. There seems to be a process. I've lain here awhile. Soon, when I'm able to get to my feet, I'll join the migration toward the mountains. Then," with a curious twitch of his head, Aquitane finished, "whatever gods will have me will come for me. Or so it seems to me."

"Migration?"

"There." He pointed his chin toward the mountain range that he could not possibly see, pinned in the grassland as he was. He laughed, scorn and mockery in his voice. "You'd better hurry, milady. You have dead to search for . . . and there's a multitude awaiting!"

Alorie slammed her heels to her stallion's flank. With a snort the beast leapt over the fallen lord, though she would not have cared if he had been trampled.

Aquitane's voice called tauntingly after. "The dead are lucky here! We do not thirst or hunger! You will die on these Paths, my fair one! Then you're mine!"

His mocking laughter did not fade from earshot for a long, long time.

Red sand crunched under the dappled's hooves, sending puffs of dust and grit into the air with every weary step. Alorie's mouth dried and her throat closed as if choked. She heard one of the Mutts at the rear make a sound halfway between a groan and a whine, and realized that Mick and Bounder rode double. She pulled to a halt.

"We'll have to stop." She shaded her eyes. "Maybe we can ride at night."

Pinch shifted his weight and flexed his shoulders. "The sun hasn't lowered in the sky one whit, milady. I think we're meant to roast out here."

The horses danced on the fiery sand, tired though they were. She looked to Jasper. His brown-splashed gelding was drenched with lather and stood with his head lower, breathing heavily. Yet he, too, could not keep hoof to sand.

She put her chin up. "Then we'll ride in the river."

"No!" Pinch cried out, but she whipped her stallion crosswise over the sands and into the water, which was dark as night. Droplets sprayed up, bits of onyx that stung as they pelted her, and the air went chill as midwinter. The dark of night shadowed her like a cloak, and both she and the horse froze in astonishment, unable to see farther.

Alorie stirred, hearing her voice faintly called, and with great effort, turned her stallion. She saw the bank and a gray land beyond it, unpeopled, devoid of life. Yet she heard Pinch's voice. She heeled the stallion toward the bank though he shook his head, thick mane cresting over his neck, unwilling to go. The Unicorn sword alone retained life, a brilliant spear of gold, and it parted the velvet ahead of her as her horse clambered reluctantly from the shade.

They reappeared so quickly that Pinch's horse reared back, the whites of its eyes showing. The dwarf curbed it down. "Milady! I thought we had lost you, sure."

"No." Alorie shivered, a chill wind still at her back. "We can't traverse it . . . wait. Have you a rope?"

Jasper fished in his saddle bag and brought out a golden length.

"A faery catch!"

The Mutt shrugged. "Lord Kithrand gave it to me."

"Aye," Pinch grumbled. "That one does prove his worth once in a while. What do you mean to do?"

"We cannot drink from it, but it'll keep the sun from baking us dry. Loop Mick's horse and hold on, no matter what happens."

The two Mutt guardsmen looked unhappy, but they guided their mare into the river. No sooner had one hoof broken water than the twain disappeared and beast too. Nor was there a ripple upon the deep blue-black stillness to show it had swallowed them. The golden rope hung in midair and ended abruptly.

Alorie waited a few minutes, then said, "Bring them back."

With a *tch* Pinch laid his great, thick hands upon the rope and hauled them back. The black mare reared out of the water, her nostrils flared. The two Mutts jumped off her back and shook themselves. Their breath frosted white on the air.

"Now you, Jasper, and then Pinch."

Jasper went eagerly and after his turn Pinch grumbled but rode in. He returned with frost on his beard, or so he declared. But they could not deny the vigor the drenching gave them.

Jasper coiled up the faery catch and looped it over his saddle horn. Pinch urged his horse ahead after one last look. He shuddered. "I'd not like to make that trip again."

"We may have to," she told him.

"Aye, that I know. Tell me something I don't."

She smiled sadly. "We're approaching a horde of dead."

The dwarf stood in his stirrups, suddenly alert. "By the horn," he swore. "You've got the sight this time. Thousands of people, afoot. That isn't shadow ahead."

"No." She reined her dappled stallion in front of him. "If you see her, Pinch, you must leave her be."

His weather-beaten face paled as he met her eyes. "My love and wife, you mean."

"Yes."

"And what if you see Rowan there?"

A death track down her spine made her shudder, but she inclined her head. "I must, too."

The armsman said nothing further to her as they kicked their horses into a trot and approached the shadowed reaches of the red-sand desert, whose umbra was not shadow at all but a mass of humanity pressing toward crimson sandstone mountains.

And though Alorie had warned Pinch, she could not help but look ahead. Would she see her father and grandfather? Perhaps even her mother, gone so many years now that she had lived half her life without her? How could she possibly sort them out from all the dead in Bethalia, from all the reaches of the High King?

As they came close to seeing limbs and heads clearly defined among the walkers, Pinch halted his mount in his tracks.

He looked to her, his face lined in desperation. "Blind me," he said.

"Blind you?"

"And deafen me, too, if you have the means, lass. I beg you."

Jasper took his dirk and ripped the hem off his cloak. He leaned out of his saddle and roughly blindfolded the dwarf.

Gruffly Pinch said, "I thank you. Now take up my reins."

Alorie reached and took the reins from his hand. Their fingers met and he grasped her hand suddenly, squeezing it tightly. "It'll be all right," she said softly. When he let go of her, she felt his tremble deep in her body.

She leaned closer yet to whisper, "She walks under a sun, Pinch . . . not buried under the earth. Remember that. The All-Mother has not condemned her to what you fear most."

He made a low sound in his throat as she pulled away. If her thought had comforted him, she could not tell.

As they caught up with the last of the stragglers, the dead scarcely noticed them. They walked with single-minded attention toward the mountains. Purple clouds at the foot of the spires promised real shade—and something more. She saw the needle eye of a pass, a black splinter in the sandstone, and even the girl felt its pull, like that of a lodestone.

They reined about the walkers, who moved as if entranced, their steps gaining them little or no headway. The dead of the last century might be here still, inching forward across the burnt sienna landscape.

Alorie tried not to look, but she could not miss the rawboned frame of the Rover healer Medra, and beside her, the doughty silhouette of Mary Rose. Like Aquitane, neither carried their death wounds, but the sallowness of their skin and their serene expression were eerie. Medra wore her Rover black and silver, covered by her long apron of many pockets, all filled with vials and tools and the many useful things she carried. A lump grew in Alorie's throat, for this was the woman she remembered most, though the careworn expression had smoothed.

As they rode past, Alorie twisted in her saddle to look back at her two friends, neither of whom seemed to notice their passage. She said nothing to Pinch, who gripped his saddle horn as if it were a lifeline to a drowning man. Then she saw a shift in Mary Rose's gaze. The small woman opened her mouth slowly, painstakingly.

"I will wait for you," she called, her voice a shadow of its former robustness.

Pinch stiffened in his leathers. He neither called back nor took off his blindfold, but tears wet his cheeks below it and ran into his curled beard. Alorie felt her own eyes brim, and kicked her horse into a gallop, heedless of the cloud of dust that rose and hovered about the host of dead.

When they had ridden farther, Pinch called out. Alorie halted and gathered his horse close so that she could free him of his mask. The tears had left dirty streaks on his face, and he cleared his throat huskily several times before saying, "Thanks, milady."

"You may have to do the same for me."

He nodded brusquely.

They rode on, keeping the multitude between them and the river, for the dead seemed unwilling to move away from the broadening waterway. Then there was a sound.

It rose lowly, like a rumbling or vibration in the air. Alorie felt it before she heard it. She pulled to a halt and turned her face from side to side, feeling out its direction. Then its pitch became higher.

Jasper shook his head, his Mutt face contorted in pain. He dropped his reins to put his stubby hands to his ears. Bounder and Mick responded likewise.

Pinch shook his head. "What is it?"

"I don't know." Beneath her the stallion moved in sudden agitation. Then, beyond the Paths of Sorrow, she saw a movement in the water.

It lashed out so quickly that she sensed rather than saw the blur of tentacles. The body it caught up and dragged into the river disappeared, and with it the sound, but not the sluggish ripples wavering as something struggled below the surface. The host never stopped shuffling forward, as if unaware anything had happened.

"Holy Mother," Pinch cried. "And we were mucking about in that! I have to warn Mary!"

She caught his arm. "No! We have no part of this. Who are you to say what happened then was natural or unnatural?"

Pinch gave her a long, measuring look. "That was no god gathering up the dead. That was a fiend out of hell."

She repeated, "Who are you to judge?"

Sweat broke out on his gnarled forehead. He tore his arm from Alorie's grip and kicked his horse savagely into motion, putting as much ground as possible between him and the abomination.

She would have been hard-pressed to catch up, but something happened among the multitudes of dead. As though released from their blindness and muteness, they noticed the living riders.

"A horse!" one called.

Jasper and Mick and Bounder joined her as faces turned toward them. What had they done to suddenly become visible in this world?

The walk to the sandstone gateway paused. In front of Pinch a wall of the host turned and, by sheer numbers, made him bring his horse to a rearing stop.

Panic rose in her as the dead began to close in on them, hands outstretched.

"What do they want?"

Jasper growled. His lips pulled back from his sharp teeth. "They want our mounts. Anything, to get to the crossover quicker."

Mick pulled his sword. As a short, burly farmer reached up to pull Bounder off their mount, he slashed downward. The being rolled aside, severed, but even as he lay in the

dust trampled by his fellows, his flesh bloodlessly pulled
back together.

"We can drive 'em into the river. Whatever is there—"

"No! We can't do that." She looked up. Pinch was being
forced back to them, step by step. Soon they would be
ringed as the dead pressed about them.

She half-opened her mouth, feeling smothered. How could
they turn aside that which was already dead?

She raised the Unicorn sword in her hand, fearful of its
powers, and it flashed in the eternal sun as their horses
jostled one another, the multitude reaching to grab them
down.

Nine

"Touch them not!" a voice roared out of the host, and Alorie twisted in her saddle, heart lurching, for she knew that voice.

A big man strode up, bare-chested, his black, too long hair drawn back from his tanned and squared face. The host parted for him, a barbarian and a warrior—and a hero. He backed the dead away from Alorie and her party by sheer force of his presence. His hand held a sword hilt, twin to the one in Alorie's grip, but his blade was one of steel while hers held the Unicorn horn. He saluted her with a grin, fierce in his joy. "Milady Alorie!"

"Gavin Bullheart," she answered. "I am both sad and happy to meet you here."

"Don't be," he told her. "I am what I always was—a farmer lad who wanted to be a great soldier. And here at least, my head still reigns upon my neck. By all the gods, what a woman you've become."

She felt her face redden. Pinch made a noise and Gavin looked to him. "Here is another face I'm glad to see still among the living. New axe?"

"Aye. Black sorcery muddled the other."

"The Corruptor?"

The multitude, who'd begun to move away and resume their long journey, caught the name. A low moan began, a keening, and the still air filled with it until the sandstone towers echoed it back before bleeding away. The sound imbued Alorie with foreboding. She looked to Gavin. "They know him?"

"All the dead know him. Even here he can touch us." Gavin pointed the sword toward the river. "We can drink from that. It sustains us. But there is *that* which lives in the river which hell uses to recruit even souls of goodness. That

is why I have my sword here. I have been given the task to
champion these who are awaiting the final trial." He smoothed
his mane of black hair away from his brow and frowned.

Jasper pointed. "That is the sword of Frenlaw."

Gavin shook his head. "No. This is but one of the many
shadows it casts. Alorie carries the only true sword . . .
though I see its blade is indeed a peculiar one. Effective?"

She made a wry face. "Very. I'm afraid I haven't got what
it takes to wield it, however."

"The gods are better at measuring us than we are ourselves. Take heart, for I've been sent to give you word."

She took up her reins to move her stallion away from
Bullheart, both afraid and compelled to hear him speak.

"Like this afterworld," the hero said solemnly, "my
auguring is both light and dark. I must warn you of treachery, Alorie, where and when you least suspect it. And I will
remind you of the sword of Frenlaw's reputation."

Pinch muttered, "It has always shattered when the need
was greatest."

Gavin looked at the armsman. "And I have words for you
too, Pinch. Though your loss has been great, greater still the
loss for all Bethalia if you do not conquer the depths of your
fears."

"The light," Alorie said desperately. "What do you have
for me to balance what you've already said?"

Gavin smiled then, a wistful smile. "Alas, milady. You
may mistake me. You already have the greatest of gifts
mortal life can bestow—hold onto it tightly and do not
throw it away. Beyond the dead lies a gate. Only we can
pass through, but it is your only way out. Make for it,
milady." He pivoted on his heel as a vibration rose from the
river. "I am called." Sword in hand, he made his way across
the dark sands to fight the Corruption that reached even
beyond death. She saw the dark water shiver. A being rose,
shrouded in fog. The dead, bound by their journey to the
banks of the river, shrank back, unable to flee.

Pinch said, "I can't look."

"Nor I." Alorie snapped the end of her rein across her
mount's shoulder, startling it into a gallop. The hilt of the
Unicorn sword cut into the tender palm of her hand, and
she thought it was a rare gift of the gods that was not also a
curse.

As they approached the range, she eyed the crowd still
following the river. She could see nothing of her father or

grandfather, though she recognized many of the townspeople of Sinobel. Even this would not be given her. Her stallion threw up his head, his muzzle foaming about the bit, and she pulled up. She cupped her hand. "Pinch, give the last of the water to the horses."

He dismounted with a scramble and brought over the water bag. Jasper followed suit after wetting his lips first. Both Mutts got off the black mare. She heaved a tired sigh and lipped the offered water with disinterest.

Bounder soothed her and said, "She won't last much farther."

"It won't be much farther," Alorie answered. "Or we'll all belong here." Still searching, she looked toward the host, found nothing, and looked down in disappointment.

Pinch sensed her thoughts and looked at her. "Meeting with the dead is cold comfort, indeed."

She tried to answer and could not, as her voice failed her. Jasper called out, "Beware, Lady. There are other riders behind us."

Other riders? She twisted in her tracks and could see little beyond a blur of movement in a dusky cloud of sand. She feared to wait until she could see clearly, knowing that the Corruptor had put Ungraven to hound their trail earlier.

"We don't want to face them," she said to Pinch.

The dwarf nodded in agreement. He pointed ahead of them at the rocks now towering high enough above them to shade them from the sun. "There's the final passing."

"Then we'll have to ask for the last they can give us," Alorie answered with a slap to her stallion's neck.

The multitude scattered from them even as they approached the impasse, but there came a point when they had to curb their mounts tightly or trample them.

"What is it?" Pinch grunted, hemmed in by the press of flesh that was no longer mortal. "They're afraid to pass the curtain!" He pointed ahead at a veil of mist like velvet night.

One of the dead was jostled forward and he screamed as he passed, a sound of terror beyond belief, a scream that brought Alorie's hands to her ears.

She lowered her hand and touched the shoulder of a woman standing at her stirrup. "What is it?"

She was surprised when the woman responded, turning up a hopeless face to her.

"The Devourer," she said. "We must face it, but we're afraid."

"Devourer? Lady, the All-Mother gathers her harvest and tucks us gently in her apron. What are you talking about?"

"One must pass the Devourer first."

Another of the multitude at the mountain's base was jostled into the gap. He went with a choking fit, too hysterical to shout for help or mercy.

Alorie took the sword out of her belt grimly, saying to Pinch, "I think we've forgotten that it's the Corruptor's art that brought us here."

Pinch flushed darkly. "Aye," he answered. "And I'm thinking I'd not want Mary Rose to suffer any longer. We've devourers enough at our heels!" He pounded his exhausted mount's rib cage, and with the Mutts at their rear, thrust themselves into the curtain of mist.

A roar split her ears, and she whirled the dappled stallion, bringing him plunging to a halt. She blinked at the sudden brightness about them even as she fought to keep her seat. The sandstone towers about them blazed in crimson light, the gravel showered down from them as the beast roared again. Its leap filled the pass. Jasper's horse whinnied in abject fear as it crashed into the stallion's crupper.

Alorie found herself with no place to go even if she had wanted to retreat. The beast spread its immense wings, shading them from the sun, and kneaded its claws into the sand. Around its neck was the sigil of her god and she knew she could not slay it—not even if she herself would be slain. At its back, water tumbled from an immense crag, pure blue water that foamed into a gem-deep pool—and disappeared.

" 'Tis true water," Pinch mumbled.

Suddenly her mouth felt incredibly dry. She could almost feel the spray of the waterfall—life it was, pouring out of the rock.

The winged lion crouched before them, his tawny, massive face eyeing them from amber eyes set deep in his wrinkled brow. "Ye shall not pass."

Alorie straightened wearily in her stirrups. She felt dirty and drained, her clothes sweat-stained and torn. "We are living. We do not belong here."

"None shall pass but the dead."

Pinch inched his axe out from his belt. "I'll take his attention. You do what you have to do."

"No! I won't leave any of you behind. And besides,

Gavin spoke to you too. We both have a part to play." Alorie dismounted and left the reins trailing the sands. "There are creatures of the Corruptor's on our trail. They will destroy us and the peace of the dead if you delay us."

On foot, the bearded jaw of the beast more than cleared her face, even crouched as it was. She watched him velvet and unvelvet his six-toed paws, great amber talons that could rip her to shreds. His flanks moved as steadily as a forge's bellows: she realized the low vibration she heard was his purr, steady if inaudible, all the time he faced her.

She unveiled the Unicorn sword from the folds of her cloak. "I too have a claw," she said.

The beast became alert, his amber eyes opened wide, golden fire in their depths. "So I see," he answered. "Twelve of mine to one of yours. Do you propose to fight a god?"

"No. But you are no god," Alorie told him. "I am the Dancer. I have pleased gods before."

"By the Apron," the lion said, and he punctuated his ire with a catlike snort. "Who are you to tell me what I am and what I am not? Who else do you think gathers up the souls All-Mother searches for?"

"Not you," Alorie countered. "This horn holds more of the All-Mother than you do." She pulled the horn from the guard that held it, and, to her surprise, it came loose easily to her touch. It fell from her grasp as it tore away and lay in the blood-red sand a moment.

A nebulous cloud rose around it, purified and whitened. Alorie gasped and stepped back as with a clarion trumpet, a beast arose from the sands, horn in its rightful socket, and a mighty unicorn faced them all.

It pawed the ground and the land trembled. Alorie's breath froze in her throat. *This*, this was the mighty unicorn who had tested her for the right to gain the horn. He snorted, and wind rushed out of his wine-red nostrils and swirled about the canyon before howling into the world.

The lion reared before him, paws curled in the air in obeisance, wings unfurled to keep his balance before the unicorn.

The unicorn said to him, "This one you shall bear at a later time. I give them passage, all five of them."

"As you wish it." The lion dropped back onto the ground and settled his wings about him again.

The stallion tossed his cloud-white head and looked back to her. "We meet again."

She dropped to the ground, forehead pressed to the sand. The horn tip touched her shoulder, branding her with its eternal fire. She feared to cry out, though a fiery pain shook her.

"Get up."

She got to her knees, then stood.

"Look at me."

The unicorn stallion filled her sight. She could not look away to save her very soul. And then she saw the blackness that stained him like night upon snow. It dappled his hindquarters and trailed into the strands of his bannerlike tail.

"What is it?"

"I was held by the Corruptor. His evil reaches into me even as it reaches into the land. Mark it well, Alorie. If you cast me aside or lose me a second time, even I cannot stand against him, and there is the Despot yet to face. Don't despair. You will find that which you thought lost along the road."

She reached out to touch the beast, then drew back, fearing to touch a god. The unicorn began to grow insubstantial again. The stallion reared against the sandstone cliff and when he came down, he struck his horn against a crimson spire. The horn belled. Its chiming note parted the vision around them. She found herself standing in the hub of an immense wheel, lands and trails spoking away from them. Part of the secret came to her then. The *Paths* of Sorrow . . . as many ways to this final parting as the mind could imagine. The horn thrilled and then fell, and as she bent to pick it up and restore it to Frenlaw's guard, she knew the beast would be gone when she straightened.

In the gold- and ivory-spiraled length of the horn she saw a splinter of black. No more, no less.

Alorie grasped the hilt until her knuckles showed white. The winged lion lay quiet at her feet, the spray of the waterfall hitting her face.

Pinch grabbed her elbow. "This way, milady!" He held the reins of their horses in his callused hand. "Quickly!"

They stepped into the shower of the falls.

Ten

He knew before they came to tell him that the quarry was lost. He could feel the shivering of air, from the quickening of power, from the breath of innocence that lay waste to his plans. And yet, though he shrank from it, that very breath of fresh air drew him irresistibly. He should have killed her then, would have to have her killed soon, but could not. He did not wish to face the loss of that which reminded him so keenly of all he had forsaken when taking up his power.

He stroked his right hand lightly where the sword had laid it open. He had not anticipated that; he thought he'd studied the weapon well enough over the past few years to hold it. In the northern wastes where unicorns were indeed a rarity, he'd hunted enough of them in experimentation. Now he had to consider that the beast that had provided Alorie with her talisman was different. A demigod perhaps, though he did not believe in such things.

With a flourish of his robes he seated himself in the altar room. He could converse with his liege, but did not wish to. He would be chided for not yet freeing him, for not having found the key to the great Barrow before he would be counseled and guided. He was not a child to be scolded for delaying a task.

The call reached him. He bent his head as he considered it. "Master . . . we have lost them beyond the gate."

"Turn back, then."

"Master, do not let us fail. Let us proceed."

He curled his hand gingerly, testing the healing of flesh that no longer lived or died. "No," he answered curtly. "You reached that realm over a road of my making, therefore you are not in the true realm, but its shadow which I

75

control. But even I cannot control the final gate. That is not shadow. I have other plans for you. Return at once."

"Yes, master." The Ungraven presence left a lingering smell of putrefaction in its wake.

He sighed deeply, wishing for one last breath of innocence and youth that the Lady Alorie brought with her. After centuries beneath the earth, it would be welcome.

Then he smiled grimly. Perhaps when he had his hands on her, she could be squeezed, pressed into an extract like a vial of perfume, and she could grace his senses forever. If not, the activity would still be gratifying.

He had other plans to set in motion. Reaching out, he grabbed up a reken kit by the scruff of the neck before it could scurry out of the way. "Find me the spy," he ordered, and the rusty beast gnashed its eyeteeth like the tusks they would become and was in motion before he even dropped it back to the flooring.

The water cascaded over them with a roar, and yet, like the rain upon the hellroad, nothing touched her, as though either she or it were insubstantial. In this realm she thought it was herself. Yet it seemed to cleanse her, sifting through not only her flesh but her mind, and when they emerged into the womblike darkness of the caves beyond, she gasped. Pinch thumped his hand upon her knee. "Let me lead, milady," he said gruffly, and she could not mistake the relief in his voice. "I can see better in the dark."

It was not unlike being guided to be reborn.

The air hit her with a rush, and even as the stallion threw up his head with a glad whicker, she knew that they had come through, for the day was full of sound. They overlooked a wilderness fresh with the blue-green grass of early spring.

She turned to Pinch, who winced as he shifted his weight in his saddle. "I never thought I'd be glad to hear the buzz of stingers."

He scrubbed at his silver eyes. "Aye, I know," he answered. "I suggest we let the horses rest. They're fair starved, and the grass smells sweet."

She slept. Littlefoot crunched under her body, giving off its aroma of healing and spring, and she gave way to an aching and weariness that blotted out everything else, even hunger. She was aware a second or two after she closed her eyes of Jasper posting a guard and the sound of the horses pulling greedily at the grass in the sun-dappled meadow, and Pinch's grunt and mumble as he settled down also. Then nothing. She did not even dream. If she had had time for a second thought, she would have been warned and known fear.

"I am here, yer worship," the squat man said and, as difficult as it would be for him to rise, went to one gnarled knee before the Corruptor.

The Corruptor let his mouth relax in a smile. "Hammersmith. I am pleased to see you."

"And I you, yer worship," the dwarf said. He got to his feet. He wore no boots, his big, tough, and hairy pads enough protection. His curled hair was black as jet, streaked with gray only at the chin-chop whiskers he wore. His chest was covered with a stained and heavy leather smithy's apron. His eyes were the color of flint.

"I have a job for you."

Hammersmith finally returned his master's smile. "It's been a long time," he said, "since I have been outside yer worship's forges."

The Corruptor waved his hand. "Littlefoot still grows among the grasses. Hawks still wing the air. And the land beyond the River Deth still awaits our conquering footstep once Bethalia is beaten down."

"Gud. How may I serve ye?"

"I need a man inside Bryant's Delvings. How long do you think the dwarves can remember a traitor?"

Hammersmith scratched his dark, curly head. "It has been three hunnerd years sith I brought the Gutrig mines down upon dwarven heads. None but sons of sons would be alive today, sith I lay those centuries at your feet in the barrows. My name be known, but not my face. I culd get inside Bryant's forges."

"Then you must do so. We go to war again soon and this time, this time, I will have the armory within my hands. Let Rathincourt plan what he can without tempered steel to back him."

Hammersmith bowed. "Yer wish is mine, yer worship." He backed away from the throne.

The Corruptor almost let him escape, then tugged on his soulstring. The dwarf froze as if nailed to the spot.

His sweat-streaked face paled. "Yer worship?"

"Hammersmith . . . what will you call yourself?"

The dwarf gave a lopsided grin. "Why, Hammersmith the True," he said. "They'll understand the dwarfish need to temper true a corrupt ore. It's a failing that'll prove fatal."

"Good." The Corruptor loosened his compulsion. "Let me know when you have gained King Bryant's trust. I do not wish the forge destroyed, only overwhelmed. It will be difficult, but that's why I'm sending you in."

The dwarf inclined his head, chin-chop whiskers trembling. He did not straighten this time or attempt to leave until he was absolutely certain his master wished him to go.

"You may awaken, Alorie of Sergius, if indeed that is your name."

She remembered lying on a tenebrous bed, not asleep and not awake, waiting for her summoning. When it came, she opened her eyes slowly. Sand clotted her lashes and the corners of her eyes. She blinked to loosen its grip on her. As she sat and brushed littlefoot from her shoulders and hair, she realized that her sleep had been neither natural nor confined to herself alone. Around her lay the three Mutts curled in slumber, and Pinch, his jaw slack and gruff throat given to husky snores, lay boldly on his back, pipe beside him.

Three robed, veiled persons stood watching her. She did not stand, for the hellride had left her bruised and sore. Her legs felt cramped and she did not trust them to hold her. She combed her hair with her fingers and said, "Who are you and why do you question my identity?"

"You have met with our ilk before. We question you as we would any who trespass us from a pathway of the Corruptor's making."

From under cover of her raven tresses as she combed them, she eyed the personages. She did not smell the Corruptor's stink upon them, but she decided she trusted them as little as she trusted her. She tucked her feet under her and got to her knees. Her longknife she'd left at Aquitane's dying body, but the Unicorn sword's brilliant length still shone alongside her within easy reach. The visitors reminded her of a man who'd come to Stonedeep when the Rovers sheltered her and insisted she search for the oracle in Cornuth.

"We traveled a hellroad because we had no choice," she retorted. "And as for trespassing, I have no idea where we are except that we've ridden the Paths of Sorrow. As for your ilk, I have met no one as arrogant or accusatory as you save for the acolyte Cranfer who came from the sanctuary of Veil." As she mentioned the city of sorcery, a visible tremor ran among the trio watching her, and Alorie knew she'd guessed right. Arrogantly she took up the sword. "And as to my identity, I carry nothing but a sword you might recognize."

"The sword we know—and we have marked the Corruptor's stain upon it. If you are Lady Sergius, then you have failed the trust put in your hands."

Anger surged through her, marking its hot blush upon her cheeks. "I didn't come here to be accused of failure. I've faced Aquitane and the Corruptor. What have you done for Bethalia?"

There was a pause in the clearing. Then the second of the veiled figures spoke, and Alorie recognized a woman's voice.

"We gave our daughter to go with you to Cornuth," the sorceress said. "It took her lifeblood to augur your pathway with the sword. And if that sacrifice was not enough for you, then know that we leave the Corruptor to you only because we save our strength for the final resurrection—and the Despot who intends to destroy us entirely."

Alorie kept her chin out defiantly, though mention of the dead Viola pierced her. She retorted, "Then, if we are indeed allies, I demand the courtesy due one. Let my companions awake."

The heavily robed woman inclined her head to look down upon Alorie. She said, "I am Luisa. You would do well to remember that Veil is a forbidden city. We are not gentle with trespassers."

"I remember," the girl answered evenly. "I had a friend once who came to Veil—and never returned. Perhaps it is here I should start looking for him."

The sorceress gestured with a black-veiled hand. Jasper stretched and whined in thinning sleep. Pinch caught up a snore in a bluster.

"Awaken," the woman said. "You are all prisoners of Veil."

Eleven

Rowan stretched gingerly in his saddle. Kithrand, mounted lightly on the withers of his cream-colored faery horse with wise eyes, looked at him with mocking amusement.

"Not as soft as a bed, eh?"

The Rover made a noise through his teeth. He ignored the gnawing ache in his side. The Barrel healer had done a credible job, it was true—the skin did not knot or pull enough to keep him from moving. But it felt as though an icicle had sliced him through and yet remained there, always cold, achingly cold. Now he knew what Pinch had borne the past few years.

"Where now?"

The elf lord shrugged. He had changed his torn and dirty clothes for new silks, and was resplendent in blue and dusky rose, the blue an echo of his elfin eyes that showed no whites. "One place is as good as another for a forbidden city."

The man did not hide his annoyance as he looked his riding companion over. He fingered the crescent scar that cleft his chin. "There is forbidden, and there is forbidden," he said. "I know a craft that will make a path."

"Courtesy of Brock, perhaps?"

"Perhaps."

Kithrand entwined his fingers in the gelding's mane. "Then I suggest that here is as good a place as any."

"What? We're barely two weeks out of Barrel. The Paths of Sorrow are another span of days from here."

Kithrand jumped down and landed on his toes. "We've berry bushes, a fresh brook, littlefoot to bed on, trees enow for shelter—come, Rover, surely you'll agree that this is a fair encampment."

"I will agree this is a fair place, but not that we've time to stay here."

The elf lord had begun building a fire ring. He looked up, his fine white-blond hair drifting about his shoulders in the afternoon breeze. His blue-encrusted circlet winked in the sunlight. "If I had known you had the power to ride forbidden paths, we could have done this in Barrel."

"What?" Rowan swung down, eager to get his hands on Kithrand. "What do you mean?"

"I mean that if they survived the Paths of Sorrow, their only exit will probably be through Veil. Veil does not take trespassing lightly. They will be taken prisoner."

"Not Alorie."

Kithrand stopped, his slender fingers gripping a flat rock for the fire ring. "Especially Alorie. They rode in on a track of the Corruptor's making. There isn't a mage in Veil who won't be crying for a show of her blood to ensure she is genuine and not of the Despot's making." He held a hand up to stem Rowan's anger. "Don't blame me, Rover. I am not and never will be a part of that conspiracy. Few elves approve and participate in Veil's politics or, indeed, any of those of the homeless children."

"And if they're not in Veil?"

"If the track did not take them where I sensed? Well, then, we might as well camp here anyway, for your Alorie may be lost for some time to come." The base for the evening fire built, Kithrand lay down on his back and watched clouds eddy across the sky.

Rowan felt his hands clench in frustration. "Explain yourself."

Kithrand's gaze flickered to him. "Ah, well, if I must, I must. Settle yourself down by me, lad, and look the sky over. If luck's in our favor, we'll see a bank of clouds scuttling by. Then you must prepare your pathway."

"Why clouds and why here?"

The elf lord gave him a brittle smile. "Why, any place is good enough to reach a city that floats in the clouds."

"Hrrumph." Pinch growled deep in his throat, his pipe stem clenched in his teeth. "A pretty enough place, but still a prison."

Alorie shivered. Jasper tore a tapestry off the stone wall of their cell and dropped it about her shoulders. She shrugged into it gratefully. "Pretty? I can't see beyond the city, what there is of it, except fog and mist. The sky above is fair enough, but always chilled. I wonder if winter ever leaves this place."

"Don't criticize what you don't know." The dwarf wagged a finger at her.

"Tell that to *them*."

He smiled slightly, the first she'd seen since their ordeal began. "Life is grand, lass, if you're tough enough."

"And I am?"

"Aye." He nodded over his pipe, struck a match stick, and began to light the tobacco he'd been tamping down. Alorie watched him, thinking that it had been Mary Rose who'd persuaded him to give up the chew of the leaf for the smoking of it. His eyes met her gaze through the thin blue-gray smoke. "I feel better," he said, "knowing that the Path we walked was but one of them, and that she may be in a far, far better place. That the netherworld was not made for mortal eyes to comprehend."

That much the mages of Veil had told them, and little else, as if to discount all that had passed.

But not the unicorn and lion, she thought. Or what the unicorn had said to her.

Or what Gavin Bullheart had said. No. She thought that no matter what path she had chosen, there would have been Gavin there to counsel her. They had a bond of love and blood between them. She said as much to Pinch.

He took a draw. "Mayhap," he answered finally. "His words rang true enough. I don't think it would hurt to remember them, milady."

"That's some comfort."

He reached out a brawny arm and drew her within the circle of his smoke rings. "Take whatever you can. Tonight we'll be on trial and I'm not thinking we'll have an easy time of it. In fact, in all of my years, I cannot remember a single tale of a dwarf who made it to Veil and returned to tell of it."

"That's supposed to make me feel better?"

"No. But it's supposed to make you aware of your enemy. You've a powerful weapon in the sword and the prophecy, Alorie. They may not believe you at first, but they'll be afraid to disbelieve you."

"And they might let us go?"

"No, but I'm thinking that the horn is powerful enough that we may be able to fight our way out."

"We never saw our way in!"

"True enough there." He paused to take a few fragrant drafts.

At Alorie's feet Jasper and the two Mutt guardsmen lay sleeping again. Their passage to Veil had not been an easy one, their heads hooded and their guardians ungentle, and the Mutts had been edgy since. Alorie did not blame them—the hood that had baffled her had cut off all sound as well as light and scent. She would not eagerly be led with such a hood again.

"Ye rattled them with your talk of Brock."

"Do you think so? I never mentioned his name."

"No, but the minions of Veil were upset that when he brought you out of Sinobel and took you to the Rovers. They knew who you meant. It's not wise to tweak the tails here."

Alorie pulled away and stood up, the tapestry curling to her feet. "I'll do more than tweak tails," she said. "Much more! The gods owe me that, if they're going to play *rool* with me and mine." She rubbed the knob at the bridge of her nose. "This is a Sergius nose. That blood runs deep in me. We'll see who's going to be on trial here."

Pinch looked at her seriously and took a solemn draw on his pipe. "That's our girl" was all he said. "Keep hold of your mettle."

"The girl has no appreciation of our danger."

Luisa looked at her opponent across a flickering torch light. "Nor of our power—for we've scarce shown any to aid or oppose our common enemy. I warn all of you here she will balk if you mistreat her, and rightly so."

A rotund mass next to her shifted her weight. "I ask, do we need to deal with a stubborn twit of a girl at all?"

"She wields the sword."

"Take it from her and give it to another."

"Even the Corruptor cannot handle that sword!" This in a hoarse, whiskey voice from the far shadows of the room. "Though taking it might be a temptation. The Prophecy! It's all we have left. Hold to it!"

"Thank you, Beldam Constance." Luisa stood. "If we're ready, I'll bring them in."

Alorie could hear, even through stone and masonry walls hung with heavy tapestry, voices beyond. They rose and fell. Satisfaction quirked the corner of her mouth. They were arguing about her already. Good.

A tile crunched behind her. She turned and saw Luisa in her somber robes standing in the archway. The sorceress inclined her head. "We are ready for you."

Alorie made note of the bright flush upon Luisa's cheek, for all her trying to check her emotions. "Good," she answered. She motioned to Jasper. The captain and his guardsmen flanked her and Pinch. They followed the sorceress into the inner sanctum.

For all the darkness and heaviness of being she'd seen in Veil, she had not expected what she saw. The walls were painted with frescoes that matched the tapestries she'd encountered so far, but not with scenes of history but rather abstracts of the elements of life. Columns braced up the ceiling. The room was filled with light, hung with baskets of gemstones from the Delvings so that they might catch up and refract every ray of candle and torch. It was as though no shadow must fall in this room. If that was what they hoped for, they were wrong, for they themselves were the blights.

Like carrion crows they perched, waiting for her. Alorie disregarded the rich and diverse clothing they wore; it was their expressions she drew her impressions from. She hid her smile in reaction. She'd been intimated by one of the best, her grandfather, and there wasn't a person in this room who could hold a candle to him! She looked about her as she came to a stop.

The Council of Veil numbered six, in a half-circle beyond a low, footed table that held a scrying bowl, now empty of the purified water that mirrored images of the future. Luisa she knew. A massive bulk of a man in subdued crimson and gold robes eyed her from slits in his obese face. Alorie knew him too, having seen him at Lord Rathincourt's in Sobor. He was a Bylantium merchant. She saw an elf lord in darkest of blues, his hair gone white, his face drawn and gaunt. An ancient woman in tattered greens who looked asleep. Another woman husky in homespuns with the chaff and dust of a mill still upon her, and a last man, who wore a harp upon his back and whose eyes examined her lecherously. At least one of the circle, she knew then, did not spend his life cloistered in Veil. Did they all have second lives in the many realms of Bethalia? They inspected her even as she inspected them, and she saw little but arrogance and hostility.

Jasper cleared his throat at her shoulder. "Trouble, mi-lady." His voice was a whining whisper in her ear.

"Perhaps," she answered. She carried the Unicorn sword and flexed her hand upon the guard. It had been cold to her touch when she'd first picked it up, but now felt warm and comfortable.

Luisa waved at Alorie. "May I present the Lady Alorie of the House of Sergius and her companions, Pinch of Gutrig Downs and Jasper, the captain of her guardsmen."

"A Mutt wearing arms! An abomination."

Jasper spread his legs and planted himself firmly upon the floor. "My litter mates and I grew up in the shadow of fallen Cornuth. Would you rather we'd died? We carried weapons from that city and learned to use them in the effort to survive until the High King came again. I see no dishonor in that!" He looked at them through the round eyes of a dog, but stood as proudly as a man.

His answer was a sniff.

Alorie put her hand on his forearm to stay his further action. She looked to the merchant. "I'm surprised," she said, "to see you here, Master Tuan. With the trade roads newly opened, I would think you most busy."

The huge man straightened up. He eyed her speculatively but silently.

"As for you, mistress miller, there is still winter wheat needing grinding and the first of the summer harvesting cannot be far away. In fact, I am surprised that all of you are met here tonight."

Luisa's lips drew downward in a peculiar expression as she said, "Our lives are not on trial here."

"One wouldn't think so. But perhaps you should be. I was told that Veil was forbidden, that you spent your entire lives cloistered here, learning how to untangle knots of evil. Instead I find a fat merchant who undoubtedly uses his power to drive persuasive bargains. And a miller who must predict bumper crops with astonishing accuracy—and raises her fees accordingly. A harpist who uses his instrument to—what? Shall I guess your abuses, master?"

The harpist straightened, his thick, square chin jutting in anger. "I think not," he said.

"Let me just say then that I doubt if it's your music that

lays a spell across your listeners. I would also doubt if you
have much trouble coaxing whatever lovers you wish into
your bed."

A crimson slash across his cheekbones confirmed Alorie's
suspicions before she looked back to Luisa. "I did not come
here for a trial."

"Nevertheless," the ancient elf lord said, leaning forward,
elbows on his knees. "That is why we brought you. You
were trespassers found on our doorstep; there is no choice
in our law."

She looked back at him levelly. "We may be many realms
since the splintering of the kingdom. We may be fields and
townships more than great halls, but *there is only one law* in
Bethalia, and that is the code of the High King. Veil is
neither above nor below it."

The beldam let out a squeaky laugh. "Above it, I'd say.
Oh, yes."

Alorie ignored the being in tattered green robes. "There
is no trespass in entering a city that is part and parcel of the
land. What you really want from me is redress for your
pettiness. Isn't that true?" Her stormy gray-blue gaze swept
the watchers. They shifted, but did not deny her words.
"Then take it. This is all the redress you'll get from me."

Pinch murmured, "Careful, lass," but she ignored him.

She laid the Unicorn sword across the scrying bowl chal-
lengingly. "If you want it, take it."

If the tension in the air had been a string from the
harper's instrument, it would have sounded. Merchant Tuan
stirred, his yellow skin paling. The crone sat up, a preternat-
ural brightness in her rheumy eyes. The miller sat winding
her thumbs around and around each other.

All gazes were fixed on the sword.

The harper cleared his throat. "You're a tease, milady.
No one can touch the sword but you."

"No one? Aquitane held it. My dwarf maid, Mary Rose,
has taken it on more than one occasion."

The miller said, "My colleague stands corrected. We mean
that no one can wield the sword but you." She dropped her
hands in her lap.

Alorie tossed her heavy wave of dark hair back off her
shoulders so that it trailed along her spine. "Surely, with all
your foresight, you can find someone. I'll leave the burden
with you and take our leave of Veil, where we should find

friends but have encountered foes. It's no wonder the Corruptor walks freely through our land!"

Luisa left her side of the council to grab Alorie's arm, saying, "You mustn't be so hasty—" but the crone's cackling amusement stopped them both as she said, "Go ahead, milady, jump for it! It'll be a long trip down."

Alorie looked in astonishment over her shoulder. "What is she talking about?"

The sorceress looked at her. "The fog that wraps about Veil is not fog, Lady Alorie. It is cloud. We're adrift."

Kithrand got up, saying, "Where is a storm when it is really needed? We'll have to hope that scrap of a nimbus there will do." He stretched indolently with animal grace. He cocked an eyebrow dancing with feelers toward Rowan. "Ready?"

The sky had darkened, and there was little rose hue of sunset without cloud, but Rowan got up anyway. He went to his pack, where they had stored their pannikins from dinner and got his out. He filled it with a cupful of clear spring water. Then he cocked his wrist, slipped his dirk from its sheath, and held it still a moment, tip to the inner part of his wrist, looking at Kithrand. "If I botch this, you'll save my ashes for Alorie?"

"If you botch this," his fey friend answered, "I'll join you. After that slash of Aquitane's, you'll get little but pink water."

Rowan smiled grimly. "You could volunteer."

"Me? You'd get naught but green sap and you know it."

The Rover jabbed sharply with the dirk, caught his gasp between clenched teeth, and let the blood flow into the water. He repeated the words Brock had taught him, harsh metallic sounds like swords being hit upon rock and echoing their distress. Then he ran his thumb over the incision, stemming the flow of blood as well as he could. Kithrand leaned over him and wrapped his wrist quickly, but both looked into the pannikin of water, where crimson swirls began to form.

Alorie found her heart beating in her throat and quelled it. "And so that is the magic that drains you, that keeps you from unleashing your strength to help us fight? Vanity? The lofty notion that you—" and she muffled a hysterical giggle— "must be lofty!"

"Milady!" But Luisa's pale face showed also a grim humor even as she pushed her lank hair from her face. "It is not what it seems. None of us here created Veil, not even Lord Balan, and he is as old an elf as Bethalia has. We only inherited it. And, true, while the keeping of Veil does drain some of us, it affects none here on this council. Our floaters work out of their homes. Here, we work only against shadow."

Alorie paused in the council room's center. Multiple rays of light struck her shadow many times over, though its intent seemed to be to omit her shadow all together. "Then you are mistaken in your efforts. Here I throw seven times as many as I would upon the land." She twirled slowly on one heel to demonstrate, arms flung out for balance, a movement of dance she had once given to a unicorn.

"Bah!" The harper stood up. "Let's take the sword and dispense with all of them. They're trespassers, and they've come by the Corrupted track. No good can come of any of this."

"Imprison me," Alorie said as she stopped—she could feel the hardness that glinted in her eyes—"and I will see that you of Veil are branded the traitors. You have what you wanted, take it. Let us go."

Tuan lifted his chin, exposing the wattle on his neck. "It is not just the sword, girl, but the prophecy. You would seem to be its core."

"You would have me die for that prophecy!"

"If necessary." He breathed hard, as if talking sapped his strength. "We all have sacrificed. You accuse me of merchant avarice, but next time you see him, ask Rathincourt who contributes most heavily to the raising of an army."

"Aye," the miller interrupted. "And the rationing of it, too!"

Luisa held her pale hands up to stop the angry flow of words. "This solves nothing."

"It solves everything," Lord Balan retorted, "if we drive her back to the prophecy."

The harper stood. "No."

He held against the sharp glances of his fellow council members. "No, and I say it because we do not know who she is—"

"The sword!"

"Or what mischief she can do us!"

Alorie sighed. "I am tired of this." She reached for the

sword, entwining her fingers about its now cold guard. As soon as she touched it, the scrying bowl filled with white mist, swirling and boiling. The council members gasped.

A scrap of a nimbus anchored itself above Rowan and Kithrand, and, as a cloud does when it rains, extended its gray veiling down. The two watched the mists slanting toward them, and even as they were touched, felt themselves drawn upward.

Kithrand drew his sword. "I feel nothing good comes of this."

Rowan echoed his movement.

Transfixed by the vision, as if the sword pinned her, Alorie looked down into the bowl. She saw the Barrows erupting as if the land vomited and a being, no, a *thing* rising there. It looked toward her and she felt her gorge fill her throat.

"It sees me!"

"Hush, child!" Luisa hissed. "Watch!"

She could not look away if her life depended on it. The palpable evil reached out, engulfing her. It was more terrifying than any malison she had ever faced, stank more of death and corruption than his lieutenant ever did, and she was not even sure if it was *human*. It lifted a hand as if in benediction and Alorie cried out, shrinking back, the sword in her hand, as she felt a cold, greasy smear across her brow.

The vision and mist vanished with the taking of the sword.

Alorie took a deep and quivering breath. Luisa's warmth brushed alongside and the sorceress said quietly, "Now you know what it is we face."

She was shaken but not too shaken to reply haughtily, "Speak only for me, sorceress. I've not seen any of you out on the Barrowlands recently."

Lord Balan pointed a slender finger. "The Barrowlands is the charge of Sinobel, a charge which the House of Sergius failed in."

The Sergius knot on the bridge of Alorie's nose went pinched and white. She could feel it. She had seen herself in a mirror when she was young and her father or grandfather had crossed her and sent her to her room. She knew what she looked like. She drew herself up and came close to the

scrying bowl that separated her from them all except Luisa.
"I would say that my house has paid for its deeds."

"Perhaps and perhaps not."

"Perhaps?" Her voice rose and she sensed Pinch at her
back becoming alert. They had spoken of winning free from
Veil the hard way, and it looked as if they had reached that
impasse. She wondered how long a jump it would be.

"There is payment and there is payment," madam miller
said. "And those are old charges. The new are more serious. You violated our taboo. And because of you, yet
another trespass."

"Because of me? I will answer for the five of us, yes, but
not for every imagined sin."

"I think you will answer for this one, though he reeks of
Corruption and we are ready to put the elfin fire to him."
Lord Balan clapped his hands, and a pair of young men
brought in a third being supported between them.

A reek filled the chamber. The tapers and lamps guttered
low, as if smothered by its presence. Labored breathing like
the sound of bellows in a smithy stopped as the being was
dragged in front of Alorie and the supporters moved away.
If it wore clothing, she could not tell. It was caked with as
rich a loam as any farmer might want, but laced with
putrefaction.

Had it been human once? She did not know. It looked
mummified now—him, she thought as she stared, and wondered if he was still alive. A hand twitched and a moan
squeezed out of his chest.

"Aaaaalorie."

Her breath caught. She opened her lips, unable to speak.
Pinch rumbled at her side and tweaked her sleeve as she
extended her free hand to him. "My God," she got out.
"Brock! Is that you?"

Pandemonium burst out in the council room. She heard
the harper yell, "Seize her! Take them all. She admits
collusion with the traitor!"

She gained Brock's side, and Pinch the other, and swung
about with her sword in hand. The horn drew in the light
and arrowed it back, yellow-gold in its shining power. Only
she could see the splinter of dark that divided it near the
hilt. Brock placed a trembling hand on her forearm to
support himself. Her flesh quivered under his touch, but she
held her ground.

With a growl Jasper slashed and cleared the doorway as

acolytes jumped for safety from the bite of his short sword. "This way!"

Luisa approached Alorie, her face pale within its cowl of dark veils. "Milady, don't do this. We are divided as a council, but we must know what has happened here."

"*You* must know? I know what I see. You've shut him away, shut him away somewhere foul, when we needed him most! Why? Because he had the nerve to ask for his powers back? Because he wasn't afraid to walk Bethalia and fight for her? I've had enough. You're all hypocrites. Pinch, find us a stairway down."

"After you, milady," the dwarf armsman muttered grimly and took a stance to protect her back.

Lord Balan was not having it. He gestured and blue fire shot the length of the room. But like the levin bolts on the hellroad, the Unicorn sword attracted the power and sucked it in, leaving only a dissolving of magic on the air, a flat taste on their tongues. The elven lord reeled back, collapsing in his chair as though shocked or spent. They took the opportunity to run, flanked by Jasper and Mick as Bounder took up the Rover mage in his arms.

"He don't weigh nothing, milady," the Mutt gasped as he sprinted after his captain.

Alorie listened to the bellows-like breathing resume and felt the hot blur of tears on her face even though she told herself it was most likely the cold mist of the clouds surrounding them.

She'd heard no alarm, but one had gone out, for from the dwellings and halls began an outpouring of folk with various weapons in their hands. They stumbled to a stop, surrounded by buildings, and Pinch said, "I think we've a spot of trouble."

Alorie raised the sword bleakly. "It won't stop an arrow or blade, Pinch."

"Aye. That I know," the armsman answered. He raised his axe. "Cover your backs."

They circled, blades outward, Brock on the inside. The poor man crumpled when Bounder set him on his feet, hands waving feebly.

Alorie did not like the looks on the faces of people she had once thought countrymen. "Attack me," she called out, "and you are traitors to what is left of Bethalia!"

Luisa drifted out of the domed building of the council, her robes brushing the ground she did not quite walk on.

Sorrow etched her face. "I'm sorry, but I have no choice."
She raised a hand to signal firing.

The mist about their feet boiled. Rowan leapt out, sword
in hand, followed on his heels by Kithrand. Alorie let out a
cry of joy involuntarily. He grabbed her about the waist and
spun her.

"Fools," panted Brock. "Leave now!" His waving hands
had spun out a grillwork of violet fire on the air, and the
mages of Veil froze.

Bounder snatched up the mage and was first to dash down
the stairs of rain and mist.

Twelve

"Will he live?"

Kithrand arched a brow. "It remains to be seen if he's alive at all." He brushed aside a crust of dirt. "Remove enough of this and we may find nothing inside." He straightened after dropping a blanket over the still figure. "Be that as it may, he's done for the night. The morning will tell."

Alorie sat on a log and hugged herself, sniffing the aroma of tea as it brewed. Her gaze flickered toward Brock and back to Rowan.

The man settled on his haunches near her. He still moved somewhat stiffly and gingerly. She noted the new bandage about his right wrist. She touched it gently. "What happened?"

"I was clumsy." He moved away slightly.

She did not pursue him. Jasper bound his stubby hand and took the brewing pot from the ashes of the fire to pour her a mug of tea. She accepted it gratefully and blew across its surface to cool it enough to sip.

"Clear night."

"Yes." She shuddered. "I'll never sleep under clouds again without wondering if Veil is up there, selfish and stupid, watching me."

Rowan settled cross-legged, putting the fire between the two of them, and watched her, his cleft chin in the palm of one hand. The campfire touched his hair and made it more than red-gold in its light. It was the elf lord who sat next to her, balancing his weight deftly on the log.

"How goes it, milady?"

"Fair enough," she answered. "But I'm of a mind to roast the two of you! What business has Rowan riding all over the countryside looking for me?"

"Business? Business?" Kithrand looked mockingly surprised. "Why, for the like of me, I suppose the business is love. At any rate, that's all he filled my ears with day and night: Alorie, Alorie, Alorie. I thank the gods you are a complicated and interesting woman, else he would have bored me to death!"

Rowan flushed deeply, but he came to his feet. "You're one to talk of riding off! Woman, when will you realize what you mean to these lands . . . to me? You cannot go charging off sword in hand whenever you get the wind up!"

"Rowan!" Alorie's head snapped back.

Pinch chuckled as he dropped by the fireside, pipe in hand. "That's telling her, bucko. But I'd watch it if I were you. She's been known to skewer her enemies."

"I have, haven't I?" Alorie said quietly. "Though it took me a long time to catch up with Aquitane." She took a deep breath. "Kithrand, you'd better whistle up a hawk or two. I need to send word to his lordship."

"As you wish, but it will be difficult."

"Why?"

"The borders are in flame again. The Corruptor has wasted no time pushing down from the north." Kithrand examined his own lightly booted feet as he brought them close to the fire's ashes. "I think he's gotten cold."

Alorie closed her eyes tightly. "Oh, damn," she whispered. Her suddenly icy right side felt a brush of heat as Rowan reseated himself close to her. He took her hands in his and guided the tea to her lips. "You can worry about that in the morning."

She looked at him, and with a sigh leaned gratefully upon his shoulder. "We won't have much time to finish what we started."

"Less time than even that, I think. Tell us what happened, from start to finish."

Pinch rumbled, "Mayhap we should tell it the way it happened to us, milady, from middle to widdershins."

Alorie smiled widely. "He means that a hellroad has no time. I know we've probably been gone close to three weeks—"

"Over four."

"—but it only seems a handful of hard riding days." With Rowan to warm her, she told the tale, interrupted once or twice by a particularly colorful description by Pinch or a pithy one by Jasper. She did not tell them of the damage done to the sword and faltered when she got to Brock's appearance.

They all looked at the mage sleeping in a hollow Kithrand had carved for him and filled with moss to ease his dreams.

"What did they do to him?"

"It looks as if he's spent the last few years in a barrow himself. Who knows what Veil has done. It is full of corrupt, jealous people. I threatened them with it, and now I declare it. They're traitors, every last one of them."

"Hasty words," Kithrand said to Alorie. "You may regret them. Besides, it's better to attend to banishments in the morning."

Rowan added, "I'll share a blanket with you if you promise not to knee me in the side. I'm still tender there."

"You're soft in the head, too," she retorted, not unkindly, and finished her mug of tea.

Bryant leaned on the carven arm of the great stone dwarven throne. "What have the scouts to say?"

"Only one group's come back, sir, and they report nothing unusual. We're waiting for the second pair."

The king looked down the length of his great hall, a dwarf who stood head and shoulders above any dwarf there. Rathincourt had sent disturbing news and as he considered it, he considered that he could not have been wrong, despite the scouting reports. He knew the stamp of armies overhead, though no sight had been found of them. Their vibrations troubled the rock of the Delvings, striking into his very heart. No marriage, no bride, no sword. The Corruptor had wrought well with his first blow.

They would be after the forge again, he thought. There would be little or no weapons and armor without the Delvings.

He said to Buckle, "It's time to fire the forges up again."

"But, my lord, we've had no sign."

Bryant got to his feet, towering above the hairy-footed dwarf. "I do not need a sign. I know what I know." Inside his crusty exterior he mourned for a dark-haired girl whose gaze was level with his own and had once not thought it repulsive that her grandfather had offered him her hand in marriage. He would kill for her to look at him as she had looked at Rowan. He looked to the stout dwarf who'd been sent to bring him the distressing news. "Well, Hammersmith. It looks as if we'll have need of you."

Hammersmith the True gave a bow. "Ye can eggspect my help wheree'r ye need it, sire. I spent but little time in

Barrel. It seemed expedient fer me to hie wi' the tidings, ill as they were."

"It's not without its good luck, for us at least. I've not talked with any of our far kinsmen from the Gutrig Downs for a long, long time. Walk with me while I show you the forge, and tell me a tale, if you will."

The dwarf pulled on his chin-chop whiskers, and his flint-dark eyes blinked to hide an enigmatic light in their depths. As he walked throughout the chasms of the Delvings, where gemstone chased the blackness away, he looked carefully and listened thoughtfully to King Bryant's words. There was a chink in the ruler's armor. Hammersmith knew it. He had but to find it.

Thirteen

"I will walk like the rest of you."

Kithrand's gem-blue eyes frowned at her. "It is best if you ride."

"We have two horses between the eight of us. I'll walk."

The elf lord's finely boned jaw tightened. "Strider will not suffer other riders, but he has agreed to accept you."

"That's very kind of him, Lord Kithrand." Alorie's eyes flashed in return. "But it's an impractical arrangement at best. Brock must be carried by litter or otherwise, and Rowan's chestnut cannot bear him alone."

Beyond her the elf lord could see amusement flashing across Rowan's face, for he and the Rover had already had this discussion, and the young man had warned him of this. Kithrand sighed. "Very well," he said. "Strider will also pull the litter when necessary."

"Thank you, Lord Kithrand." Alorie quickly ducked her face to avoid letting her triumphant look be seen.

The elf lord watched her walk away and bend over the Rover mage, checking him, and said to Rowan, "She'll have it her way or not at all."

"So it seems."

He ran slender fingers through a wave of white-blond hair. "Take care of her, Rowan. The future doesn't bode well for any of us."

"Tell me something I don't know," the auburn man replied. Worry creased the corners of his brown eyes.

Neither had the courage to mention his portion of the prophecy from the wall of Cornuth to the other.

To Rowan it meant acknowledging his loss of her. And to Kithrand it meant revealing his cowardice.

They watched as the three Mutts pulled the litter into place and gently strapped Brock in. The dark-skinned mage

slept in a daze, waking only briefly to ask for water in a
hoarse voice, and to return to sleep. The two men turned
away from the sight. A long day's walk awaited them, for
they had no way of knowing when—or if—Rathincourt would
send an escort with extra horses for them.

They stopped at noon, the brook having pooled into a
sun-dappled pond, and the banks of it grassy and beckoning. Rowan put Mick on point and sent out Jasper and
Bounder to hunt for lunch. He and the elf lord took on the
difficult task of bathing the mage while Pinch grumbled and
set up camp.

They eyed each other over the litter and both said, at
once, "It's all or nothing," having decided it was useless to
strip the man down when he was so encrusted they could
not even tell if he wore clothes.

"I'll take his ankles," Kithrand offered.

"And I've got the shoulders."

They lifted him carefully from the litter and found him so
light to be insubstantial. "He is only a shell," Kithrand
said, and lowered him into the sun-warmed pond. The water
lapped up to his chin and the man flinched as it touched
him, then lay quietly, his eyes closed as if he was still lost to
sleep.

Alorie watched critically. "More like a dried fruit," she
commented. "I wonder if he would plump up if we stewed
him there all day."

Rowan shuddered as he watched the dirt soak into mud
and puddle off the mage. A maggot wriggled in a clod as it
washed up and eddied into the brook. In his mind, Brock
had always been vigorous. He could not imagine what had
been done to the man to bring him so low. And at the back
of his mind, Rowan remembered the dungeons of Trela'ar,
where the malison Ayah had tormented him. He took an
involuntary step backward, as though Brock were responsi-
ble for the memory. Gooseflesh quickened on his arms.

Brock's hazel eyes opened, their gaze fastening on Rowan's face. Greenwood and smoke, he'd always thought of
those eyes, with a hardness that could pierce armor like an
arrow. They caught him now.

"Traitor," Brock said huskily.

Alorie made a soothing noise and knelt at the pond's
edge. Part of the bank crumbled under her knee and the

water dampened her, but she did not move. "It's us," she said. "You're free now."

The stare did not leave Rowan's face. "Like my son," the mage croaked. "And now a traitor."

Rowan's face went white. "He knows what he says," he snapped to Alorie before swinging around and stalking off.

She watched him go but did not call him back. Instead she reached out a trembling hand to Brock's twiglike fingers floating in the water. "You're safe now."

He closed his eyes with a sigh. She dabbled water over his face, trying to dislodge the dirt and cleanse the sores there. Kithrand stood hesitantly over them a moment, and Alorie looked up.

She smiled. "It's all right," she said. "I've got him for a while."

The elf lord nodded in relief and strode off in search of Rowan. After a moment he took his bow and quiver from his tack and ran off in search of game. His feet barely touched the ground as he raced through the trees, his white-blond hair streaming behind him. Rowan strode after him before breaking into the ground-eating lope of the Rover.

The fingers in her grip twitched slightly. She looked back to find Brock watching her.

"The ring," he croaked. "Where is my ring?"

"Safe. It's with my things in Barrel."

"The wedding canopy was . . . in Barrel?"

"Yes. Didn't you know where you were sending?"

He squeezed his eyes shut and shook his head, a palsied movement. Then he looked back to her. "I . . . told you to wear the ring always."

Alorie felt shame catch in her throat. She looked to the brook, where the water eased up against Brock and carried away filth. "So many things happened. There was war and then, suddenly, there was peace. I thought my time had passed. Cranfer told us you'd been killed . . . I thought the ring had died, too."

"Cranfer. Of Veil." There was a twisting across the mage's face.

"Yes." Alorie began to splash water onto the fingers she held and, as she would a child, washed his hand. "He died with our forces when Aquitane attacked, later." It remained difficult to tell what was dirt and scar and skin, but finally she had cleansed it. Underneath the grime and scabs, he was painfully thin. Obsessed with uncovering him, she be-

gan to work her way up the arm. The pink-brown patches of
skin surfacing were crisscrossed with tiny scars. He said
nothing, though her labors must have hurt as scab floated
away with dirt. Her tears blurred hotly and she kept working, remembering the vital man in the last years of his prime
who'd come to Sinobel and challenged her grandfather for
her. Rowan, whom she dearly loved, was a great deal like
this man had been.

As she worked, she could not believe what she saw,
despite the hostility encountered at Veil. The Rover mage
had been tortured horribly, then buried alive . . . but not to
die. To be bound somehow, as near as she could tell. What
human being could do this to another?

The hunters had returned, some successful and some not.
Their catch was skinned and either roasting or boiling before she finished washing Brock down. The man had drifted
back into sleep as she uncovered the lines of his face. He
wore a simple leathern vest that covered his chest and faded
black breeches, but his feet were bare . . . if the network of
callused scar tissue on them could be called bare. The sun
was no longer directly overhead, and the water in the pool
was coarse with the filth strained off his form. She looked
over her shoulder, saw Pinch nearby, and called for help.

"Help me pull him out."

The dwarf came over and muttered as he grabbed the
limp man by his shoulders, "Now, aye, here's a man I
remember." But his joviality was forced, whether for Alorie's
hearing or Brock's she didn't know.

They carried the mage onto the sweet meadow grass and
left him lying comfortably in the sun. It was a hot day and
she didn't worry about Brock catching cold. She looked
back as the smells of the luncheon came to her. "We probably should have stripped him and washed him better."

"One thing at a time," the armsman reassured her. "He's
better off than he's been in a long time. When he wakes,
we'll have quail stew for him, with broth."

"Good." She sniffed deeply. "Who found the onions?"

Jasper's sharp face stretched in a grin. "I did, milady."

Kithrand snorted. "Superior sense of smell," he remarked.

The Mutt did not take offense, though nearby Mick rolled
an unappreciative eye at the elf.

They had roasted onions and rabbit, quail stewed with
sweet and mustard grass and tubers. All in all it was a
princely lunch. There was a brace of quail slowly smoking,

to be eaten cold at the evening camp, and Kithrand had flat cakes of his sourdough bread baking on hot rocks to accompany them. Though she'd eaten well enough in Veil, Alorie felt as though her senses had all finally awakened after the sterility of the Paths of Sorrow. She would pick berries when they started out again, using her cloak for an apron.

Rowan gave her lunch on a broad, waxy green leaf. "How's the patient?"

"Cleaner."

Kithrand showed his sharp and neat white teeth before biting into an onion. "He could hardly be dirtier."

"Oh, stop it. You'd think we'd brought out a drunkard or a villain."

Rowan examined his quail as he said slowly, "We have talked, and we have our doubts it is Brock."

"Not Brock? You've spring fever. Pinch, you'll help me gather up a tonic." Alorie kept her tone light, but she watched Rowan as she tore off a piece of quail and crunched it.

The Rover shook his head, auburn hair falling onto his forehead. "We were fooled once by the Corruptor. We could be fooled again."

"That man is flesh and blood!"

"Of that we have no doubt," Pinch countered. "But the Despot is said to have troubled with the forces of creation itself, and I've no doubt his lieutenant could do the same, though with great effort."

She set her lunch down. "And replacing Brock with a creature of his own would be worth that effort."

"We think so."

She balanced on her heels. "But why let Veil capture him?"

"You think so, and he thinks so, but we've no proof it was Veil who imprisoned him." Rowan licked the juices off the corner of his mouth and added sadly, "If he makes the journey, we'll have plenty of time to find out what happened."

Their gazes tangled a moment, and the look on his face struck a chord deep inside Alorie. She remembered his plea to marry him before she'd left. Now there would be little time. Suddenly she understood why Brock had called Rowan a traitor. The Rover mage had always had a fate in mind for her: that was why he'd come to Sinobel, and why he'd sent Rowan to bring her out.

It was also why his sending had interrupted the binding.

She looked away, unable to bear the longing in her lover's eyes. The quail no longer smelled so savory or tasted so tender in her mouth. The spring they had eagerly planned to share had turned cold and lonely, a false season of even falser hopes.

Her thoughts were shattered when the mage began to rave.

They traveled painstakingly the next few days through warm weather and rain, by brook and over raging river, on foot and occasionally on horseback. She sat watch by Brock's fevered body, unable to help him other than the mild tonics she and Pinch could prepare from herbs in the locale. Kithrand's elfin talents precluded healing, so all the lord could do was run lightly, tirelessly, after the herbs Alorie hoped to find. Sometimes he was successful and sometimes not.

Most often Brock was incoherent, though he rambled and shouted constantly, sending rabbits running from thickets and birds to wing as the litter bore him cross-country. As Pinch drily put it, "If there're any reken about, he's given them ample time to bushwhack us."

There was nothing anyone could do, though occasionally just the light stroke of her hand across his brow would quiet him. One evening Rowan joined her, though the sight of him normally set the mage shouting again.

"How is he?"

"The same. I wish Medra would be meeting us at Barrel." She dropped her hand from the mage's forehead.

That brought silence between them. It was broken by Brock's mumbling. Rowan turned away before Alorie could see the despair on his face, but the ill man's words turned his head.

"Bring up the guard! Quickly. They are foresworn, but nothing less will do! Frenlaw . . . the baron has left, but they will hold now—"

Alorie saw the intensity that gripped Rowan. "What is it? What is he saying?"

The Rover said grimly, "He's talking about the betrayal that stripped our forefathers of station and land. You've heard the stories."

"And the sword of Frenlaw I know well." Irony colored her answer. "None of you ever forget."

"No. And we won't ever, either, until we've earned our

rightful place once more. He's returned to remind us of many things we forgot." Rowan touched her chin. "Come on, and leave him now. Let Jasper bring him soup."

She nodded wearily and as the night shadowed close about them made her way to the camp.

Kithrand watched them go by and said to no one in particular, "That's a fever that will burn us all before this is over."

Fourteen

Bryant returned to his rooms wearily, pondering his immediate choices for the future. His scouts had ridden into death traps, proving his intuition correct at the cost of lives he could ill afford to lose. He took his helm off and tossed it at a corner desk, where it landed with a dull ring. He left his surcoat on. He would be wearing it night and day for some time now, he thought, and he'd best get used to the weight again.

A cleverly carved dwarven chair welcomed his tired bones as he dropped into it, kicked around a small stool, and put his feet up. A fire had been built for him—he had his rooms off one of the air chimneys that ran from top to bottom in the Delvings—and he watched the dance of the flames now. He leaned on an elbow, scrubbing a hand through his curly brown hair, his thoughts taking him far away.

Down a trading road this time. Supplies had been slow coming in, but the Despot's forces had tried unsuccessfully to besiege the Delvings before. Bryant did not figure the trading road was closed off, but harried, hit-and-run, to slow the traders down without expending much time or energy. The lessons they were teaching on the trading road would linger for some time. So the enemy's activities remained an inconvenience, little more, and with nothing he could do about it. The Delvings were flanked to the north and east by fallen Cornuth and south and east by fallen Sinobel.

The dwarf king spied pen and paper still lying on the table, along with a covered platter for his dinner. He could perhaps write and urge Rathincourt to consider retaking Sinobel and garrisoning there. Yes, there was an option that would be advantageous to both of them. The Barrowlands should be watched closely now. The Corruptor was an apt lieutenant. It would not be long before he unbound his liege and set the Despot free once more.

Lamplight guttered in his room, as though thought alone could darken it. Bryant heaved a weary sigh. A hawk had winged through the giant stone teeth of his gates that morning, bringing word that the Lady Alorie had retrieved her talismanic sword and was returning to Barrel. Further, her quest had led her to the lost mage Brock and she was restoring him also. Not all news was ill, though he'd been sorrowed to hear his kinswoman had died in Aquitane's raid. Odd that Hammersmith the Truth had not mentioned Mary Rose's death with his other news, but it was unlikely the Gutrig smithy had known of their relation. Still, dwarves being dwarves, they were keenly interested in the doings of their people, outnumbered as they were by the rest of the Seven True Races.

The news that the wedding had been disrupted had been even more fortuitous. Bryant smiled a little and scratched an annoying spot on his chin deep inside his beard. Dropping his chin on his chest, he grew pensive and his eyes closed while the fire burned down. No, he was not at all unhappy that the marriage had not taken place.

In a corner of long shadows Hammersmith stirred. He cursed himself for having been caught in the king's chambers, for if discovered, he would undoubtedly be put to death and the Corruptor's mission would go unfulfilled. He was not worried about the possible loss of his life. He had not thought of it when he'd destroyed the mines of Gutrig Downs, when fortune had saved his life, and was not so worried now. It was the cause that flamed his blood and will, and if he failed, it was the cause that would suffer.

Fortune still watched over him, it seemed, as the king grew wistful and then sleepy in his chair. Hammersmith ignored the pins and needles pricking his limbs, and waited for the breathing to become low and rhythmic and the hands slack upon the chair arms. When that happened, he had two choices: he could either strangle Bryant or leave quietly. Killing the dwarf king must bring on the chaos his master needed to invade it . . . but it might not. No, he had time yet. He could bide awhile on that choice. Bryant was an admirable dwarf with few vices. A chink in the armor of the Delvings might not exist, but the Corruptor had ordered and so Hammersmith would obey. He hunkered down to wait.

Bryant grew restive and opened his eyes, not surprised to see the fire reduced to glowing embers. He would go to bed, he thought, but not before he took one last look and thought again upon the fate of Lady Alorie.

He reached under the carved hand rest and found a small indentation, which he pressed. A tiny spring clicked and a panel popped out on the arm. Reaching in, he took out a scroll and shook it out of its protective cover. Careful not to crumble the waxen seal of Sergius the Third, he unrolled the missive and read it again. His face was melancholy as he wound it tightly and replaced it in its secret cupboard. This time when he lay his head back against the chair, it was to sleep.

Hammersmith crept out carefully when his time came, though it was difficult because his pulse thundered in his ears. It would take watching and timing to return unnoticed to the king's chambers, but it would be done. Yes, it would certainly be done. Because whatever it was Bryant had hidden in his wooden chair, it was a key to the fall of the Delvings!

Brock's fever broke three days after Rathincourt's escort found them a week's ride from Barrel. They rode on after a brief visit, taking the Mutts with them. Alorie did not hide her relief as she wearily brushed her hair back from her forehead and knotted it out of her way.

"I couldn't take it if he died this close to Barrel."

Rowan watched her fingers flashing through her black hair and waited until she'd finished before capturing a hand. "He's too tough to let go." He considered Brock a moment while the mage evidently slumbered peacefully as they struck camp. "I think you were right about his being a dried fruit. All that bathing and all that soup seems to have plumped him up. Now he looks more like a man instead of a twig."

Alorie watched the mage fondly. She remembered the first time she'd met him. He had suddenly appeared in the Inner Ring of Sinobel, bowed under an old cloak, covered with dust of the road, his hair grayed. She'd thought him old then. But when he'd stood up to grandfather to ask for her, he'd been straight and proud in Rover black and silver, the gray washed out of his hair except for a fleck here and there. He'd had a peeled wood staff, a bow across his back, his sword on his left hip for an easy pull, and a dagger strapped to his right wrist. Marked more by his life on a Rover road than by years, he'd given the immediate impression of being not only quick on his feet, but experienced, a dangerous combination. A sadness passed over her now.

Rowan tugged on her hair. "Come on. He's still asleep and it'll be awhile before his soup is ready. You need to rest."

They walked away, hip to hip, his arm about her waist in easy familiarity.

Brock turned his head to watch them leave, his hazel eyes suddenly sharp and knowing. There was no mistaking the aspect of their nearness, and his gaze narrowed. Damn it all. The lad had been warned beforehand, and warned away again. The mage took a deep breath, feeling mustiness and cobwebs still in his lungs, then exhaled. Something would have to be done as soon as he regained his strength.

Rowan refilled her mug of tea. As he settled back, sprawled on the ground and leaning on one elbow, he frowned at her. "You're thinking again."

She looked up from the mug and tried to relax that tight spot between her brows. "Always," she said. "I was asking myself what I would do if this was a game of *rool*."

"And?"

"And I think it would be wise to let the chiefest of my pieces know all that I know."

He stood up. "Then there is no time like now, for in three days of hard riding, we'll be up to our necks in Rathincourt's councils." He offered his elbow. "Shall we walk a ways in the dusk?"

Alorie stood up and took his elbow, holding her tea in her other hand as they left the campsite. The others noted their leaving, but only Pinch commented.

He clamped down tightly on his pipe stem. "Does my heart good," he said as the figures disappeared from sight. He dug around in the ashes, trying to fish out the last roasted egg.

Kithrand said nothing, but watched after them with a speculative look.

When they were out of earshot, Rowan found a knoll still

wárm from the sun and pulled her down upon it with him, curling an arm about her shoulders. "Now, what is it you would have me know?"

Braced against his knee, she told him first of the unicorn's rebuff of her on their marriage morning. He listened well, drawing out her hesitant words, and gradually she told him more of what had happened along the Paths of Sorrow. When she reached the unicorn stained with darkness, he had no questions.

She paused. "What do you think it means?"

"I think it means," he said quietly, "that we will have little of our lives left to ourselves. The prophecy—"

"Damn the prophecy! You know what I think of it."

"That can't be helped. The prophecy is a foreseeing, our one hope in the dark times to come, because it does say that despite all, we shall persevere." He put his face to her cheek. "We may only have this night."

Alorie threw aside her mug of tea and turned into his arms.

Kithrand faded from the shrubbery, unwilling to witness anything more. He found his own moon-dappled glen, where he stood, head bowed in thought, the tiny, hairlike antenna in his brows as quiet as the woods about him. The Unicorn sword had been tainted by the Corruptor. There was discord in Veil. None of this was good news.

Disquieted and torn by loyalties, he gave a sharp whistle. The note pierced the woods until it found a sleeping hawk and awakened it, and the raptor answered.

Kithrand heard the beat of wings upon the night wind. He put his arms up to absorb the blow of the landing bird. He had no paper or ink with which to write, but stared into the creature's amber eyes, willing it the message to take back to forbidden Charlbet. Then he flung the hawk into the air, watched it gain the air, wheel, and soar away west. He sighed. He had come to the crossroads of his life, where he must betray either friend or family to protect the other. Having reached the crossroads, he did not like it. As the hawk faded into velvet night, Kithrand wondered if there was a portion left of his long life ahead of him that he would ever enjoy at all.

Alorie checked Brock's litter when they returned to camp. As she touched the back of her hand to his forehead, she found her fingers grasped tightly and imprisoned.

"Do not cry out," Brock said.

"If I did, it would be in joy." She folded her legs and sat down next to the litter. "You've been very feverish."

"What I have been," he said, shuddering, "is far worse than that." He loosened her hand. "Where are we?"

"Not far from Barrel."

"Barrel?" The brown-skinned mage relaxed his gaze. "Where a peasant can live like a king. Or at least drink like one."

Alorie found herself smiling. "You remember."

"Did you think I wouldn't?"

"Your senses have been muddled. We've been worried."

"Have you, last of the House of Sergius?"

"Yes, we have." Alorie tucked in his blanket against a mist that began oozing up from the ground. They had borrowed a change of clothing from one of Rathincourt's men before the detail had gone on its way, and the shirt and breeches hung upon Brock's frame. But he was clean now, and healing.

"I have questions."

"Then ask them, though I can't promise you'll remember the answers." Alorie smiled gently. Over the past few days there had been a few lucid moments, and she had answered questions then, too.

"How long have I been gone?"

"Three-and-a-half years, give or take a month."

"Ah." Expressionless, he looked up at the leafy canopy that hid the moon and the stars from view. "Doubtless much has happened in that time."

She laughed. "Doubtless!"

"Then there is too much for me to learn at once. I remember—I remember escaping and using what strength I had left to send to you." His face grew stern. "They mocked me with your wedding. It gave me the will to escape. And I remember being taken again."

Uneasiness swept over her. She drew away, but though he'd loosened his grip on her hand, he held it still.

"You must wait for me," he told her, even as fatigue thinned his voice. "You must wait for me to get well before you do anything. There are things you must know."

She had seen this moment coming and turned her head away, not wanting to face it. "Brock—"

"Promise me. All I ask is a delay."

"That you'll have without asking me to make vows. The

woods hereabouts were thick with reken when we left. Rathincourt had been cleaning the vermin out."

"Make me a vow."

He'd had his lucid moments, but never like this. Alorie felt a cold aching through her body. She looked away and watched the white curls of fog rising from the ground in wispy fingers.

He squeezed her hand slightly.

She looked back. "All right, then," she answered. "I promise to hear you out. But you know my heart, you must."

"I've seen you look at Rowan."

He released her and she stood over him for a wordless moment, then tucked his blankets about him one last time.

"My father," she said softly, "was a wise and good man. But if he'd had your iron will, he'd be alive today."

With that she left him.

Brock watched her go, the smell of Rowan still upon her. He sighed and loosened one hand from the blanket to cover his eyes. She had been destined for the High King. How could he let her go?

Fifteen

The elfin woman stroked the hawk gently, then settled him on a branch lofting near the council platform. It remained, though days out of its territory with a yearning like fire in its heart to return to the nest and winds it knew best. It blinked, then watched them keenly.

"You've questioned Kit's loyalties once too often. I think this message is the proof of him."

"Perhaps." Drussander wore his red hair tucked behind his ears, proudly exposing their tips. When he was younger, it had been to get attention, and now that he was older, it still was. His flesh was still as firm as it had ever been, his jawline smooth and unsagging. "The boy has entangled himself in their affairs. He hasn't yet learned the lesson the rest of us have."

Lady Orthea knelt at the table. No one else stirred or deigned to speak. Her eyes glimmered. "And what lesson is that, Dru?"

"That we far outlive them. It is heartbreak to become attached to any one of them."

"Ahhhh." Her voice, in understanding—or perhaps it was only a wind sighing through the treetops of Charlbet.

Gillus, to her right, lay on the cushions, his head pillowed on the council table's edge as he looked out over the city, not even appearing to be listening. He stirred. "And that is only one of the lessons they've taught us."

The lady urged him. "Yes?"

"You want others? War. Pestilence. Destruction of the natural order. They tear out trees and wonder why the soil washes away. They fill dry riverbeds with garbage."

"Children wanting lessons from us, perhaps." The lady smoothed her dark green dress. "They have taught us other

111

things. Love. Passion for the moment. They have given us back fertility.''

Dru made an angry gesture. The lady stared him down. "Do you deny it? All of us have their blood in our young. In our ancestors. They gave us back the ability to bear children. You may choose to forget it now . . . but even you, Dru, had a human grandfather."

"There is no history of theirs that records it."

"But ours do. We remember what they were once, even if they do not. And here is another thing they gave us: the will to survive against all odds." She glared about the table. "Without that, the malisons would be eating our souls even now."

Gillus swung around and came to attention at the table. The silver streak in his jet hair matched the gleam of his silver torque. "We can treat with the malisons."

"Oh? Can we?"

"Coexist, then."

Orthea tapped her elegant nails on the tabletop as Drussander said, "I agree on this with milady. The malisons are too many now, and their appetite too great."

Another stirred, one who had remained silent through this debate, and when Kithrand had asked for permission to attend the wedding. She was lovely, in her prime, white-gold hair down to her waist, and eyes of pale blue gem. Her stomach curved with the life she carried under the soft blue folds of her waiting-gown. Liandra said softly, "Gillus wishes to force us to a choice before the battle is enjoined. The malisons or the homeless children."

Orthea's lips compressed tightly. "To make such a choice disturbs the balance."

Gillus made a rude noise, then added, "There is no balance! Has not been since mankind flooded our kingdoms, an endless parade of chattering, quick-lived flesh."

"Nonetheless, we strive for balance. We live within the elements, not without. Beyond Bethalia the balance was horribly tipped and little remains. We do not wish this here." Orthea put out her chin. "If you wish otherwise, and wish to press the point, Gillus, then we shall have to call for a full council."

"Perhaps we should," the round-bellied elf answered darkly. "In either case, it will be a choice of the lesser of two evils. None of us is wise enough to make the determination hastily."

Liandra murmured, "Done, then. I will send a calling for

the full council. You have until the harvest moon, Lady Orthea, to cozen your homeless children."

As if sensing dismissal, the hawk took to wing and left the hidden city.

Rathincourt had cleared the entire tavern for housing for himself and his officers. Alorie entered to find it strangely quiet, but the innkeeper seemed content enough. She went upstairs to her rooms and found them full of the remnants of other people: Mary Rose, who'd shared them with her while preparing for the wedding, and Rowan while he'd been recuperating. Now the room was quiet. The lid of her bridal trunk remained open. She took the sword from her belt, wrapped it in her frayed and muddied cloak, and put it away. She dipped inside it, found the sigil ring wedged in an inside crack, and retrieved it. Cupped in her palm, she could feel its inner fire.

Feet dragged along the corridor, feet of men burdened by carrying the litter. Alorie threw the door open wider. "In here!" she called. "And send for Karlin as soon as you put him down."

"Aye, miss," the gruff soldier said, bearing the litter weight to the fore.

Brock made a sound as they half-dropped him to the floor, but waved away their help as he rolled out and got to his feet. "Which cot?"

Rowan had left hers rumpled and bloodstained. She pointed to Mary Rose's even as she quickly gathered her things and those of the maid to fill the trunk. "There's a smaller room next door. Rowan will want to stay here with you until you're fully recovered." She waited until she heard the door shut and the cot creak with the Rover mage's weight before she turned.

She crossed the room to take his hand and pressed the ring into the pinkness of his palm. "I did keep it," she told him. "Even if not properly."

Brock looked at her. "You've met all my greatest hopes— and more," he said after a moment. "The ring is for you to keep."

She had had no choice before—the mage had appeared in a sending, a phantom, no more, and left the ring behind. Now she had a feeling that there was much, much more to Brock's offering than he told her, and she didn't like it.

Alorie shook her head. "It belongs to you," she insisted

gently. "And, like you, it still has occasional flashes of power."

Brock stayed propped on his elbow, but he curled his fingers about the ring. "I spoke truth when I said that Veil had stripped me of my magic."

"Did you? Then you owe me a wedding ceremony." She picked up a dress for a shield and began to fold it over her arm for packing.

"I could not let you go through with it. I told Rowan, and I told you: you are the last of the House of Sergius. The fates have something different in mind for you."

Alorie put the dress in the trunk and picked up a cloak, doing the same to it, keeping it between them. "The fates did not seem to care one way or another," she answered. "It was your seeming which interrupted. From where did you dredge up the power for that?"

"It came from desperation. No one, not even the Council of Veil, can shut me off entirely. I cannot make love potions or enslave demons, but once in a while—yes, once in a while, I can make a difference." With a tired sigh the mage lowered himself onto the cot. "Not that it's predictable. If it had been, I would have saved your city."

She might have questioned him further, but she thought of the sword, and her own inadequacies. How could she allow him to be any less fallible than herself? Oh, it was easy enough to slice with it, but the healing—that she could not do, and she could not bear to destroy without the balance. And now, with the dark lieutenant's stain upon it, could she trust it at all? She had nothing to else to say, so she turned her back and busily cleared her things.

Brock lay his head back, watching her. He'd felt the authority of the talisman when she'd put it away, even though she'd kept it shielded after that first thrust in Veil. He ached to have the weapon, to examine what she'd wrought in his absence, but he told himself he'd have time. The return of the High King was close, very close. He shut his eyes against the light streaming in through open-shuttered windows. His thoughts shifted. Was he the reincarnation of the High King . . . or merely waiting for him? His enemies must be very powerful indeed if they could make a man forget all that he had been and all that he was destined to be.

Signing with his signet ring, Brock returned it to his hand and let sleep take him.

*   *   *

Hammersmith crept across the stone floor. He paused before the chair, his flint-hard eyes examining the minute detailing for traps that might tell of his trespass. He saw nothing. With a grunt of satisfaction he ran his black-nailed fingers over the burled wood, searching for the hidden lever.

Bryant's hands must have traveled this path often, for it was slightly worn, and Hammersmith's fingertip found the groove that hid the lever. He pressed it and deftly moved aside as the panel in the arm snapped out.

He took the scroll and slipped it from its cover. In the tremulous light from the single candle he'd brought with him, he read the letter carefully. When he was done, the dwarf smiled a bitter smile. He returned the object and restored the chair as though he'd never been there.

But he had.

Hammersmith's hard, callused feet slapped against the cave floor as he made his way to his modest cubicle. He sat at his desk a moment and encoded his message before reaching into the corner under his humble bed. There he opened a box trap he'd made earlier. Two red slits eyed him from the trap. Hammersmith agilely fetched out its denizen.

The rat twisted and squirmed in his hands, showing massive yellow teeth, but it could not duck the collar being fastened upon its neck.

Hammersmith grinned. "We're alike, ye and I," he muttered. "We both know to leave when the pickings are poor. And we both like to travel dark, twisty paths. Now find the master, damn yer hide, and quickly!"

He set the rat loose. It snaked on the floor a moment in a vain attempt to loose its collar. Then, hugging the dim recesses of the inner chambers, it was gone. A reken patrol would find it outside.

Hammersmith rocked back in his chair and hugged himself in delight. He'd done all his master would want of him, and more.

The Delvings had already begun to totter and did not even realize it.

Sixteen

Rowan caught her by the shoulders. She fell into his quick embrace, saying, "I've missed you. It's been days." He smelled of sweat and the dust of the trail.

"And I've missed you." He smoothed her hair off her shoulders, then bent and kissed the shoulder he had bared. "I don't know where they come from. The fields are crawling with them, like mice. Reken everywhere. They're pouring out of the north like a flood. They've got the trade road to the Delvings blockaded when they wish. Wagon loads go through on a whim."

"Are they laying siege to Bryant?"

"No. Not that we've seen." He sighed. "At least councils have some good result. It was the only good excuse I could find for coming back in to see you."

Alorie tilted her face. "The only good excuse?" she teased.

He fell into her trap and kissed her long and hard. When she broke away, it was with a breathless gasp. "Not here in the hall."

"And why not? You're as good as my wife." Rowan seemed pressed for breath as well. "We've an assembly gathering down there. They'll be good witness for the ceremony we've put off long enough."

Alorie hesitated, then caught his enthusiasm. "All right! I'll send for Karlin—"

"No," said a flat voice wedging between them.

The two turned and saw Brock leaning in his doorway. A cane braced him, a wooden cane cut and iron-shod by Rowan before leaving on patrol. The mage looked better, but his face was still gaunt. It was the first time she'd seen him on his feet without aid. His dark, curled hair held more gray flecks than she remembered.

Alorie felt Rowan's muscles tense. "I forgave you your

words on the road," Rowan said. "I blamed your fever for them. But now, by god, I want to know what the problem is."

Brock inclined his head. "In the room, then."

"No," Alorie protested, but Rowan curled hard fingers about her upper arm and steered her inside after the mage.

Immediately he turned upon his once comrade. "What do you want from us?"

Brock sat down on the window seat, easing his lame leg. "Obedience," he answered. "Complete and unutterable obedience. But I can tell I'll never get that. You're no longer children."

"A Rover," Rowan said harshly, "has little time in which to be a child. You learn the ways of the road quickly or you die. And I shouldn't have to remind *you* of that."

Brock leaned forward. "Then I shouldn't have to remind you that the prophecy takes us from that road—and restores us to house and land. To honor! To our place beside the High King!"

"I'm sick of hearing about the prophecy," Alorie said. She found herself shaking. "I won't be molded to fit some obscure ciphering of it!"

"You have no choice."

"I have all the choices I want! If we're to face the Corruptor in my lifetime, then I'll do it with Rowan!"

"You can't," Brock said softly, sadly. "Not if you wish your people to survive. And I think you know that."

The image of the jet-stained Unicorn nudged into her mind, and she pushed it away. "I won't hear that from you."

Brock got up and came to her, taking her by the shoulders. "If I remember correctly, it was you who first asked me of unicorns."

"I was a girl then. I thought they made a beautiful tale." She could not look into his eyes. "Sinobel was still alive then."

"And it was I who warned you what the beasts demanded of you."

"I know."

Rowan stirred. "She's done all you asked and more."

"Not all. The Corruptor distracted all of you, sent you to Cornuth for a traitorous weapon. It was not until Alorie remembered what I had told her that you even had a chance against the north. And now it begins again."

She could barely speak against the lump in her throat. "I need Rowan." All the questions he'd asked of her, all the lost history she'd given him, he now turned against her.

Brock denied her. "You cannot have him."

"By what right?" Rowan protested. Brock slapped his face, the sound as sharp as a leather strap popping. The Rover recoiled, the welt as dark as his auburn hair. His brown eyes blazed with fury. "I wash my hands of you, old man. You've lost your senses." Rowan bolted from the room, but Brock caught Alorie by the wrists before she could follow.

"Damn you! Damn you and your damned prophecy!"

Brock's voice lowered dangerously. "Don't cross me on this, Alorie."

"And why not?"

"If you wish to keep him alive, you will stop your heresy and listen to me. I've come back, against all the odds, because you need me, and Bethalia needs you. If you need Rowan, so be it, but what you have now is all you'll ever have of him—or I will dispense of him."

"*Dispense* of him?"

"I will do what I have to do to see the prophecy fulfilled. It's the only way we can withstand the return of the Despot and see the Corruptor destroyed."

Her blood went cold at the mage's words. She dared to look him full in the face, and she saw the truth in his green-gray eyes, the mad sincerity. Brock would have Rowan killed before he'd let them marry. She took a fluttery breath.

"I'll be content," she said. "For now."

The light in his eyes died down and his fingers eased upon her wrists, but the lump in her throat did not abate.

"Rest," she told him. "I'll be back for you when the assembly is ready. It'll be late." She fled from him then, unable to stay in his presence a moment longer.

"It won't be what you expect," Alorie cautioned the Rover mage when she returned for him. He seemed quieter now.

"Where's Rowan?" he asked mildly.

Astonished, she gaped at him.

"Alorie, you'll swallow flies that way. Is he still out on patrol?"

How could he not remember what had happened between them? She stammered an answer and Brock patted her hand. "We'll do it alone, then. And what do you think I'm expecting?"

"A council of war with barons, lords, counts, and kings. Few are left after the swath the Corruptor cut through our ranks three years ago. We're a land of mayors now, Brock, not dukes."

The mage came to a stop, leaning heavily upon the cane. He wore Rover black and silver, setting a burnish to his own dark skin, and his hazel eyes looked at her critically. "Had they no heirs? No sons to follow in their steps?"

She looked away, unsure how to deal with him. "We did what we could," she answered softly. "We survive, township by township. But Bethalia is not what it was."

"How do you expect to raise an army?"

"Lord Rathincourt has proved able in that direction." She waited as Brock ventured a step with the cane to brace himself, and tensed if he should begin to fall. He might never lose the drag to his right leg. He had told her days past that he could not remember what caused the original injuries, but thought perhaps he might have broken it while struggling against being overcome.

Brock ignored her intent scrutiny of his ability to walk and continued his passage toward the doorway. "And next I suppose you'll tell me the Rovers have failed in their stewardship of the open lands."

"No. Never. But there are a handful more havens than before. Quickentree and Flaxendown domains hold two. I don't know for sure of the location of the others, though I'm told one is on the shores of Lake Sobor."

"Rathincourt's holdings?"

"Yes."

Brock gave a short laugh. "That must please his lordship. He disliked being at beck and call. Now he has Rovers under his own thumb if the need arises."

He gained the doorway and paused, breathing in short gasps. "And who are these mayors? Farmers? Merchants?"

Was he pretending that nothing had happened? Two could play at that game. "And more." Alorie, her mettle up now, met his eyes. "And you'll find they're all veterans."

"Ah." The corner of his mouth quirked. "I deserve that, I suppose."

"Yes, you do, you old curmudgeon. Who do you think you are?"

The quirk gave way to rueful smile. "A musty-smelling

old Rover. You do well to remind me, Alorie. Well, since they're waiting for me, I guess you'd better help me down the stairs."

She looked over her shoulder. "Jasper and Mick are going to take that duty. They're stronger." She moved aside to let the Mutts approach Brock.

The mage's spine went stiff and he put his head back as the two came near. Jasper was in leather armor, his sword at his side, and Mick wore the breastplate Pinch had found for him two days ago, with bracers to match. Brock sucked his breath in sharply and pulled himself from their reach.

"Who gave weapons to *these*?"

"Brock—" She remembered then that he had been raving when the Mutts escorted them. They had gone with Rathincourt's men before Brock had really come around.

"I said, who dared to arm these Mutts? They're an abomination to the Seven True Races, milady. I don't care how desperate we are to win against the Corruptor, we are less than him if we've come to this!"

Jasper's round eyes flashed and his ears perked. "No one *gave* me a weapon, Rover—I was birthed in the shadow of Cornuth and I earned my arms! Am I less than you? Do I not deserve to protect my own?"

Alorie thrust herself between them as the Mutt bristled and his hand covered the hilt of his sword, ready for a draw. Mick showed his sharp teeth in a wolflike grin. "Stop it, both of you. Brock, I don't understand." She put her hand out toward the mage's face, thinking he'd grown feverish again.

In a fury the mage knocked her hand aside with his cane. He seemed not to hear the smack of wood against flesh or see the way her face went white and she recoiled in pain.

"You are not Mutts, you're hyenas! Corrupted whether you know it or not."

Jasper could not pale, for his brown and white pelt did not allow it, but the whites showed at the corners of his eyes. "You call me black-hearted? I've spent the last few years fighting for milady—where have you been? I've always judged a man by his actions, yet I've seen none of yours. Tell me where you stand!"

"My standing is not in question here!"

Their raised voices filled the upper floor of the tavern, and Alorie was not surprised as Rathincourt mounted the stairs, his eyes icy blue and his white hair a shock upon his tanned and handsome face. "That is where you are mistaken, Brock."

The mage turned to him. "Rathincourt. I thought you fought only large battles."

"This is the biggest battle of all if it divides our forces." The warlord motioned to Jasper. "Stand aside, Captain. Let the mage make it downstairs under his own wind. If he's well enough to fight, he's well enough to walk."

As the lanky Mutt took a calming breath, he moved aside and Brock shoved forward, now leaning almost desperately on his cane. Alorie nursed her hand silently, unwilling to let any of them know what had happened, frightened by the division she'd seen before her. First Rowan and now Rathincourt—was she the only one who did not doubt Brock's authenticity?

Rowan stared at her from across the room. Her resolve wavered. She knew he thought she should defy the mage, but she did not dare, not at the price he'd named. Nor did she dare tell Rowan, for the rift between them could well divide all of the Rovers. In the All-Mother's name, what had she brought back from Veil?

Not what, but who—and she knew she had gotten Brock. She had to hold to that truth and build from it. The mage had not always been terribly popular. He was brash and radical, keeping secrets even from other Rovers. But she could not stand aside and let him be questioned. Absently she let Rathincourt seat her as she watched the Rover band that guarded the exits, their faded black and silver uniforms like banded shadows beneath their green and russet cloaks of the forests they roamed. Their return to honor, as well as the safety of Bethalia, depended on her. She reminded herself of it, clutching at her sanity.

Rathincourt did not seat himself. He returned to the tavern table where his adjuncts sat, and took off his riding gloves. His red uniform was dusty and sweat-soaked as he slapped his leather gloves onto the table. "I'm just in from detail, my lords and ladies, and council," he began, "and the news is not good."

Ethan, Mayor of Bylantium stood. He was young and pimply-faced, referred to as a robber baron of that city. Gladly distracted, Alorie watched him now, wondering if he was under the thumb of Tuan of Veil. Ethan bowed his head even as he interrupted Rathincourt. "With all due respect, warlord, I don't think it's a good idea to discuss news good, bad, or indifferent with strangers in our midst. Unproven strangers."

Brock had been leaning upon the bar. Harsh lines were etched into his face, but he turned slowly and eyed the young merchant. "Perhaps it is I who should ask for your credentials. When I . . . retired . . . from the scene, it was Duke Latham who stood in succession in Bylantium. The Thieves Guild ran a poor second."

Ethan's face was ashen now, his pimples standing out like sore boils. "I'm no thief."

"No? Then perhaps you could return the elven dirk up your left sleeve to the gentleman sitting next to you from whom you borrowed it."

The farrier who had sat next to Ethan grabbed his great, wide belt, and then glared at the young man.

With a fluid shrug Ethan brought out the dagger and with an ironic flourish offered it back to the farrier, who took it with more than a little distrust written across his craggy face. "I found it upon the floor, a blade too valuable to be trampled by boots."

Alorie shrank back. More dissension. Brock would not prove himself by humiliating Ethan. What did Brock hope to gain by taking their allies and turning them against one another? How could she defend him or his insane actions? Before she could stir, the robber baron said, "Duke Latham is dead, Rover. He fell to the black unicorn. In grief, his father the grand duke went to Trela'on to help defend it against Aquitane's siege. But he fell, as did Trela'on. So no one runs the city now, except the Guild which was always there. Like rats we are, but we are willing to deal with the dross as well as the gold, and in Bylantium today we survive." And though his emotions stood out starkly upon his face, the young man did not hesitate to meet Brock's stare.

The mage seemed to consider something. "Arvon still runs the docks?"

"Aye."

"An honest man, for a smuggler. I take it with the royal family gone, smuggling is now fair trade."

"Aye again. As it should be." Ethan inclined his head. "I am Arvon's second oldest son."

"Then remind him of the strange thing the three-legged dog did. He will give you my credentials." Brock looked away and the youth swayed a second, then realized he'd been dismissed. Alorie let out her breath, realizing that

Brock did not need her aid here. His mind had sharpened again.

Rathincourt said, "I cannot wait until the lad sees his father again and be convinced you are who you say you are. The Council of Veil said you'd been found dead upon the Paths of Sorrow."

"Who from Veil helped you defend Dirtellak?" Brock retorted. "Did they loose their powers to protect you from the malisons and the reken? No? Then why would you take their word over mine?"

"Because, old friend, you have been in places unknown by any of us."

"Is Veil any more known?"

"You know it is not."

"Indeed." Brock tapped his cane upon the tavern's plank flooring. "If I must convince you of where I've been, then we're both unfortunate, Rathincourt. I do not know where I've been! Too deep for sleep or memory, I was kept until one of our enemy decided to taunt me with the news of Alorie's wedding." The mage's hazel eyes smoked about the room. "Anyone else doubt me?"

The tavern was silent a moment. Rowan shifted weight at the front entrance, bracing both feet upon the floor and resting his hands upon his hips.

"I do, mage."

The room turned at the sound of Alorie's voice cutting across the faint mumblings of the council.

Brock's head snapped around in surprise, his body clumsily following its lead as he stood propped upon the cane. "Why you, of all people?" he murmured.

Alorie stood, hiding her injured hand in a fold of her skirt. "Because I alone represent all the people of Bethalia. If they doubt, I doubt. If I am convinced, they must be . . . or forsake the last shred of authority we have that survived the fall of Cornuth." She held her head high. "Or have you all forgotten that I am the heir to the High Counselor?"

Cries of no and no answered her.

The surprise faded from Brock's expression. He looked to her. "Ask, then, Lady Alorie, and I'll answer, if I can."

"Do you swear to answer the truth?"

"By the Horn, is this a trial?"

"Do you swear?" she asked relentlessly and clenched her hand, though its throbbing distressed her.

He smiled wearily and said, "I swear, but if I am the creature you fear me to be, it will mean nothing."

Rathincourt sat down heavily in his fighting gear. "If you are the creature we fear you to be, we'll burn you at sunset."

Kithrand came in behind the Rovers guarding the side door. One of them nearly skewered him, but the elf lord jumped agilely aside and held his hands up, saying, "Peace." With little more noise he found a chair and sat. Brock and he stared at each other a second, then the mage looked back to Alorie.

She read his expression as clearly as if he asked, *Do you know what you're doing?* And she hoped she did.

"Who are you?"

"I'm called Brock, a woodsman with some skill as a mage."

"Who here can speak for you among the Rovers?"

Brock looked over the crowd. His gaze lingered on Rowan. Alorie looked there, too.

"Rowan can."

Her lover shifted weight. The crescent-cleft scar in his chin whitened slightly. Just before he spoke, she could tell from the look on his face that she had made a grave mistake.

"You all know me. I knew the mage Brock well. He was one of the fathers who fostered me. *But I have been at the hands of the Corruptor and his malisons, and I can tell you that this may or may not be the man I knew.*"

A stir ran throughout the room as Alorie's heart went cold. She could not blame Rowan. Despite the fight with Brock, he spoke the truth. He had not forgotten the terrible tortures he'd suffered in the dungeons of Trela'ar. Dreams still waked him at night, lurching from her side in cold sweat and tears, and yet he would not share them with her. All he had said was "They can make and unmake whatever they wish until a man doesn't know what is real and what isn't—and what is alive and what is not." But then the Sergius blood awakened in her, and she smiled coldly, knowing how to turn this to their advantage.

"Thank you, Rover, for the truth—for it is only the truth we want here, not some conspiratorial porridge cooked up to make us feel better."

A murmur of approval ran through the tavern, and Alorie knew she at least had their attention.

"How would you characterize the Brock you knew?"

Rowan warily encircled his thumb and forefinger about

his sword hilt. "A stern man. He was steeped in the traditions of the road, and also that of the prophecy that would take us from the road and return us to our rightful place."

"Was he a mage?"

"Yes."

"A powerful one?"

Here the man paused. He looked at her as if she could throw him the answer she wanted across the room, but she could not. Brock's punishment by Veil had not been widely known. His skill had come from knowledge and wisdom as well as from herbs and sleight of hand. And, occasionally, a flash of true power. He said hesitantly, "He had been, once."

"Once? What happened?"

Pinch spoke up from the smokelaced corner where he'd been sitting quietly. "Tell the truth, bucko."

"I don't know the truth, Pinchweed. All I know is that the Council of Veil took his magicks away, most of them. The Brock I know died going back to Veil with the intention of getting his power back, because he knew he needed it to fight."

Alorie pitched her voice to rise above the growing undercurrent in the tavern. "And would you then say it would not have been difficult to overcome the Brock you knew, and keep him imprisoned?"

"Not easy." Rowan grinned. "But possible."

"But the enemy would not have known of his weakness."

"No." Rowan's voice gained in strength. "No, they wouldn't have. The Corruptor wouldn't even have tried it."

"Which brings us back to the Council of Veil, which did know . . . and which did spread the rumors of Brock's death. But that is another matter to take up presently." Alorie cleared her throat. The barmaid touched her on the elbow as she made her way through the crowd to offer her a mug of beer. She took it gratefully. "Rover Rowan, did you hear the altercation that chanced upstairs just now?"

"I did. I think the whole damn town heard it."

Laughter flooded the tavern. Alorie took the break to wet her throat. When the sound had died out, she said, "How did the Brock you knew feel about Mutts?"

There was an intense silence. Jasper, holding guard at the rear of the room, moved visibly. Rowan looked there, then back at Alorie. "I'd say, milady, that he was well versed in the stories of creation. He often told me that the Mutts were some of the good that came out of the ancient wars."

"Why were Mutts said to have been created?"

"To be soldiers. To replace mankind as fighters."

"And did they?"

"No . . . not generally. Most Mutts are too kind and gentle."

"What is their place today?"

"Farming and serving. They are loyal to a pup and extremely good companions."

Alorie flicked a glance at Brock, who seemed to be weakening upon his cane. She must hurry before the mage collapsed and the council dismissed. They still had urgent work to do. "How would the Brock you knew have taken a Mutt fully armed and geared for war?"

"He would have been furious," Rowan said before he realized what he said, and then looked to the mage.

The hearing came apart in a roar of sound, and Alorie stood triumphant, having proved her case. She waited until the noise died down before saying, "You have convinced me, Rover, that the man you knew is the man who faces us now."

But in the silence that greeted her decision, Kithrand rose. From his place, she could not see the feelers that bobbed up from his brows, or guess his intention. He said, "One final test, milady, to convince us all." He pointed slender fingers and spoke, and blue fire raged across the room, enveloping the mage in flame.

Seventeen

Someone screamed. It might have been the bargirl as she dropped her tray to the ground, mugs flying everywhere, or it might have come from the throat of young Barth, his voice breaking under the strain. Brock threw his hands up, the cane toppling, as a curtain of blue flame roared to life. It licked him from head to toe.

The innkeeper grabbed a pail of slop water, but Rathincourt yelled, "Halt! The elf lord is right. I've never seen any of the Corrupted who could withstand that."

Brock lowered his hands slowly, palm down. The flames died as he did so until there was just a ring of them dancing about his boots. Then, with a snap, they were gone without a scorch mark to show they had been there.

Alorie's knees had turned to water. She fought to remain standing as she said, "Can there be any doubt?"

She sat down as the tavern erupted in furor again. Kithrand faded to the side door where he had entered. He and Brock exchanged a look, the meaning of which she could not fathom, and the elf lord left as the white-haired warlord shouted, "A round for the house, man, and then we're down to business."

The farrier retrieved Brock's cane. Brock said nothing as he took it and settled himself in a chair the farrier shoved forth.

"And now to the business," Rathincourt said, dabbing the cuff of his sleeve along his mouth in a genteel manner. "We've horse troops to train, and home guards to set up. Skirmishes in the north keep my regulars busy—I haven't trained troops to quarter down here. We've got to build an army again."

"Second," Brock interrupted. "We have this business of Mutts to settle. I wish them disarmed."

Rathincourt gave him an incredulous look, and settled it
by saying, "We need every hand we can find to hold a
weapon. We're getting slaughtered out there."

The mage retreated into silence, and the serious discussion began.

The Corruptor stroked the message received from his
courier thoughtfully. "My spies are well placed. First Hammersmith's revelation, and now this. Interesting," he added,
"that there should be any doubt at all about Brock's identity."

"But helpful."

"Immensely," the man agreed. He held out the paper
scrap and let the malison take it from his fingers, the shrouded
nimbus about the being brushing his hand intimately. The
gesture brought gooseflesh to the man's hand, but he showed
no reaction. To do so might whip the malison into a frenzy
and make it difficult to calm him.

He got to his feet and paced a few steps. "I never could
get him to reveal what was in that powder he used so
effectively."

"Distressing."

"Yes." He paused. "We could expend one or two of you
at Barrel along with the reken. He'd be bound to respond.
We might be able to obtain a sample."

Ayah's nimbus radiated anger. The Corruptor stood rock
still as the air crackled about him, and he could feel the
being sifting his very thoughts. Then the malison appeared
to recede slightly.

"It was," the man said, "just a thought."

"And a good one. It is a possibility," the malison answered. Its shroud parted. A leathern pseudopod reached
out enticingly. "I hunger."

The Corruptor swung around on one heel before it could
touch him. "There are prisoners," he said abruptly, "downstairs."

The malison faded from the hall, leaving behind an aura
that made even *him* uneasy. The scrap of paper wafted
down to a broken tile and lay there, a greasy stain upon it.

He pursed his lips, then sat down again and pulled up a
lap desk from underneath the seat. Conjuring up the image
of Alorie Sergius, he frowned, then began to scratch upon
the paper in a ladylike scrawl a missive to Bryant of the
Delvings. It would be unimportant—an apology for delay in
expressing an appreciation of the water clock, a few lines

about the strife in Barrel. When Bryant finished reading it, he would be touched once again by Alorie's vulnerability.

The Corruptor knew no such letter had gone forth. He had the courier road well secured and Rathincourt's green troops unable to break his stranglehold if such a letter did begin a journey. He sealed it with blue wax and a sigil bearing a cursive A. He whistled for a runner, pleased that with this action he had begun to seal the fate of the Delvings.

The horse troop returned to their garrison long after the midnight star had reached its zenith. The horses chewed tiredly on foamy bits and dragged their hooves through the grass and dirt. Five of them rolled white-rimmed eyes and trotted sideways, unnerved by the blood-splashed bodies draped across their backs.

Alorie, sleepless, came out to meet the troop. She held Rathincourt's reins for him as he dismounted. "What happened?"

"It's late, milady. Best wait until morning."

She ran her eyes over the wounded and dispirited men as they led the dead away. "News like this will darken any day. Are you all right?"

Rathincourt shook his head. "I'm too old to lead raids like this. Damn me, but I can't teach them the difference between a battlefield and hit-and-run bushwhackers—yet they've got to learn how to fight both."

"Take the Rovers out with you next time."

"They can't do it all. But you're right. It takes a Rover to know how to ferret out the reken from hill and dale." Rathincourt's stallion whuffed at them tiredly, and she walked with the warlord as he led him to the livery to care for it. "What are you doing up?"

She could not tell him that Brock's raving had awakened her again. He had not known her when she came in to check on him. His incoherence had fled after a moment, but she could not blame his lapse on fever. She picked out a concern that had bothered her sleep before that. "I've been considering your proposal to pull back to Sobor and build a regular army there. I think you're right. The logistics will be easier handled there, and we'll be closer to strike at them as they swing down from Cornuth."

Rathincourt pulled off his saddle and bridle and began to wipe the great roan warhorse off. Alorie pulled a bucket down from a hook and, dipping her hands into the pungent

ointment, began to rub liniment into the feathered pasterns.
The stallion made a noise of contentment and lipped the top
of her head as she knelt between his great hooves.

"Don't slobber on me," she scolded him.

Rathincourt smiled wearily. "Mind your manners, Lane.
It's not every day a princess rubs you down."

"Ah," she said. "I'm no princess."

"No? Then I've a mind to speak to someone about that."
He drew her up. "Now go and wash your hands or the
whole tavern will smell of liniment. I'll tend to my horse-
flesh myself, like a soldier should. You go and tend to
yourself for what's left of this night."

He gave her a fatherly hug to send her on her way.

She paused and hesitated briefly outside the livery. The
embalmist was the only one to gain so far from the death
toll taken in Barrel. She watched the handcart being wheeled
past, trailed by a sobbing girl not even as old as she was.

She thought of Rowan then, and turned away so quickly
she almost ran down the elf lord of Charlbet.

"Kithrand!"

"Pardon, Alorie. It was clumsy of me."

That made her laugh. "You, clumsy?"

In the dim light the tavern cast, she could see his half
smile. "Senseless, then. I would have to be not to smell the
horse ointment presaging your journey."

She wrinkled her nose. "One does what one has to."

He paced her to the outside pump and held a washing
bucket for her as she took up a bag of herbed soft sand to
scrub at her hands. He said nothing for a few moments as he
levered the water up to splash over her, but she noted his
frown. As she stood and took a towel off a hook, he said,
"It was bad, wasn't it?"

"Yes. The casualties are high. I can't stand to think about
it. If we have to take the field tomorrow, the Corruptor
would walk through us as if we weren't even there. I told
Rathincourt I like his idea of withdrawing to Sobor to
recruit—but even at that we won't get some of our veterans
until after harvest. And I don't blame them—I can't! I was
hoping that was all I would have to worry about for a while
myself: planting, hoeing out the weeds, herbing against the
insects, and then the harvesting." She sighed and replaced
the towel.

"You have a weapon at your disposal which could fore-
stall all that."

"The sword?" She paused at the inn's doorway.

"The sword and more. Veil won't help you, but my folk are not ineffectual at magick. The Corruptor is an unnatural man, milady. There must be ways to undo him. I have been . . . empowered to invite you to Charlbet. Our librarians have offered their assistance. Such a simple thing as knowing his name may make him vulnerable to us."

"Invited to Charlbet?" Shock showed through her fatigue.

He nodded. "And it may remove you from some of the things which worry you."

"Ah." She sighed as she ran her fingers through her hair, pushing its ebony length back from her pale face. "Does it show?"

"Not unless one knows you well."

Which, of course, the elf lord did. He knew all three of them exceedingly well. "Let Rowan and Brock settle this between them. You are not the sole cause of their friction."

"Am I not?"

"No. Rowan, despite his youth, has become the informal leader of the foresters. Brock was used to holding that position, and he is attempting to take up those reins again. This is something above and beyond your marriage."

"And you think it might be settled better if I was out of the way?"

The elf lord nodded again, the faint movement giving his jeweled circlet that bound his hair a wink in the twilight. "And it is not often I give out invitations to Charlbet."

She pushed her hands into her skirt. The scabbard of her longknife rustled. "I cannot think of any time anyone's ever been invited."

"It has been a long, long time . . . even for elves."

Alorie glanced at the sky, which showed faint signs of lightening. "If there's any left tonight, I'll sleep on it." She gave him a tired smile, leaned forward, and brushed a kiss along his temple, just under the circlet, and left.

Kithrand stayed poised in the doorway. His jaw tightened. *Bring her to Charlbet,* he'd been told, so he had set those wheels in motion. They would fight him, he knew, to keep her from the library, but if she was going to make the journey, she might as well get some benefit out of it. He was not going to bring her in like some caged bird to sing for their fancy. Nor could he tell her that the fate and judgment of the homeless children would rest on her shoulders. She had enough burdens to carry for the moment.

*   *   *

The reken stayed downwind of the pungent smell of the horse liniment. No hound or horse in Barrel caught its scent because of it. There was shadow enough for it to keep to. Shoved into its weapon belt was a newly skinned pelt—dog or Mutt, the hair long and silky, a burnished chestnut color. It dragged as the reken made a leap to the tavern's eave. Its claws scrabbled for a purchase on the wood, bringing up splinters and leaving scratches. The pelt shed hairs that caught on the rough wood as the beast pulled itself over. The reken smiled, sharp tusks clashing as it did so. There were ways for an assassin to come and go, but it had been told to leave sign, and leave sign it would.

It balanced on its haunches a moment, long back aching. Standing on rears was difficult, though the masters demanded the posture of it. It slewed around and caught sight of the window it had been sent to enter.

A mage slept beyond that window.

The assassin paused. It had been told the mage was powerless, but the reken feared elven fire more than its soul in the Corruptor's hands. It flicked a glance toward the sky. It could hesitate no longer. Soon even the men would be waking.

It drew its needlelike dagger and crept to the window. As it slipped the latch and opened it, the assassin took care to rub the Mutt pelt upon the framing. Its talons dug soundlessly into the wood. It was leaving sign.

Brock's yell brought Rathincourt running from the livery. The warlord had his sword pulled before his boots struck the front door, kicking it open, but the mage met him halfway.

"Did you find him?"

"Who?"

"An assassin. Did he come this way?"

"No. My god, the Lady Alorie—" but Rathincourt was pulled to a stop by Brock.

"She's all right."

"Are you sure?"

Brock pulled open his sleeping robe and pulled the needle-sharp dagger from his leather vest, where its blade had been turned and bent. "Exceedingly sure. This fellow meant for me."

"By the horn." Rathincourt looked upstairs. "If he didn't come out the doors, then we'd better try the window."

They bypassed the innkeeper's wife, apron pulled up to her ample bosom, floured from head to toe. "What is it, gentlemen?"

"Thieves in the night, good woman. Nothing to worry about." Rathincourt sniffed. "Your bread smells delicious."

She beamed, saying, "And I better return before the loaves are burned."

Brock led Rathincourt's long stride up the stairs with painstaking ones of his own, cramped though no longer dependent upon the cane.

"Your devilish luck has held again."

Brock raised an eyebrow as he pushed open the door to his room.

Rathincourt followed him in, explaining, "You should be dead a dozen times over. I've never seen a man so good at cheating it."

"Hmmm. Give me a moment to ponder on whether I've been insulted or not." Wearily Brock dropped onto his rumpled cot.

Rathincourt strode to the window. "Well, my Rover lad, while you're resting from a full night's sleep, let me tell you that this is where he came in and left."

"What have you found?" Brock got up and limped to the windowsill. He followed Rathincourt's finger to the gouges. Deftly he picked out a tuft of silken hair. "Now," he said. "I want no argument from you."

Rathincourt picked the tuft from Brock. He looked beyond to the edge of the roof, where more gouges and silken hair in the splinters caught his gaze. "Ah, no," he sighed. "Not the Mutts."

Eighteen

Rowan led his tired horse across the field. Barrel lay shrouded in an early morning haze. As he stumbled over a dirt clod, a scrap of fog broke away and drifted into the air. His gelding nibbled his shoulder as if in concern.

"Recovered, eh?" the Rover asked and rubbed the beast's green-stained muzzle, feeling stubby whiskers grind into his palm. "Never mind, we're so close now I might as well walk the distance." He slapped the nibbling lips away affectionately. Riding down reken was a difficult task and the Rover horses had been all but run to ground. He'd been sent back to Barrel to get supplies and new arrows while the rest of the detail stayed out, and he looked forward to being with Alorie briefly. If he had any sense and the domain was not full of reken, he'd throw her over his shoulder and take her with him. Not that she'd go willingly.

He did not doubt her love. But he could not understand Brock's influence over her now. It was plain enough to Rowan that the mage had lost his mind while imprisoned. Though it came and went, there was not enough left to cling to, to hope any longer that Brock could be the hope that might change the tide of the new attacks. She seemed to have lost all faith in herself and the sword.

He searched his memory for what it was that could have happened to cause that as the outbuildings of Barrel cast a pall over him. Out of that shadow, as though he'd summoned her, ran the woman he thought of.

Her dark hair was tangled and her face pale as she ran across the outer edge of the field, holding her hem high so she could run better. "Rowan, hurry! Please, this is madness and you've got to stop it!"

He grabbed her up. He could feel her heart pounding desperately as if she were a frightened doe. "What is it?"

"An assassin came for Brock. He says it's one of the Mutts—he's disarming them, and if they won't do it, he'll kill them!"

His old friend's mind had finally snapped like a piece of tinder. Pushing his reins into her trembling hands, he said, "Catch up with me." He broke into the Rover's famous long stride, though his thighs felt like wet bags of meal. His steps carried him far past Alorie and toward the faint sounds of argument.

"—without a trial!"

"This does not merit a trial."

". . . unfounded accusation—"

"Were it better I was dead!" Brock's voice raised in rage, something Rowan was not used to in the old Brock, but had heard often since bringing him out of imprisonment. "Then you might be lynched instead of disarmed!"

An angry whine broke off as Rowan rounded a building's edge, and he saw them in front of the tavern. Jasper held his guard behind him as if shielding it. Rathincourt was flanked by his adjuncts, Flask and Deanmuth. He could tell from their postures they were ready for trouble, but on whose side they were, he could not tell. Brock seemed to stand alone.

Jasper stepped back, his hand curled near to his sword. "I won't let you take our weapons from us."

"Then get out." Brock half turned, presenting his back to them, even as Rathincourt wearily shuffled a boot in the dirt. "Neither door nor field in all Bethalia will be open for you."

"Now see here, Brock, this is uncalled for—" At last the warlord spoke, and his deep voice cut through the low snarls issuing from the pack behind Jasper.

Rowan's voice overrode them all. "This is madness," he said. "The enemy won't need to beat us—we defeat ourselves."

The mage swung on him. "By what right do you meddle?"

"By the right of sanity . . . and for the Lady Alorie, who came to me for help." Rowan came to a halt, his chest moving heavily in exertion, and he fought to keep his voice steady. "I've heard enough. Jasper, one of the Mutts stands accused of attempting to kill Brock."

"Aye."

"True?"

The multicolored Mutt shifted weight. He met Rowan's

gaze with a steady one of his own. "Not that I know of, though it seems a fair idea."

Rathincourt put in, "We've found signs."

"A witness?"

"No, it happened while still dark."

Rowan angrily looked to Brock. "No witness? And you rely on signs alone? How many times have you and I led reken down a false trail? Who's to say they don't now lead us?"

"A fighting Mutt is an abomination to the Seven True Races. To the All-Mother." Brock's voice was petulant.

Jasper made a sound that was a strangled bark. Then he said, "You offered us exile. We'll take it, with every *man's* hand against us, before we put down our arms."

"Then go!"

Rathincourt shambled forward. He shook his snow-white mane. "Brock, you're fighting the wrong enemy!"

The mage pointed a finger at him as though it were the point of a sword. "They are Corrupted. If they can't stand being purified, then they must be driven out!"

Rowan felt Alorie at his elbow. Her breath came in tiny gasps of distress. "There's no talking sense to him," he muttered aside to her.

She took his arm. "I know."

Jasper saw her. He gave a half bow, his eyebrows tight together in a frown. "By your leave, milady. We brought with us mounts, supplies—"

"Of course, Captain. Take with you whatever you need. And if you must be exiled," she raised her voice, "I will let it be known that no man is free to hunt you, or he will answer to my justice!"

Rowan caught the Mutt's sleeve and said to him lowly, "Go to Stonedeep. They'll take you in there."

Jasper nodded. He brushed past the two of them, the others grumbling on his heels, but Bounder paused. He looked at Alorie.

"There is no justice in Bethalia," he said.

She stepped back a pace, caught herself, and answered, "In time. As long as I am alive, I will see that all things, even justice, have their time!"

Rowan stepped gently between them, but the Mutt seemed satisfied and loped off after his leader.

The warlord looked astonished at Alorie. "You cannot side with him."

"I have no choice. To keep them here will keep them under a cloud of guilt. But as long as our mage has given them two choices, I have chosen the lesser of the two evils."

Fatigue puffed the warlord's face. His expression ran from disbelief to disapproval. He slapped his hand against his leg. "I cannot dissuade you."

"No."

"Very well." He turned away, not even facing her as he added, "It's been a long night. I am retiring." Rathincourt left.

Brock dropped his hand. He panted once or twice as if he'd been running hard. Then he looked to Alorie and Rowan, his hazel gaze sharp. "Milady. Have you forgotten our agreement?"

She looked back at him. Rowan was startled to find her moving away as she answered sadly, "No, I have not." She left him standing solitary in the dust.

"The whole world," he said to himself, "is going mad." With a sigh he realized he had no answer to it except to find Pinch, wake him, and have the two of them ferret out a hearty breakfast.

Alorie made up her mind as she mounted the tavern's rough stair. Brock was making his hesitant way up behind her as she stopped. She said, "I've decided to take Lord Kithrand up on his invitation."

"Invitation?" Brock raised eyebrows that were like soft, kinked wool. They were the only things about his face that were not harsh.

"Yes. The elders have invited me to Charlbet."

He was thunderstruck. "Charlbet? Charlbet?"

"Yes. I'll take Pinch and one or two guards with me. You won't talk me out of this."

"I'm not sure that I want to." Consideration swept over his expression. "Charlbet."

"He tells me the library will be at my disposal." She sighed and tightened her grip on the handrail. "This isn't a new fight. Even the High King faced it. Maybe I can find out how to win. If not, then perhaps how not to lose."

Brock's voice sharpened. "You'll not be taking Rowan."

"No. Neither Rowan—nor you."

"You might be able to use a good mage in the domain of the elves."

"Perhaps. But I'm not a bone for the two of you to snarl over. I need to get away."

Brock blinked slowly. "I understand," he said. "It will have to be done secretly, for your own protection."

"I had a guard before you drove them away," she retorted.

She turned and pelted up the stairs before he could threaten Rowan's life again.

The mage resumed his shuffling pace. Below, in the dusky dawn corners of the tavern's main floor, his shadow tangled. As he passed into the corridor, the shadow enlarged, then separated, as an eavesdropper emerged. The darker being stared upward a moment, then hurried to send a message.

A dwarf courier writhed on the stained tile flooring at the Corruptor's feet. He kicked the dwarf over with a black-booted toe, uncaring of the freshet of blood trickling forth.

A message pouch dangled from his knife. He slit its strap and pulled it open. Various receipts and requests lay within—but he stopped when he came to the parchment folded thrice and wax-sealed.

With a smile that stretched his lips thin, the man drew it out. Wax crumbled as he ripped it open for reading.

His laughter rumbled throughout the nearly empty room. "Perfect! This is perfect!" He nudged the dying dwarf again. "And incredibly timed. I could not have planned it better. But you really should go to hawks for couriers, little man. It's really quite a bit faster. This morning, for instance, I have already heard the Lady Alorie plans a secret visit to Charlbet."

The parchment snapped shut in his fingers. The Corruptor said over his shoulder to the pale being waiting in the corner, "Do you know what this is, Viola?"

"No," the Ungraven whispered back.

"A love letter. And the writer isn't even aware of it. He commiserates with Alorie. He sends to her, and asks her to visit, thinking to remove her from her troubles for a while, using an inspection of the armory and forge as an excuse."

As the dwarf gargled into a horrible death rattle, the Corruptor dropped the letter onto him, where it soaked up blood like a blotter, and stepped over the body.

A shiver ran through the Ungraven, who had been waiting for sustenance. Her master examined an excellent example of cartography pinned to the wall. "The timing could not be better." He turned even as the Ungraven bent a knee and dipped to the black blood clotting upon the floor.

"I'll use you, Viola."

She looked up, darkness staining her ashen face. "Master?"

He smiled. Yes, it would be better with Viola. She would not have to be given the scent to find her victim in Charlbet. She had, after all, once been a quest companion of the Sergius girl and knew the sword intimately as well. He would have her death and its retrieval in one fell swoop.

And as for the Delvings—the Corruptor felt a joy burn inside his chest. "Leave me, Viola. I have an invitation to accept."

The Ungraven swept away, the hem of her silken gown sullied by her kill.

Nineteen

Rowan found Pinch in the basement of the Broken Barrel, sitting contentedly near an empty keg, filling the cellar with fragrant smoke rings and singing a broken song around the stem of the pipe clenched firmly in his teeth. The Rover kicked aside another empty keg as he entered, saying, "I might have known I'd find you here. I've been looking for you for days."

Bleary silver eyes winked at him. "Go 'way," the dwarf said. "I'm grieving."

"The whole town is packing up and you're grieving? By the Apron, man, why? It's been weeks." Rowan upended a keg and sat on it after belaying his first intention of picking the dwarf up by the scruff of the neck and shaking him. The intention needed postponing anyway, considering Pinch weighed close to what Rowan did.

Pinch blew out another gust of smoke. "Oh, aye, man, I know what you're thinking. I'm to go with Alorie and you'll be making the march to Sobor and then we'll be meeting again. But it's not the same, Rover." Pinch unclenched his jaw and waved his pipe around. "We won't be coming back here again . . . and this is where Mary Rose's ashes are scattered."

Rowan fought the impulse to look about the cellar. "You can come back later if you wish. Barrel's not a bad place for a veteran to hang up his sword and axe." To his astonishment his friend dropped his pipe, bowed his head, and treated the young man to the gusty, snorting sounds of a crying dwarf. "What is it, man?" He reached out awkwardly and thumped Pinch on the shoulder to comfort him. "It's not like you to be crying in your beer."

Pinch lifted his head, his nose red and swollen and teardrops glistening in the curls of his yellow-gold beard. "Ah, bucko. If it were only that simple. I'd be in the cups for the rest of my life. No. I found this while packing for the march. I could not throw out her things yet." With a trembling, gnarled hand, the dwarf thrust a logbook at Rowan.

The Rover took it.

"Open it!"

Rowan did so and found himself confronted with the round and looping handwriting of the apple-cheek dwarf maid who'd come out of the Delvings to marry his armsman and take care of Alorie, too. The log opened to the last entry—its spine had been broken there.

"Read it," Pinch said gruffly. "If you want to know why I weep."

He did so, and then shut the book carefully. "Pinch, I—I don't know what to say. I'm sorry, man. By all the gods, I'm sorry!"

The dwarf clenched his pipe tightly again, then took the pipe out and said fiercely, "She was with child! I lost both of them to that murdering bastard!"

It was not easy for dwarf women to bear children. His wife had not wanted to tell him until she was sure she would be carrying it past the first troublesome months. Rowan had nothing he could say which would be enough. "I'm sorry, Pinch."

"I know you are. No sorrier than me." Pinch scrubbed at his eyes and got to his feet, albeit a tad wobbly. "The memory of Alorie gutting him becomes more satisfying by the day." He looked about the cellar. "It's time we were on our way. I paid for three kegs of the best, and I've had them."

"Three kegs!"

"Aye." Pinch put his chin up. "And don't be making fun of me. I know I'm off my feed a bit. But I didn't want to be too drunk to ride out with our lady." He stomped off toward the cellar ladder.

Rowan followed him in awe.

Barrel emptied slowly as great wains were filled and then hauled out of the crossroads town. A homeguard rode sentry to the outskirts, then circled back. Many of the tradesmen were going with the troops to Sobor, but the farmers remained to nurse along what promised to be a bountiful harvest, and the homeguard's job was to ensure their and its safety. Rowan escorted Pinch to a cot to sleep off his intemperance—with the dwarf's capacity, Rowan didn't think he could call it anything else—and decided to find Alorie, for it would be one of his last chances to say good-bye.

Toward dusk, the innkeeper's wife told him she had retired early. Rowan debated with himself a moment, but knew that Brock would be busy charting troop movement with the warlord. He took the stairs eagerly and found the door to Alorie's room.

As he lifted the latch and entered, the blackness of the sleeping room engulfed him, the windows shuttered tightly against the coming night. The hair at the nape of his neck crawled, for Alorie disliked the dark and often slept with a taper burning nearby. The velvet that claimed him now was both unlikely and unnatural as he shut the door behind him.

His mouth had dried. It was difficult to call her name gently. Fear pricked at him as no answer came. Had the enemy struck again? "Alorie!" he called urgently.

A light flared in the darkness, blinding him, but not before he saw the mage sitting there, green-eyed like a cat in the night and Rowan staggered back.

"Come in," said Brock, as the oil lamp guttered down to a steady light.

"I don't need your invitation. Where's Alorie?"

"Mapping with Kithrand and Rathincourt. She did not object when I suggested it, so I take it this tryst is your idea."

Rowan crossed his arms over his chest and leaned against the door frame with insolent grace. "Like it or not, Brock, when this latest attack is turned back, she'll be my wife."

Brock's eyes had returned to their normal smoky-hazel coloring. The dark skinned mage answered mildly, "I think not. But that is not why I met you here."

Rowan said nothing, so the older man continued, "I know your mind. You spent your first seasons on the road striding next to me like a long-legged colt. I know your dreams and their manifestations."

"I wish I could say the same of you."

"Do you doubt me still?" Brock rolled the cane he held between the palms of his hands. "I would not think much of you if you didn't. I taught you better."

"All right, then, dammit. I still wonder."

"Good. This is a hell of a time to go soft." Brock rose and leaned heavily on the cane as though his leg had weakened again. "He turns in the Barrows. I can feel it. Why the

Corruptor has not released him yet, I don't know . . . but soon I'll have to go find out." He raised the iron-shod foot of the cane to unlatch the shutters and open them, letting in the night. "Do you remember what we found the last time?"

Rowan shifted. "A trap and an empty grave."

"Yes. Someone with a great deal of power had helped the Corruptor break free. We never did find out who."

The young man ran his fingers through his hair, brushing it off his forehead. "Corey—" He named the now dead, traitorous Rover.

"No. A traitor, yes, a sorcerer, never." Brock kept his back to him as he looked out the window. "I've always suspected Veil." Abruptly his voice changed tone. "I know you well enough to know your mind. I tell you now that you're forbidden to go with Alorie tomorrow morning."

"Brock—"

"No. She'll be safe at Charlbet. Pinch and Kithrand will watch over her."

Even in the twilight Rowan's face heated, for the mage did know him well, for that was what he had planned.

Brock continued smoothly, "And I have other plans for you."

"What?"

"I want you to ride out from Barrel. Strike out for Stonedeep . . . meet with Ashcroft. I want the haven disbanded and brought to Sobor."

At the mention of his disabled older brother, Rowan straightened. "In god's name, why? Why should he or any other cater to your whims?"

Brock turned and faced him. The cane went back into its place at his right side, bracing him. "I know he's suffered. I may not have been at your side, but I'm not unaware of the battles you fought. There's a greater one yet to come. It's time to raise the Raltarian Guard. I want every Rover ready to resume his rightful place."

The statement shocked Rowan to his core. "Raise the Guard? On whose word?"

"Alorie has left a letter of authority with me."

"You surely don't mean to use it for that."

"Among other things. *He* is nearly ready. It's time for the Guard. It's time to make ready for the return of the King. 'When moon overshadows paling sun, evil everlasting shall be undone.' Who knows when that time will come? But soon, I feel it. And we need to be ready."

Rowan's throat felt tight. "You can't expect to get away with it."

Brock made his way across the tavern sleeping room until they were shoulder to shoulder, and he reached for the latch. "I don't *expect*, Rowan. I have done it. The Guard is to be gathered and you are its captain. Ride off with us in the morning, as I am sure the Corruptor has his spies among us, then branch off. You have your orders."

"Yes," Rowan answered, his stomach clenching.

Horses whuffed softly in the morning air, already hot and humid and promising to be more so as spring gave way to summer. Rowan came out of the livery, a roan gelding following him with a pack lashed to its back. He put the lead into Pinch's callused palm as they waited for Alorie and Kithrand to take their leave of Rathincourt and Brock and join them.

"What's this? He's not made for packing!" Pinch glared at the roan, who rolled an eye right back at him.

"Clamp your lips shut around that pipe and keep them that way."

"What's up, bucko?"

"Nothing. I want you to be able to cover ground as fast and as safely as you can. That's why I'm sending Banner with you as I can't come."

" 'Twon't be the same." Pinch glared at him. "And I don't like being up to my neck in elves!"

"You'll get by."

"Sure I will. But I may have to knock a few flighty noggins together to do so!"

"You behave yourself. It's a great honor to be invited into Charlbet."

His armsman made a disbelieving sound. Rowan stepped close to Pinch's horse and gripped his thick boot. "I cannot come with you. Brock's forbidden me."

"Aye. Tell me something I don't know that muddle-headed mage has done."

"He's reinstituted the Raltarian Guard."

"What!?" That fairly knocked the dwarf back in his saddle, and he grabbed for his falling pipe.

"No one's to know of it yet. He told me to close down Stonedeep and bring them in to Sobor. We'll be sending word to the rest of the havens."

"He can't. Rathincourt will have his head for sure. Brock hasn't the authority. Only the High King can do that."

Rowan shook his head. "Never mind that now. I'm not going to Stonedeep. I'll send Ashcroft word by hawk and he'll bring them around."

Pinch looked at him. "And what will you be doing, then? Pitching camp at the Barrowlands?"

"Not quite. I'll be rendezvousing with you."

The dwarf shut his eyes and opened them again, saying, "And I'm a thick-skulled lump of rock. Well, I'll console Banner then with the news he's not to be a packhorse for long."

"Do that." Rowan broke off as Alorie approached. She did not quite meet his eye as she went to the bay mare Pinch held for her. She wore a long riding skirt, and he caught a flash of her shapely leg as she kicked over and then settled in the saddle. She wore the Unicorn sword in its scabbard on her left hip.

He caught the mare's headstall. "No kiss for luck?"

"You'll have better luck if I don't kiss you," she said softly. "But you know you carry my heart. I'll see you in Sobor." Her stormy blue eyes had gone gray with sorrow.

"It's a short parting," he said to cheer her. "Don't be sad."

Alorie pointed her chin away from him so he could not see her face. "It's not sadness," she said faintly. "It's fear." With that she kicked the mare over, putting Pinch between them.

Rowan said nothing else as Kithrand brought Strider up from his pasturing, and the lanky youth from Barrel made rich by Rathincourt's uniform joined them. Barth wore an ear-to-ear grin. "It's a great morning for adventuring! Think of it! I'm to go to Charlbet."

The Rover slapped Barth's calf. "Do that, lad, and remember to tell me all about it." He stepped back as the party moved out. They would ride with Rathincourt's troops for a bit, then peel off, hoping their movements would be hidden from spying, just as Rowan would do the same.

But all their machinations were already too late.

Bryant stood in the gaping stone jaws that gated the Delvings from their enemies. He put one booted foot up on a tooth.

"Do you see them yet?" the dwarf king said.

"No, sir," the guard at the winch answered dutifully. He blinked a little as Bryant's breastplate glinted in the sun and blinded him momentarily.

There was a shuffle in the dust behind the king. He turned and saw Hammersmith waiting, a shimmering glimmer lying across his open palms.

"What is it?"

"A gift," Hammersmith said. Sweat glistened off his balding head and in his mutton-chop whiskers. "For the lady." He held out an intricate gold link belt.

Bryant grabbed it up in delight. "You think of everything." He stretched its length in the air. "She will be most pleased. Do you think her waist is really this tiny?"

Hammersmith gave a quick bow, saying, "I've been told it is. If not, a link or two will be easy to add." He turned to go.

"Stay," Bryant said.

"There's work at the forges."

Bryant poured the gold link belt into one hand and resumed his watch across the valley. "I know. But she'll be here soon, and I'd like her to meet the craftsman of such a magnificent gift."

Pleased to stay, Hammersmith bowed again, lowly. His sweat had dried to crust by the time hoofbeats could be heard echoing off the mountainous towers surrounding the valley floor.

Bryant's heart pounded in his chest like the hammers off the anvils below. Then he saw her, riding to the fore, wrapped in traveling cloak and veils against the dust of the journey, her dark horse mincing his way through the rock and gravel of the road. An escort of close to a hundred men paced her.

"So many," he murmured in quiet surprise.

Hammersmith spoke up quickly. "Perhaps they've come for fittings. Our moldings are ancient. These Men sprout like weeds with every generation."

Reassured, Bryant smiled. He waved at the dwarf guardsman. "Open the jaws."

With a sound of chain and stone, the gates to the Delvings began to open wide. They were ready when the procession reached them. Without a word they rode into the Delvings, crowding Bryant back until all of them were inside.

The dwarf king held out a hand to Lady Alorie, saying, "Welcome, milady, to the Delvings once again. May I present Hammersmith, who carried out my commission of this gift to you."

He placed the gold link belt in her gloved hand.

"Thank you, King Bryant, but this is the first I have been to the Delvings, though I accept with great pleasure. Hammersmith I know well." The cowl pushed back, and the veils were torn off, and the Corruptor grinned cruelly into the face of the dwarf king. He placed the belt about Bryant's neck before the shocked king could move, and his eyes went flat as the faery catch subdued him. Thus it was the Delvings fell without even a single stroke.

Twenty

As soon as Rathincourt's destrier stepped foot in his domain, the warlord knew it by the thrill that ran through his frame. The very wind held a different scent, the loam a more fertile color as the horses kicked it over. And five days later, as he pulled up to the last crest before Lake Sobor, the pride had swelled to an almost overwhelming pain in his chest.

He halted Lane and looked downslope. This would not be a bad place to house a king. Old stories had it that the High King had taken Cornuth because of the straits and commerce that boated inland that way, and because he had liked snow. Lake Sobor was rumored to have been a second choice. Now that Cornuth was fallen, there was no court, no center of Bethalia. With Rowan and with Alorie, Rathincourt saw a second chance.

His son had been killed following Gavin Bullheart. His wife had died birthing their second child many years ago. He had no heir. That no longer bothered Rathincourt. The whole of Bethalia would be his heir if he could start a second monarchy.

Lane lifted his head and trumpeted, the stallion winding the horse lines below. With a laugh Rathincourt kicked him back into motion. From the looks of it, thousands awaited him. The freshwater fish and the beasts of the bountiful fields and forests of Sobor would support the army far better than the limited capabilities of Barrel. Not only would he build the Lady Alorie an army, he would build her a kingdom.

As he rode down to the bivouacks, what he saw made him slightly grave. Tattered men made ragged by the harrowing of reken before gaining the safety of his kingdom squatted by their fires. Their swords were bent, blunt, and rusty. There was no armor to speak of.

Rathincourt beckoned Deanmuth forward. The adjunct drew even, their horses bumping shoulders, then Lane nipped the other mount into submission. The adjunct's young face was limned with the fatigue of their journey, but he snapped off a trim salute. "Yessir?"

"Get them into troops. And for god's sakes, show them how to oil and sharpen their weapons. Get grindstones set up as soon as you can."

Deanmuth nodded.

"Flask!"

The colonel rode close as Deanmuth peeled off. Colonel Flask was nearly Rathincourt's age. It had been his daughter the warlord had married. Flask was bald and jowly, but his limbs had stayed lean, his legs perpetually bowed by a life on horseback. The colonel looked at him with an unfathomable expression.

"Post to King Bryant immediately. Tell him we have an army, and we need weaponry as soon as he can ship it to us."

"Yes, Lord Rathincourt."

"And then set up drills. The men are here, but they were whipped by the reken getting here. We've got to put the heart back in them."

Flask nodded, his jowls wagging as he did so.

"And Flask—"

"Yes, milord?"

"Don't let that damned mage countermand my orders."

This time a glint awoke in Flask's eyes, and he nodded sharply before wheeling his mount.

Rathincourt reined his stallion in a second longer and overlooked the encampment. With a little bit of luck and a lot of hard work, he'd have them whipped into shape by the time Lady Alorie returned at midsummer from Charlbet. Provided that damned mage stayed out of his way.

Alorie shivered into her cloak. The bay mare, worn and tired, stumbled upon an icy rock and went to her knee, nearly pitching Alorie from the saddle headfirst. She held on as the mare regained her feet, but Kithrand was there, saying, "Are you all right, milady?" even as he ran his slender hands over the mare's tender knee.

"Yes. No thanks to these mountains of yours."

The elf lord gave her a sardonic smile. "Ah, but these mountains are what keeps Charlbet hidden."

Hoarfrost made the ground brittle around them. Pinch kneed his horse up, grumbling, "Ye could have told me to bring my cap."

Kithrand turned his smile to the dwarf. "A little farther. The air is thin here, and always chill, but it makes Charlbet that much more beautiful. We're almost through the pass." The wind whistled behind his words as if to emphasize them.

Young Barth suffered the worst of any of them, chilblains swelling his hands so that he found it difficult to cup his reins. The packhorses moved up behind them, crowding to keep the warmth of the herd from being blown away.

"If you're quite all right?" Kithrand said.

"I'm fine. Let's see if we can make this wondrous home of yours closer."

"Done." He turned and gained Strider's tall back with a single bound, touching the gelding's cream-colored withers to push him forward.

The mare followed of her own accord as Alorie tried to shrug her cloak about her. The very clouds that misted the mountains hung about them. She felt their dampness upon her cheeks and hands as the elf lord led them onward. As the fog swallowed them up, she put her hand to the hilt of the sword and felt its warmth answer her reassuringly.

When they had finally wound their way beneath the clouds and discovered the light of day, Kithrand turned a corner and abruptly threw his hands up to halt the party behind him. A fire burned across their path, stones banking it against the wind, and in the ashes, from a leaf-wrapped bundle came the sizzle of cooking fat and a heavenly aroma.

The welcome of the fire did not penetrate to Kithrand, however, and he would not let Alorie, Pinch, or Barth pass.

"It may be a trap."

"If so, 'tis a pretty one," rumbled Pinch. "I'd say let's have lunch before it's burnt." The dwarf did not seem at all surprised at the find. He reined his horse around Kithrand and dismounted with a grunt as he bent to build the fire up yet more. "Tea, milady?"

"That sounds wonderful."

Strider threw up his head in alarm as gravel and dust slid and a dark shadow leaped from the rocks above their head. Banner let out a loud neigh and shook, pack rattling.

Steel filled Kithrand's hand. Alorie's mare shied around between them, and she felt a hand on her knee.

"Pinch is right," he said. "It wouldn't do to let lunch burn."

She gasped, then said, "Oh god. What are you doing here?"

Rowan smiled and grabbed her by the waist to pull her down off her fidgeting mare. "Do you think one crazy old man could come between us?"

Kithrand's face did not lighten in expression, though he sheathed his throwing dagger. "You do take risks, forester. How did you find us?"

Rowan did not answer for a moment, being busy warming Alorie's chilled lips with his burning ones. The elf lord cleared his throat and decided to join Pinch at the fire. Young Barth hurriedly pitched a line for the horses and bent with his trailmates.

"My heart's been cold these past two weeks," Alorie said.

Rowan laughed. "I'd have caught up sooner, but Rathincourt miscalculated. Reken followed you by the drove. I've been dispatching them as I came."

Kithrand filled a pannikin with water for tea. "A better question is—how did you find us?"

"Ah, Kithrand. Did you think a Rover could look at your hawks and not tell a mountain bird from a forest one? And there's only one pass through this range, though we don't traverse here . . . it's said a devourer waits beyond and Rovers never return."

"Charlbet," Kithrand said tightly, "is hidden for a purpose."

"That I know. Do you think I would have breached it for any other reason than to find my lady and protect her?"

The two stared at one another, one brash and auburn-haired man, one lithe and white-blond elf. Kithrand blinked, a shuttering of his gem-blue eyes that held no white. He smiled. "I suppose I had better say well met, or we're in for ill fortune."

They clasped hands.

A week later found them leaving the pass and looking upon a sight that made Alorie catch her breath.

Charlbet ruled the forest and valley below, overlooked by purple mountains capped with white. In the summer they had left before climbing the mountain pass, grass had already passed its springtime lushness, but here it stayed verdant. She had expected an elf realm carved out of wood and rock, but never what she saw.

It had grown. The trees embraced Charlbet, thrust it up, passed it from lofting branch to another, and formed its roofs and walls and flooring. Its spires rose from platforms, works of elfin hands upon nature. She saw bridges soaring across chasms of stone from grove to grove. And beyond, the fields and orchards. She saw cream-colored horses chasing one another down leafy glens and sun-dappled fields without fence or bridle to slow them.

Pinch hawked and spat. "Impressive," he said.

Kithrand looked quickly at him, but the dwarf's face stayed expressionless. The elf remarked, "I'll ask you to keep your pipe cold and in your pocket, shortman. Fire is one of our enemies." He lifted his hand, and Strider stepped out to lead them down into the valley.

Twenty-One

"You did what?" Gillus wore the long robes of leisure, but his antennae vibrated madly and his cataracted right eye twitched slightly as if trying to force clear vision. He grasped his potbelly with his hand as if protecting it from a mortal wound.

Lady Orthea repeated Kithrand's announcement calmly. "He promised her the use of the libraries."

"You're mad! You've been drinking silverweed—"

"Peace, milord." Kithrand held up his palm, but his face was smeared by anger. "I've vices, but not that one! You wanted her here for evaluation. They face a war. What did you expect me to use for persuasion? I told her what I hope will be the truth."

The roof leaves of the house huddled close upon the rooms, muffling their voices. Lady Orthea took Kithrand's hand and patted it. "What's done is done," she said. "And perhaps not such a bad idea. The Corruptor is our enemy also. After he finishes with the homeless children, he may remember our part in his binding."

Gillus paced his room, kicking aside cushions like a piqued child. Then he glanced up and pinioned Kithrand. "Perhaps he will forget," he said. "The homeless children are notorious for their short memories."

"Their memories are no shorter than their lives." Kithrand would not back down. He looked to Lady Orthea. "You are our regent. My guests are resting, but anxious to begin their search. Give me a decision."

Orthea tilted her head. The lines deepened in her heart-shaped face. "I am regent, but Gillus is the librarian."

And Gillus, still clutching his robes of midnight and goldfire, seemed horrified at the prospect. He relaxed only when

Kithrand held his silence. Then he said, "Does Drussander know?"

"Not yet."

The elder elf ran a hand through his graying ebony hair. "Very well, then. But secretly. I do not wish to have this trespass made public."

Kithrand smiled. "If you've said yes, Uncle, then it's no trespass. But no one will hear it from me."

"Go on, then." Gillus rubbed his failing eye. "Take care of your guests. I'll be along presently to direct them."

"And translate? I can't do all the work."

"Yes! And translate." Gillus flapped the hem of his robe at him as if shooing a bird off a tree limb.

Kithrand jumped nimbly out the window instead of leaving by the door like a civilized elf.

"It's even more beautiful than the city." Alorie's voice sounded hollow in the huge chamber.

"It's one of the few stone buildings here. But we couldn't trust a library otherwise. Termites like the scrolls too much. So do midges." Kithrand stopped lightly behind her.

"I could spend a lifetime reading here."

Rowan flanked her other side. "It's only one of life's pleasures," he murmured, bringing a flush to Alorie's face. He swung on the elf. "Where do we begin?"

Gillus entered on their heels. His elfin face showed clear disapproval of Pinch, but the dwarf clamped down on his cold pipe and ignored him. The librarian counted their number and said, "There is one more. Where is he?"

"Barth is with our horses, seeing to them and our tack. He cannot scribe, Lord Gillus," explained Alorie.

"Neither, I wager, can the stunted man, but you have brought him nonetheless."

Pinch rolled a silvery eye at the elf lord. "Fash me," he said, "and I'll be lighting my pipe when you least expect it."

Gillus blanched and Kithrand moved swiftly between the two, saying, "It's my fault, Lord Gillus. I have a sharp tongue and Pinchweed does not appreciate my humor. He's actually a very good reader."

The elder elf gathered his sleeves and held his arm out stiffly for Kithrand to fasten bands upon, keeping the material in place. Alorie watched, wondering what they had in mind.

Gillus told them soon enough. "The scrolls can be dirty

and, in some cases, quite inky. My skin can be cleansed. The fabric, alas, is a little more difficult to deal with. All right, now. Though I sense you are interested in everything we have here, you have a specific need."

"Kithrand thought we might find out the Corruptor's background," Alorie said softly. "We need to deal with him—and soon."

"But you have a sword, do you not? A magnificent artifact."

She found his jewel-blue eyes, though one of them was clouding, disconcerting. She felt as though the elf lord looked directly through her and, what's more, did not care that he could do so. "Only one person can carry a sword. An entire army can use knowledge."

A bitter smile swept across Lord Gillus's face. He turned to look at Kithrand. "I can see why you brought her," he said. "Very well, then." He swept an arm behind him at an alcove. "Confine yourself to this area. It covers the histories you are looking for."

Rowan pursed his lips for a low whistle. "There must be several thousand scrolls and books in there."

"Or more."

"Perhaps we could narrow it down a little?"

"Perhaps," said Gillus, privately amused. "But then you might overlook what you are seeking. You see, we don't know who the Corruptor is or where he came from. He may have erupted on the scene when the Despot began to wrestle with the High King for power, or he may have been around for several hundred years before that."

Alorie pushed her own sleeves up. "Then I guess we had better start reading."

Over the high passes a wisp came to ground near the cooled ashes of a campfire. It coalesced into a being, a feather-thin woman with silver hair, in robes nearly as insubstantial as she was herself. She hovered close to the fire as a wind howled through the pass. Her robes shimmered and crested in the gust, but she stayed intent upon the ash, sifting it through her fingers.

She had already felt the heat from her quarry. The sword called to her, a beacon of fire, and she had no trouble homing in on it. But it was the ash that drew her now, a troubled memory of ash and blue fire.

The Ungraven straightened. She faced into the wind and

floated off across the rock and stone as if she were no longer of that world. She would encounter wards across the boundaries of Charlbet, but her master had friends. One of them awaited her.

Alorie swept her hair from her face a last time, as annoyed at its continual unknotting as she was at her failure. The gesture left a smear upon her eyebrow. She pushed the tome aside and tried to adjust her scabbard upon her hip for greater comfort. "It's no use. It's as though his name was wiped from history."

Gillus sat on a cushion nearby. A feeler quirked up as he arced his brow. "Or his name was so well known it was not thought it could be forgotten." He beckoned. "Come here, child."

Alorie crawled to him, unwilling to bend her knees one more time to stand up and then sit down. She felt his lighter-than-air gesture upon her hair and then a snap.

"There," the elder lord said. "That should keep a few of those locks in place." His fingers lingered there a moment longer and he smiled.

Kithrand snapped, "We've barely begun to search."

Gillus looked at him mildly and said, "Perhaps I could continue after they have returned. Hawks can carry the information."

Alorie, sensing the tension between the two elves, returned to her cushion chair after murmuring a thank you, and picked up her tome. Instead of reading page by page, she began to leaf through the volume. Of the traitorous Frenlaw and the purloined sword and the last High King whose name had been forbidden to be spoken or written until his return, she had found much. Also the Despot often referred to as the Iron Liege and the Miscreant and Deathwalker. A cold chill swept through her.

What set her to thinking so oddly? But the gooseflesh that had broken out on her arms and the back of her spine stayed, in spite of her efforts to chafe it away. She looked about the library, which was now beginning to shadow as the day progressed.

Rowan looked up. "What is it?"

She shrugged. "I feel as if we're being watched."

"We are," and he laughed shortly. "By hundreds of kings and Rovers and maids long dead."

She twisted her face with a rueful "Thank you. I needed that."

Gillus held up a scroll. "Here, perhaps, is something— Baron Frenlaw provided the guard for the High King."

"The Raltarian Guard," countered Rowan. "That is history I don't have to read."

The librarian's expression became stern and he began, "There is more, young man—" but his words were drowned out by a chilling wail, and a cloud swept over Alorie.

Pinch jumped, his axe swinging as Rowan grabbed her by the wrist, flattening her to the cushions underneath her. She felt a yank upon her hair and a powerful twist upon her weapon belt that threatened to drag her away.

"Rowan!"

With a flex of his wrist his dagger was in hand as he yelled, "Keep down! It's an Ungraven!"

Alorie flattened herself to the library floor, her cheek impressed upon the embroidered cushions, smelling now the rancid air within the chill that covered her. She dug her nails into the wood planking beneath the cushions as the inexorable hold on her belt pulled her slowly across the floor.

"Don't let it make the window," Pinch warned and shifted his axe from hand to hand. She could make out his short height, but dared not shove her head higher.

The librarian's voice quailed. "She carries fire. Kithrand—"

"Stay down, Alorie, for god's sake," Kithrand shouted.

But Alorie could not. Fire would destroy the knowledge they needed. Fire would char the forest around them. Fire would be the death of Charlbet.

She kicked out violently, felt ice jab her knees with a stab of pain, and heard a scream interrupt the wailing as she came loose. The weapon belt tore free, and the scabbard slid before her.

Alorie grabbed the sword and hugged it to her chest, rolled over, and pulled it free. The Ungraven held its hands high, a torch within them, made a gigantic sweep, and let the torch go. Fire shattered into a thousand sparks and the stench of burning paper filled the air.

She caught a glimpse of gray and silver and darkness as the thing hurled itself at her throat and met the Unicorn sword instead.

Blood so cold it burned splashed upon her. Alorie gagged as Rowan grabbed her by the elbow and tore her out from under the Corrupted being. He mopped her face and hands as she stood shivering and Pinch made the last stroke.

Kithrand said urgently, "Out, all of you," while Gillus stood, his voice caught in an endless litany of "Burning! It's all burning!"

Alorie got to her knees and saw the being Pinch stood over, his axe limp in his hands. In death she recognized her. "Viola." She looked little like the stern-faced, silver-haired sorceress whom Pinch had loved briefly upon their disastrous quest to Cornuth. Alorie read upon her face the same cold beauty that her mother, Luisa of Veil, still possessed. Then the thing curled into char and ashes upon the library floor.

The dwarf looked up, his face contorted. "Does he never stop? Must he take everything!"

"Pinch, you didn't kill her. She was dead long before—" Alorie stopped as Rowan grabbed her by the shoulders.

"Get out of here," he said urgently. "It's a trap."

Gillus looked up, stricken. "Do you think, man, that we would burn this to gain the sword?"

"Is the city not warded? How did she get in, then?"

Kithrand stepped backward, sweeping them with him. "I can't do anything. Lord Gillus, Rowan is right—our magic augments this being. We must argue later—" His words halted as another alcove went up with a tremendous *whoosh* and burst of flame and spark. Smoke curled toward them.

"My books! The history!"

"I've warded what I can. Now it's the city we must fight for. Go! That way, and quickly!"

Rowan took her hand and they ran toward the doors. As they flung the carved oak panels open and halted upon the stone dias leading to the building, they could look out upon the whole of Charlbet.

Orange raged in the sky. Birds took flight in clouds of panic, their chirping and calls piercing their ears. She could see individual trees explode into an inferno of flame, spiraling into the blue sky. A bridge crumbled into red sparks and embers, curling into the chasm below it, where another fire guttered up to receive it. Clouds boiled up where water hit the flame.

At her back Kithrand said, "My god. Lady Orthea."

Gillus said, "She's there. See her? Directing the water." He took Kithrand's hand. "Go quickly. I'll see your guests out of here."

Rowan said grimly, "I'll stay to help."

"No. You cannot. It is your presence that does this. Your presence and that of a traitor within our own ranks. You're right, the Ungraven could never have passed within our boundaries without help. Nor could she have spread this much fire. Come with me."

Kithrand hesitated a moment, torn, his hand upon Alorie's arm. "Milady—"

"Go on! They need you."

The elf lord leapt away from them, his agile body springing onto a nearby tree limb.

Alorie called after him, "Kithrand! Fight fire with fire! The blue fire doesn't burn!"

A look of hope passed over his pale face, then, with a toss of his flaxen hair, circlet of blue gem sparkling upon it, he jumped from their view.

Gillus pressed. "Come quickly."

She heard the roar and agonizing sound of a greenwood tree exploding in conflagration. Cinders began to swirl in the air, edges glowing red. She coughed and put her hand to her face.

At the green field where the horses were pastured, Barth met them. He had all of them tacked up and packed, his hands shaking. Already wildfire licked the far end of the meadow. Brush went up in flame too quickly to see and the fire jumped closer in bursts.

Banner danced impatiently at the end of his lead as Rowan took up the reins. They mounted and looked down at the elder elf lord.

"I'm sorry," Alorie said.

His antennae trembled in the wind. "Do not apologize to me, Lady Sergius. It is I who should apologize to you. We thought of standing with our enemy, briefly, to avoid losing all, but that is death in itself. I know that now. If you could have stayed, I think I might even have been tempted to show you the histories that our law says must never be revealed to you."

She curbed her nervous bay mare. "Why?"

"Because you deserve to know. These lands are not yours, except that you came to overwhelm them. Overwhelm them with your will and your industry and your fertility."

His words struck her deeply, and she opened her mouth to ask more of the librarian, but Barth screamed as a curtain of wildfire swept down the field toward them.

Rowan jerked the bay mare's reins out of her hand, snapping her mount into a panicked run out of the field and the forest toward the mountains that sheltered the hidden city of the elves. The pounding of horses hooves as they galloped for their lives almost drowned out the death wails of the burning city.

On the ridge they halted and turned, pulling cloaks out of their packs against the harsh chill of the looming mountains. Alorie blinked from the cinders and stinging smoke hanging low over the forests.

"They'll save most of it," Rowan said.

She turned away, hot tears blurring what little vision she had. How could he see to say that? Had he said it to comfort her? She did not know. She prayed to all the gods he was right, turned the bay mare's head toward home, and dug her heels into her flanks.

The sword had extracted yet another price of her.

Twenty-Two

Rathincourt hunched over his desk, trying to ignore the heat and humidity creeping into his fortress room, bringing sweat to his brow. He overlooked the reports again and clenched his teeth in frustration.

It was difficult enough making soldiers out of plowmen and cobblers, but without weapons it was damn near impossible. The trade road from the Delvings was open, but not one single wagon had returned from King Bryant's holdings. Rathincourt drummed his nails as he read. He wanted victory, even in a minor skirmish. His men needed to know they could win, would win if something more dire came along. The reken kept harrying them, picking open sores upon their flanks.

He heard the hollow booming of boot steps upon the stairs long before his door flung open and Deanmuth came in hastily, gulping for breath.

"My lord!"

"What is it?"

"A messenger from the Delvings." Deanmuth moved aside as other quickening steps caught up with him, and Rathincourt, his heart leaping at the sound of his colonel's voice, stood.

Messenger was a misnomer. The wretched being who hobbled into Rathincourt's study with Flask's aid was a refugee, not a courier.

"Get him a chair," Rathincourt rapped out, and the dwarf was seated. He drew his bare, thickly callused yet bleeding feet up underneath him and sat, hugging his ribs for air. Flask dashed a glass full of ale and passed it to the dwarf.

The gnarled man grabbed it thankfully and drained it before he could regain his voice to speak. Then he looked at Rathincourt. " 'Tis the warlord himself?"

"Yes. What's happened? Were you ambushed on the road?"

"Nay. 'Tis the wurst, the wurst. I hied out a bolt hole to get away, then knew I must tell ye, if I could make it here." The dwarf wiped ale foam from his mutton chop whiskers while the room went silent, waiting for him to finish. "The Delvings is fallen."

"Fallen?" Flask stepped back, his jowls waggling. "To whom? And how?"

"And," Rathincourt added darkly, "when?"

"To th' dark lieutenant, two weeks ago, if my reckoning is right enow. And the how is the wurst of it. Treachery. Foul deceit. He came disguised as the Lady Alorie, come to inspect the forges. King Bryant had messages. We thought 'twas from her hand. He welcomed the villain in himself."

A sound belled upon the stone steps. Rathincourt flinched. He knew the noise well enough and lifted his gaze to watch the Rover mage push his way unbidden into the study, tapping his cane upon the flagstone.

"By whose authority was this man brought here first?"

Rathincourt bridled at the imperious tone. "By my authority," he fairly roared back. "Though you seem fit to ignore it, with Lady Alorie absent."

They glared at each other. The canny dwarf took a look, then buried his nose in his refilled glass.

Brock seemed to shrink a little before the veteran soldier and nodded at the refugee. "What message does he bring?"

Rathincourt growled. "Nothing good, mage. He tells me the Delvings has fallen."

"What?"

" 'Tis true, honored sir," the dwarf got out. "Overrun without a stroke."

"Are the forges cold?"

"No," the refugee said, returning the mage's piercing stare with a steady look of his own. "Leastways, nay when I left. The Corruptor has armies of his own."

Rathincourt sighed. "That's a hope, then. Flask, Deanmuth, make this man comfortable in the barracks. Have you a name, brave dwarf?"

"Aye," the ragged man said. "Hammersmith the True, they call me." He was helped out of his chair and flanked by the two colonels.

Brock lifted his cane as if to detain them, then let the tip fall back into place. He held his peace until the two adjuncts had closed the door behind them. "Hammersmith is not a good name among dwarves," he said to Rathincourt, who paced the study irritably.

The warlord came to a stop, his white head frazzled about his lined but still handsome face. "If you look hard enough," he said, "I'm sure the name Brock could be found among the histories with a black mark or two beside it."

Brock took up the empty chair. "This is not good," he muttered. "First the disaster at Gutrig Downs, and now this."

"Gutrig? By the Horn, what's happened at Gutrig?"

Brock looked up mildly. He rubbed his left brow. "The mines have been flooded."

"The mines flooded?" Rathincourt's voice fairly thundered. "Good god, man, that happened before the fall of the High King—and you sit there prattling about it as though it was fresh news!"

"But—" Brock fumbled to a halt. He seemed disoriented.

Rathincourt relented. "Old friend, you've not had an easy time of it—or made an easy time for me! Your place is by Alorie's side, as adviser. I don't expect you to help me lead the fore of the army as you did once. We all slow down!" He poured a glass of the refreshing ale and gave it to Brock. He had to push it into the mage's hand and close his fingers about the drink.

Brock took a long draft. He shut his eyes momentarily, then opened them. "You don't grow older."

"Bah! This next year or two will see the end of me in the saddle. Deanmuth is my hope for the future, though the Apron knows I wish the Lady Alorie could make a quick end of this." Rathincourt pulled his great chair out and sat down. He slapped the palm of his hand upon his thigh. "We've no choice. We've got to retake the Delvings."

"Can't be done. Once those stone jaws clench shut, nothing can pry them out of there."

Rathincourt's face flushed heavily. "We'll have to try."

"From where? Where will you pull back and quarter?"

Warlord eyed mage. "We'll take Sinobel first. My men are crying for confidence. They need a good fight, a victory—and sight of that god-blessed sword!"

Brock hunched his shoulders. He said, "She'll never agree to it. She's not been back since the massacre."

"All the more reason. She—all of us—need to exorcise that ghost!"

"She's given all she has."

"This is no gift I'm requesting. It's a necessity. We have to have the Delvings if we're to even stand a chance against the north."

Brock shifted to ease his leg and rubbed his knee absently. "Any word from Rowan or Ashcroft?"

"None. Were you expecting any?"

An unreadable expression flickered through Brock's hazel eyes. He sat back in the chair and said, "Not yet."

Rathincourt thrust himself out of the chair. "Are we agreed, Brock?"

"On what?"

"Taking Sinobel, and then aiming at the forges."

"I don't see as we have much choice."

"All right, then. I'll take to the road myself to find them . . . too much time is lost if we wait." He strode to the wall and grabbed for the bell cord, ringing out Colonel Flask's code. "I'll leave Flask in charge. He'll ready the men."

Brock stayed inert in the chair, as though it were suddenly too much for him to move. Rathincourt slapped him on the shoulder. "Stay here a moment. Ring for Deanmuth if you need help. I'll meet you on the field."

"Yes," Brock agreed faintly as Rathincourt strode out of the room. "Do that. But watch for Frenlaw. He can't be trusted."

The snow-haired warlord neither heard nor heeded him.

The smell of smoke stayed in her clothes for days until either the fierceness of the wind finally cleansed them, or her nostrils refused to recognize the odor any longer. They spoke little to one another, bowed against the wind, hunched against the cold. Before they came out of the mountains, Rowan turned them north.

Alorie caught up with him. "I thought there was only one pass to Charlbet."

"Only one in . . . several out," he said enigmatically and led the way. Nor did he explain himself to her further at night when they shared blankets for warmth, as did Pinch and Barth. The horses slept huddled nose to tail as the wind howled after them with a vengeance and, hanging in the smell of snow and hail, she swore she could still smell burning leaves.

When they came out of the mountains, she feared the worst. She woke at night, quivering, feeling Rowan shake beside her. Nightmares gripped him again. The dungeons of Trela'ar? She lay back down, curling around him to comfort him, fearing to wake him because they were all tired and even troubled sleep was better than none.

It was then she heard the reken drums. They were far away and muffled, too far to be on their trail. It had been years since she'd heard their drums, but she knew what it was to be hunted by them, to be their single quarry.

She reached out and shook Rowan lightly. He came awake with a strangled gasp, and she put her hand to his cheek.

"It's me," she said.

The night hid his expression. "I'm all right," he said flatly.

"Quiet. Listen. They're drumming tonight."

He lay still beside her, and from the tension in his body she could tell he listened. "They're after someone."

"Us?"

"No. They're coming over the Broken Wagon trail, west, toward us."

The sounds stopped. He rolled over on his side and drew her in, and she held her breath a moment, for the intimacy awoke feelings in her she'd had to put aside. The neck of his shirt had come open, and she could touch the tiny, curled hairs upon his chest.

The drumming began again. She held her breath, confusing the sound with that of her pulse.

Rowan gave a low laugh. "I think we'd better head that way and help out."

"What? And ride into a reken trap?"

"Oh, it's a trap all right, but not for us."

"Who's their quarry then?"

"A certain white-haired warlord riding hell-bent for leather."

"Rathincourt!"

Rowan lay flat. "I'd say so . . . and further, that he's probably looking for us. With any luck they'll hear the drum message as far north as Stonedeep as well."

"Will you two be shutting your mouths and letting the rest of us sleep?" Pinch's voice grumbled at them from across the banked fire.

Alorie smothered a giggle as Rowan's hand twitched, and Pinch exploded with a curse as a handful of moss dampened his bare head. They ducked under the blankets as the dwarf responded in kind.

Then Rowan decided they could do something a little quieter under the blankets.

Rowan made a noise of pleasure as he crawled upon the ridge. He reached down to his belt quiver. "These bows have been useless for too long."

"I'll say," ventured young Barth. "I thought you could hunt with 'em."

Alorie put her hand over her mouth as Pinch rumbled, "Bite your tongue, bucko. We've done well enough keeping the stewpot full."

Barth's face flushed awkwardly. "I only meant—"

"Hist! Reken moving below," Pinch said, cutting him off.

Rowan flattened himself even more as they watched the rocks below, rippling with the rust and black of reken moving into place. He nocked an arrow.

"Hold yer fire, lad," rumbled the dwarf.

"Don't tell me how to fire an arrow," Rowan returned. He crept forward, out of Alorie's reach. "Make your shots count. Rathincourt hasn't a chance if we give them time to shoot."

She held a shorter bow, one scaled down for her pull, and as she looked below, she doubted she could hit a target at this range. The drums had long since stopped so as not to alert the prey.

Pinch had his big dwarf ear to the ground. He looked up and nodded. Rowan got up on one knee, knowing the reken would be too busy to look uphill as their quarry galloped into the pass.

The horse was covered in foam, and the rider a muddied brown hunched over his neck. As the reken boiled out, Rowan, Pinch, and Barth came to the ridge's edge and let fly.

Alorie picked a target close to her and did the same. She was surprised to see the reken tumble off his rock, paw clenched to shoulder in barking agony.

Howls and yelps split the air even as Rathincourt's stallion plunged to a rearing halt, reken arrows going astray because of the attack to their back. Pinch and Rowan scarcely paused in nocking and letting fly, their movements smooth, not waiting for the thunk of an arrowhead striking target before drawing again. Barth fumbled for his third arrow, but his shots were respectable.

It was over in moments. A last reken burst out of the

rocks, then bolted in the other direction. Pinch took off after him, short sword in hand. Rowan stood up as Rathincourt put back the mailed hood of his surcoat and looked up in surprise.

"Well," the warlord said. "I've finally found a use for a Rover."

Rowan grinned insolently. "Don't press your luck, milord. By nightfall, you'll be surrounded by us."

That night they camped on the banks of the Frostflower. Its waters flowed still and wide here rather than steep and swift, but they still retained the icy chill of Alorie's memories. The Frostflower flowed past Sinobel and to the south, and she remembered its waters well. Rathincourt held a conference with Rowan and Ashcroft, and he seemed shocked at what the Rover brothers had to say, though they left Alorie out of their conversation.

"By the Horn, you said," the warlord burst out once. "And how do you suppose he means to back that one up?"

Rowan gave her a sidelong look across the fire and said something that lowered the lord's voice but not his vehemence as they argued across the lamp. Suddenly the conversation came to a halt, and she realized the trio watched her. She got up from her seat by the fire, where she had been contemplating riding down to the Rovers' main encampment just to have the companionship of a woman again—oh, how she missed Medra and hearty Mary Rose—when she saw them and went to their fire.

"How bad is the news?" she said.

"What do you mean?"

She looked fondly at her older brother-to-be, his left sleeve pinned against his ribs, his fair skin and auburn-haired good looks an echo of Rowan. "I mean, Ashcroft, that you don't have to be a Rover to read this sign. Rathincourt routed from training his army at Sobor. Three men huddled over a fire while their dinner grows cold and their wine warm. Stonedeep emptied and moving, lock, stock, and barrel cross-country. What has the enemy done?"

In the awkward silence Rathincourt cleared his throat before answering, "Taken the Delvings."

"What?" She staggered, and Rowan caught her, helping her to sit on a log stump next to him. "Are you sure?"

"Reasonably."

"But what about Stonedeep? Why empty it? The Rovers are as safe there as anywhere."

Rowan looked at her. "That is the doing of another."

"Who? Why?"

"Brock has reinstated the Raltarian Guard."

Her thoughts whirled and she put her hand to her head to steady herself. "That can't be."

"No, but he's done it."

She met Rathincourt's icy-blue gaze. "Has it been made public?"

"Not when I'd left."

"Blasphemy. There's no other reaction for it." She stood then, paced a step away from the stump, then went back to it and sat down, feeling helpless. "He's dividing loyalties. If I didn't know better . . ." Her voice trailed off.

"Don't think it," Rowan said. "He's not been Corrupted. There's a method to his thinking, I know there is."

"Milady," the warlord said to gain her attention. "The situation at the forges is more important. We have no choice. We have to march north to face it, and we'll have to take Sinobel first."

No, her heart cried silently, but she made a fist of her trembling hands and answered, "Yes. I understand."

Twenty-Three

Midsummer rain followed them all the way north and east. It helped to wash their tracks away and dampened their body heat—for the reken tracked by temperature as well—but it gave Pinch a deep cough. The resulting mud mired down the wains bringing most of Stonedeep who were to journey on to Sobor. The Rovers who had mounts and wished to, peeled away to ride with them, leaving the wagons behind. The riders were also, Alorie knew in her heart, the core of the newly recommissioned Raltarian Guard.

At the edge of grasslands and hills, where the Frostflower grew swift, a hawk reached them. Rowan threw up an arm wrapped around with his much-worn cloak and lured the bird down. Its jesses were colored a brilliant blue. If Alorie had ever doubted Kithrand sent it, she did not when Rowan held the raptor out for her to be hooded while he fumbled to get the scroll loose.

"Greetings, this new dawned day, as Charlbet rises out of the ashes like the legendary firebird, to the Lady Alorie Sergius, from her humble admirer, Kithrand." Rowan cleared his throat at this.

Alorie laughed softly. "Never a servant, not one of the elf lords. Can you blame him?"

The man looked at her with his brown eyes and said, "You've enough admirers for me." He continued to read: "The news of the capture of the Delvings has reached us. By the time you encamp at Sinobel, I will be joining you with a troop of horse knights, veterans all, to ride at your side."

Rathincourt interrupted, "How did he know about Sinobel?"

"It's a foregone conclusion." All humor fled, Alorie answered, her voice barely audible. "We have no choice but to take Sinobel if we're to strike at the Corruptor. We all know it, even I." She pinched the bridge of her nose. "Go on."

"Not much after that: The library suffers greatly, but Gillus has been sifting the ashes and regrets he has not found the information needed. Until we are met in the road to victory, yours, Lord Kithrand." Rowan snapped the missive shut.

Pinch coughed, hawked, then said, "I suppose that's all we could expect of them."

"All?" Alorie kneed her bay mare around and glared at the dwarf. His bright yellow curls were matted and his beard needed trimming; his silver eyes were dull with his cold. She curbed her tongue at his misery, but said, "Because of us, Charlbet burned."

Rathincourt heeled his roan stallion. "Don't believe it, milady. The Corruptor would have burned it sooner or later if he thought it would keep you from defeating him."

"But we failed."

The warlord took his half-helm off. Sweat darkened his snowy hair. "But *he* doesn't know that, does he?" He pointed off to the horizon. "We'll be caught up with the foot soldiers by tomorrow dusk. The horse troops the day following. Then, milady, you will have to deal with what you've been avoiding. We must council our attack for Sinobel."

They arrived at night, and Alorie was grateful for the hands that helped her from her saddle and into her tent. They had a canvas tub ready with buckets of steaming water by its side, and the ladies bathed her and put her to sleep gently. She knew one lady, whose hair was already gray among its amber and also had eyes of the same piercing blue, the younger half sister of Lord Rathincourt. Alorie felt a twinge that Rathincourt would have endangered his own half sister to wait on her, but pushed it aside. It had been a long time since anyone of bearing had waited on her.

The maids giggled at her rough hands, but their voices grew hushed when they laid her in the bath water and began to lave the saddle sores that had begun to eat into her thighs and buttocks. One of them murmured, "She's so pale."

"The House of Sergius doesn't brown," the lady answered.

She clucked at the freckles sprinkled over her arms and face, and when they toweled her, Alorie stayed limp and only half awake as they rubbed in soothing ointments and pulled on a nightshirt. Lady Marne tucked a coverlet under her chin, saying, "I will bring a cream for the freckles in the morning, Lady Alorie," and left with a whispered command to her two maids to follow her. Alorie knew nothing more.

Nothing but the nightmare of the black unicorn, the same one that had awakened her months before in early spring. But this time she knew the dark beast she faced, knew him well, and saw the anguish in his eyes as he attacked, for she had failed him.

Pinch awoke stiff and tired, and rolled out of his blankets, which smelled like pipe smoke and woodfire. His chest ached relentlessly. Rowan had promised him a draught of silverweed and ale for sleep and the cough, but Pinch had gone under without it. For a time he'd dreamt suffocatingly of being underground, pent up under rock and stone—his greatest fear. Then he'd drifted into more peaceful sleep, though his nightmares still nagged at him. He awoke feeling guilty—he'd learned long ago the virtue of sleeping with only one ear and one eye shut, but the past weeks of hard riding had sapped him of his strength.

Or perhaps it had been the death of Mary Rose. He sat and hugged himself against the cough that threatened to burgeon, and mourned his wife. If she were about now, she'd be fussing with a mustard plaster and steaming water with foolstaff in it for him to breathe under a blanket. If she were about now, he would be fussing that she'd come to war with him. Pinch scratched his curly beard.

He got to his feet with difficulty. He wore his summer drawers, cut off just above the knee, and looked down at his legs. They'd be bowed before long, stuck as he'd been riding horses instead of his sturdy ponies from the Downs. He'd had no choice if he wanted to keep up, but their girth bowed his legs almost beyond bearing. He'd waddle like an old dame into the meeting this morning.

Rowan's blankets were cold, as were Barth's. Pinch bared his teeth at that. So they let the old dwarf sleep in this morning, eh? He unburied his pipe from his vest pocket and lit it before sauntering out of the tent. He scampered back in as two women let out a shrill scream and the third, with her chin up, said, "Well, I *never!*"

With greater dignity he washed, dressed, and emerged into the world a little later then he had planned, visiting the latrines first and the line of horses second. He found Rowan grooming Banner and Alorie's bay mare. Pinch scratched the bay mare's whiskers as she shoved her muzzle at him. Little bits of grain and chaff clung to her lips.

"Been into it headfirst, old gal?" the dwarf said. He sized up the mare. She'd lost flesh on their journey. The hollow above her eyes were greatly sunken in, but they were graining her this morning and she'd soon be fit as a fiddle. He checked his gelding, ran a hand over the legs, and, to his pleasure, found them cool and solid.

"Thought you would never greet the sun," Rowan said as Banner grunted and leaned into the brushing he was getting.

Pinch's lips tightened. "You young squirts may be forgetting, but I'm old by your reckoning."

"But not by dwarf reckoning. Just stubborn and lazy." Rowan ducked as Pinch threw a handful of dirt and chaff at him, sprinkling Banner's newly groomed back. With a cluck the man began to clean him all over again.

"When's the meeting?"

"Soon. They're giving Alorie a chance to rest. She was done in. I heard she fell asleep in the bath."

"That one has a fair amount of grit," Pinch said.

Rowan paused. A proud look passed over his expression, and his cleft deepened. "I know."

"Where's the seer?"

"Stay clear of him, Pinchweed. He and Rathincourt have been into it already."

The dwarf's golden-yellow eyebrows went up. "Over the Guard?"

"What else? While we slept the sleep of the overworked and innocent, he made his announcement to the camp." Rowan sighed as he scrubbed away on his horse's rump, his hands making graceful circuit with the brush. "They think he's lost his mind."

"How about you? What do you think?"

"He's not the man I knew."

Pinch pointed his pipe stem at his friend. "Neither are you. Like a flower, bucko, we're either still growing . . . or we've begun to die."

Rowan finished with his grooming and stepped out of the picket line. "Since when have you become a philosopher, you sawed-off excuse for an armsman?"

"Since ye fell in love and lost what little wit you had!" the dwarf retorted. His stomach growled. "What about breaking fast?"

"There's to be rolls and fruit at the council."

"That'll do to fend off lunch. In the meantime, let's you and I find a real feed."

They strolled off in search of the food wagons. It took Pinch no time at all, for the air was filled with the aroma of meat strips and potatoes and onions. He drew a mug of ale, heaped his crust full, and found a place at a table, with a bench and all. He forked a mouthful of grilled onions. "Ah," he said. "Here's an advantage to the situation."

A rough-looking footman to his right jostled him slightly as he grumbled, "Eat hearty, short stuff. The Guardian of the Prophecy's liable to see all our throats cut before this is over."

Rowan seated himself opposite Pinch. He still wore his Rover brown and russet, not having had time to change to his ceremonial black and silvers. The young man slid over an extra mug of ale to the footman. "What's this?"

"You never heared of the Guardian? Where you two been? I thank ye," the footman added as his big paw of a hand slid the mug close to his breadloaf trencher.

"Down south," Pinch said. He shoveled in some potatoes in appreciation. "What's the grumble?"

"Oh, the lord's a fine man, right enough. But the mage, the dark-skinned one, he's the one to watch out for. Thinks he's the bleeding guardian of all Bethalia's future. Says we're to see the return of the High King before all this is through."

"Does he now?" Rowan chewed thoughtfully.

"And you're not looking forward to that?"

The man put his mug down. "I ask you, does this lot look like a bunch of bleeding heroes? The reken been driving us crazy. I'd pee my pants running if I saw a malison, and I don't mind telling you. We came to fight, but we don't need our ears filled with crazy talk to puff us up."

Rowan had finished scraping his trencher. He said quietly, "What would you say if I said it wasn't crazy talk?"

The table grew quiet. The footman scrubbed at his bristling jaw and then said, "By the Apron, I'd say you were drinking silverweed. I'll follow the warlord wherever he wants to lead us, but I ain't going on no crusade to the Barrowlands and the Iron Liege. I wasn't born to be no hero!" With that he pushed away from the table after throwing his trencher to the great dogs hungrily pacing the benches.

Pinch finished his heap of onions, licked his fork, and said reflectively, "Morale isn't the best I've ever seen."

Rowan held his trencher out to a grizzle-coated hunter, who snatched it with sharp white teeth. "I don't like it."

"Ye don't have to like it," Pinch said. A brindle bitch sniffed his hand before delicately taking his crust. He patted the dog as he swung his legs around and stood.

"We live by the prophecy," Rowan said as he joined his friend in walking back toward the pavilion that housed Rathincourt. "It's our hope."

"And your hope is the dread of most of these common folk. To them you're talking war such as they've never seen, and the return of the Despot. It comes to that, as well." Pinch grew silent, thinking of his portion read to him off the wall at Cornuth. He had thought to pass it down to a son. Now he knew that, baffling as the command had been, it was his to decipher. "I don't think any of us feels grown enough to fill those boots."

Rowan dropped a hand upon his shoulder. "You're right, as usual. Instead of inspiring these men, Brock has put the fear of death into them."

Pinch said solemnly, "Where the Corruptor's concerned, even death isn't beyond his reach."

They stood before the tent where a war would be planned. The two men guarding it saluted and pulled aside for them to enter.

Brock looked into the polished shield Alorie had once used for a mirror. He had appropriated it and brought it along for her use, but now it stood in his tent. As he looked, his image seemed to diffuse and three brown-skinned men looked back at him. He stabbed a finger at them. They shimmered and disappeared altogether.

The Corruptor's too pale face smiled back at him. The slash of a mouth widened.

Brock jumped a step back, reaching for his cloak to throw over the image, then stopped.

"You," he said, remembering. "It was you who had me."

The grin widened until the skin on the lips grew white with tension, threatening to split.

"Yes," the image said with satisfaction. "But now Veil has been branded traitor. Who would believe you? You have blasphemed. You have divided. You have accused falsely. Tell them you were wrong, Brock. Who will believe you? The war is lost before it's even begun."

"What have you done to me?"

"I? Nothing. You have done it all to yourself. I remember you, old friend . . . do you remember me? And if you do, when you tell them, will they believe you? Will they trust you?" The image began to laugh.

He flung the cloak. Its weight knocked the shield askew as it draped across the image. From within its folds came a fading laugh. Shaken, the mage went to his knees, and that's the way he was found when Flask came to tell him the meeting had convened. The colonel paused, startled.

"Are you all right, sir?"

Brock turned to him, unhearing at first, then stumbled to his feet. He leaned to get the cane Rowan had made for him. Unknowingly the lad had carved him a wizard's staff, albeit short, his own having been lost years ago on one of the many Paths of Sorrow. Perhaps the shortness was apt, considering his own paucity of magic. "No, Colonel, I'm not all right," Brock said heavily. "But they must be waiting for us." He brushed past the veteran and limped toward Rathincourt's pavilion. He closed his eyes briefly, but he could not forget one of the visions the shield had shown him. Was it another trap of the Corruptor's *or had it been truth?*

His hand clenched tightly about the cane's handle until his knuckles showed white. Time had run its course for him. Now he must remember and he must not fail.

"This is the best approach to the Delvings." Rathincourt tapped the map he had had drawn up. Rock paperweights and an inkwell weighed it down across the table.

"It's straight down the valley," Rowan said. "When we came down last time, we came through here."

"You cannot march an army down a mountainside to get there."

Pinch grinned. He had his axe on the table, head down, and was leaning on its handle. "Ye can if you're being chased."

The warlord shook his head. Alorie murmured, "Peace, gentlemen," but she smiled softly.

"I see no other choice. If we had found some other way to bring the lieutenant down . . ."

"But we failed," Alorie answered.

The warlord gave her a kindly look. "You did your best. The answer was not in Charlbet. Perhaps we'll find it in the Delvings."

Pinch rocked back a little, as if he'd been punched in the chest.

"What is it?" Rowan said, but the dwarf shook his head. "Naught."

"You look like you've seen a ghost."

"Heard one, is all. Do ye know the Delvings is the oldest inhabitation in the records of the lands?"

Rathincourt looked sharply at him. "What are you saying?"

"It's a warren of runs and tunnels. The Pit itself is reputed to be a bottomless hole, running to the middle of the earth itself, where a second sun is trapped and spews up the heat that keeps the forges hot. We came out a rabbit hole the first time."

"That's what the survivor who got out told me. A 'bolt hole' he called it."

"If someone could get back in . . ."

"Forget it," Rathincourt told the dwarf. "You'd have to fight your way through the entire Delvings to get to the gates. We've had one or two others out of there since. Aquitane's renegades have iron-fisted control, and they're squeezing it tighter."

Alorie leaned over to Pinch, saying, "How old is oldest?"

"All of the Seven Races sprang from there, according to dwarf history. When we fell from Her Lap, ye see, we made quite a dent in the earth. We stayed there for a while, afraid to leave."

"That's quite a tale."

He put his axe down. "Indeed it is. You'd have to get to the bottom of it to know if 'tis true or not."

Alorie laughed delightedly when the tent flap pulled back and Brock came into the pavilion.

He nodded to her and Rathincourt. "My lady, my lord, and gentlemen."

"Brock."

Rowan said nothing. The mage looked him up and down. "Where is your uniform?"

"My black and silvers are in my pack."

"You're on duty, Captain."

Rowan's eyes stayed levelly on him.

Rathincourt cleared his throat nervously and sat down at the table's head. He dropped his quill pen. "All right. We won't get any work done until we have it out. Brock, have you lost your mind?"

The mage refused the chair Flask drew out for him. He stayed, leaning on his cane as though his life depended on it. "It's time for the Raltarian Guard. There's never been a better time."

"That may be, but it's not up to you. We can't pick the time. It's not up to us to decide."

"Perhaps not up to you, but it's most certainly up to me."

Alorie broke in. "I've heard you called the guardian of the prophecy in camp, Brock. What have you been doing while we've been gone?"

"Preparing the army." The mage looked to her. There was a weariness in the depths of his expression.

She straightened in her chair. "I don't know about these farmers, and merchants, and sons of millers and candlestick makers, but if I knew for sure I was going to face the Despot rising out of the Barrows, *I* wouldn't follow you for two leagues. Can't you see what you've done?"

"I've done what I had to do. You must pass around the Barrowlands once we've taken Sinobel. Then, it stays at our back when we march on the forges. Alorie, I can feel him shift. I can feel him *breathe* under that dirt, and with every breath he takes, the bindings grow weaker! The Corruptor knows now what it takes to free him, and he's just biding his time."

Pinch said in his deep, rumbling tone, "You guess, mage. You cannot know. You've not had a full measure of strength in many years."

Brock looked to him, opened his mouth as if to say something, then sagged into the chair the adjunct had held for him. Then he shook his head. "You are right and wrong, shortman. I do feel. I cannot see, but I do feel."

"And you expect this little chit of a lass to stand up to him when he does break loose?"

Alorie said warningly, "Pinch—"

"No, don't stop me. I'm not a warlord or a Rover or a mage, but I am one of the Seven True Races. You've overlooked me on many an account, but I'll have my say. He was not there when you read the final prophecy. I was. He's banished the Mutts because no one stood up to him. Now he'll bully you into the Barrowlands. I won't have it. Who do you think you are?"

The mage sighed. "I was hoping you wouldn't ask me, old friend. I was hoping you would all stand by me until the time came. I'm not ready for it, but I'll tell you." He lifted his chin. "I am the High King."

Twenty-Four

Rathincourt pushed back his chair with a strangled sound. His face turned a brilliant crimson as Rowan straightened, his face turning livid under his woodsman's tan. "By the Horn," the warlord sputtered. "I've had enough. Deanmuth, remove this man."

"You do," said Brock without moving his head to look at the adjunct, "and you've come dangerously close to treason."

"What treason? You'd have to be the king before that. I've known you for years, man. Give it up." Rathincourt beckoned vigorously for Deanmuth, who stood hesitating to obey him.

"No," Alorie said. "No, don't. He believes what he's saying."

The mage met her troubled gaze. "I'm not deranged. This is no delusion."

She started to put out her hand, then paused. "There's a big difference between being the guardian of the prophecy and the High King."

"Don't coddle him, milady," Rathincourt interrupted. "He's asked us to believe, after three hundred years, the unbelievable. The impossible."

"Perhaps we could trace the bloodline . . ."

Rowan stirred and spoke his first words, though his eyes never left Alorie. "The libraries at Charlbet are in shambles. Stonedeep has been evacuated"—he did not mention the exiled Mutts who had stayed behind—"and dwarf histories are unlikely to mention Rovers. It would be difficult to prove his claim to be a descendent."

Brock slapped his cane upon the table. Sparks flew inexplicably as the furniture vibrated. "Are you all deaf? I did not claim to be a descendent, nor am I speaking of reincarnation! I am what I say I am. I am the High King."

His words hung on the air a moment. Alorie sat back in the great chair. Her heart felt like a lump of ice hanging in her chest. Since that first moment when Brock had appeared in court to request her from her grandfather, he had been pointed toward this moment. He had threatened Rowan because of this. She was to be his wife instead. The prophecy was all, and she was its daughter. While they sat in that pavilion in disbelief, she accepted his words. "Why," she asked lowly. "Why didn't you tell us earlier? Couldn't we be trusted? How did you expect to rebuild a kingdom without allies?"

The mage lifted his cane into his lap, balancing it across his knees. He ran his hands up and down the length of the wood. "I didn't know who I was," he finally answered. "And how I have lived as I have, I don't know. I have some power . . . it comes and goes. I suspect that I was taken away after the battle to lie dormant for some years, and when I arose, I became a Rover. Memories—" His fingers gripped the cane. "I can't tell you any more because I don't know myself."

"Then we're to accept your word on blind faith." Rathincourt thrust himself to his feet. "I've put up with your meddling long enough. Milady, I've never yet abandoned a battlefield before being defeated, but I renounce this man. Veil has scrambled his brains, and the sooner you recognize it, the better off we are." The veteran soldier pushed his way out of the tent, Deanmuth following.

The dwarf got down off his chair, hiked up his belt, and stuck the axe into it.

"Pinch," Alorie said in an agonized voice.

He shook his head, yellow curls bouncing. "We all have prophecies to follow, milady." He disappeared as well, leaving the three of them alone in the tent.

She sat, stricken. Rowan moved to her side and Brock stared at the two of them.

"Captain, you're to find yourself a proper uniform as soon as possible. Please escort the lady back to her quarters and remove yourself from her company. *Is that understood?*"

Rowan did not answer. He put his hand upon Alorie's shoulder and she felt the tremble of his anger. "Rowan," she pleaded. "Please do as he says." His hand moved, and he came around to help her to her feet. They were halfway out the tent when Brock yelled after them.

"She's mine. Remember that! She's mine!"

* * *

Rowan paced Alorie's quarters. "You can't stand with him. You need Rathincourt to lead the army. They won't follow Brock. Alorie, for the love of god, you can't believe him."

"I have to."

"Why?"

She hid her face from him. "You yourself said there was a method to his actions."

"That was before. There was a lad at Stonedeep who fell into one of the caverns . . . thought he was a chicken after that, *but that didn't make him one*." He caught her by the shoulders. "Come with me. Let me take you back to Sobor, where you'll be safe. Leave me the sword. I'll lead the damned army. And when I come back, marry me."

She shook her head. "I can't."

"Alorie—"

"I can't!" She shook herself free of his hold.

He moved back as if stung. "Can't or won't."

"If he's right, my love, if he's right, the outcome of all we do depends on me."

"And if he's wrong, you'll be dead. This isn't a game of *rool*."

She twisted around. Tears glistened upon her face. "Perhaps it is," she said. "And I've sacrificed the queen. Please go. Don't make me throw you out."

He turned on heel and left. She stood for a bare second more, then tumbled to the ground, pillowed her face on her arms, and wept as her heart broke.

"No, I don't mind," Rathincourt said gruffly. "Take anything you need. And don't go denouncing me for abandoning my lady."

"I said nothing," Pinch returned. "But ye two old goats butting heads won't be winning this war."

"He's lost his mind."

The silver-eyed dwarf shrugged into his pack of battle gear. "Then he needs his friends to help him find it. 'Tisn't true, of course, not after three hundred years—but if that's so, then the Corruptor isn't true either, and we've had a heap of trouble from that one these past years."

"Do you believe him, then?"

Pinch took his pipe out and scraped the bowl clean. "Don't know," he finally answered. "What's the harm in believing him? If he's wrong, we've got no more trouble than we have now. But if he's right . . . we'd better grit our teeth, for the Iron Liege makes his lieutenant look like a snow-white lily."

"I have my pride," the warlord returned. "And this has the stench of the Corruptor about it."

"Mayhap." Pinch hiked his pack up. "I'll be seeing your lordship."

Rathincourt nodded absently. He sat in a chair in his private tent overlooking the bivouacks. He said suddenly, remembering, "Say, Pinch—that refugee dwarf I told you about. Said his name was Hammersmith and he came from your part of the country—Gutrig Downs—"

But the dwarf was gone.

Alorie stayed in her tent until dawn when the army decamped. The air was filled with the neighing of horses alert to new action, the stamp of boots and creak of leathers, the clang of weapons and armor being gathered. She dressed in clothing Lady Marne had found for her and then sat, huddled until she heard the clearing of a throat at the door.

She knew the voice. "Come in, Lady Marne."

The woman entered, dipped a knee, and stood, her cheeks reddening. "I'm sorry, milady, but—my brother is leaving and I cannot stay."

"I understand." Alorie put her shoulders back. She stared across the tent, where the Unicorn sword lay in its sheath. "What's happening out there? I can't bear to look."

"He's declaring himself. It's not . . . it's not an inspiring sight." The woman fumbled for words. "With camp gossip, most of the men already knew by dawn anyway. My lady, Rathincourt says one man in five left during the night. More will probably drop off during the march to Sinobel."

"I see." Alorie stood and picked up a traveling cloak. Its deep blue weave accented the blue of her eyes. "Is your brother already gone?"

"He's without, waiting for me."

"Will you see if he'll have one last word with me?"

Hesitantly Lady Marne left. Alorie waited for several breath-stopping minutes, wondering if the snow-haired man would meet her request. When at last his broad shoulders brushed through the tent flap, she saw he was fully armored, his half-helm in his hands.

"Milady?"

"How bad is it?"

A muscle quirked along his jaw. "It is not good. You may face the loss of half your army by the time you reach Sinobel."

"Stop it."

Rathincourt looked at a spot somewhere over the top of her head and beyond. "I'm no longer your commander," he said stiffly.

"But you're still my friend. For the love of life, stop them."

"I can't. If I go back before them now, they'll think me insane as well . . . or bewitched. They won't listen to me just yet."

Fear quickened through her body. She fought to keep her voice even. "Then what can be done? Anything?"

"Kithrand's been sighted. His troop should be joining by midday."

"The elf lord hardly makes up for losing half an army," she said bitterly. "What else?"

Rathincourt lowered his gaze. "Take up the sword. Ride out in front of them, by his side if necessary. They'll follow you and the sword down the gullet of hell."

Her throat tightened because she knew it was true, and she feared Sinobel as much as the gullet of hell. It had not rained enough in four years, could not rain enough in a lifetime, to wash the streets clean of her people's blood. "Thank you," she said. Her voice had dropped to a whisper.

Rathincourt turned to go. He paused at the tent flap. "I'll be guarding your back, milady. When he goes down, send for me. I'm not abandoning you."

"Thank you," she answered after him as the veteran disappeared from her view. She stood and stared at the sword, then retrieved it. As she pulled its length from the scabbard, a dark shadow grew until its splinter-fine length had run from tip to guard.

Alorie stared in horror. "I've done everything," she protested. "Everything you demanded of me and more." She turned the guard overhand. The splinter stayed in place, a hairlike fracturing of the gold and ivory-shot horn. She had years ago lost the ability to heal with it—what if she could no longer make war with it, either? Her courage fled a moment, but she planted her booted feet firmly and took deep breaths until she knew she would do what Lord Rathincourt had said was the only thing she could do. As she belted on the scabbard and emerged from the tent, sword in hand, horns winded and she saw Brock mounted on a chestnut destrier as red as blood awaiting her.

Kithrand let Strider put his head down and drink deeply of the tiny brook. Its freshet wound through summer grass going yellow and wildflowers beginning to wilt in the relentless sun. The brook was muddied, he saw. There had been many comings and goings that day and no reken sign among them. His own troop had dismounted in the shade of the grove, he being the last to water his mount. As he looked up, he saw a foot soldier striding across the grasslands, his pack on one shoulder, his armor patched.

The elf lord gave a whistle as the man stopped upstream and went to one knee to scoop up a mouthful of water.

His antennae danced in sardonic amusement as the soldier looked up. "Careless of me," Kithrand said. "But isn't Sinobel north of here?"

"Aye," the man answered.

"Then you must be marching in the wrong direction."

"Not me. I've missed midsummer harvest, but if I make good time, I'll make the second crop."

Kithrand carefully put his hand on Strider's withers, keeping his wrist sheath straight. The cream-colored gelding continued to suck at the water. "Where I come from, that is called desertion."

The farmer cum soldier straightened. "Call it what you will, lord elf. But when Rathincourt himself takes leave, the rest of us figured we could do what we wanted. And I want to go home. My armor is patched, and my sword rusty. I could do more damage with a hoe if I had one!"

"Rathincourt gone?"

"Since yesterday. I won't follow a crazy man, so it's home for me." The farmer saluted him and jumped the brook.

Kithrand stopped him. "One last question, good man. What character of dubious wits now leads the army?"

"The dark mage Brock. He says he's the High King returned to lead us to glory. If Rathincourt didn't believe him, why should I?"

"I see." The elf lord moved back lightly and let the farmer pass. When he was out of earshot, Kithrand murmured to Strider, "I see not all news comes by hawk."

Strider, disinterested, lifted his dripping muzzle and nodded back down for a pull of sweet grass.

* * *

"I won't let you put her to the fore tomorrow," Rowan said angrily.

"We haven't any choice. The troops will rally to her and she knows Sinobel better than anyone here." Brock remained impassive. He sat, peeling a greenfruit. "From what I've heard, it didn't seem to bother you last time there was a war."

"That was different. The horn had a . . . an aura about it. Arrows shot at her fell short. Malisons fell before it. Reken ran. Even the Corruptor and Aquitane took to their heels."

"And that was before you loved her."

Rowan's face went still. "I loved her," he said, "the first moment I saw her."

The peel fell to Brock's feet. "I suggest you remember she is to be my wife."

"Only if she survives fighting your battles. You only want to be High King to make her yours."

The mage came to his feet. "You're insubordinate."

"And you know what I think of you."

"Stay away from her!"

Rowan looked at the mage. He searched the brown face intently for some sign of the man who'd once been his friend and found none. "You may wed her, if it comes to that. But she'll never love you." He pulled himself tall. "You may count me among your deserters." He ducked under the open-air canopy and strode away from the command post, brushing past Kithrand dismounting at the pavilion's edge.

The elf did a quick about-face and raced to keep up with Rowan. "Did I hear a falling out?"

"You did." Rowan made the picket line. He took Banner's reins and jerked them free. His fellow Rovers stayed mounted, Ashcroft, Tien, Corbet, and others, twenty in all on duty.

The elf lord reached out his slender hand. "What is going on here?"

Rowan mounted. As he found purchase in the stirrups and pushed his boots through, he looked down. "If you decide to stay, promise me one thing."

"If I can." Kithrand's fair blond hair tangled in the afternoon breeze. "What is it?"

"Stay by Alorie. She'll need all the help you can give her."

The lord bowed. "Done. Where will you be?"

He looked grim. "Trying to put her army back together."
He reined away from the elf lord, and the Rovers left in a
cloud of dust that hung on the warm summer day and
obscured the visage of fallen Sinobel.

Dawn came. Despite the heat that would later follow, a
fog roiled up from the ground. It clung to the horses' hooves
and the foot soldiers' boots and obscured them, as if the
entire army floated several hands above the ground. Alorie
emerged and found herself looking at a sight she had been
avoiding: the ringed city of her birth.

It held a mountain, a stony crag actually, and each walled
portion ranged up that crag until the Inner Ring overlooked
and ruled the valley. The forest had gone wild or the towers
could also have overlooked the Barrowlands. She remembered a wide trade road leading up to the gates, terraced
fields and orchards to the east, grasslands that made approach difficult. She remembered green and the river that
flowed from the foot of the crag to be blue, not muddy, and
gentle, not harsh and erratic, to the orchards. Scouts had
gone through the trees yesterday, hoping for a harvest of
fruit to augment marching rations. What they had returned
with had been withered and wormy and had to be boiled
down to make a thin jam for the journeybread. The trade
road was ripped up, and the grasslands were sere weeds. So
far the only thing she'd seen prospering was the forest: so
green it was near black, and more wild and broken than
before.

Kithrand held the headstall to her little bay mare and
stood rubbing her chin and talking softly to her in his lilting
language. He smiled as Alorie approached. They had dined
last evening and she felt some comfort with the elf friend by
her side. Rowan and Rathincourt gone, Pinch off on some
errand of his own, only Brock remained—and now he was a
stranger to her. The lord gave her a leg up and settled the
reins in her hand.

"I'm with you," he said softly before gathering a handful
of Strider's mane and vaulting onto his back. The gelding
whickered softly and pricked his ears forward.

Brock rode up. What was left of the foot soldiers got to
their feet en masse. She noted the new line across his brow,
the intensity of the ones about his eyes.

"The city is quiet now."

"We were attacked last night," she said.

He raised an eyebrow.

"Did you think I wouldn't find out?" Alorie returned angrily. "I heard that two score men were dragged off, blooded, and that our dogs whine and howl when shown the bodies."

Brock looked across the troops. "Not quite that many, but accurate."

"Malisons."

"Probably."

"And does your new memory include the receipt for the herbed powder to drive them away? No? A shame."

He turned to her. "I don't remember a sharp tongue among your assets."

"You'd better get used to it." The weight of the Unicorn sword sheathed upon her back burned into her like a brand. She twitched the reins, moving her horse forward. "At least I'll die a better death in Sinobel than my father did."

Brock grabbed her shoulder as the two horses brushed into one another. His hazel eyes burned. "If I had my power, I would ward you."

Alorie sighed. "I know. Since you can't—I will wrap this army about me like a shield."

The mage let go of her as he moved to the fore, and raised her hand and pulled forth the Unicorn sword. It caught the last of the dawn's rays like a beacon, calling forth and drawing the army after her.

she looked about. The cobblestone streets stirred with no lurking enemy. A scant troop of horse met her with weary cheers. The words she cast in a matter of . . .

Twenty-Five

Rowan ducked an arrow, hauled Banner around, and bolted under a hanging branch, taking what shelter in the wildwood as he could. He bumped into Kithrand, hanging onto his cream gelding's back by sheer will. Both were gory.

"Where the bloody hell is Alorie?"

"We were cut off at the gate. They let us think the city near deserted. They let us ride right in, up to the second wall, then snapped the trap on us. I lost her almost immediately. Five thousand reken they have in that stinkhole."

Rowan grinned fiercely. "We outmatch them, then."

"What? Are you as mad as Brock? There's two times more of them."

"We figure five reken to a Rover, elf lord."

Strider danced impatiently and snorted. Kithrand gave a weary shake of his head and ran his hand down the gelding's neck to quiet him. "Such bravado from a deserter."

"Deserter no more. I'm commander of milady's army, a free and independent branch of the armed forces." Rowan waved an arm, and Kithrand looked out of the wildwood to see fresh troops sweeping in.

"Ah," he said, and with that word the elf lord spoke volumes.

The little mare spilled out from under her, slipping in blood and gore. Alorie felt her go and bailed out, kicking free of the stirrups and landing if not on her feet, somewhat reasonably. Without looking to see, she swung the sword about her viciously, heard a reken squeal, and stumbled up. The mare wallowed, unable to get up on a dangling left foreleg. With a sigh Alorie gave her a mercy stroke. Hot blood spattered her and she scarcely knew its difference from the hot tears that nearly blinded her.

She looked about. The cobblestone streets surged with troops fighting hand to hand amid broken bodies. Her men, still pitifully short of swords and armor, were picking up reken weapons as they went. She knew she ought to cry out, to inspire them, to bugle, "To me! To me! For Bethalia!" but a lump stuck in her throat and threatened to strangle any word.

A human soldier loomed in front of her. He was covered in dirt, and she hesitated, but when she saw the blue and silver of Quickentree, she ran him through. Aquitane's renegade ate the dust in front of her, and the dagger he'd been hiding in his hand clattered to the street. She kicked it away.

Her riding skirt tangled about her ankles as she plunged uphill. A loose horse clopped past her. Alorie ran after it in hopes of catching it, but it flushed an ambush of hungry reken and they were upon it in spite of their orders to murder other prey before they saw her.

The three that did went up on their rear legs and clashed their tusks with pleasure. They split apart, giving her too big a target for her sword. They snarled as she stepped back and drew her dagger from the inside of her boot sleeve.

She ducked and spun to the right, slicing the reken across the inside of its white-furred belly hanging over its belt before it could react.

"That leaves two of you," she said, and repositioned herself.

Feeding reken at the stray horse's body looked up. She had only a few moments before they would be after her, too.

The left-hand reken snarled. Alorie hefted her dagger and threw. The right-hand reken went down, mewling and clawing its throat. She kicked it in the teeth and pulled her dagger out.

The remaining reken let out a sharp bark. Its feeding companions all looked up and seemed to recognize her as prey for the first time.

Alorie turned and ran.

Her riding boots were too well-heeled to allow her much speed, but she hotfooted it over the stone and bodies as fast as she could, the pack of reken breathing down her back. She turned the corner of an abandoned building—the fleeting memory ran through her mind that she remembered a soap seller here, his wares sweetly scented—and plowed to a halt. Reken at her back faded away.

She smelled the malevolence. Every hair in her pores stood on end as the being drifted cloudlike out of the yawning doorway toward her. Its sheer evil froze her, rooted her to the bloody street. She could not move if her life depended on it—which it did. Malison, *souleater*, devourer of minds as well as bodies. It rippled. She sensed a nebulous thing reaching toward her and reacted by bringing up the horn in defense. The arc of its sweep cut off the creeping sense she had of being violated. Alorie staggered back abruptly.

She had a moment in which to see the doorway issuing other clouds of menace before she let out a squeak instead of a scream and darted up the street. Hoofbeats thundered down on her as she reached the main road to the Inner Circles. Flashes of cream-colored skin and mane and wise blue eyes swept by her, and she slowed long enough for an arm to embrace her, pulling her aboard a faery horse.

She recognized the long chestnut locks and pure green eyes of Lord Torrey, Kithrand's second, as he squeezed an arm about her. Kithrand, in front, brought Strider to a rearing halt.

"Get her out of here!"

"Yes, milord!" the elf warrior said. He put heel to his steed, which jumped to his command, and Alorie grabbed his mane with both hands. Kithrand led the way, clearing the street of reken stragglers as they made their way downhill.

The nape of her neck prickled with disaster. They fairly flew toward the gate of Sinobel, but not fast enough, no— and when Torrey's horse slipped among the bodies as her own mare had, Alorie threw a look backward.

The street was filled with malison clouds, boiling toward them like a storm in a high wind.

"Kit!" she screamed, her voice shrill over the panicked neighing of Torrey's horse.

The elf lord pulled to a stop, turned, and looked. She clung to the stallion's mane, feeling Torrey's body behind her as he kneed and leaned, urging the horse to kick and bite his way free. Dying rekens in the mass of bodies imprisoning his hooves clutched at his pasterns, trying to drag him down. The stallion squealed in fury, his teeth snapping, head snaking from side to side. Alorie saw with confidence Kithrand signal his gelding, and she knew he was putting himself between them and the malisons. Even a moment of time would save them.

Whistling with the voice of a tempest, the malisons drew close—and Kithrand bolted. He kicked his gelding violently, slapping his hand down upon the haunch. The cream steed lunged into a gallop, carrying them free of the malisons and leaving Alorie and Lord Torrey at their mercy.

Her heart leapt. There was no mistaking his action into thinking he drew the malisons away. She and Torrey were between them and Kithrand. Tears beat down her face as she leaned from the stallion's withers and literally clubbed her sword at the fiends trying to tear them down.

The stallion ripped loose with a bugling note of pain and terror. Torrey pulled her straight and held her tightly into his chest as he grimly said, "Hold on, milady!"

She could feel the malisons straining toward them.

The faery stallion hurtled the last pile of bodies and flung himself at the gate. Two more elf warriors rode there, aimed their slender hands, and shouted words, and blue fire roared before them. They leapt the barrier. She felt fire crackle in her ears, and sing upon the strands of her loosened hair. They hit ground and thundered safely out of Sinobel.

"He left you there."

Alorie took a folded cloth, dampened it, and patted her face once more, trying uselessly to cleanse away the blood and smoke and tears staining it. "Yes," she said flatly. "He ran. He could face anything but the malisons. He found me and then he ran."

Brock held his cane between his hands as if he would break it. Then he said, "Well, he hasn't come back. If he does—"

"If he does, you'll let him go."

"He's a coward!"

"He, my liege, is an ambassador of the elves, and he's here by his own free will, not because of any fealty owed to you or to the realm. You'll let him go."

A fleeting expression passed over his face, then Brock smiled. "By the Horn, you surprise me. I had forgotten what it took to rule a kingdom. You will be an asset to us all."

She dropped the cloth into the battered helmet she was using as a bucket. Tiredly she overlooked the field. Battalions of foot soldiers were gaining the ringed walls, spelling other troops staggering out and regrouping. Sinobel was as good as theirs—but at what cost?

"What happened to the malisons?"

Brock shook his head. "I don't know. I've reports of two killed, but we've seen nothing of the phenomenon you described. Into the mountain perhaps?"

She shuddered at the thought of the inward passages . . . dark and confining. Only one went to safety. Several of the others to dungeons, two to the underground river pent up for use as a water supply, a thoroughly horrible canal for sewage runoff—and at least a handful of decoy tunnels. "Maybe," she agreed reluctantly. She put a hand out and put it on the mage's knee. He wore jet and silver.

"We never would have won today without Rowan's free troops."

Brock's jaw tightened. "They're deserters and looters. My men have orders to take bow and arrow to them if they camp within range."

"You can't be serious."

"He walked out on me!" Brock pulled away and stood up, stalked out of her reach, his back tense with his anger. "I am the king!"

"You can't blame them for not wanting to accept it. It seems so . . . impossible."

He looked back at her. "But not for you. Or are you a paragon among the Seven True Races?"

"I'm a nearsighted, knot-nosed, hardheaded Sergius! And it's my right to be among the first to bow to your return. But I won't be the last. Give them time, Brock."

He gazed across the wildwood toward the Barrowlands, and his tone was grim as he answered, "We haven't got time." He clenched a fist and raised it toward the wood. "But I'll have my powers back."

Alorie sighed and lapsed into silence. She watched the gates of Sinobel wrenched open, trampled down, and the ringed walls being breached one by one. It was a ghost city ruled by bonfire as night fell.

She was asleep when they came for her. She awoke at Brock's touch upon her wrist. He led her outside the tent where the army knelt. Confused, she turned to the mage-king.

"What do they want?"

"They've taken Sinobel for you. They want to take you inside."

She looked to the crag. Smoke and flame roiled from gaping windows behind broken walls. The moon above was a clear silver disk, barely a lesser sister of the sun. Her shadow was cast crisply upon the ground. She shivered. "It's haunted," she murmured quietly.

"All the better. Take the sword through." Brock held out the scabbard, and she could see the glow of the sword through its leather seams. The army saw it, too. A ragged cheer went up.

She protested softly. "I can't."

"You must. For me if no one else. Look to the west, to the Barrows. And tell me what you see when you return."

"You're not coming with me?" Alarm edged her voice.

He smiled. "The army came for you, not me. And they'll be at your back every step of the way." He pressed the sheathed talisman into her hand.

Alorie shuddered as she took it. "Kithrand's still up there," she said.

"Or dead."

The elf lord did not believe in an afterlife. Her fingers were cold as Brock helped her buckle on her weapon belt. She'd eaten and changed clothes, then slept in them, knowing a battlefield was no place to be taken unawares. One of Rathincourt's veterans, a rough-hewn sergeant, with a chewed-off right ear, knelt in front of her to brace her while she put her boots on.

"Forgive me," she said. "I remember your face, but not your name."

"Owl, miss. His lordship called me Owl."

She looked into the battered face. "Why didn't you leave with Rathincourt?"

Owl stood, ignoring the dusty, baggy knees of his trousers. He was only half-armored, and in leather at that. A leg cut would be the end of his fighting career. He answered her in a raspy voice, "The warlord bade me stay and watch over you."

Alorie made herself smile. "You've done us both proud," she told him, and followed him up the slope to the shattered gates of a city once prosperous and arrogant.

Twenty-Six

Strider let out a single human scream as they pulled him out from under Kithrand. The elf lord hit running, lightfooted with his terror. He never drew his sword to protect either his mount or himself and he never looked back. He slithered through the grasp of *something* and, panting, lost himself in the sacked ruins of the upper circles.

He ran until he thought he'd lost them, and then, like a hunted animal, went to ground. He found a dark corner and hid there, his face in his hands, gasping. The cold sweat poured off him. He did not stop shaking until the sun went down, and then he realized he'd trapped himself.

He unrolled into a crouch. The dappled half-light dazzled his eyes for a moment. Then he realized he watched bonfire and moonlight, still bright to his eyes. There was a mop-up maneuver going on in the lower rings. He was in the warrens of the High Counselor's wing.

And there were still malisons between him and freedom.

Kithrand bit his lip until his bluish blood flowed. He deserved no better. Alorie and Torrey were lost because of his cowardice. Strider had been shredded alive. And all because of him. His nerve had shattered. He had disgraced himself and his nation. He should stand up now, draw his sword, and hack his way through whatever of the souleaters he could before they closed upon the battalions working their way inward.

But he could not. His knees would not hold his slim weight. His fingers were numb. His eyes—Kithrand jerked his hands up to touch them—were dimmed from long hours of weeping in silent fear. He stood. His joints ached. A throbbing cold made him clench his teeth. He was damned, damned beyond redemption—and it had all happened so quickly.

Kithrand threw up his chin. In a voice barely audible, he began to recite a litany of elfin good-byes and placations to his ancestors. Blue motes sparked and drifted upon the dusky air as if his very words were empowered. His whisper fell away. He tilted his head to one side, listening. The air remained charged, but there was no response. Kithrand sighed. At least he had not been denounced. His soul was still hanging in the balance.

He looked back from his spy hole in the warren. Malisons still ringed the Inner Circle. No matter what the reward, he could not find redemption in an act of bravery there. He knew his limitations. Kithrand palmed the hilt of his sword. He would have to find a way out soon, one that was beyond the reach of the malisons.

Alorie strode between the gate posts. Built of stone, they alone remained standing. She looked at them. The years had eroded their carved surfaces. She did not need a torch; the Unicorn sword flared brighter. Owl held his sword ready and slipped a makeshift shield onto his left forearm. She watched. "I thought the city had been taken."

"Aye, miss, it has. But there's stragglers about and I wouldn't want to take chances with our lady." Owl looked up the hill. "And I've heard tales tonight of ghosts and such."

She could feel a prickling along her spine. In the brittle light of the moon she could feel the restlessness of the city. Too many dead, too much blood. She needed to lay them and her own fear to rest. She stepped beyond the gateway and onto the stone-paved streets, determined to trace a pathway of cleansing and blessing up to the final watchtower at the crag's peak. The Unicorn horn would blaze from its dark, slitted windows before this night was over.

Brock watched from below. He could see the movement of the horn, a golden fire that left its track behind it, a river of liquid light upon the twilight within the city walls, yet it seemed to circumscribe it. Its trailing never faltered. He balled a fist. "May you never waver," he muttered. He felt a stab of awareness striking at him from beyond the wildwood. He repelled it but not easily, sloughing it off as if he peeled his own skin away, sweat beading up on his forehead. When he was done, he felt dizzy, faint, triumphant.

He was not the man he had been, but there was a great deal of hope in the man he was to become.

He pointed his fist toward the unseen Barrows beyond the woods. "Our time is not yet come!"

Horses squealed and stamped on the picket lines, despite their weariness from the day's battle. Brock leaned back onto his cane.

Inside the Second Ring, Alorie paused. The moon tipped in the sky. She was tired and her wrist trembled from upholding the talisman. Her mind ached with the effort to keep it lit. She tried not to think of what the army would do if she let it dim. Owl paused beside her. He breathed heavily as well, and his sword was stained from dispatching of the straggler or two he'd warned her of. The streets had been cleaned of their own casualties and great bonfires lit to burn the piles of enemy dead. Their stench rankled upon the air and smoke made her eyes sting, but where she had walked with the horn, the air had sweetened despite the pyres and the abominations burning within.

Although she rested her elbow now upon the parapet of the stone ring, the sword still blazed as it had not since those first days of battle long ago. The splinter of Corruption within it was the barest fraction of a shadow, a flaw of eyesight, a twitch of a blink, no more. If only she could always wield the sword this way.

Owl waited a few more minutes, then gave a rough bow. His mannerisms reminded her of a Mutt valet of her father's. She hid her smile behind a hand and straightened. Only the Inner Circle remained to be traversed.

The gate here, big enough to admit a wain of distinction, was whole. The vast oaken panels depicted the installation of a High Counselor, the passing of the small, boxy black hat worn as sign of the office. The man carved there possessed the distinctive Sergius knotted nose that her own was a feminine echo of, though she didn't otherwise recognize his long face. Owl twisted the immense rings hanging there and pulled the gate open.

The malison waiting beyond launched. Alorie fell back, sword point out, unable to help Owl as her boot twisted under her awkwardly. The armsman froze, not for lack of courage, for Alorie had seen it happen time and time again and experienced it herself. The malevolent aura of the thing simply paralyzed its opponent.

The sword flared. Golden sparks spit into the air, drifting into the nimbus shroud of the malison. The thing jerked back as if burnt and squealed with a high whine almost beyond her hearing. Owl snapped into motion. He made a cut chest-high at the fiend. It curled down.

Alorie got her feet under her despite a twinge of pain and made a stabbing lunge. As the Unicorn sword pierced the shroud, the thing screamed in agony and burst into black flame. It burned in a flash, and as its ash drifted away, only an oily spot was left upon the paving.

"Thank you, milady," Owl huffed.

She smiled tightly. "Oh, no. Thank *you*," for Owl, frozen in the malison's grip or not, had kept himself between her and the beast. She thumped the sergeant on his shoulder and passed him into the Inner Circle.

Memories swept through her. She had to put both hands upon the sword hilt to extend it in front of her. Moonlight flooded the archer's step where she had sat and listened to children's tales from a Rover mage disguised as a story-teller. Her heart drummed as loud as nightmare hoofbeats from her dreams. Across the courtyard were the doors to the Great Hall, where her father and grandfather had been murdered in stealth in the aftermath of celebration. Not far from here she had sulked over the duties of a lord's daughter, unable to go riding in the morning. How far away that time, and that person, was from her now.

"Where to from here, my lady?" Owl waited for her.

Behind them she could hear the shuffle of boots as the rest of the troops flooded the Second Ring. She could hear a muffled curse or two, as well as the creak of armor and clash of weapon upon stone.

"The Great Hall," she said. "From there, the watchtower."

He shrugged into his leather surcoat and nodded, and kicked the doors open. Milk-white, the haunts floated out. Owl yelled and sprang back. Alorie braced herself with the sword.

"Illusion," she cried out. "It's only what you see!"

The sergeant went to a knee and shielded himself with his arm as the night sky filled with wails and howls. She felt herself begin to shake as she knew this trap had been planned for her and her alone. The enemy knew her well. She would have to enter if Sinobel was ever to be regained.

Her feet stayed rooted to the flagstone. She couldn't. It was too much to be asked. Would she see her father's

decapitated body holding his severed head aloft? Her grandfather's split torso gushing upon the tiles? She fought to
hold fast. To force a breath at a time into her aching throat.
She could not run. She would stand but a second longer.

Out of the fog and mist a massive form strode and laughed
at her, arrogant in his blue and silver uniform, his blond
hair ruffled by a ghostwind, his too small eyes crinkled as he
smiled. Aquitane!

Alorie found movement to her feet. She had dealt with
that lord already. The Corruptor was not as clever as he had
thought—this trap had been laid before she had taken her
vengeance. She walked through the doors of the Great Hall,
sword ready, bursting the illusion into spinning motes as she
passed.

Inside stank of reken spoor and litter. Tiny bones crunched
under her soles. No moonlight penetrated here, even through
the high, slanted windows. The horn guttered low, its blaze
faltering. She could see little through the velvet shadows
draping the hall's interior. Owl's hesitant boot steps clomped
behind her.

Pinch reined up the little pony and scrubbed her lathered
neck with his knuckles. "Here's where we part, my little
lady," he said lowly. "I'd put a charm upon you to take you
home, if I could. Use your head and keep to the path where
the littlefoot grows. The filthy beasts dislike it for some
reason."

The pony had her neck down, breathing gustily, for the
dwarf had ridden hard these past two days to come in the
back way of the Delvings. For a borrowed mount, she had
shown all the endurance and canny knowledge of a mountain pony, and he was proud of her. He swung down,
lightening its load considerably, and heaved his pack to the
ground. Then he tossed the stirrup back and unbuckled the
saddle, pulling it off her lathered back. She flipped her ears
back and forth in astonishment as he reached up for the
headstall, unlatched it, and slipped the bit from her teeth.

"Now go on with you," he said, and pushed her head
away even as she nuzzled him in puzzlement. He dragged
summer shrub gone brittle and dry over the tack, hiked up
his pack, and left. The pony made as if to follow him. He
stamped at her, and she rolled her eyes and instead began to
crop the last of the sweet grass.

Pinch put his chin back, eyed the massive mountains

rearing in front of him, and prepared to enter the future prophesied for him.

Velvet darkness parted in front of Alorie and her father stepped from the dias where the Sergius judgment chair reigned. He was pale, drawn, but just as she remembered him, a mild-eyed, dark-haired man, compact and slight. He wore dark green, a color he had loved, and he held his hands out to her in welcome.

"Ghost!" Alorie screamed and ran him through. To her shock and horror the sword met solid meat, twisting and ramming. Blood gushed. She screamed again as the *thing* flailed at the sword and went to its knees with a gasp, tearing the sword from her hold.

"Ungraven!" Owl snarled. He bent to wrench the sword out of its guts, but Alorie said, her voice breaking harshly, "No! Don't touch it! Only I can." She pulled the sword out, the wound sucking at it and letting it go reluctantly.

"Alorie," the thing said, crimson fountaining from lips going slack. "Daughter. Free me."

She stood in shock, unable to turn from it, knowing that this being was no illusion. It *had* once been her father. She could not heal it, and now she could not stand to kill it. Owl, with both hands, brought his sword blade down, severing the head from the shoulders, and the Ungraven died with a clacking of its sharp teeth.

Alorie lurched aside and vomited, spewing bile and her meager dinner upon the floor. Owl gripped her shoulder.

"Milady?"

"I'll—I'll be all right!" She pulled her head up and wiped her mouth on her sleeve.

The imperious ring of an iron-shod staff hitting stone belled in the hall. It echoed harshly. She knew its emanation before she slowly turned. From the dark about the chair of judgment her grandfather appeared, as stern and erect as ever.

He sneered at her. "Nathen begged for freedom, but I cling to the life I have. Last of the house, you disgrace us. You have become a Rover whore. Last of my blood, I renounce you!"

"You cannot cling to life," she said unsteadily. "You're not alive! Aquitane split you, grandfather. The Corruptor brought you back and now you mimic life in *his* will."

"Do I? Perhaps. But who will deny me life here? Not you, girl. You haven't the spine!"

"Oh, haven't I!" Alorie bit her lip and charged at him.

The quarterstaff came up, blocking her lunge. She gained the edge of the dias anyway, and circled, on equal footing with the old man. The horn sputtered in its light, bright then dim then bright again. He aimed a blow with the staff. She caught its weight with a grunt and fended it off. He struck again, trying to force her off the narrow platform.

Her arms quivered with the effort of holding him back. Her muscles cramped, sending violent pain and unresponsive numbness up to her palms. She could hear Owl fencing with something in the corner of the hall. She and her grandfather crossed arms and held a moment, staring at each other, he with an unholy light in his eyes.

The sword went out, plunging them into darkness.

Twenty-Seven

Alorie pulled back and stabbed before she could think about it. As the sword bit deep, it flared again, strong as the white light of the sun into which they dared not look. Blood fountained, staining the light red-gold, as Sergius went down. An incredulous expression passed over his pale face.

Then he smiled. "Run, last of the house of Sergius! Run with our honor . . . and our love."

And the thing that was her grandfather and that was not died.

She pulled the sword free, blinked, and turned to look for Owl. He stood, breathing heavily, over an Ungraven she did not recognize. The hall was empty.

"There will be more traps," she said unevenly. "I have something to do before we reach the watchtower. I must go alone."

Owl hesitated, then nodded. "Milady."

Alorie pivoted and ran for the staircase that dominated the back of the hall. She took its steps two at a time and headed for the wing that had housed the High Counselor in ages past.

The sword now limned a bedroom. She found a tapestry lying in a heap at the base of a wall, revealing a secret panel. Reken claws had scoured it, but not tripped it. Alorie found the lever and stood back as the panel creaked open. A black maw yawned in front of her.

If she thought about it too long, she would not enter. Her old fears hammered at her pulse. Her ears rang. But she pushed the thoughts away and entered the maze of tunnels.

Holding the sword like a torch, she stood a moment, sorting through her lessons. Then she selected the passageway to her far right. It should carry her to the underground river.

Cobwebs obscured the tunnel. They crackled stickily about her as she brushed through them. From the corner of her eye she saw furry dark bodies run to the walls of the tunnel and affix themselves. The webs told her only that nothing had passed her recently, but she'd seen spiders in the forest spin a web overnight that could catch a man on horseback—though these seemed to have caught only dust.

A clever break in the wall hid an alcove while the tunnel carried on. It would lead to a dire pit. She turned into the alcove as soon as the torch revealed it. The walls became slick with a gray-green moss. Its furled edges were tough as leather. The tunnel path dipped down, turned, and brought her to the edge of a river.

This was the lifeblood of Sinobel. She had always been told that it flowed away under the stony ground and became part of the Frostflower—since she had never swum it, she didn't know. She doubted if anyone could. Water might drill through rock and ground, but she'd have to breathe water to traverse the journey. Here it was leashed to serve the purposes of the city. Wells were drilled down in public squares. On the far side, latrines were made to utilize the runoff. In this cavern the river bubbled and frothed, its scent clean. Alorie reflectively looked up where the sword outlined the granite ceiling. Above, the occupation of Sinobel had befouled it. More traps of illusion and cunning were undoubtedly planted throughout. She knew of only one way to cleanse it.

Here, Nathen had said gently, touching the iron wheel set into the wall. *Turn this, and you will stem the river. It will back up until it floods the city from the ways we have chosen for it. If we ever have an enemy within our walls, remember this.*

There had not been time that fateful night, nor had she been able to reach it in this morning's battle. But now she had the wheel under her hands. She shoved the sword guard first into the wall as if it were a torch and grasped the wheel. It groaned and squealed with an eerie voice as she took a deep breath and budged it. It gave unwillingly. The cords on her neck stood out with effort. Her mind spun. She took another breath, dug her boot heels in, and prayed the wheel would give.

It broke loose with a spray of rust and then settled to a

smooth turning under her effort. She heard the water churn and boil. A muffled sound of chains and plates moving came to her. Then the wheel turned no more. Alorie took the sword. She had to get out, and quickly, and warn the men trying to scourge the city for her.

She found Owl above, waiting for her, fresh black blood upon his blade. "Call retreat. Get the men out of the city as quickly as possible."

He did not hesitate, but grabbed up the battered tin horn at his waist and brought it to his lips. It gave out a mellow call as beautiful as a court musician's song, and he winded it several times as they walked to the parapets of the Inner Circle.

She leaned below and saw from the movement of torches that her army responded.

Owl put the horn down to ask, "Why?"

"I've flooded Sinobel."

He winced. "Had I known that yesterday—"

She gave a rueful smile. "Yesterday we could not have gotten to the device. Today it purges Sinobel. Tomorrow we sweep out and garrison here." She drew away from the parapets. "Come on. I want to see the watchtower."

Owl led the way, being left-handed and a natural for fighting in the spiraled tower. She followed in his steps, noting the puffs of dirt as they climbed. Nothing had been this way for a long time. Her lips tightened as she remembered how long Aquitane's illusion might have been waiting for her. The guard of Frenlaw was warm in her sweaty palm.

Nothing met their search but the round room of wood and stone, occupied by a straight-backed chair at a musty smelling desk, and scattered papers, their edges nibbled and fronts molded. Archers' windows slit the horizon at regular paces. Shutters with crescent sickles carved into them were wide open. She could remember lying in this room as a child, looking out through the moon shapes. The wind whistled through, carrying with it the smell of rain. She looked out and saw the Inner Circle boiling with water. It had begun.

She lifted the sword. Its light blazed out, flooding the room with fire. She knew her beacon would be seen on the grasslands below.

After a moment, her arms aching, she lowered it and put

it in its sheath. The light was hooded immediately. She waited for her sight to adjust. Owl shifted uneasily.

"Anything in here you want me to take down for you, miss?"

"No. Thank you anyway. We're almost done here."

The sergeant sighed gratefully. Alorie felt herself smile. It had been a long day and night.

She stepped to the archers' window overlooking the wildwood. Beyond lay the Barrows. At night it was a series of ridges and little could be distinguished.

Except for the aurora borealis of magefire that played over it. It was not elven blue but a yellowish green, unhealthy in its pallor. Alorie watched it a moment, thinking of bile and feeling its burn at the back of her throat. Brock was not going to be happy with her report. She closed the shutters on the view.

Sinobel blazed like a torch over the hillocks. Pinch paused and spit on his rock-torn hands, looking across the dizzying heights at it, unable to cipher if the blaze meant victory or defeat. Gravel slid from his precarious anchor. The moon hung so close overhead, it was like having a lantern resting on his shoulder. He took his eyes from the ringed city and glanced down at the boulder bracing him.

A runic *R* was scratched in its surface. Pinch smiled. As hastily as they had made their way down this mountain once, the Rover had still stopped to mark his trail. He climbed upward, carefully searching the area hand over hand. Then he found a boulder with another runic *R* etched into it. The dwarf sat down contentedly and took out his pipe. Stone awaited him, old and evil rock, and the Corruptor. He had time for a smoke before levering the boulder away and beginning his descent into the depths of his greatest fear.

Twenty-Eight

Kithrand skidded to a stop. He balled a fist and slammed it against the tunnel wall. A pit in the floor yawned before him, eager to gulp down an unwary trespasser without night vision. The lord turned on his heel and thought of the way back. He had not given the homeless children credit for such devious minds—but here he was, wandering cold stone trails for the better part of what he was certain to be at least a day or night. His tunic hung on him, sweat-streaked and torn. His stomach was racked with spasms of hunger and his lips were parched. Underneath his boots he could feel the thrill of water booming through the rock. Wild water, from the force of it, as inaccessible to him now as the light of the sun.

He tilted his head, antennae perked to help him discern which way to go. Fresh air stirred, ever so gently. Kithrand smiled, picking a new tunnel from the air, backtracked, and found an alcove. He slipped into it.

The underlying vibration of the wild water grew louder, numbing his usually keen senses, so that he was not forewarned when the tunnel blossomed suddenly and he stumbled into the open. The illumination of several lamps blinded him momentarily, though they were partially screened. He stayed on one bent knee, his circlet tight upon the throbbing of his head. He was in danger, and he knew it without lifting his head.

He'd seen the cells and oubliettes, could still smell the lingering aroma of a charnel, and his quivering feelers picked out the echo of stifled screams. His path had brought him to the dungeon, appropriately housed in the bowels of Sinobel—and he was not alone.

The tickling of every fine hair on his body played over him. Danger prickled every sense that he had, but he dared not move. His empty stomach found bile to force up the back of this throat and he swallowed once, convulsively.

A chill descended. A caress cupped the air above him. His antenna detected the thermal moving and his body cried out with the agony of staying, head bent. If a sword blade were to fall now, he would be decapitated before he could begin to move.

Kithrand's skin shivered. He was afraid what stood over him now was far, far worse than the quick death of a blade. He sucked in what was perhaps his last breath. Slowly he began to turn and lift his head upon his shoulders as a shroud, a nimbus of light and dark, lowered over him.

Rowan reined Banner to a halt. Men poured out of the broken gates of Sinobel, their faces pale with terror. He caught a soldier by the scruff of his neck. "What is it?"

"Haunted. Worse than the reken. We've seen the dead walk—" The man gasped. He twisted in Rowan's grip. "They blew retreat. We've lost the city."

"But why? Who blew retreat?"

"Who knows? But I'll not stand a moment longer in that hellhole!" The soldier ducked, his shirt tore out of Rowan's hand, and the man ran, joining the wave of soldiers. Banner shied away from their torches. He heard a cry of "Water! The upper rings are flooding! Run for it!"

He had no choice but to ride or be caught in the stampede. Men screamed as they trampled one another in their hurry to get out of the city. Torches were dropped and abandoned along with packs and weapons. One grizzled veteran reached up and tried to drag Rowan from horseback. The Rover clubbed him with the hilt of his sword. The man fell, his scalp split, and crawled away from Banner's vengeful hooves.

Alorie was in there somewhere. He brought his gelding to safety and stood in the stirrups, overlooking the gates. There was no way he could breast the tide of fleeing men. All he could do was sit and wait, and then see if the flooding could be crossed. He shut his jaws tightly, grimly, and wondered what could have happened. Had she been killed? What had they met in a city that was supposed to have been conquered?

It was a rout. Even if the waters receded, he'd have to whip these men to get them to follow him back in. He had his own troop of men, but not enough. If they could not hold Sinobel, how in god's name could they hope to march on the Delvings?

The panic had to be stopped and stopped now. It might mean his head, but he knew of only one man who could do it.

Brock sat in his pavilion, his dark face shadowed by the night. His fire had burned down to flowing coals. Rowan brought his horse to a standstill and did not dismount.

"They're fleeing," he said flatly. "They've seen ghosts and who knows what else up there. You've got to stop them."

"I do not listen to traitors."

"I'm not a traitor."

"Or deserters," the mage said listlessly. He turned the cane in his hands.

"Damn it all, Brock, Alorie's up there!"

The mage stood heavily. He pointed as he said, "Yes, I know."

Rowan shifted in the saddle and looked back. The watch-tower suddenly flickered with light. He frowned. "What is it—"

"The sword."

The tower blazed for a moment, then went out.

"Is she—" The Rover paused. "If the sword is that powerful . . ." Confused, he pivoted Banner. "What's going on up there? Who flooded the city?"

"Perhaps she did. If I know the Sergius turn of mind, it would be difficult for an enemy to find the mechanism. She, on the other hand, would have been shown it long ago."

"Why in god's name would she flood Sinobel?"

"The dark lieutenant has been waiting for us to attack. There are things in there that steel cannot kill." A keenness returned to Brock's vision. "You should know that."

Rowan smoothed the reins wrapped about his hand as he thought. "And she had retreat blown to clear the walls?"

Brock limped forward to where moonlight could reveal his face. "I think so."

"Your army doesn't know that—they're running. By dawn you won't have an army left."

"I no longer need an army."

Brock's response rocked Rowan back in the saddle. "She does! How the hell do you expect her to get out of there alive?" He sat for a moment, his ears filled with the noise of the fleeing army: screams and yells, the brawling for horses and equipment.

"She has the sword and the prophecy."

"Damn the prophecy," Rowan began when out of the darkness a snow-haired man charged up, his stallion blowing foam.

"We're losing the men!"

Brock shrugged at Rathincourt and turned away as if the two of them did not exist. The warlord shook a mailed fist and called out, "No king would let this happen!"

The mage froze in his tracks. He veered around. "There are battles and there are battles."

Rowan said, "You're not man enough to stop them. They followed Alorie here, not you."

Brock's lip curled. A sharp whistle split the air, and the nervous chestnut stallion that was the mage's destrier came trotting from the grass to the pavilion's edge. Brock took up the reins and mounted him. He rode toward Sinobel without a word to them.

Rathincourt pulled his sword. The two who had been fighting in the rear of the army rather than the vanguard looked at each other. Rowan tightened his hold within the guard of his sword.

"It had to be done."

The warlord nodded. "I know. I've clubbed more deserters today than enemy." He reined in beside the woodsman and they followed.

Brock faced a tide of men at the picket lines. Their orange torches limned his face, always shadowed, now barely visible in the night except for the touch of moonlight upon it. His shouted words had no effect on the tide of men bearing him farther and farther away from the gates, his chestnut showing his teeth and snapping, unable to keep the men at a distance.

"I am the king!"

One of the soldiers hurled himself at the chestnut's shoulder. His lips curled in a feral sneer. "Then you try fighting the bastards with a rusty hoe!"

Lord Rathincourt kneed his mount into the fray, disregarding the mob. Men moved hastily lest they be trampled. Rowan rode at his back.

"Hold!" Brock shouted. The multitude of soldiers slowed, fixed on the man they had trapped in their midst. His destrier could not stand firm, carried by the press of soldiers about him, and threw his head up with a whinny of panic. Brock curbed the bit violently and stood in his leathers. "I forbid it!" His brown fingers sketched a sign in the air. Rathincourt let out a curse as the magic failed. He heeled his roan stallion, charging the king.

"Damn your witchery!" the farmer/fighter snarled and swung his hoe amid catcalls and whistles of scorn.

The blow was a wide, swinging one that Brock, inundated in the backwash of power that had failed him, could see but not react to. It was Rathincourt, leaping off his roan at Brock's shoulders to bring him down before the blow struck who caught it.

There was a sickening thunk. With an "oof!" the white-haired lord went limp and bounced to the ground between the horses' bodies. A pool of crimson stained the crushed grasses beneath his head. The farmer fell back immediately and went to his knees. As Rowan cleared a pathway with curses and blows, the deserters fell quiet. A circle opened about the fallen warlord's body and his attacker. He looked up at Brock with a stricken expression.

"I meant that for you—I never meant to hurt his lordship!"

The mage pointed downward. "Seize that man!"

In the silence Rowan sprang from his saddle. He kneeled at Rathincourt's side, saying, "Give me a light!"

A torch brushed so near his forehead as to sear him with heat, but it gave off a circle of illumination that showed the warlord still breathed. "He's alive!" Rowan called. "You men—you and you—get a litter. And you, run for a healer—they're sleeping in the green tents to the rear. And as for you"—he looked the farmer in the eye—"We've won Sinobel. Our lady is up there flooding the city to make it safe for you to garrison there."

They took up his words, repeating them throughout the crowd. "Our lady . . . our lady . . . safe . . ."

"I'm no braver than you," Rowan added. "But I stood a little longer, and that is all the difference between any of us! Stand tonight until dawn and I promise you, we'll find victory instead of defeat!"

His voice gone strident, Brock ordered again, "Seize that man!"

No one moved to obey him. Rowan pinched together the scalp wound's edge, trying to stem the flow of blood. He looked at the attacker. "If you've not addled his brains,"

Rowan said, "he'll commend you in the morning for a blow well struck. Next time, hit the enemy!"

The farmer stumbled to his feet. "Yessir. I will." With a trembling hand he picked up his hoe.

Rowan could not stand, but he looked up and pitched his voice to carry. "As for the rest of you, we've got a walled city to garrison in. The Unicorn sword carried by our lady has purged it for you like a spring tonic—unless, of course, you wish to sleep on these muddy flats."

In the mumbled hush a voice so young it broke called out, "We'll go if you're in front of us!"

Brock's horse overshadowed Rowan. He looked up. The mage king sat there, his lips set in a thin line.

"Lead them in," the ranger said, "and they're yours again."

The king put his thin shoulders back. "I'll take nothing from you. Nothing!" He whipped his horse, and with a startled noise it bolted away from them.

Rathincourt stirred under Rowan's hand as the litter bearers arrived. A pale-faced, tired healer staggered in their wake, but the wiry man came alert as Rowan pressed his hand into place over the scalp wound.

He straightened as they bore Rathincourt off. The need to find Alorie pressed at him, but first he had to bring order to the army and wait for the waters to recede. He missed Pinch and Kithrand and wondered, as he looked to the smudged horizon, where his friends were and how they fared.

The army met Alorie and Owl at dawn just inside the shattered gates. The waters had flooded everywhere, carrying away all but the rock and wooden buildings and walls of the ringed city. On the muddied plains Rowan had set the men to building new pyres, scourging the grasslands of the death and scavenged bodies swept out, or there would be disease and carrion eaters everywhere. There was no sign of Brock, who had taken to his tent and refused to come out. As the smoke filled the new sky, Rowan mounted his horse to see what the flood had wrought, and found Alorie, wan and besmirched but safe, walking down the winding cobbled street.

She paused as she tucked back a long dark strand of hair. No fire showed from the sword sheathed and muted at her side. Owl stood ready to brace her if she faltered, but she put out her pointed chin and looked at the army.

"If any one of you tracks mud on these clean streets," she called out, "I'll have you hung! Clean your boots before you enter my city!"

The Delvings reeked of sweat and fire and blood. Pinch clamped his teeth as the foul scent filled his nostrils. He kept his head down as he crawled through the burrow on his hands and knees, sweat pouring off his knotted brow, his heart pounding like a hammer on an anvil in his chest. It's not dark, I can see, he told himself, yet his ears roared with his pulse. He would not fear, he told himself. But they were empty words inside his tormented mind. The stone of the Delvings was old, old as dwarfdom could be. It had been carved out by sacrifice and death in bygone days, and he could hear its silent cry for more. Pinch bit his lip until he drew blood, not red blood like human blood, but dark as stone where sunlight never falls. He might be called a shortman, but he was dwarf and thereby lay all the difference and all his pride.

That pride took a beating now. The rock pressed in all about him—he could feel it leaning on his back and closing in all about him. He hugged the tunnel floor and his pace became a crawl. Never mind that when he and Rowan and the others had fled here before, all could walk, though hunched over. The mountain and caves that held the Delvings stood on him now with all its weight and the dwarf groaned beneath it.

He broke. With a muffled cry he got to his feet and scuttled through the tunnel in blind panic, not stopping until he slammed into an overhang in the passage and the sting of gravel cracking open his forehead brought him to a stunned, reeling halt.

Pinch put his hands to his forehead as he sniveled with the pain. The real injury as opposed to the imaginary one brought clarity to his whirling thoughts. He stood and carefully patted out the knob on his brow, and winced as his fingers came away sticky from where the skin had split.

"Well, Pinchweed," he told himself. "You've done it now. That could have been your pipe as well as your noggin and then where would ye be!"

He ducked under the outcropping and found the mouth of the tunnel breaking into open cavern. When he hunkered down this time, it was to wedge his stocky body into a crevice where he might see and be unseen by the enemy who had overwhelmed the Delvings.

The stamp and shuffle of boots reached him before the chain gang rounded the corner and he could see them. Pinch's lip curled in hatred as Aquitane's blue and silver renegades goaded a shackled line of his kinsmen, women, and children, ore buckets balanced upon their bloodied heads. A whip cracked. A girl went down, her callused dwarfish feet black with blisters and welts. Her ore bucket clattered loudly as it rolled to the side. She crawled frantically to keep up the march, unable to get back on her feet. The dwarf boy chained behind her, his beard still a fuzzy smear upon his chin, hauled her up by the shackles by sheer will as the cords stood out in his neck and his arms. With a cry the girl settled back into the pace of the forced march as the whip cracked again.

His mission could wait, Pinch told himself, for a small detour. He let the chain gang pass him. Then, with a cautious distance between them, he left his crevice to follow it. They passed a Y-intersection as Pinch eased his axe out of his belt and began to catch up with the last soldier pacing the chain gang.

A heavy hand fell on his shoulder from behind, crimping his neck muscles. "Just where do you think you're going, bucko?"

Twenty-Nine

"It's his victory, too," Alorie said. "Why are you shutting him away?"

Rowan rubbed his face. He'd found clean water to wash before sitting at the breakfast table, but it was barely enough. There was a ring of grime about his wrist. He moved stiffly and she wondered if his side still hurt him after all these weeks. She found herself thinking that if she had been able to lie with him, run her fingers over the scarring, she would know. Other feelings surfaced, but she was too exhausted to blush or do more than lean on the table herself as one of the cooks filled a trencher for her. Rowan took up a goblet of the pungent watered wine and took a drink before answering, "It's not his victory. That simple. He wasn't there when you needed him most."

The bitter edge of his words told her Rowan wanted to argue. He needed to, but she did not take the bait. Instead she turned her attention to the meal before her, knowing that once she'd drunk her glass of wine, she would sleep until mid-afternoon.

Rowan added before stabbing at a strip of meat, "And I haven't shut him away. He won't come out. He hasn't spoken to anyone since Rathincourt went down."

"How is my lord?"

"We've got him upstairs—your father's room, I think."

"Then I'll be there, too." She looked at him over a slice of freshly baked bread. "All right?"

"Good enough. Owl's nursing him now, but he'll need to be spelled. Flask has taken half the troops with him to the Delvings. We've decided to soften them up before attacking with our main force."

That she hadn't heard. "The Delvings is under siege now?"

"By midday, day after tomorrow." Rowan watched her finish her bite before asking, "What happened to Kithrand?"

Alorie winced. She felt her left eye brim suddenly with tears and put her sleeve up to it quickly. "Ah, gods," she said, and swallowed hard. "I'm too tired for this."

Rowan put out his hand across the rough-hewn table, but she wouldn't take it.

"I found a nest of malisons. The troop from Charlbet swept in to save me, but Kit had no idea what was on my heels. I'd been unhorsed—"

"Riding in where you had no business to be."

"—and Torrey picked me up. I thought Kithrand knew what we were facing . . . he saw them and broke. Just plain broke, left us to their mercy. Torrey got us out of there by sheer nerve. As for Kithrand—he ran right into their nest. I don't see how he could have made it out."

"And even if he did, I doubt he could face us." Rowan heaped a forkful and chewed it thoughtfully.

Alorie dabbed at her face again. "I wouldn't care," she said, "if he were all right."

"Ummm." Rowan asked, "Are you sure you want to sit with Rathincourt? His sister's camped half a day back. I had hoped you and I—"

Alorie got up abruptly. "Don't hope that. You can't ever think like that again." She shoved the bench away and reached down for her goblet. "I was meant for the king. I will be his."

"You can't believe Brock."

"I believe that he believes. I can't *not* believe. It's not just you and me anymore. Don't hope for me, Rowan. Please."

"Then, this is the game of *rool*."

"Yes," she whispered. "And I've sacrificed the queen." She turned around so fiercely the wine from her goblet splashed out. She walked toward Brock's pavilion.

Rowan watched her go. His breakfast went cold and one of the dogs pushed his muzzle up to the table and ate it without the forester even noticing.

The heavy hand on his shoulder dragged him back into the dark fastness of a tunnel mouth and shoved him to the ground. Pinch blinked, getting back his vision, but he hardly recognized the ragged dwarf leaning over him.

Then he sputtered, "Bryant!"

"Aye. You're looking well, Master Pinch."

Pinch could not return the greeting. Indeed, the dwarf king of the Delvings looked like death warmed over. A deep brand burned into his once handsome cheek. It was festering with ugly red and purpled edges. A collar dug into his neck, rubbing sores there the size of Pinch's fist. His mail, the pride of dwarf kings the decades down, had been stripped off, and he had only a tattered shirt flapping about his ribs and knee-length trousers knotted about his waist. The dwarf stood up and drew his knife.

"Let me get that off you."

Bryant's hand flashed up and caught him by the wrist. "I'll take it off when my people are free." The king's sudden strength left him as he began to cough and doubled over. Pinch caught him and they both sank to the dirt and gravel bed of the tunnel.

"I've water and journey rations. Not much, but more than you've seen, by the looks of you."

Bryant took the water bag with grateful hands. He choked his cough back. The journey rations Pinch could spare he split on a clean handkerchief spread on the ground. Pinch watched him with a worried eye.

"Why did ye stop me back there?"

"You couldn't have taken out all the guards. All you'd have done is given away our position. They were decoys, anyway."

"The dark lieutenant knows you're loose?"

"Knows?" Bryant gave a harsh, barking laugh. "He set me free. But first he tortured, then branded me."

Pinch looked at the last honey cake, then pushed it over by Bryant. "Why?"

"Because he's very shrewd." Bryant picked up the honey cake, broke it into two solemnly, and laid the half in front of Pinch. "Because he couldn't gather up all of us, no matter how he tried, and try he did. So he set me free. That way the forges are kept hot. Our people keep working. They've not given up and they're no longer sabotaging the armory. There's the barest glint of hope, you see, that I'll be able to come back and drive them out."

Pinch took up his piece of cake, broke it into two again, and laid the last piece in front of the defeated king. "The man's a demon."

"No truer words ever spoken." Bryant eyed his last bite as if he'd divide it again, but took it and ate it instead. "I haven't a chance, but they work better with those embers of hope still glowing. He keeps the forges going, and he has his entertainment trying to ferret me out."

"How did this happen to you?"

The king sat back against the rock, a faraway look in his eye. He stroked the water bag as if it contained wine. "I carried a secret, and they found it out and used it like a key for a lock."

Pinch, knowing something of what had happened, looked away shamefaced. "They trapped you using Alorie."

"Yes. I was too blind to wonder about it all." Bryant sighed and took another swig of water. He said then, "Have you anything for fever?"

"As a matter of fact . . ." Pinch rummaged through his pack and came up with a packet. "Mary Rose always swore by it."

"And how is my dear cousin?" Then it was Bryant's turn to feel shame. "Ah, no—forgive me, I'd forgotten. By the hammer, I even heard the reken march through—"

"It wasn't in the raids, no. When Aquitane attacked and carried off the sword . . ." Pinch told him what had happened.

Bryant sat very still. Then he shook his head. "Half truths. All I've gotten for months, from anyone, has been half the truth."

"It wasn't milady's fault!"

"No. I'll wager her couriers were waylaid and the Corruptor's messages substituted. If I came out once in a while instead of hiding here in the rock, maybe I would have known . . ."

Pinch closed his callused fist about Bryant's, crushing the packet of herbs. "I've heard enough," he said roughly. "If I had told Mary Rose to wear mail, she'd still be dead! The villain sliced her in the throat. Mayhaps will not stand us in good stead. So long as the embers of the Delvings keep burning, we've a chance of setting a backfire that will burn our enemy proper."

"So they sent you here? Whose idea was it, Rathincourt's?"

"No. I came on my own."

Bryant shook half the packet out into his trembling hand, put it to his lips, and downed it, followed by another swig of water. He then passed the supplies to Pinch. "Tell me," he said, "the whole truth of what is happenng."

When he stirred finally, he did so with pain in his eyes. "Do ye believe him, Pinch?"

"It doesn't matter if I believe in him. He believes in himself, and you can hardly deny that the Corruptor walks free enough."

"And it's said Deathwalker is far worse. After what I've seen of the other . . ." Bryant's low voice trailed off.

"One step at a time," Pinch said. "That's what I've come to do. One step at a time. Like milady is trying to do. We'll get the Corruptor, then worry about what comes after. The libraries at Charlbet are rubble, but the elves are not the only folk who keep histories."

"You want to find the First Warrens."

"Yes."

The king pushed up to his feet. Already his flushed face looked better and his eyes clearer, but the herbs could not purge the sorrow in their depths. "Old tales," he said.

"But they must be here."

"Cave-ins and worse."

"They're here somewhere!"

And Bryant, who knew something of Pinch's innermost fear, answered, "They're deep, if they're anywhere, Pinch. Deep and cunning in the old stone. Lost to us, but—there might be a way."

"I'll take it."

"Ye haven't heard it yet. The main warrens can't be used, but if they could be reached, it would be through the Pit. The Pit travels from the top of this old mountain to the roots of the earth."

"It's bottomless," Pinch whispered hoarsely.

"It's the only way."

Monsters crawled out of that Pit—primitive beasts that did not care he'd come to find the means to defeat the enemy. Even worse than his fear of being closed in under the stone was his fear of falling. And as the sweat beaded up on his forehead, the dwarf knew all his nightmares of the prophecy had come to life.

Kithrand hunched over, his guts clenched, and thought to himself that he had already gone through the worst. Nothing could be worse than the shame he had brought to himself and his ancestors through his cowardice. He had abandoned lady Alorie publicly, in front of witnesses, though all in the street who had seen him might be dead now. The prophecy had done its damage. It could no longer haunt him. He had carried its forewarning of cravenness and betrayal all these years, and now that it had happened, he almost felt relieved.

But what he thought and what he felt were two different things. His body shook in fear and his bladder spent what little water it carried. He was a stinking heap of shame as he looked up to see the malison lowering itself over him.

Rock boomed. The dungeon cavern shivered and the malison paused. They both listened, it seemed, to the pounding of an angry tide within Sinobel's crest. Kithrand grit his teeth.

"Get it over with!"

The souleater rippled inside its cloud. *In time, noble one,* it answered. A leathern tentacle emerged, wrapped itself about his wrist and drew him to his feet. *Come.*

Kithrand had no choice, for his feet obeyed the malison far sooner than they obeyed him. Like a blind elder dependent upon his guide, he trailed the malison to where a cell door lay open. The souleater whipped him inside, where he fell like a stringless, broken puppet and lay on straw cleaner than himself as the iron door clanged shut. The malison hovered outside a moment, and Kithrand had the impression the door was no barrier to it. Then the souleater left, drifting out of sight in the dungeon.

"Lay still," a husky voice counseled him. "Our energy excites it. If it gets too excited, it'll attack."

Kithrand propped himself up. The paralysis of fear slowly drained from him. He felt wrung out, as empty of sap and life as a brown autumn leaf. "Who?" he got out finally, his voice a croak.

"Nelbar, milord . . . Torrey's cousin."

Kirthrand put his head against the bars, felt the rust crackle and bite into his skin. "What are you doing here?"

"It likes us better than homeless children. So it feeds on them and . . . experiments with us." Nelbar's voice was young and reedy. Kithrand could picture him if he closed his eyes: stockier than most elves, eyes a dark amber, hair the rich color of tree bark. He wore amber and citrine in his circlet—if he still had a circlet. And he wondered most of all if Nelbar knew of his cowardice.

It seemed there was more of his shame yet to come.

Kit lifted his chin. Across the cell, water trickled damply down the cave wall. He crawled in its direction to lick the stone. The water tasted fresh and clean. He could not wash, but he could slake his thirst somewhat. When he crawled back to sprawl on the dusty hay of the cell, Nelbar said, "You needn't have much fear it'll use you."

"Why?"

"It seems to be searching for something. Bravery, I think," the unseen elf answered bitterly.

Kithrand curled in upon himself as the air brought no further words to him. For lack of anything else to do, he slept.

He woke to the sound of a cell door being opened, but not his. He heard the scrape of heels upon the floor and the crunch of straw. Going to the bars, he could see the malison's shuddering cloud as it wrestled with his kindred. Thinking of what Nelbar had said, he called out, "Don't fight him, Nelbar! Cower if you must."

His words were drowned out by the sound of the elf being dragged from his cell. The malison gripped his mane of hair and, though Nelbar's face had gone blue-gray with fear, the captive went on his own two feet, his expression defiant. The malison threw Nelbar to the flooring, and Kithrand saw the sparks of magic flash. Nelbar lay unmoving. The stink of its soulbinding lay on the air.

Then the souleater came for him. *It is time*, it said, *for me to taste you.*

Thirty

"I'll come with you," Kithrand said, forcing serenity into his voice. "There's no need to drag me."

The malison shuddered slightly as it threw open the cell door and stood aside. The elf lord gathered himself, for its odor filled his nostrils and the senses of his antennae. It tensed as he drew near it. Beyond, on the dungeon floor, Kithrand saw that Nelbar saw and heard, but could not respond.

He would run, the lord told himself—but not now, not leaving Nelbar behind. He felt numbed to the horror that floated beside him. Was this bravery? He did not think so. He was too spent to run, that was all.

A caress touched him, parting his hair. He knew that bone-crackling sensation of being invaded as the souleater said, *Do you not fear me?* Its inner voice was like the wind across a hollow reed.

"I fear you more than death itself," Kithrand answered. "I'm just too tired." He sat cross-legged next to Nelbar.

The malison made a move. Auras shimmered around it, and suddenly Nelbar sat up. He shook himself as if shedding water and put his chin out. "I'll die before you break me."

That is most probable. In which case, you will become an Ungraven when I take your body. That is not what I desire.

Kithrand's ears perked. "The Corruptor makes Ungraven," he countered.

But how does he do that? Have you ever asked yourself?

The elf lord sat next to his kindred from whom he had been sundered by his act of cowardice and betrayal. Terror pierced his numbness. He began to tremble again.

Nelbar talked, as if that could ease their fear. "The lady made it out," he said. "And she has need of me!" Nelbar burst to his feet. He bolted toward an exit as quick and nimble as any elf could be.

The malison was quicker.

It met the fleeing elf where the walls narrowed. It surrounded Nelbar with the edge of its fog. The stocky elf went down with a strangled cry and lay convulsed on the floor, heels beating the stone.

Why, said the malison rhetorically, *should my partner*—Kithrand had a confused mental picture of a raw egg being split into two—*have all the glory of having power? He has forgotten my taste.* Again, what Kithrand felt and heard conflicted. Taste was a pattern. A name? He struggled with confusion, watched Nelbar laid low, and knew it was his chance to run, but he couldn't as he watched with horrified fascination the souleater lower itself over, around, *into*—by all the gods!—Nelbar.

Then there was nothing in the dungeon but Nelbar and Kithrand.

Kit got up slowly. His feelers tested the air. There was a metallic aftertaste, much as when one sucked on a small cut or sore. Nelbar's heels continued to beat a staccato on the floor. The elf lord approached his possessed kinsman cautiously.

Nelbar foamed at the mouth. He spat at Kithrand, who jumped back, and as Kit recoiled, the stocky elf stumbled to his feet. With a choked curse he began to batter himself at the rock walls surrounding them. He flung himself until his blue-green blood began to run, slowly at first and then copiously, his chest panting and heaving, the air filled with obscenities that tainted the lilting elfin tongue as Kithrand had known and cherished it.

Then the abomination went to its knees and began to vomit. It spewed up bile and blood until it could vomit no more.

Kithrand moaned, "Stop it. Stop it. You're killing him!" He hugged himself helplessly.

A mist spurted out of Nelbar, and as the elf keeled over into its own discharge, the malison became solid again. It lashed out at Nelbar. Kithrand heard his kinsman let out a sob of breath, a death rattle, and perish.

The malison turned toward Kithrand. *Perhaps,* it said, *it will be better tasting with you.*

Kithrand backed up a step and held up his hand. "I have seen what you do, and heard what you wish to do. I think I know what is it you must do to succeed. Let's talk." He clenched his jaw tightly to keep it from chattering as the malison paused. There were secrets here to be learned, though he doubted he would live long enough to pass them on.

Alorie found her father's bedroom and stood just inside it a moment. The locking bar had been shattered when Aquitane's men rammed it years ago. but the great carven door, dented and imprinted, remained. New drop bars inside and out had been put up. Rathincourt lay quietly on the cot made up for him, his head swaddled like a newborn babe's. A patch had spread beneath the wrappings, but as she bent over him to check it, she could see the bleeding had stopped.

"You old warhorse," she murmured, so as not to awaken him. "If you get yourself killed by a plowboy, I'll never forgive you." She brushed her fingers across his face. The skin was firm and warm, but not hot.

The immense bedstead that had been her father's and mother's beckoned. Someone had pulled aside the dusty blankets on top, leaving cleaner, if musty-smelling, covers for her. She sat down wearily and unbuckled the sword. The cup of wine at breakfast had fired her veins and now lulled them. She was almost too weary to think.

Brock had not responded to her report of magefire across the Barrowlands. It was almost as if he already knew what she had seen. It was not until she turned to leave that he had asked, "Are you going with Rowan?"

"No," she'd answered.

The mage had sighed, through she could not tell if it carried relief or exhaustion. He did not speak another word as she left.

Alorie held the scabbard in her hands now. The sword held no life as it had. She pulled it. The dark splinter it carried had grown, lengthened, widened, until it looked like a fissure within. She remembered its sudden failure in her hands that was but a forecast of the things to come. Their only true hope against the Corruptor was itself being Corrupted.

But there was much of the sword still pure. It had to be enough. She had to hold to that firmly and never waver. She could not afford to be afraid.

If only, she thought, this really was a game of *rool* and I was just a game piece of polished wood.

She sheathed the Unicorn horn and laid it down on the bed beside her. Before she fell asleep, she put her hands over her head and let her fingers trace the elaborate wooden carvings of the wardrobe headboard. She lapsed into dreams, remembering the night she'd opened the headboard into the secret passage beyond, fleeing Sinobel's massacre and meeting Rowan in the dawn. With that dawn meeting her dream changed as she greeted her lover, and in her sleep, tears spilled down her face.

The Corruptor sat on the dwarfish throne of the Delvings. A stone carving of a winged sun pressed into his spine, and his hands rested in grooves worn by shorter, more muscular arms than his. The doors to the hall were shut, massive wooden doors shielded with plates of bronze. The long table before him stayed empty. He sat alone. Hammersmith had not returned to him from the courts of the warlord Rathincourt at Sobor. He wondered if the dwarf had been found out—or if he played at waiting until the victory was in hand before putting himself into jeopardy.

His spies reported that rebel activity within the Delvings had slowed, and he wondered what Bryant was up to. Perhaps he would summon Ayah, and the malison would hunt for him. The malison possessed rock with more difficulty than flesh, but once set upon a search, little could escape it. He shivered and brought his dark wool cloak closer about his shoulders. Ayah was ambitious, even jealous of the egg-brother that possessed *him*. No, he would not call for the malison just yet. Besides, there were indications Ayah was off on designs of its own.

A searching touch reached him and before the Corruptor could get his shields up, that touch gripped him by the throat. He hunched and groveled on the seat of the stone throne. "Sire!" he gasped.

Had you forgotten me?

"Never, Deathwalker. Your time is close. Very, very close. I listen for the summonings to the Barrows even now." The Corruptor shuddered. The Iron Liege's power was strong, far greater than he anticipated. The knowledge filled him with both joy and dread.

The touch left him. *I await you.*

The Corruptor straightened in the abrupt silence. He put

his scarred hand to his throat and rubbed it pensively, though no mark had been left on it.

Rowan whistled the hawk down to him out of the afternoon sky. It came, jesses trailing, its talons out to grip the padded glove he wore. He stroked it and spoke an encouraging word before taking the hood Deanmuth handed him and slipping it over the raptor's head.

Deanmuth took the scroll eagerly. He grinned. "They're in position, Flask reports, and by the time we reach this, they'll be hammering at the Delving's stone face."

"Good." Rowan handed the hawk to Owl, who walked away with it. He took his glove off. "The rest of the foot soldiers should be in place by tomorrow morning. The horse troop will join them by midday tomorrow."

"Rathincourt?"

The forester smiled, deepening the cleft in his chin. "Try keeping the old man down. But you watch him, Colonel. This battle promises to be a long and hard one—without much chance of success. We need him for the next campaign. The Corruptor will be damn near impossible to dig out of the forges—but by the same token, we'll have him and most of his forces bottled up where they can't do us much harm. I don't intend to let him out until the fall rains force us to break siege." Rowan's expression became grim. "This year's bounty will carry us through until next spring. Then, *then*, is when I worry. We'll have all winter to get an armory going. If we're successful, we stand a chance. If not—"

Deanmuth broke stride next to him, and caught himself as he cleared his throat and said, "If not, it will be a long war."

"Pray," Rowan said, "that our exiled Mutts at Stonedeep have what it takes to get the new forge going."

The two men walked shoulder to shoulder, each deep in his own thoughts.

It took a day-and-a-half to creep from the mining tunnels to the point where Bryant thought they could safely approach the pit. They shared the meager remains of his rations. Pinch found water, and they were grateful for its brackish flavor, saving the contents of his skin for future needs. The dwarf king fought off his fever. Pinch scraped a poultice of moss off a cavern wall to draw the heat and infection out of his brand, and it began to heal. The scar would never go away, the armsman reflected as he peeled off his poultice. If they all lived beyond these apocryphal days, Bryant would no longer be a dwarf as handsome as any man.

They stole a sturdy length of rope in the first excitement of the siege, and then another, and then a third. Bryant showed Pinch how to braid the ends into one another so their junctures were sturdier than the rest of their span. Coiled up, the rope was nearly as large and heavy as Pinch. They studied it on the cave floor as if it had a life of its own.

"It needs to be long," Bryant said, "to reach far enough down into the Pit to find the lower tunnels."

"If any intersect that blasted hole."

"They have to. The first forges took fire from the Pit before we moved them. There are some abandoned runs down there. I'll wager the First Warrens are there, if anywhere. You'll have to swing in, anchor the rope, and go down again." The deposed king smiled kindly. "At least ye won't have to take torches with you like a tallman!"

"No," Pinch agreed, an odd gleam to his silver eyes. "That I won't." He hooked his thumbs into his belt. "When do ye think I should drop?"

"We'll nap first. I'll need my strength to lower ye."

The armsman looked up in wonder. The edge of the Pit was open, and it was unsafe to Bryant to expose himself to the Corruptor's guards. The tallest, once most handsome of all the dwarves, shrugged. "Who else?" he said. "I have to be able to throw the rope down to ye when ye signal. Or hold the anchor if need be."

"In that case," Pinch answered. "Care to share a pipe with me?"

"If I have to split your skull again, you're not getting out of bed!"

Rathincourt lay down under Alorie's none-too-gentle prodding, his fair skin flushing. "I'll not lie here and let you tend me one day longer."

"Fair enough. Lady Marne has taken up residence down the hall. When she's settled in, your litter will be moved down to her apartments. Then she can threaten to pound some sense into that thick noggin of yours." Alorie crossed her arms and mock-glared at her general.

Rathincourt groaned and closed his eyes. "I cannot stand to see the two of you frowning at me like that."

"I'm the only one here, milord—and if you're seeing double, it's your own damned fault."

"Hist," the general said, his ice-blue eyes shut tight. "Have a care with your language, woman."

There was a rap at the door. Alorie moved past the litter to admit two brawny aides with Lady Marne at their rear. Rathincourt's sister gave a twisted smile.

"Is he being his usual patient self?"

"Of course." Alorie waited until the aides passed with the litter in hand, and leaned down to brush a kiss across Rathincourt's furrowed brow. "At least," she whispered saucily, "now you won't have to part your hair."

Rathincourt groaned and put a hand to his swaddled head as the litter swayed back into motion.

Lady Marne hesitated long enough to give Alorie a quick handclasp, her cool fingers pressing tightly. "Thank you," she said.

"I love him, too," she answered. From the doorway she watched the small party until they disappeared into the second wing. She turned with a sweep of her long velvet riding skirt across the planks. The room was hers again, blue with shadow although the sun was bright outside. There were no windows to this room, only one way in and out—apparently. The House of Sergius had been a cautious lot, to no avail.

"I am the last Sergius," she said softly aloud. "And I'm home."

A pulsing glow from the Unicorn sword answered her. Its fire burned through its sheathing, the scabbard unable to contain it.

Alorie froze. "Ah, no," she said, and her heartbeat answered with its own drumming. "Not now!" She grabbed it up and ran from the room to the watchtower.

Thirty-One

Pinch knotted the rope sling tightly about him. He looked up. The immense cavern roof arched over him, swords and spears of rock crystal shimmering, their gem-light brightness piercing his vision. A stone staircase led from the caverns above. They were in the open now, and vulnerable. They had stolen a massive bow with a quiver of arrows. It lay at the king's feet as Bryant braced himself.

"I'm ready," he said.

Pinch was not. His heart resided somewhere in his throat instead of in his chest. As he stood on the yawning lip of the immense Pit, he could not help but think of his pipe falling from his pocket and dropping into the bottomless sink. The two dwarves looked into each other's eyes. A light flickered in the dark brown depths of the king's.

"Do your best," he said. "It's all anyone can ask."

Pinch gave an abrupt nod, flexed his knees, and shoved away from the Pit's edge. For a brief, dizzying moment he dropped like a rock.

Brock sat at his pavilion's edge, overlooking the newly barren field where an army had camped. It was his army, given to him to restore Bethalia, but not an army that could fight the upcoming battle for him. The Raltarian Guard had turned against him once more. He stayed in quiet thought as he had these past few days, trying to gather up the memories long denied him, memories necessary to survive—perhaps even win—the coming war. Clouds eddied across the sky, paling the sun's harsh gleam on a late summer day. He looked up, then saw a glint, a mirror flash far brighter that caught his eye.

The mage king got to his feet. It came again, unmistakably, from the east—a crescent-shaped flash that all but

blinded him. He could not see that it came from the watchtower on Sinobel's crest.

*When moon overshadows paling sun, evil everlasting shall
be undone . . .*

He must strike now, ready or not.

Brock whistled for his stallion. His aide, Rowan's guard,
Tien, had been nodding at his post. The Rover snapped to
his feet now.

The mage king swung onto his destrier and leaned down
as the forester came to him, brown eyes unreadable in his
yellow face as he looked at Brock.

"Guardsman," Brock said, "you've failed me once. Fail
me now and all hope is lost. Do you understand?"

"I'm listening."

"Do more than listen! Bring me the Lady Alorie. Tell her
the time has come, and tell her to bring the sword with
her." His nervous chestnut danced away, and Brock kneed
him to bring him back in line. "I'll wait for her as long as I
can."

Tien hesitated.

Fury twisted Brock's face. "Damn your soul, then. Damn
all of you! I'll stand alone at the Barrows!" He whipped his
stallion into a leaping run away from the Rover.

Tien fingered the hilt of his longknife, then looked up to
Sinobel. What would it hurt, he thought, to pass the message along?

Rowan mounted the stairs in the Great Hall as Deanmuth
said, "His lordship will be pleased with Flask."

"True enough, but you're his fair-haired boy."

The adjunct flushed, then said, "I couldn't love him more
if he was my own father. I'm glad he's going to be around
for a few more years to bully me—"

The boom of leaping steps upon wooden stairs above
interrupted them. Rowan looked up the stairwell, past the
wing that had housed the High Counselor, to the well that
housed the watchtower. He could see the illumination sending leaping shadows down toward them as molten gold
spilled out from the object Alorie held in her hand. Her
dark hair was a cloud upon her shoulders. She wore dark
blue velvet with a silken cream blouse under her riding
jacket, and her face was as pale as moonlight.

"Rowan—the sword—"

She had nearly reached him and the bottom step as Tien

ran gasping across the Great Hall. Rowan turned, caught between them.

"Milady, captain. The High King sent me—" The Rover paused and gulped for wind.

"What is it?" Alorie's voice went thin.

"He says to come to him, and bring the sword. He says not to fail him now. He says—"

"Where is he going?" Rowan interrupted harshly.

"The Barrowlands."

Shocked, Deanmuth said, "He's raving again."

But Alorie said nothing. She leapt from the stair, her slim body poised for the bottom, as if nothing but flying could be fast enough.

The sword wound in his side went ice cold, thrilling through him, sending fear through him. "No!" Rowan shouted and caught her in midair by her waist, the sword's light spilling over him as he grabbed her roughly.

"Put me down!"

He embraced her. "You're not going to the Barrows with him."

"Rowan!"

He dragged her up the staircase with him. Deanmuth stood, jaw agape, watching him.

"Send someone after Brock. Bring him back before he does something stupid. Forget his kingly dignity. Throw him in prison if necessary."

Deanmuth snapped his mouth shut. He turned to Tien. "You heard him!"

Alorie squirmed, held fast, the sword in her hand pinned against her body, too close to even threaten with it. She kicked and screamed, but the riding skirt hampered her, tangling her feet. Her lover shoved his sleeve into her mouth, muffling her screams. She bit down, hard.

"Damn it!" Rowan cursed and pulled her head back against his chest. She could hear the pounding of his heart, beating to match her own. She made him drag her down the hall, fighting all the time to free her sword arm.

"Let me go!"

"All right!" He flung her out and she stumbled into the bedroom. The massive door slammed at her heels.

Alorie threw herself against it. "Rowan! Let me out! Rowan! You've got to let me go!"

His reply was muffled. "No. He wins alone or he dies alone. You're staying here!"

She could hear a lock bar being forced into place. She fingered the one on her side. It was heavy, but not heavy enough to batter the door down. She could hear Rowan moving away as he shouted for a guard. She reached out once to stroke the door.

"Ah, love." She had hoped he would go with her. Now it was impossible. Alorie sheathed the Unicorn sword and turned. She was in her own quarters, and the massive headboard that concealed a secret passage beckoned to her. She knelt on the bed, found the carving, and pressed it. The wardrobe opened.

Kithrand collapsed, writhing. His jaws opened in a silent scream and his mind recoiled. He was being turned inside out, all his senses raped, and something foul left in its stead . . .

He went blind. His limbs would not obey his needs.

Quiet.

A voice inside him. The elf lord stopped his thrashing and did as he had been bid.

Do you taste me?

Kithrand fought to order his mind, to think, to realize what was happening to him . . . and it came to him, an anchor in the cyclone of his mind—*possessed*—he'd allowed himself to be *possessed*.

Was it better than dying?

He sensed the malison waiting. "Yes," he rasped. His voice literally tore out of his throat, and he tasted blood with his words. "I taste you." With that he began to get his sanity back, reeling it in on a tenuous thread, and remembering he'd been working with the creature toward this moment.

The malison withdrew. Kithrand felt sucked dry and empty, but his sight returned and he blinked as the dungeon swam in brilliant colors, motes drifting in prismatic swirls before his eyes.

In a shimmering cloud the malison hovered before him. It put out a tentacle and before the elf lord could shrink back, it caressed him. The skin was dry, mildly scaly, and warm. Kithrand sensed pleasure in the creature.

Again, the malison said.

"Not . . . not just yet." Kit swallowed a mouthful of blood. He'd evidently bitten his tongue badly. "I need your pattern again." Pattern was the creature's essence. Once Kithrand had that in his grasp, he could separate the creature's being from his own. He eyed the malison. It called itself Ayah, and it was to be greatly feared. Its twin had possessed the Corruptor.

He was going to die here, he knew, but he could not stop hoping that he might learn the pattern of the malison that made the Corruptor what he was. It was that hope that kept him going.

The malison quaked. Then it stilled itself. *Learn this time. My pattern.*

Kithrand clenched his fists and sent a silent prayer to the ancestors who had disowned him. If he succeeded in what he was doing, might he not hope for redemption, even in death?

His scream tore from his throat as the malison enveloped him.

The rope swung taut. It snapped against him and held, vibrating. Pinch gulped and closed his eyes a moment. Gravel fell from overhead. It pummeled him, bounced off the sides of the Pit, and fell in a never ending shower.

"Pinch!"

"I'm all right," he got out. He grasped the rope. Its rough twist tore the palms of his hands and he wished for gloves. He lay against the rock and readied to let another coil of the rope go, springing backward and away from the stone face as he did so, trying to spring and drop a coil and spring again before the jerking halt rattled his brains. He could hear Bryant above grunt with each plunge.

On the fourth one, his boots slipped. He bounced to a bruising stop against the rock face.

"Lower me," he called back when he'd swallowed his heart down enough to speak.

The rope let him down gently. He found himself facing a tunnel mouth. The moment of surprise almost chased away his fear as he looked inward. The plan at this point was for him to swing in, cast off and land, and then Bryant would throw the rope down to him, and he would anchor it and lower himself again.

Pinch canceled that strategy as he looked at an unsavory pile of bone and skull, some still with flesh hanging in strips from them. On this level the Pit monsters lurked. He had fought them before and had no desire to do it again.

He called back, "No good. Brace yourself." His words echoed, blurred, and he heard Bryant call back, "Go on. On. On."

He checked the sling, then shrugged the coil off and let it drop him with a sickening *twang* as it jerked him to a halt. Once more, and then he was able to push off on the stone again, giving him some control. His palms and his face were slick. His stomach bubbled and warned him of disaster. Pinch closed his eyes a moment and tried to think of matters beyond him, of great deeds. Of prophecies and nearsighted, feisty ladies with talismanic swords.

He opened his eyes to see Mary Rose. She floated quite calmly upon the air. "Do the best you can, dearest. It's all anyone can ask," she said. "I'll hold you fast."

His hand shook so he could barely mop his forehead. "I don't see ye," he muttered to himself. "I don't see ye."

"Of course you do," the dwarf maid answered. "Don't fash yourself, Pinch, or hang there with your mouth gaping, gathering flies. Is that smelly pipe in your pocket?"

He could feel its comforting bulge against his rump. "Yes," he answered hesitantly.

"I should drop it while I have the chance," his ghostly wife told him. "But it wouldn't be fair. Now you've a job to do. Get to it!"

Pinch shut his eyes and let himself drop. Push, swing out and drop, catch himself with his knees bent. And again.

"Open your eyes, dearest, or you'll miss the tunnels," Mary Rose called before she faded from his sight.

The coil of rope upon his shoulder disappeared at an alarming rate. He had scarcely any length left when his boots met emptiness again, and he knew he'd found the mouth of another tunnel.

But this one was not in his direct path. He would have to swing to his left to catch it. Pinch fumbled in his sling for an iron peg. He let himself down until he hung in midair across the tunnel's entrance. He eased his axe from his pack and hammered in the peg, then looped the rope about it to secure it. Someday, he thought, he'd develop a real technique for this. It might be useful for mountains as well as caves. When he was done, he let himself down a hair more and, trusting to the gods and his dearly departed wife, he swung himself inward.

"No more," Kit cried. He clung to the dungeon wall, his

nails scraping its gritty surface until they tore to the quick. "Please. No more."

We're so close.

The elf lord sagged to the floor. "I know," he forced out. "But I've got to rest. To eat. Water, if you have any."

The malison seemed to consider him. Then it said, *I hunger also. You will stay and wait for me. Do not try to escape.*

Before Kithrand could cry out in protest, the malison put a soulbinding on him, and then hovered out of view.

He lay unresisting, gem-blue eyes staring unfocused at the rock above him. He thought for a moment of all the poor souls tortured in this room and smiled mockingly at the knowledge that none of them had suffered as he had.

Do not try to escape . . . escape . . . escape. . . .

Kit blinked. The sparkling afterglow of the malison's sorcery faded from his eyes. His life seemed to follow after and fade with it. He remembered being tested for Veil. He had some talent—elven fire came easily to his fingertips, and the charming of small animals—but his talent was more for unmaking than making, and as such, distasteful to elves. But if he could unweave this binding now. He had the malison's pattern and more, the pattern of the twin bound to the Corruptor. He might actually be of some value to someone again.

Kithrand frowned in concentration as he made an effort to unravel the strands of sorcery that bound him and his fate.

Alorie fastened her weapon belt tightly about her waist before stepping into the corridor beyond the wardrobe. She snapped shut the door behind her. The sword's gleam sputtered about her, golden sparks cascading to the dust and granite under her boots. She had no fear of the dark this time.

"The third time pays for all," she said, remembering the times she had traveled this way alone.

The first was when her mother had died and she had tumbled accidently into this passage and had had no choice but to crawl its length throughout the mountain. The second had been fleeing the massacre.

She did not flee this time, and she did not crawl. Alorie ran, jumping and leaping fallen rock in her way, the sword showering out its light. She had a prophecy to fulfill.

*   *   *

Ayah felt the shuddering and vibration within the mountain. Above, it knew the city crawled with game and any one of them would be a fair meal, but it could not resist the easier prey within. The malison put out a questing touch and found its quarry. It shivered with delight. Such energy! Such an aura. It melded into the stone, slowly, achingly, seeking its victim.

She barely kept her feet under her as she ran, sprinting on the edge of being out of control, boot soles skittering upon loose gravel. She slid around the corner, put her hand out to steady herself—and came face-to-face with the malison blocking the tunnel.

Her throat closed. Its dark presence sealed itself around her. She scarcely had a second to think before her arm moved of its own volition. The Unicorn sword sliced through it and the malison collapsed with a wailing sound. Its molten light dimmed a second, then renewed, as the creature battered itself at her feet. Alorie gave it a merciful thrust, and the thing ceased to move.

It blocked her path. Was it dead? She prodded it with her toe, thinking it had almost been too easy.

She sliced across it with the sword once more, and oily black smoke leaked out upon the ground. It was quite dead when she left it. Alorie hopped over it without a second thought as to where it had come from.

The rope burned through his palms before he released it and landed with an "oof!" and an "ugh!" among a pile of rubbish. Pinch doubled over in a coughing fit prolonged by the cloud of dust in the air about him. As tears came to his eyes, he finally caught his breath.

If these were the First Warrens, he thought, looking about him, they were left looking like someone's cellar. Junk was piled everywhere. It was some old grandad's chair that had broken his fall and now lay splintered under him. He got up and dusted himself off, though cautiously, not wanting to set off another fit.

He scratched his curled beard. He had no fear that the invaders had come this far. No one had been down here for a long, long time. Pinch hiked up his pants, squinted in the dusky light, and began to pick his way through the junk. He fell over a trunk, a rusty-locked, wormy-lumbered contraption of a trunk. It burst open. A wedding canopy spilled out and, wrapped in its oilcloth folds, a thick-bound book.

Pinch signed himself, a gesture he did not use often, in thanks to the All-Mother. "And Mary Rose, too," he added as an afterthought. He bent over to pick up the book with trembling hands.

The Corruptor sat head bowed, on his usurped throne. He had tasks to attend to, but did not feel like seeing to them. He contemplated the full meaning of his relegation to lieutenant once more when the Iron Liege arose, and did not find his thoughts pleasant.

An alarm tingled as someone set foot upon the Barrowlands. The Corruptor stood up abruptly, black eyes looking across the hall as if he could see through stone and over the distances. He waited. Another footfall sounded. This was no mistake. A man walked the Barrowlands, and he knew well which man it was.

His lips thinned in a cruel smile. "I hear you, old friend. I hear you. Hold on. I shall join you in a moment." He bowed his head, crossed his arms over his chest, and gathered the strength to open a hellroad from the Delvings to the Barrows.

Thirty-Two

She stole a horse from the cooks. He was round-barreled, with hooves the size of pannikins. Alorie's feet stuck out either side of his rib cage, and she thought that if she lived through these next few days, he would have stretched her enough to make childbearing easy.

The brown-splotched stallion had one advantage aside from being easy to steal. He'd been born with the soul of a hotblood and knew his destiny was to race the wind. The moment she'd pointed his head toward the wildwood and he discovered he did not have a heavy wagon hitched to his harness, he let out a shrill whinny of joy and let fly. Alorie threw her arms about his neck and hung on as her boots were dislodged from the stirrups.

The horse pounded along the track and ducked instinctively as she turned onto the overgrown trail that pierced the forest. She'd ridden it often as a child, though never very far. Overgrown as the pathway was now, it had been worse when she was young. There had been traffic from Sinobel to the Barrows since the massacre. She did not like to think why.

The forest slowed her intrepid mount. He settled into a smooth, gliding walk that ate the distance up nearly as fast as a gallop. The pace pleasantly surprised her. If that walk could be bred into his get—Alorie shook her head. She had no business thinking of tomorrow. Though the sword now hung upon her hip, she could feel its fire. It was still awake and burning. But for how long?

She rode until the sun dipped low through overhead branches. A thrashing sounded in the brush. The splotched stallion swung his heavy head through the shrubbery and bugled a note of inquiry.

Brock's nervous chestnut answered. He minced in the

undergrowth, his eyes rolling white. The big cook's stallion blew a distainful *whuff* that made him paw the ground.

Brock sat confidently astride it, as if unaware he rode a powder keg. "Alorie! You give me hope."

"You called and I came," she answered, uneasy at the tone of his voice.

He nodded. "I need you. I cannot succeed without you." The chestnut gathered himself and made a little sideways hop that would have unseated a lesser rider. Brock did not seem to notice it. He beckoned at the trail. "The track is narrow, so you'll have to ride behind me instead of by my side. Still, I can't think of a better person to have at my back." Before she could answer, he looked at her sharply. "Or did the traitors send you?"

"What?"

"They're everywhere. Worse now than when Cornuth fell. I was like a father to them . . . I should not have been. You would do well to learn from their example." He pivoted the chestnut and this time succeeded in guiding the destrier through the bracken.

Alorie sat absolutely still for a moment. The hair at the nape of her neck crawled. He had sounded like Brock yet strangely unlike him. What if the mage was wrong and the only one of them meant for this time was the sword—and that growing more Corrupt by the day? She touched a heel to the cook's stallion and bounded after the disappearing chestnut.

Pinch closed the faded book slowly and raised his left hand. It trembled and he clenched it shut. "*Human*," he said and his voice echoed anger throughout the cavern. "I am human, not dwarf. *Human*—but twisted and ugly to their eyes. I'm to be pitied and scorned!"

And changed. He listened to the echoes die away. Changed by wars that left all countries blackened and ruptured, forcing the humans to flee. They had sailed a poisoned sea that crippled them and changed them further. It forced them to cast out misshapen children, who fled to the mountains and lived as far from the sight of their parents as they could delve.

The All-Mother hadn't made him. His only role in Her eyes was as flesh to be pitied!

Pinch pounded his fist upon his thigh, as if he could hammer the pain away. The Seven True Races had no

legacy but war. Of them all, the only true race was that of
the elves.

The rest of them had come from nowhere—abandoned,
homeless, landless after their wars with the malisons and
each other. The elves had taken them in. Then war had
erupted, the continent destroyed, and all were forced to
leave. It was a pattern repeated seven times over.

Bethalia was the last continent.

It would be better, he thought, if we let it stop here.

But that was defeat, and even in this book, which spoke a
truth so foreign he at first thought it might have been lies,
the malisons were a consuming evil.

Pinch opened the volume to its last entry, skimmed it,
then unbuttoned his shirt and put it inside. He would bring
the book to Alorie and let her decide what to tell the lands
of Bethalia. He drew himself from the pile of junk and
looked around. He picked up a toy, a badly whittled bird,
its wings stiff and its head monstrously tucked into its body.
The shortman shook his head and let the toy drop. Perhaps
another day he would come here and try to understand all
that he saw. And perhaps he would not.

He gathered the rope in his hands and reattached the
sling, giving it a mighty jerk as he shouted, "Ready!"

The rope quivered and danced. Pinch gained purchase on
the rock face as soon as he could, and the rope drew him
slowly upward. He dangled a moment before the last tunnel
mouth, the lair of a Pit monster.

With a roar something darted at him from the maw.

With a jangle of nerves Alorie reined in at the edge of the
Barrowlands. The wildwood skirted the east side until it
met the broken jumble of bare rock and spires that skirted it
on the west. Both pushed toward a narrow pass that had
earned the name the Jaws of Death. It had once been called
the Eye of Cornuth, the main passageway that swung down
and around from the capitol city which ruled the harbor
where the straits came to an end.

Here the land was ridged in immense graves that stretched
to the north. The land was all gray ash and feathery green
moss, a sickly moss with purple eyes that opened to the sun
and shut again at dusk. Great standards were speared into
the mounds, their silver tarnished black by the centuries,
their medals tinkling in the wind, their fading runes telling
who had fought under the name of what god and why, and

how the dead beneath were shackled. Plowing under the dead from that war, and the likes of the Corruptor and the Despot, had been like plowing salt into the soil. The land was dead.

She sat her horse now and recognized the black scorch of pitch to her right—a ditch that had been fired by a blazing arrow years ago. To her left lay a ditch that had been filled but never used, its pitch still waiting to be fired up against an enemy that had been defeated.

The High King had fallen here. But not right here, she thought. To the north, where the Barrows were so immense they blocked out sight of the pass. The king had been defeated, routed, and driven from Cornuth. The Iron Liege and his lieutenant had followed, determined to grind him under their heel. When he had reached here, the Eye of Cornuth, he had turned and let the Jaws of Death snap shut upon his enemy. Elves and dwarves and humans alike had stood here waiting.

He had given all his power in the fight. The Corruptor fell, and so did his dire master. And then the king.

Alorie watched Brock's back and wondered.

The mage cleared his throat. He seemed to hesitate to ride onto the Barrows.

She brought her horse even and let the two stallions sniff at each other and bare their teeth.

"What is it, Brock?"

The mage turned to her. His dark skin was burnished in the last light of the sun. "Sometimes," he said. "I don't remember everything."

"You're the heir to the High King."

"No!" The chestnut threw up his head and started at Brock's vehement denial. "No," Brock repeated, lowering his voice. "That much I do know. I am the High King."

"No delusion."

"No. Though *he* delights in having made it seem so." Brock stretched in his saddle, easing his legs and back.

Alorie felt her insides quiver. "I believe you."

"Do you? I know you accepted the idea, but I don't think you really accepted the reality." He looked away, north. "That hardly matters now. It's time for my power to be returned to me. Then my kingdom." He snapped the rein ends against his mount's rump, and the startled animal took a hop onto the Barrowlands and sank up to his pasterns in ash.

A wind too brisk for late summer rattled the standards and medallions. Alorie clucked to her horse and urged him to follow, though he snorted to tell her better sense dictated otherwise.

Kithrand found the last knot and undid it. He was freed. He lay stupefied on the dungeon floor a moment. He tried to stand and could not. Weakened by days of deprivation, his constitution had been feeding on itself. He fell back to his stomach. "If I have to crawl," he told himself, "I will get out of here."

True to his word, the once high elf lord began to drag himself through the dust and gore of the prison.

Bryant heard Pinch's shout of alarm. He set himself firmly, looped the rope about the anchor they had rigged, and went down on his stomach to crawl to the lip. He smelled the acrid odor wafting upward and knew what Pinch fought below. He backed up, got the bow and arrows, and ran to the far rim of the Pit.

The silvery flat-headed beast seemed baffled by the bait dangling in front of it. Pinch yelled and danced at the rope's end, axe in hand, as the Pit monster reared. Its multitude of legs clawed in an attempt to grasp the juicy morsel making such a noise.

Bryant nocked an arrow and drew.

He let fly, knowing he might hit Pinch as well. The arrow clattered harmlessly against the stone and began its eternal drop.

"If you're going to shoot," Pinch yelled, "at least take aim!"

Bryant smiled grimly and nocked another arrow. He watched as the armsman hacked off a claw-tipped leg that had gripped him about the boot and yanked him up and down. He drew the string back and let go, the arrow whistling sweetly and thunking deeply.

The Pit monster squealed in outrage. Its venom-tipped tail curled up.

Bryant drew and shot again. The arrow hit deep. Pinch stopped whirling at the end of his rope as the flat-headed beast reared and exposed his throat. He cocked his axe and threw.

The weapon buried itself halfway up the handle in the silvery wattle. With a piercing hiss the monster pitched forward and tumbled down the shaft. Its bulk brushed past Pinch and set him whirling again.

Bryant did not move for a second. His arms trembled. Then the king looked down and saw Pinch looking up.

"Well, you woolly-headed nobleman," the dwarf said. "Are ye going to let me swing here all day? Or are ye fishing for another beastie?"

Bryant began the slow task of hauling Pinch back up. The dwarf was almost at the top before Bryant let out his breath freely.

"It's out the bolt hole you go."

Pinch clasped Bryant's bloodied hand. "I'd rather go to the gates with you and see if we can let in a surprise or two."

The dwarf king shook his head. "It's too dangerous." He thumped Pinch's chest. "You have to get that book back to Lady Alorie."

"Or my head, at the very least." Pinch tapped his temple solemnly. "For whatever help it will be."

"Anything, any scrap of help at all, may turn this tide," Bryant said. "Look what you've done for me."

"Me? Help you?"

"Yes. Wandering around, thinking that was all I could do. No. Don't you worry, Pinch, the dark lieutenant will have a surprise or two down his gullet."

The two grinned at each other, then clasped their forearms tightly, knowing that behind their smiles was a veil of tears. Neither knew what the next day could bring.

Pinch gave a snuffle, hiked his pack, and put his shoulder to the boulder that blocked the warren. It let him out into a darkening night. He left without a word about the book.

Kithrand tumbled out a wall of mud and down the broken hedge of what had once been a vegetable garden, and the small pony that had freed him by yanking up parched stems gave him a suspicious look. The elf lord sat a moment, stunned by his sudden fall from the earthen tunnel to freedom. It had rained in this ring of the city, or so it appeared from the sodden ground he rested upon. The sky overhead grew sullen with dusk. The small, wiry-haired pony rolled its eyes and flared its nostrils at the fey being.

Kithrand saw hope on four legs. He held out a begrimed, death-smeared hand. "Come, my beauty. Come to me," he called in his lilting tongue, and the pony took a halting step forward. Kithrand's sensitive ears could hear battle on the wind.

The Lady Alorie needed him at the Delvings. His slender fingers stretched achingly toward the suspicious pony. "Come to me," he called again.

Low thunder rumbled. Alorie looked overhead, ever suspicious of clouds and thunder. Brock paid no attention. He dismounted the chestnut, which had come to a halt and refused to budge. Alorie kicked off her immense stallion and patted it fondly before letting it trail off after the destrier. She thought the horses had greater sense than the two of them.

They passed the open welt that had been the Corruptor's grave. (The silver standards, last of the magic to bind him, were burned to slag.) Brock paused a moment, then went to the last great ridge.

It blocked the mountains from view. It was gray earth and purple shadows. Standards pierced its back as though bearing a long and serpentine creature to the ground. Alorie watched the medallions hanging on their blackened silver threads. *Tink, tink, tink*, they tapped. Kithrand had once read one of the standards to her:

"Set here in this day in the Jaws of Death by Myrlianne, of the star-shone people." Prayers had been uttered here. Incense was burned and magicks worked by the hands of all involved. And they had been victorious once.

Alorie looked away. Once, it appeared, was not to be enough.

Brock strode up the mound and ripped the standard away, then the next and the next until he had walked its length. He threw all ten to one side.

"What are you doing?" Her voice cracked. She could feel a leaping awareness of their presence.

The mage hardly looked at her. "I'm getting my powers back," he said. "And that monster is bound with them. Pull the sword, Alorie. When I take up my magic, he'll be loosened. Strike once, straight up under the rib cage for the heart."

She stood, rooted to the ground. "You're raising him."

"I must. It's the only way I'll be whole again."

She held the Unicorn sword in her hand, half out of its

sheath. It took fire, a sun in itself, as the solar disk hung low in the sky. "Brock—"

"Shut up, woman and do as I tell you!" Brock held up his hands, palm upward, to the sky. He began to chant.

She felt the rise of bidden evil, palpable, around her. She took a step backward. "No . . ." It wasn't supposed to be this way.

Green fire shivered over the barrow. A rift opened, she felt her ears pop, and a figure jumped out of the doorway between her and Brock.

The Corruptor put his hood down and laughed, a hollow, booming laugh. "Old friend! I see you've come to the truth at last. It was always your role to release *him*." He ran his gloved hand under her chin. "Always faithful."

Alorie slapped away his touch.

The Corruptor turned on boot heel, seemingly unafraid of the sword point to his back.

"Come to help me?" Brock said ironically.

"No, actually." The sorcerer flinched aside as violet fire spurted upward from the mound and thunder rumbled.

Levin bolts danced along Brock's shoulders and hands. The Rover mage threw back his head. "You can't stop me now!"

With a roar the magic began to return to him. The air shivered. Its boom rattled the very mountains to the west. Brock made an incoherent sound of joy.

"Pity," the Corruptor said. "You've done it now." He turned, his fist flashing toward her.

Alorie felt the smack, the shock of the blow against her wrist as the sword went flying. The Corruptor reached up and grasped it in midair. Scarcely pausing, he thrust it deep into Brock's chest.

The lightning ran across the sword and into the dark lieutenant. His black hair rose with a crackle, and St. Elmo's fire illuminated him. He laughed and pulled the sword from Brock's torso and threw the talisman to one side.

The Corruptor strode to the doorway of his hellroad. He paused, a stride up in midair. He held his hand palm down. Yellow-green fire came up to greet him. His glove sucked it up eagerly. He swallowed up the power birthing from the grave—power that had been Brock's and had been sacrificed to bind the Despot. Then there was nothing but silence. The barrow caved in upon itself.

The Corruptor took another stride and gained the sill of his

doorway. He smiled at Alorie. "So much for prophecies."
With an ear-wrenching shatter the hellroad disappeared.

Brock went to his knees. Alorie dove for him, took him in
her arms, but she could not stop his fall. He rolled over.
Crimson blood spattered his chin.

"While he's weak, replace the standards!"

She hesitated, then left him to do what he said. She knew
nothing of elfin chants or mage magic, but she said a prayer
to the All-Mother with each stabbing placement of the tarnished silver spears. With each stab, something below retreated farther. Then she returned to Brock and took his head
in her lap.

The Unicorn sword lay in the dust, its gold and ivory
length charred darker than night. Useless. Spent.

He grasped her hand. His fingers were cold and slick. "I'm
. . . sorry," he said. "I did not remember . . . enough."

She held to him tightly. Things stirred in the night that had
befallen the Barrowlands, things loosened in that one moment, however brief. She heard their hungry mouths drooling
for them. Hungry eyes burning for sight of them. The horses
had fled in terror.

"I am the king," Brock whispered. "I know I am. And
. . . I had a son. And he had a son. I can't remember their
names just yet. You'll have to find him on your own, Alorie."

"Don't talk."

"I must. Three hundred years. But I have a descendent.
You'll look—"

Her voice caught. "I'll look," she got out.

"You'll have to fight *him* . . . on your own. But you have
the sword . . ."

She did not tell him the sword was destroyed. The sword
of Frenlaw, failed again. When she finally had choked back
her voice to say something, she realized Brock had left her
all alone.

No one even knew she was there in the Barrowlands.

Thirty-Three

  The guard at Alorie's door snapped off a salute.
Rowan gave him a smile. "Quiet?"

"Yes, sir, very quiet." The guard took a deep smell of the
covered platter Rowan carried. "She'll be grateful for that,
sir."

"There's a trencher in here for you, too." Rowan held the
tray out and let the guard retrieve his dinner. As he balanced it, he knocked on the door with some misgivings.

There was no answer. He sighed. He knew the ways of
women well enough to know he might be getting the silent
treatment for days to come. He also knew Alorie well
enough to know he had better enter the room cautiously or
she might bolt for it. He handed the tray to the guard and
pulled aside the drop bar.

With care he kicked the door open and entered the unlit
room. Lantern light from the corridor flowed in and around
him, throwing his shadow across the floor. Rowan's breath
caught in his chest. He pivoted slowly, making sure there
was no mistake.

Alorie was not there.

"Guard!"

Trencher and tray went clattering as the man bolted in.

"Where is she?"

The man went livid. "Nowhere, I swear, captain. No one
has gone in or out!"

Rowan clenched his jaw. Damn that Sergius blood, that
stubborn, devious Sergius blood! The manor must be rife
with secret passages. No matter—she was gone, and he
knew where she'd gone.

Rowan took the stairs to the watchtower two and three at
a time. The room had been shuttered. He threw the archers'
windows open and looked out across the expanse to the far

mountains where the Barrows lay huddled. It was night.
Even the moon was gone in her cycle, to reappear in a night
or two. He heard the dull, heavy roll of summer thunder.

Magefire flashed. It could have been sheet lightning, but
he thought he could smell the burn of sorcery even half a
day's ride away. He stood rooted to the floor. Violet flashed
again, then the vile green of Corrupted magic, and he knew
greater fear than he'd ever felt before.

Damn the prophecy! Damn all oracles! He'd been told he
would lose Alorie—and now he had.

And Deathwalker was arisen unless Brock could best him
on the field of sorcery.

Rowan unfroze himself. He took the stairs headlong,
gained the landing, and burst in on Lord Rathincourt. Lady
Marne stood up with a gasp, and the veteran warlord twisted
in his sickbed, his snowy hair standing up like a thicket from
his bandages.

"Rowan. What is it?"

"I've got to go. I haven't time to find Deanmuth, but the
horse troop goes out tomorrow morning on schedule. Tell
him to hammer away at the Delvings with everything he
has—that he has to do more than hold his position. He has
to win."

"What is it?" Rathincourt's expression became grave. He
beckoned for his younger sister to calm down.

"Brock is gone. So is Alorie. And there is magefire in the
Barrowlands."

"Good god."

"There's still hope. If the Despot is freed, we've an army
between him and his lieutenant. Tell Deanmuth I'd like to
keep it that way."

The injured man struggled to his feet. He wore a crumpled nightshirt that revealed pasty white legs with knobby
knees—skin that had spent a lifetime inside battle armor.
"I'll go with you."

"No. You won't be able to keep up."

"You'll go alone?"

Rowan nodded. He added grimly, "By the time I get
there, it'll be long over."

The warlord let himself sink back to the edge of his bed.
"I was wrong. I never thought to see this in my lifetime. I
never wanted to see this."

"None of us did. You'll tell Deanmuth?"

"Of course. Go on, you've wasted enough time on me. Luck go with you. May our lady be safe."

Rowan snatched a cloak off the hook by the door—Rathincourt's good red woolen one—and ran through the corridors to the stables. He took a pair of matched bays, the pride of Sobor, from Rathincourt's stock. He tacked them lightly and spoke to them gently as he readied them, for he intended to use them badly. Let him get to the Barrows. He would return on foot if he had to. A summer storm threatened and spoke loudly in the west. He could feel its dampness on the air.

As he led them down through the ringed city, he cursed himself. He cursed himself for thinking his portion of the prophecy engraved on the last standing wall in Cornuth could have been any different. He had been told it would take the blood of the last of the House of Sergius to free the Despot. And when he rose, he would take all the dead in the Barrows with him before the blood of the House of Sergius would put him down. Deathwalker, the elves called him, with an eerie prescience. He had been told he was doomed to love and lose. But he had never thought Alorie would leave him.

As he reached the shattered gates of Sinobel, he did a running mount and pointed the horses west. He could use a companion, and while he was cursing, he laid a mild one on Pinch, wherever that crusty shortman could be this night. If ever he needed a friend to protect his back, now was the time.

But he rode alone.

Pinch struggled down the mountain. The moon had gone. Was it two or three days ago it had hung over his shoulder like a lantern? Now the lightless velvet stretched overhead, overcast clouds hiding even the stars. He looked up once or twice, thinking of Veil.

His breath grew hot and raspy in his chest as he half-fell, half-climbed down the mountain. Bracken and thornberries pricked and snagged at him. As he reached the bottom, his pack was nearly torn off his shoulder. He paused to shrug it back on, and found the rip in his shirt and the hot festering skin that met his touch through it.

The dwarf went to his knees to examine the tear. Sweat beaded up along his eyebrows and he dashed it away impatiently as he bent his chin at a nearly impossible angle to eye the wound. He could see little of it. Had he been touched by the Pit beast somehow?

And then he remembered the curling stinger in the creature's tail. He'd been struck. How or when he was not sure, but the venom coursed through his veins as surely as his own black blood. He fished through his pack and found the crumpled half pack of herbs. His fever could not be stopped, not now, but the medicines might keep him going long enough to find Alorie. He choked it down and washed the bitter taste from his mouth with a last gulp of brackish water.

"Well, bucko," he said to himself. "Next time, perhaps you'll take a friend or two along with ye, to make sure the job gets done." He got to his feet. He left his pack on the ground. Empty, it had served its purpose. He would keep his water skin in case he found a freshet or brook somewhere, but he could not carry deadweight. He thumped his chest where the book rested warmly. That was now a part of him—he could no more leave behind than an arm or a leg.

He pulled his pipe from his pocket. His leather pouch was nearly empty, but he scraped together a fresh bowl, tamped it down, and lit it, ignoring the tremor of his hands. A good smoke could make up for a lot of inconveniences.

The dwarf strode along the flatlands as reken howls and barks sounded and bonfires of a besieging army turned the western sky a smoky orange.

Kithrand gained the pony's back after a great deal of trial. Straight-legged the beast hopped down through the city, shied, and threw him in the washing well near the foot of the first walls. The elf sat up sputtering. But the pony did not trot away as he held out a hand once more and continued his lilting quest of its friendship. At last the recalcitrant beast whuffed noisily and lipped the well for a drink.

Kithrand scrubbed himself hastily as long as he was there, got out, and shook himself. The city was stripped bare of troops and the plain below empty. Had there been victory here or defeat? The still of the night gave him no hints. It was best that he go cautiously, then. He grabbed the pony by the ear and pinched it tightly until he was settled firmly on its back.

"Now then, you lop-eared excuse for an equine. We've a long ride ahead and before we're done, your legs will be a great deal shorter." The elf lord gripped his calves tightly and forced the squealing pony into a run. He pointed it north, toward the Delvings and beyond, to the pass known as the Eye of Cornuth. As he rode, he read the telltale sign of an army's passage, but reken signs and even those of malisons crisscrossed it. He could not tell whose army he followed.

If victorious, Rathincourt and Brock would have led them onto the Delvings. If not, Alorie would have been captured and taken to the Corruptor at the dwarf forges. He saw little choice in his destination. His heart cowered but for once he did not listen to it. He only prayed that he would not be alone when he reached the trail's end.

The even star had just peaked when Rowan slipped off the back of his foaming mount and let it and its running mate put their muzzles to the ground. The horses took deep, shuddering breaths as he overlooked the Barrows. A reken barked. He listened and placed it north of the Barrows—somewhere in the canyons of the Eye. The threatening storm had disappeared, but he could still taste its quickening upon the air. A splintered edge of bone snagged the toe of his boot. Rowan dug it up and put his flint to it after wrapping its knob with dried grasses. The rushes flared up, burning furiously as he held it overhead.

The stillness of the dead grounds gave him some hope. The lesser burrows lay undisturbed. Whatever had happened here, it had not been the worst . . . yet. He strode to the farthest graves, his sputtering torch consuming itself with a fierce intensity.

The Despot's mound was closed, but the ash and soil over it was charred to a glassy coating. Atop it, his arms folded across his chest, lay Brock's body. Rowan caught his breath. Glowing sparks from the crude torch spit into the night wind. Magefire had blazed here; he saw its sign everywhere. The very ground crackled and spat as he walked upon it. He knelt by Brock, saw the blood-soaked front of his shirt, and knew his friend was dead. He stood.

"Alorie!"

A pebble crunched. He turned quickly and leapt off the mound. The torch's light set off green reflections in the slitted eyes that watched him. The reken snarled and jumped as Rowan pulled his sword and parried the attack. Before the beast could recover, the woodsman skewered him. He kicked the body to one side.

"Alorie!" His voice echoed throughout the Barrows. As long as the torch burned, he pored over the land, searching for sign, and saw little beyond the fact she had stood here and then—nothing.

She had vanished.

Thirty-Four

Hammersmith paused in his machinations in Sobor. His gnarled body grew stiff as he felt his master's call. His eyes watered, and he hugged himself, throwing back in defiance, "No, I willna attend ye! There are other matters here. . . ."

His master's strength had grown. Hammersmith felt it batter him down until he was a sore, bruised lump upon the fortress steps. Then, abruptly, it left him. The dwarf lay hugging the stone a moment, licked his lips, then sat up. It was time for him to flee. Whoever triumphed in the upcoming battle would have no good uses for him, and he had business in the stone depths of Bethalia. There were forces far older than either the Corruptor or the prophecy beckoning him. Hammersmith got to his feet laboriously, planning his escape.

Alorie hugged Brock's body until it grew stiff and cold in her arms, and she realized she had cried until her eyes were dry.

If only the despair had flooded out with the tears. But it had not. She heard reken barks along the edges of the fields. She searched Brock's shirt for a short sword, dagger, anything, and found in an inner pocket of his cloak the cane Rowan had made for him.

She ran her fingers over it. Runes had been carved into the hardwood. The oil of many rubbings had polished it. What she had in her hands was no longer an implement for walking, but a wizard's staff of power. She put it through her belt and then decided to put Brock's body on the barrow. She wished for Kithrand and his blue elven fire to honor it—a hollow wish. Taking a deep breath, she grabbed him by the shoulders and dragged him until he rested atop his enemy's grave. She folded his arms over his chest and whispered, "I would have gone with you. I could never have loved you like I love Rowan, but I would have gone with you."

Standing on the barrow's crest, she tried to make sense of Brock's death. All she knew for sure was that the Corruptor was even more powerful than he had been before—powerful enough to even temporarily usurp the return of the Iron Liege. Her hair streamed loosely in the tempest as it swept across the Barrowlands.

What could she do now? All their hope had been tied in the prophecy. It was broken now, shattered. There was no High King. No return of the force prophesied to sweep the land, cleansing away evil and right wrongs. No mystic weapon to fill the protector's hand.

And no longer a need to be queen.

Alorie put her hand to her face. She was free! She could return to Rowan, marry and take whatever time they had left together.

But how long would that be, without someone to oppose the dark lieutenant? Years perhaps . . . or possibly only months. And what kind of a fool was she to think it could be at all?

Alorie left the grave mound and bent to pick up the sword. She gripped the blackened guard. To hell with prophecy. She would make her own fate, and it would be everything she wanted, or she would die trying. Beyond prophecy lay destiny.

She filled her left hand with Brock's staff and her right with the sword, and pointed them toward the clouds rushing in overhead.

"Hear me, city of Veil! Let down your stairs! I have business with you tonight!"

It was a gamble, but not an unreasonable one. The magefire would draw them, of that she was sure, in curiosity if for no other reason. The mountain peaks cracked with a lightning bolt, and thunder rumbled after, its vibration shaking the ground she stood on. The sky filled with boiling cloud and the wind whipped to a howling frenzy.

She knew a second of doubt before the storm swallowed her.

Luisa grabbed her by the end of the staff and pulled her over the cloud bank. The pale sorceress held her tightly a moment, and her black cloak furled over both of them.

"Hurry," she said. "Whatever I have that you need is yours."

A sheet of lightning broke over their heads, dazzling Alorie's vision. The mists under them roiled.

"What is it?"

"We're under attack. All in the outer village are dead or dying. Veil is falling. The Corruptor is here and we can't stand against him. We waited too long to fight."

Alorie held out the deadened Unicorn sword. Luisa held trembling fingers over it. "All is lost."

"No! I won't give up."

"The High King is dead. I saw you in the scrying bowl." The sorceress's thin face tightened. "When we found him, just out of the Corruptor's vault, we didn't trust him. We did not believe. Only you did."

Alorie turned her face away, ashamed that she had only believed for the sake of unity among her people, until the end. "There must be something we can do."

Luisa gazed across Veil. Fog and mist tore loose as the wind whipped her silver hair over her face. She looked back. "You are the Dancer" was all she said.

Alorie regarded the sword in her hands. She remembered throwing the horn down on the Paths of Sorrow, and having the Unicorn manifest itself. How dead was the sword? How dark its Corrupted power?

She had only one way of finding out even if it meant summoning the beast of her nightmares. She looked to Luisa. "Ward me," she said. "If you can."

The sorceress nodded gravely and stepped back. Here, on this edge of Veil, the temples had fallen. Starlight illuminated rubble and broken beams. Alorie stepped out onto what had once been a courtyard. Its tiles were buckled and shattered. She wrenched the horn from the guard of Frenlaw and threw both to the moonlit ground.

The ground tilted. Alorie fancied she heard the screams of a multitude upon the wind, but it might have been her imagination—or it might have been the death knell of Veil. Lightning shivered across the dome of the sky—blue, red, green, white-yellow. Black lightning flashed upward from the ground and reared, and she saw the ebony unicorn rampant before her.

His jaws snapped. He pounded the misty ground with the drum of thunder in his hooves. His lance gleamed wickedly sharp.

But she saw his eyes, and they held still the colors of purity, and she knew she faced the Unicorn—her unicorn—and all was not quite lost.

He lunged at her. Alorie spun away, her sleeve going with a sharp rip. She caught her breath as her ankle turned upon a mosaic shard. The beast essayed a stab at Luisa, who ducked behind a fallen column, then he pivoted and returned for her.

"You are an elemental, a god," she said as he pounded down on her. "You are fire or maybe wind. Fight him! Don't let him do this to you!"

She threw herself aside at the last second. He anticipated her jump and snaked his head with her, the horn slashing across her brow. It tangled in her hair. She felt the rip of strands from her scalp, gave a yelp, and stumbled farther back.

The pain smarted. Alorie put her hand to her forehead, but found no blood. Her long riding skirt hampered her legs, but she managed a twirling step.

How long they bobbed and weaved, she did not know. Her feet went raw inside her boots—her velvet jacket shredded and drifted away on the storm winds—her silken blouse stuck to her body with sweat. She dodged and danced until she could scarcely breathe, and still the beast hunted her relentlessly. Dawn had come and the sun blazed relentlessly down on them. The roll of the storm was matched by the thunder of war machines from below.

They came to a stop. The black unicorn lowered his head to watch her. Alorie managed a laugh of fierce joy. "I'm still here!" she cried. "I'm still alive!"

The beast lunged. Her foot slipped as she moved to the side, she put her hand out to slap the attack away—and where her hand touched, it came away blackened as with soot, and white stained the creature's flank.

She let out a shout and flung herself at the unicorn as he tucked his hindquarters under him, plunging to a halt. She slapped him, danced away from a lashing kick, and let her hand stroke down his flanks.

White! Everywhere she touched, dazzling white!

"I love you!" Alorie cried in exultation. She danced about the Unicorn as he thrust and snapped at her, and she touched him everywhere she could.

Luisa screamed, "Alorie!" as the tile broke under her feet and she went down.

The obsidian horn pointed to her eyes and stayed there. Alorie gathered a shaken breath, reached out and grasped it, heedless of the searing fire through her palms. As she pulled herself up, the beast went to his knees with a racking shudder.

Beneath her touch, gold gleamed. And then, like a cloud burning away from the sun, the black fled until the beast that knelt before her was as powdered snow.

Alorie went to her knees beside him, and threw her arms about the Unicorn's neck.

He faded within her embrace until all she held was a gold-and-ivory-shot horn.

She stood up and kicked aside the guard of Frenlaw. Its cursed hilt would never betray another sword if she could help it.

Veil crashed asunder. It drifted tilting across the sky in a wild run. A dark figure loomed to block the sun.

Luisa screamed a second time, "Run, Alorie! Now!" She darted out from behind her shelter and stood, taking the green bolt from the Corruptor's hands dead on. She shriveled to a stinking mass at his feet.

He looked over the sorceress's body to Alorie. "Well," he said. "I am beginning to understand why Brock chose you. I won't toy with you. You've suddenly become too dangerous." He threw all his malevolent power at her.

She had a split second to bring the sword up in front of her like a shield. The sky exploded.

The mists opened up under her feet and she fell from the heavens.

Rowan overlooked the battlefield. His heart was not in the Delvings, though he'd had little choice where to go from the Barrows. Deanmuth reined in his horse, and the colonel's big destrier crushed against his knee.

"It's not going well," the adjunct said.

Rowan rubbed the back of his neck with a sigh. "He's toying with us. He comes out of there to harry us, but before we can get a grip on him, he scurries back inside the mountain."

"We've little hope of digging him out."

"I know." The ranger shifted and overlooked the mountains. On the other side of that range was the Eye of Cornuth. His auburn hair was plastered dark brown with sweat under his borrowed helm. He made do with a leather

surcoat and bracers, and he'd stolen black bloodstained shin
guards off a reken. He'd also stolen a good-sized black
gelding from one of Aquitane's deceased officers. He grudg-
ingly gave the dead lord credit for having well-trained troops.

"Do you think he has her?"

Rowan licked his dry lips. He did not want to think so.
He shrugged. "If he has, we can expect to be taunted with
her fairly soon. He already has most of us wondering what
we're doing here. He can expect to break us if he shows
her."

Deanmuth took off his helm and ran his gauntlet through
his hair. He examined the helm minutely. "What will you
do," he asked finally, "if he has her?"

"I don't know."

"But—"

"I don't know! And pray to god you'll never have to find
out." Rowan fiercely reined his gelding away from Deanmuth
and left him sitting there staring after him.

The colonel's reverie was broken as a wild shouting started
at the fore of the lines, and he could see from his position
that they were being overrun. Humans and reken and malisons burst out of the Delvings and plowed over the volunteer army. He saw Flask on his plunging horse, trying to get
a line up, to send a wing to protect their flanks.

He blinked, and Flask went down, his horse rolling violently over him. Deanmuth took a deep breath as he waited
for the bandy-legged colonel to get up from the troddened
ground—but he did not. Deanmuth dug his heels into his
horse and headed for the front. They would have to hold.
They had no choice.

This was the final battle. If the Corruptor won here, there
would be no place to hide.

"Hold fast!" he shouted, and whistled for the bugler.

He only wished he knew how to perform miracles.

Barth gripped his sword tightly and wished he were home
in Barrel. His shield had been ripped from him by one of their
own troops, and the man had disappeared in a hail of arrows
from the stony crag of the Delvings. Now Barth had nothing
to fight with but his sword. His mother had been right, he
thought. He should have left the fighting to heroes and
learned how to cobble. His boots had hopeless holes in
them, blistering the tender bottoms of his feet.

He saw the wave of reken, rusty-furred faces above their

leather vests, white tusks gleaming as they charged. The only good thing about the charge was that there would be no arrows for a while.

He flexed his big, awkward hands about a sword hilt too small for him. It had been slippery, too, until he'd torn the hem off his shirt and wrapped it. He stood a moment, looking down the gullet of the enemy, and then he realized he stood alone—and that was when he broke and ran for the rugged foot of the mountain.

He prayed his back was not a tempting target.

Rowan wrapped his reins about his hand. "Get me a spear."

His trail mate looked askance at him.

"Get me a spear!"

Tien moved to do what he was told. He approached Rowan's blowing horse. "What are you going to do?"

"That bastard's down on the field now. See him—there . . . that scarecrow of shadow. We're beaten here unless he goes down."

Litters of wounded were being carried past the Rover encampment. The men were resting for a moment before mounting back up and going out again. The stink of the battlefield enshrouded them, the scent of fire and gore and death. Ashcroft lay by the fire, his sides wrapped heavily, his eyes closed. Rowan looked briefly at his older brother. Tien said, "I'll tell him."

"Right."

The Rover gripped the toe of his boot in a tight fist, a farewell embrace. "Good luck" was all he said.

Rowan swallowed and set heel to his mount. He heard movement at his back, horses' hooves. When he turned to look, he saw that most of his fellows had re-mounted and followed him.

They picked up straggling foot soldiers as well until they formed a solid wedge and by the time they met the first edges of the fight, they drove through it. Rowan's horse picked up speed until he was nearly at a dead run, and the rest of the company charged behind.

The wall of protection in front of the Corruptor opened up and left him bare. Rowan saw it. He knew then that the time for Alorie to be used against them, if ever, was then.

Bile souring his throat and air burning his lungs, Barth

stumbled against a boulder and came to a halt, sagging against the rock and stone, black spots swimming before his eyes.

"Hist, young'un! Watch where ye plant yer clumsy boots!"

The lad looked down and saw he had not kicked a rock, but a rock-hard dwarf crumpled upon the ground. There had been dwarves among the enemy's fighting forces, but the Barrel lad thought he recognized the raspy voice. He reached out and hauled the body up.

"Master Pinch!"

"Aye, or what's left of him." The dwarf struggled to stay upright, his face flushed red with fever, and the rest of his complexion as pale as death. He gulped for breath: "Could ye give me a hand, or are ye too busy attacking in the wrong direction?"

"I didn't mean—I'm sorry, master, but I was the only one—I was so scared—"

"I know the feeling." Pinch put his head against the stone at his back and fought for breath. "I can be of some help, but it's too far for me t'go on my own. Is the lady about?"

"Lady?"

The dwarf panted heavily and got out, "Alorie, fer god's sakes."

Barth shook his head. "There were rumors . . . lost in the Barrowlands last night, but I don't know. The colonel said *he* might have her as hostage."

Pinch shook his head violently as if to clear it. "Then it's up to us to do it."

"Do what?"

"The dark lieutenant's an unnatural being. He's wrought of mortal flesh and sorcery—and I'm of a mind to cleave him in two! Boost me up, bucko. D'ye want to go down swinging—or would ye rather the reken harry you to death?"

Barth took a gulping swallow of air. It made him hiccough his answer. "I'll f—fight, master!"

"That's my boy. Now hike me up to them lofty shoulders and let's be off."

Kithrand could smell the battlefield before they rounded the bend—and trotted into a troop of reken, jabbing and snarling at something in their midst. The canyon walls echoed their cries as whatever they had cornered fought back. The elf lord paused, pony gripped between his knees, knowing that it had to be a deserter this far from the actual battle, but he couldn't help admire the unseen fighter's mettle.

With a sigh he raised his hand and let fly a small bolt of elven fire. He regretted it immediately, feeling his breath suck back into a sore chest. He had not the strength to waste. The reken yipped and boiled apart, and the swordsman aimed a few well-chosen epitaphs after them.

When the dust cleared, an amazed Kithrand faced Alorie on the road.

"Milady," he said and bowed, every fiber of his being in pain, "fancy meeting you here."

She limped to his side. "Will nothing stop your mocking tongue?" She threw her arms about him, Unicorn sword and all, and hugged him till he could scarcely breathe. "Brock is dead. The prophecy is nothing. We're on our own, friend, and I need your help."

And to her astonishment, the elf lord began to weep.

Alorie pointed as she finished her tale. "See that copse of trees down the road? If we survive this, I am dedicating it to the All-Mother. One of those lofty crowns broke my fall—several times—on the way to the ground."

Kithrand shook his head again, feelers bobbing. "You lead a charmed life."

She sobered. "No, Kit. But my destined death is elsewhere." She stood. "Are you rested enough?"

He was not. He would never be again, his elfin flesh wasted beyond a point of recovery. If suddenly his world returned to normal, and he to his platform in Charlbet, he would still be a shadow of himself, his hold tenuous upon this life. But he did not tell her that.

Nor had he the nerve to tell her what he knew of the malisons. She would think him raving as they had thought of Brock, and he must stay at her elbow, despite his fear of dying. His scrap of knowledge was all he had to gift her with—and it might save her life.

He whistled up the pony. "After you, milady."

A pallor lay over the battlefield. Alorie slipped down off the pony and sidestepped its ill-tempered nip. She felt as she had riding the hellroad and looked to the elf lord for confirmation. "What is it?"

He shrugged. "Not good, whatever it is. The calm before the storm perhaps."

She could feel a gathering in the air about her. The horn attuned her to magic. She sensed it now. "I think you're more than right, Kit. And I think the Corruptor's behind it."

He gave her a bittersweet smile. "Only one other person I can think of knows me well enough to call me Kit."

She paused. "Who?"

"My mother, the Lady Orthea." He jumped off the pony and landed lightly behind her. He felt insubstantial, like a wisp in the wind. With a slap he sent the beast crow-hopping down the road. "Show your sword, milady. Hold it like a triumphant banner."

"A banner of the Seven True Races and the star-shone people?"

He gave her a sideways glance from gem blue eyes. His white-blond hair needed combing, and his jeweled circlet had been lost days ago. But he nodded. "Yes."

He made a path for her through the weary troops. Here at the rear they were either wounded or cowardly or so tired they were beyond all hope. But they saw her and remembered Sinobel.

"Our lady! The sword!"

Their whispers grew bolder. She sensed a following at her heels. "The sword! Look at the sword!"

It burned with white fire shot through with gold, a light that overturned the sun. Its molten illumination cascaded over her.

Rowan pulled his horse to a plunging halt. They had beaten and wedged their way close—and now the Corruptor had sight of him. Perhaps it was the banner carrier who paced him. But the dark lieutenant had sent out a signal, and now the field opened. The fool was going to let him get a shot at him!

Then he heard the cries.

"Our lady! Our lady!"

He cursed himself for having human eyes instead of those of a hawk. The Corruptor had to be bringing her out, parading her.

The boy with the banner tugged on his sleeve. "They're shouting at the rear."

"The rear?" Puzzled, Rowan spurred the horse around. He still could not see—the battlefield was anything but level. But he could hear now. "Our lady! And the sword!" By all the gods, she lived and she was free!

His moment of joy stopped cold as he realized she was stepping into the fate from which he had done everything he could to protect her.

With a yell Rowan whipped his horse at the Corruptor, spear in hand.

The dark lieutenant met him arrogantly. When he was within hailing distance, Rowan shouted, "A challenge, master! A challenge to win the battle!"

The Corruptor laughed. He signaled his reken and traitors to hold their arms a moment. He stepped out from the battle machine that half-shielded him.

"Why risk myself to win what I've already won?"

"Is it that certain? Nothing in life is but death, and you've already beaten that, my lord. But I can guarantee you that as long as I or others like me stand, you'll be fighting. Here or elsewhere." Rowan paced his horse closer, close enough to see that too-white face with its black brows arced high in sardonic amusement. The ranger swung down. "I give you a challenge, by the codes of honor, and a victory—if you win."

"And if you should win?"

Rowan shrugged. "Your death, and your forces withdrawn."

"Reasonable. Even entertaining. A chance to show my power. All right." The man threw off his hooded cloak, drew his sword, and strode near.

Barth ambled through the ruin of bodies and armor on the field. A curious thing was happening—a space was opening to the front, and arms were being held, though ready, and the reken and hovering malisons pulling back. The village lad pushed his way through, talking constantly to the odd companion riding his shoulders.

He stopped at the lack of response. He tugged on the heavy, hobnailed boot of the master dwarf. "Pinch—I said, what d'you think is going on?"

"Just get me to our lady." With a gasp, the dwarf pitched headfirst into the dust. Barth knelt beside him. The shortman's face was mottled red and white, his breath like a bellows in his chest. Barth put his hand to Pinch's throat and felt the pulse there, rapid and unsteady. With a sudden tear in his eye he picked the dwarf up in his arms and cradled him to his chest.

He'd gathered a crowd. To them he addressed his question. "What's happening?"

A weather-beaten soldier with nothing at hand but a rusty short sword answered. "The dark one has accepted a challenge. It'll be just the two of them. 'Course, if ourn dies, we'll be mowed down anyway. But it gives Rowan a chance at the other."

"Honor combat?"

"Aye."

Barth held the dwarf uncertainly. He heard the other's breath rattle against his chest. To have come all this way, and fail—this was surely a hero he carried, if a short one. As long as Master Pinch breathed, he deserved to reach the end of his journey. The village boy kept a hold of his heavy burden and made his way down to the arena of onlookers.

She could hear shouts to the front, but the broken field of hillocks and boulders hid the stone gates of the Delvings from her. A courser galloped through the ranks, scattering the soldiers, followed by a cream-colored faery steed.

Deanmuth pulled up. "By all the gods, it is you!"

Lord Torrey joined him. He hesitated a moment, then swung down from his stallion. He offered Kithrand the reins, saying, "Milord."

Kithrand's hands trembled as he took them. He bent to give Alorie a leg up.

Deanmuth reached out to stop them. "Don't let her down there. He's hacking him to bits."

"Who? What's going on?"

"A challenge, milady, to win the field. Although," Deanmuth's expression was grim, "we know our opponent too well to know that if we lose, we're out of this."

Kithrand tossed her up. Torrey gave him a leg up, and the elf landed at her back. He slipped an arm about her waist and tightened it. With foresight riding him as well as doom, he said, "There's no time to waste!"

"No!" Deanmuth cried at their backs, but the faery horse jumped away, hurtled a barrier, and was down away the hill before he could be stopped.

She had never cursed her nearness of sight before, but now she did. She could see the figures in the challenge ring, and heard the clash of steel, and watch them circle one another, one smoothly, one stumbling in pain and weariness. Kithrand held her fiercely.

"Who could it be?" she asked. "Rathincourt's not here, Brock is dead—" Then she sucked in her breath with an icy chill. "Oh, *god*! It has to be Rowan!"

He went down. Alorie screamed as Kithrand brought the horse to a plunging halt and lifted her to the ground. She watched the Corruptor overwhelm his opponent and smelled the stink of sorcery and heard the echo of her cry.

Rowan rolled before the blow struck. He staggered to his feet. She ran forward, but a linked row of soldiers caught her and threw her back.

"It's a challenge. No one passes until one or the other is dead."

She stood in numb defeat, tears blinding her now, as bound by the code of honor as the Corruptor was not. Someone nudged her.

"Milady, the sword . . . the horn . . . can you help me?"

She looked, finally, to her elbow and saw Barth standing there, his gangly arms filled with a heap of filthy rags and boots. Her failure to wield the horn to its full potential cut at her. She blinked. "No," she cried. "It does not heal! It kills! If it healed, don't you think I'd help Rowan!"

The heap of rags stirred. "Don't fash yourself, lass. He wouldn't want that."

She stared in horror at Pinch's revealed face. Kithrand had come up behind her. The elf lord reached out and took one dry and callused hand.

"Well, shortman. At least I'll have company."

The dwarf turned a bleary eye at his old sparring partner. "I wouldn't be seen dead with the likes of you."

The elf smiled crookedly. "I wouldn't be too sure about that."

Pinch reached out his free hand and pawed at Alorie. "When Rowan goes down, strike then."

"It's a challenge."

"The Corruptor knows no such rules." Pinch interrupted himself with a racking cough. He thumped his chest. The sound of a book being struck under the rags came to her. "I have the name, milady. I have the name!"

"What?!"

"I've been to the Delvings. I've brought our history out of its pit."

She knew she heard his dying words and that there could be nothing but truth in their ring. For the first time, more than mere hope filled her. Alorie looked desperately over the heads of the onlookers. She could do it—she could strike the dark Lieutenant down—though Rowan would have to die first to give her the opportunity. She balled her left hand into a fist so tight her nails drew blood.

Kithrand said at her ear, "I can help also. The Corruptor is more than a man . . . he is possessed, and I have the name which can split him in two—"

"Kit?"

"Shall we chance it?"

"Yes, damn your mocking tongue. Yes!" She hammered at the beefy foot soldier in front of her. "Let me through!"

Rowan fought with desperate skill. His left arm hung at his side, his shirt bloodied and damp. He circled on a right leg with a wicked-looking gash across the top of his thigh. He worked at his sixes, meeting blow after blow, side to side and top to bottom. He had no strength left and it was just a matter of time until a thrust came through or his opponent cut his leg out from under him.

He seemed not to know she was there, and she dared not let him know for fear of distracting him. She gripped the horn tightly, the stump of its end throbbing in her hand as if it were a living thing.

Barth jostled her. Pinch plucked her sleeve. "It'll be close," he said. "The name is Frenlaw."

"What?" She turned to him in surprise.

"None other. The grand traitor himself."

No wonder the books had not mentioned it—the name of the traitor so well known it needed no repeating. But over the centuries one had gotten separated from the other. She could have kissed him, but there was a sound from the audience as Rowan stumbled.

Her heart stopped in her throat. She saw him crumple, a second thrust to his chest, and heard his death cry.

She opened her mouth and cried his name soundlessly.

Kithrand pushed her into the circle, where she stood in shock as the Corruptor turned. She thought she saw Rowan's chest in a shallow rise and fall. Down, then, but not yet dead.

The dark lieutenant's look of rapacious joy fled. "What do you want?"

She smiled tightly. "Your blood upon this ground. Or don't you think you can dispatch me as easily as you did him?"

The Corruptor made as if to leave and raised a palm. She

felt a tug of power and saw the glimmering of sorcery leave it. She shouted, "Frenlaw!" before he could complete his act.

She rooted him to his place. Sweat sprung upon his pale forehead. She brought the horn into position as if it were a rapier.

The sky filled with foul clouds, the nimbus-shrouded bodies of souleaters, hundreds of them. They shuddered with frenzy, waiting for their master to unleash them on the battlefield.

Kithrand wanted to run. He could not breathe. He went blind to the sight of Alorie facing the Corruptor. His ears rang with his pulse.

The dark lieutenant moved about stiffly to face her. "Very well," he said. "But the code of honor is forfeit."

"Like a good game of *rool*," she answered. "If you may remember, the House of Sergius does well at that."

They touched weapons.

The sword trembled in her hand. She felt its fear thrill up her arm. The Corruptor made his cruel slash of a smile. With his free hand he pointed, and she saw the jagged splinter of darkness being reborn within the horn.

With that, he did not fence with her. He went to the attack, vicious thrusts and cuts that she did all she could to parry. Her balance was off—she'd been taught with the longknife and the horn was all wrong—the wrong weight, the wrong length. She pulled Brock's short staff from her waistband and used it as she would a shield.

His sword flashed. Her sleeve ripped. Now she had both arms bared. She parried an uppercut he telegraphed, and it was well she did, the slice was meant to take her head off.

"No quarter," she said, borrowing Kithrand's irony.

The Corruptor frowned and she stepped back just in time, remembering his facile feet. The blow missed, and she lashed out, the horn's white fire ripping at the back of his kneecap.

He staggered, but recovered his balance. His dark eyes glittered. "More than sinew knits me together, my lady," he said.

She did not listen to him. She must do more than distract him from completing his sorcery—she must finish him off. The horn gave her power, but no skill. All she had were the lessons her love had given her. In the dust behind her Rowan bled. She went on the offensive then, and drove him back, back so that his reken foemen scattered. She could feel the knot on her nose tighten in determination.

"Enough of this," the Corruptor siad. He began to sketch a sign in the air. The blanket of sorcery overlying the struggle began to tighten.

"What is it you have in mind for us? Firestorm? Ghostwind? A rain of blood perhaps, before you set the malisons on us?" She punctuated each word with a thrust. The jagged splinter of darkness grew larger with each attack. Without a hilt to steady it, the talisman twisted in her palm.

The Corruptor's mouth curled. "You are mine, milady. *Taste me*." And he set upon her with an attack she could not turn away.

With those words, Kithrand froze. Now he felt the destruction the dark lieutenant planned to summon with his cloud of sorcery—he could feel them quaking on just the other side of the hellroad door. Malisons. Their malevolence probed him like curious tongues licking the meal to come. From where Frenlaw could summon such a mass, he could not begin to guess. But his very marrow froze and he forgot what he had to do to help Alorie.

She danced back, bobbing and weaving. She gripped the unicorn horn dearly as the splinter of Corruption threatened it again. She could no longer hold Frenlaw with his mortal name and she did not know what possessed him. All she could do was use the sword, and that was not enough.

His sword bit at her. She blocked it with Brock's cane. There was a spat and sparks as if magic met magic. Her wrist trembled as the Corruptor stepped close, bearing his weight down upon the blade, and the staff trembled in her left hand. She crossed it with the horn in her right to hold him and knew her strength was failing.

The moment she slipped, she knew.

The Corruptor let out a purr, leapt back, and sliced.

She scarcely felt her left leg part, and then she tumbled down, and there was nothing but the crimson wound spurting from thigh to kneecap. "Kithrand!" she screamed in agony.

Her warm blood spattered him. Kithrand shuddered back to life. *Taste me*, he heard as Alorie struggled to get to her feet, to parry the sword and ward off the sorcery aimed at her. He leapt into the circle with hands full of blue fire as she fell again. He laid his hands on the gaping wound, her velvet skirt in tatters. Flesh seared.

"Kit!" she screamed. The sword blade swung by his head. With fading elven agility he dodged. With the last of his elven fire, he sketched the pattern of the malison's name, the possessor. It had to answer, drawn to an aura it could not resist tasting. "Frenlaw!" he shouted, and saw the abomination thrust at him.

Leaning heavily on Brock's runic cane in her left hand, Alorie got up. As Frenlaw pierced Kithrand's almost translucent body, she ran the Corruptor through, the horn driving deep with her off-balance weight behind it. It tore out of her hand as Frenlaw fell back. The human flesh gave way, but the malison shivered out of him, parting from mortality it had shared too long, and came at them in a feeding frenzy.

Kit saw it come. He knew he could not stand before it. It leapt upon him, shredding his feeble attempt to keep it off. He felt his blue-green blood splatter and heard screams of horror, though not from his throat.

White fire slashed across his agony, ripping into the malison. Alorie had the sword once more, and with its force cutting before him, Kithrand made his final unraveling of power. The act took him with it.

Thirty-Five

Deanmuth swept past, driving the reken into the mountains as dwarves burst out of their rocky stronghold, Bryant to their fore. The Corruptor's cloudburst of malisons boiled over, met by Torrey and his kindred, attacking with blue fire and steel until the horizon cleared. Alorie watched the armies converge in a last feeble charge, but the wall of soldiers protecting them held and she knew the battle was over. Of Kithrand, Frenlaw, and his possessor, nothing remained but ash.

The shock of her injury began to set in. Kithrand's fire had cauterized the bleeding and she felt no pain. That would come later. She tore a strip of fabric off her skirt and tried to bind the gaping slash closed. Leaning heavily on the cane, she limped to Rowan's body. She put her hand on his chest and could feel nothing. Too late. She dropped the horn and threw herself over him, sobbing as if her heart would break.

"Trying to . . . squeeze . . . what's left . . . out?"

Alorie looked up. Rowan dragged a hand up and wove his fingers into her hair.

"Use the horn," he whispered.

She could not. Had not been able to. Not even for herself. "Oh, gods," she cried as she picked it up. "It's been Corrupted. Oh, love—" But the talisman flared in her hands. It was a candle of power. She touched it to his chest, plunging it into the wound that was killing him. With a gasp, she felt her very life pulled out of her. She clenched her teeth and flung her soul after, the soul he had saved with his love, determined to heal him even if she could not heal herself. He arched his back in pain, his heels drumming the ground, harsh cries pulled out of him.

Then he sagged back. He took a deep, quavering breath.

"Now," he said. "Could you try that on my leg? A little gentler?"

She kissed him. She kissed his mouth and his cleft and his brows and his mouth again, and his chest where only a pink scarring revealed the deadly wound.

He drew her back to his lips. "Not here, woman. I'm hardly in any condition."

In spite, she healed not only his leg but his limp left arm. He cried only when he weakly tried to stand. She could not help him, her body quivering in shock, and he saw her wound. As they brought a litter up to carry her off the field, it was already occupied by a feisty, disreputable lump.

"Shove over," Rowan said.

The dwarf opened an eye. "Do ye know who you're messing with, bucko? Y're messing with a dwarf meaner than poison itself."

The Rover ignored him and dropped Alorie down on the litter anyway. She clenched her teeth against the bone-racking shudders of her body's reaction to her wound. Pinch gave over with a grumble, saying, "I think ye broke my pipe."

Alorie kissed his yellow-gold crown. The heat of his fever warmed her. "I'll buy you a new one."

"In truth? Ah, there's a fine looking one in a certain tobacco shop in Sobor—his lordship will point it out—"

Rowan, his face still unearthly pale, said, "Shut up, Pinch."

The dwarf clamped his lips shut with a pleased look on his sickly face.

The woodsman walked by the litter's side, unwilling to leave her. She beckoned him down. "How soon can you stand for a wedding?"

Rowan stroked her hair. "Ah, my lady. Didn't you know we've already been wed? There is spirit as well as flesh, if we'd only had the sense to recognize the bonding. But I'll make you legal as soon as you're fit."

Alorie smiled. This, then, was the gift she had tried to throw away, more precious than any other she could have had from the gods. She closed her eyes and grasped his hand as if she would never let go.

In the spring, she sought the unicorn out. She dressed in white, though it hardly stood for virginity, the slight roundness of her stomach flush with new life, and she leaned heavily on Brock's cane, her wound laming her for life. It was not

the forest where they first met—but she had come to know
any forest would do. But she paused in the wooded stillness
and listened and when she heard the bend of branches and
an arrogant bugling, she followed it until she reached a
sunlit glen.

A trio of unicorns approached her. Two lesser beasts
supported the third, a great exultant beast, hornless, his
flesh nearly translucent. They stepped aside, and the Unicorn dropped to his knees before her.

"I am still the Dancer," she declared. Awkwardly at first,
then warming to her ability changed by her leg, she did a
sword dance. She brandished the talisman with a fierce joy,
its edges singing in the air, and when she twirled to a stop,
she presented it to the Unicorn.

"Thank you," she said. "For all the pain and sorrow and
joy. You have changed me immeasurably. You have taken
away my city and given me a country. Taken away a country
and given me continents. You have taken away my history
and given me truth." She had spent the long nights of her
convalescence reading Pinch's journal and wondering on her
newfound world.

The beast lowered his head, resting his beard upon her
bended knee. "And this makes you happy?"

She put the horn into the gory socket in his brow. "Yes.
And it terrifies me. The Despot slumbers deeply. I know
he'll rise someday. Perhaps my child or my grandchild will
have to face him. But I know, with love, they'll be strong
enough."

"Then I have given you nothing. You won it for yourself."

Alorie smiled. A whistle split the air, a ranger's whistle.
She touched a hand to the Unicorn's jaw.

The beast said, "Has he no respect for a demigod?"

"No. I don't think so. But he has love." And she kissed
the creature good-bye.

The Unicorn got to his feet. "I leave you with one last
quest."

Alorie paused at the edge of the meadow. Sunlight dappled her. It followed the gentle swell of her stomach. Almost afraid, she asked, "What?"

"To follow after the truth."

"Is there war in truth?"

"Sometimes. There will definitely be war without it."

She looked to the ground where the steps of her dance
mingled with the prints of the unicorn. "Then I will do what

I have to. In the memory of those who have died, and in the hope of those to come." She left the glen, leaning upon the cane, her head high, ebony hair streaming down her back, the graceful lines of her body not diminished by her injury. Rather, her posture held a dignity that came not from birth, but through life.

ABOUT THE AUTHOR

R. A. V. SALSITZ was born in Phoenix, Arizona, and raised mainly in Southern California, with time out for stints in Alaska, Oregon, and Colorado. Having a birthplace named for such a mythical and mystical beast has always pushed her toward SF and fantasy.

Encouraged from an early age to write, she majored in journalism in high school and college. Although Rhondi has yet to drive a truck carrying nitro, work experience has been varied—from electronics to furniture to computer industries—until she settled down to work full-time at a word processor.

Married, the author matches wits daily with a spouse and four lively children, of various ages, heights, and sexes. Hobbies and interests include traveling, tennis, horses, computers, and writing.